Apple Blossom Honey

by

Mary Lesser

Also by Mary Lesser

The Lemon Juice Summer
The gifts of Mr Karim

Acknowledgements

The Japanese Garden Society
www.jgs.org.uk

Apple Blossom Honey

When jilted ex-nurse and celebration cake maker Lucy Huccaby unexpectedly lands a job at Trelerric House overlooking the River Tamar in Cornwall, looking after Flick Latchley the one time B-movies starlet Felicity Gray, she finds herself embarking on a plan to help the Latchley family put Trelerric on the map. She didn't expect that her own family origins would be revealed nor anticipate that her heart would be captured by more than just the house.

If you enjoyed *The Lemon Juice Summer* you might recognise one or two characters in this book.

****

For Nicola

ONE

It was New Year's Eve and I was not in a party mood. The past twelve months had been foul. Last Christmas I'd been wearing a small but classy diamond cluster and getting ready to go to a party with my fiancé Peter and Emma my best friend, who was also my business partner. The future had all seemed set, a successful business, a wedding planned, rose tinted glasses set firmly in place. Now it was twelve months later, I was still on my own and I was borrowing my sister Megan's spare room in Plymouth while I tried to make sense of my future.

Peter and Emma had gone off together leaving me jobless and homeless. Megan had come to my rescue and been endlessly patient with my tears and anger and disappointment.

'Condiments of the house.' Megan was handing me a glass of champagne. I'd opened the bottle as she didn't want to damage her new gel nails. She was an elfin blonde with legs up to her armpits. A lovely sapphire engagement ring which matched her dark blue eyes was flashing on her ring finger.

'Thanks, but sod making any New Year revolutions.'

'Touché.'

We liked to play with words. It was a family thing.

It was typical of Megan to produce champagne and to share it with me. We were both adopted and had been blessed with a caring and loving family. That was the wellspring of Megan's optimism, the fact that someone had wanted her and provided a safe and supportive home life were nothing short of miraculous to her. Mostly I shared her optimism. It was just that, well, it had been a shit year. Now I'd had enough of it.

'I feel like revolting and doing things differently.'

'Well, you've certainly been revolting, you'd gone right off the railings, but I'll drink to change.'

I took the glass and raised it to her. 'For looking after me Meg. Thank you, I really mean it. I've been a world class pain but that stops now. I shall find a way of thanking you properly one day. Cheers.'

'To infinity.' Megan said solemnly.

'In a cupcake.' I replied. It was one of our silly secret childhood codes. We were very close.

We chinked glasses and drank, the bubbles having a party up my nose. I sneezed and Megan giggled.

'It gets you every time Luce.' Calling me Luce meant that I was in her good books. She drained her glass. 'I've got to finish getting ready, Mike will be here shortly. Can you let him in and keep him talking?'

'What about? Sex and drugs and rock 'n roll?'

I was being unfair. Mike, Megan's fiancé, was gorgeous. He had his own music business which specialised in finding and managing emerging talent and he was very good at it. He and Megan were crazy about each other. They'd met at some corporate events shindig which Megan had organised and had exchanged private contact details almost immediately. Four months later she was wearing a shiny ring and planning an Easter wedding. By the time they were married they would have known each other for just ten months. It's like that for some people.

Taking the bottle of champagne I wandered into the sitting room. I wasn't invited to the party and my hot date was with the television. The only way to cope with the endless hobbit movies and pathetic New Year celebrity quiz games was to get pissed so I planned on finishing the champagne and going to bed. I couldn't wait to get this year over.

The doorbell shook me out of my reverie. I heard Megan yell to me to let Mike in.

'Hi Mike.' I stood back as he loomed into the small hall, wearing a purple velvet jacket with a pink and lilac patterned shirt and black jeans. 'You look very, er' ... I waved my hand searching for a description. 'Impressive.'

'You think I look like a prat don't you.'

Mike, who usually dressed in casual clothes kissed me briefly on the cheek. He had nice manners.

'Actually I was thinking how festive you look. A bit like Peter Rabbit on crack with the purple velvet. It's rather nice.'

He looked good with his floppy dark hair and lean grace.

'The children throwing the bash are a bit nouveau, they'll expect a bit of bling.'

'In that case shouldn't you be wearing a medallion and at least an earring?' I said.

One of Mike's clients was throwing the party, a local boy band he'd discovered and helped along the road with promotions and they'd hit the golden time.

Mike was looking at me. 'You okay Lucy?'

I nodded. 'I am. Tomorrow's a fresh start. I've always loved New Year. I'm fine. Really. But I'm not going to watch the Hogmanay crap on the telly or I'll have to stick pins in my eyeballs.'

'Megan anywhere near ready yet?'

'Dunno. Come through into the sitting room, you'll match Megan's festive lilac Christmas tree. Can I get you anything, we've just opened some champagne.'

Mike shuddered and declined. 'Thanks but no thanks. Got anything soft?'

It wasn't just that he was driving, Mike was one of those rare people who actually didn't like alcohol. For a moment I saw the forthcoming evening through his eyes; everybody getting progressively sloshed while you stayed sober must be extremely tedious.

'How do you cope on pissfests like tonight?' I asked him, offering him a small glass of orange juice.

'Slimline tonic water with a slice.'

'What?' I raised my eyebrows.

'Everyone thinks I'm a hardened gin and tonic man. And in a champagne flute you can't tell it's not champagne. I know it's sad and pathetic isn't it. Doesn't do my image any good, in my line of work I should be a hardened spirits and spliff man with a small ponytail. Don't tell anyone about my clean living please.'

I was about to say his secret was safe when Megan appeared. She was wearing a sexy dark blue cocktail dress, a spangly fitted number which flared to one side at the knee and had one fitted sleeve and one bare shoulder. She'd had a pale golden spray tan a couple of days earlier and looked sensational.

'Wow.' Mike and I spoke in unrehearsed harmony.

'But won't you be cold?' I asked, knowing there would be an outdoor firework display at midnight.

'I shall watch from an upstairs window. I'm not catching my death for a load of bangs and sparks.' Megan might look like a ditzy fairy princess but she was the most level headed and practical woman I knew. She was also very fit; we swam, cycled and ran together and she outdid me at everything, probably because she was much more disciplined.

Mike helped her into a white fake fur coat and they promised not to be too noisy when they got back. I watched them from the apartment window, Mike solicitously assisting Megan into his car. I liked him and his emotional baggage wasn't too heavy. Travis, a teenaged son as a result of an early liaison with a music studio manager from Cardiff's Tiger Bay was showing musical promise of his own. Mike didn't see as much of Travis as he would like, since he was currently living in New York with his mother.

Briefly I thought back to my own disappointed dreams. I'd been focussed on some marriage mirage that promised happy-ever-after, thinking that starting my own family would somehow confirm me as a real person and make up for the real family I'd never had. I poured some more champagne and mentally kicked myself for my disloyalty. I'd had a safe and happy childhood with loving parents and Megan was proof of the closeness we all had. As if on cue the phone rang and I answered.

'Lucy? Is that you Lucy?'

'Hi mum, happy new thing almost. I'm already drinking Megan's champagne. They've just gone out to a party. How are you both?'

I spent some time reassuring my mum that I really was ok.

'I'm over it all now mum, I've gone past acceptance and I'm at the bored-with-it stage of grief. Tomorrow's a brand new year and I'm going to go out and get a job and start again. Peter and Emma are history.'

'Are you going back to nursing?' Mum asked hopefully. She'd come to England from Ireland as a nurse.

'I don't know. I'll have to see what's out there. I fancy a change.'

I'd gone into nursing to live mum's dream of what a decent girl should do, and then given it up to go into business with my best school friend. Emma and I had done our nursing degrees together and shared a flat with some other students before working at the hospital in Hereford. In our spare time we'd made cakes for colleagues. We'd started this as schoolgirls to make pocket money and as students we'd continued because not only did we make money we got invited to more parties. There were always birthdays and occasions to celebrate in a large establishment and eventually the demands on our skills had become sufficient for us to decide to quit nursing and go full time into celebration cakes. We'd had a good two years and I'd got engaged to Peter who was the brother of a medical colleague. Somehow I'd failed to observe the easy friendship between Peter and my business partner develop into something serious. At Christmas he'd turned up and asked me to take a walk with him. On Hereford Cathedral green he'd told me that he couldn't go through with the wedding because he'd fallen in love with Emma and she felt the same. My world had fallen apart. I'd gone back to the flat above the business I'd shared with Emma and unplugged the Christmas tree and thrown the whole thing onto her bed. Then I'd really lost it and smashed some wine glasses we'd bought together. Eaten up with rage and shock I hadn't recognised myself. Mum and dad had taken me home and then Megan had moved me to Plymouth where she was based saying that it wasn't healthy for me to be near Hereford. I just hadn't expected to stay with her for almost twelve months.

Obviously I couldn't work with Emma any more so we'd closed the business. Orders had to be cancelled and deposits paid back. Eventually we managed to sell the flat and the business. I'd felt utterly betrayed and furiously angry. Being jilted and dealing with the humiliation of a cancelled wedding with presents to return had left me in tatters but mum had been pragmatic, grateful that the wedding hadn't gone ahead because she'd never taken to Peter. She'd described him as a spineless piece of work not fit to kiss the soles of my boots. She'd also told me to thank my guardian angel and all the saints for saving me from a well of tears, as she'd described it in her lovely Irish accent, still reminiscent of County Cavan.

After chatting to mum she passed the phone over and I spoke to dad briefly. He told me that whatever I decided to do they loved me and that I was a good girl.

'But it's time to get back up on the horse now Lucy. Everything happens for a reason. It's as clear as mud now but all will be well maid. I'm sure of it.'

I loved his west country endearment. Wishing him Happy New Year I blew a few kisses to them both and put the phone down. My adopted parents had strong faith in the ultimate goodness of things which I didn't always agree with, but they meant well. I didn't fancy the remains of the champagne now and it wouldn't get drunk so I poured it away and made myself a comforting mug of hot chocolate instead. After staring mindlessly at a film for a while and then watching the fireworks I tidied up and went to bed, leaving the hall lights on for Megan and Mike. I didn't hear them come home.

I was making toast the next morning when Mike appeared with damp hair after his shower and pinched a piece. I made some more for both of us and sat down to eat.

Is Megan surfacing yet?'

'Nope. She's crashed out with her face in the pillow and making little snuffling noises.' Mike smiled indulgently as he loaded his toast with marmite.

'Good party?' I asked.

Mike shrugged. 'The catering was good but I knew it would be since we'd recommended they used Helena Fox-Harvey. The fireworks were very good too. The conversation was infantile but what do you expect with that age group when they're just out of kindergarten. The parents were all quite decent and Megan was marvellous with them. She made all the right noises and moves but we managed to get away when people started jumping into the hotel swimming pool.'

I spread honey on my toast. 'Are the boy band going to be big this time next year?

'Doubt it. One will go solo if I've anything to do with it. He could go far. The others are one night wonders fuelled by hormones and I hate to think what else. They'll just have a good story to tell their grandchildren one day.'

We ate in silence. Mike got up to look for orange juice and spoke casually.

'I heard of a job last night Lucy, more of a position really. You might be interested, but then again you might not since I don't know what your plans are.'

I stared at him, momentarily interested by the use of the word *position*. I had a mental image of myself poised on point like a ballerina, about to take a great leap forward. I knew I had to move on because Megan's apartment was going on the market shortly. I'd known that for a while because she was moving into Mike's place on the side of Dartmoor after their wedding.

'I haven't made any plans Mike but I'm ready to start looking for something. I said so to mum and dad last night.'

'Okay. Well Helena said she'd done a children's birthday party at Trelerric House last week. It's owned by the Latchley family. Apparently Mrs Latchley's in the market for a live in help.'

I immediately felt doubtful.

'I don't know that I'm keen to look after children Mike. But what and where is Trelerric House?' I asked politely.

Megan and I had grown up on the Welsh borders. My knowledge of the West Country was solely summer holidays in Looe with the grandparents and latterly, Megan's flat in a handsome converted Victorian house outside Plymouth.

'Helena described it as a lovely old place on the Cornish side of the Tamar. She said it was a time warp outside and a tarts boudoir inside. Mrs Latchley is an elderly lady, not the mother of the children.' Mike answered.

'Sounds interesting. How do I find out more?' I was being kind really, the idea of a live in job didn't really appeal, but I wasn't sure what did at this point in my life. I'd got nursing experience and I could make extremely good celebration cakes. And where was that going to take me I wondered. Lately I'd been considering joining up or going to work on a cruise ship except that I hated taking orders and I suffered from seasickness.

Mike fiddled with his phone. 'I've sent you Helena's number. Give her a bell and tell her I've spoken to you. She can fill you in. She knows the Latchley family.'

There was the sound of a yawn and Megan came into the tiny kitchen. She was tousled and dozy in a sugar pink and orange satin dressing gown. On anyone else it would have looked tawdry but she looked right in it. She shook her head at the offer of toast and kissed the top of Mike's head before selecting a plain yoghurt from the fridge to which she added a few blueberries. Mike poured her tea and gave her his chair. Her self discipline for the pre-wedding diet had started today.

'I've got to go my wordless beauty, business calls for the self-employed even on this day of the year. I'll see you tonight.' Mike kissed Megan on the forehead and raised a hand in farewell to me. 'Think about it Lucy. Have a nice day together cackling like banshees over your cauldrons.'

Megan looked at me and raised her eyebrows.

'Mike told me about a job at a place called Trelerric House. Some woman called Helena Fox-Harvey told him about it. Do you know anything?'

Megan shook her head. 'I saw him talking to the predatory Helena. She's so desperate for a man she ought to wear a "for hire" sign on her head. He didn't say anything about a job. We were both busy networking last night.' She yawned. 'I think Trelerric used to have a reputation hereabouts for being a fast place where the county set used to hang out. You know, car keys in a basket and that sort of debauchery.'

'Mike said Helena had done a children's party there and that the owner needed a live in help. Maybe the wild party days are a thing of the past.' I said.

'If last night's party was anything to go by you're not missing anything.' Megan responded. 'It was a total success for the party planner but a nightmare for whoever has to clean up afterwards. Just cleaning food and broken champagne glasses out of the swimming pool will cost shedloads. I hope the hotel charges them top dollar for it. But the boys are enjoying the transient pleasures of fame and need something for their social websites to show how fabulous and wonderful their tiny lives are.'

Megan poured more tea, emptying the teapot so I got up and made some fresh while she checked her phone.

'Thanks.' Megan said when I put the pot on the table. 'I've just sent Mike a text telling him he's gorgeous.' She was still tapping away.

I thought it would have been more along the lines of telling him he was her best bunnykins but I kept that to myself.

'And here's something about Trelerric House.' She was reading aloud. 'Tudor origins, fine mullions - whatever they are, something Georgian added, attractive old chapel on site, owned by the Latchley family since forever, gardens being restored, several open days last year. Quite a place.'

Outside it was dull and unpromising and rain was falling in short bad tempered squalls. This was the year Megan was going to be married and there were lots of things to discuss. We spent the day indoors occupying ourselves with glossy wedding magazines, laughing at the dresses worn by minor celebrities and shrieking over impossibly ugly and ornate wedding cakes. As an events manager she was pulling in some favours but there was still personal stuff to arrange. I was really happy for her and glad to help.

The following day I called Helena Fox-Harvey and introduced myself as Megan's sister.

'Sorry if I'm bothering you but Mike Bartlett said something about a job at Trelerric House. I wondered if you knew anything else. I'm looking for something now.'

Helena had a posh, quacky sounding voice. 'Oh ya, I'm rather good friends with the Latchley's. I'm friendly with Alice, Mrs Latchley's niece. It was her daughter's party I catered for. Mrs Latchley is in her seventies, she's an amazing character. Apart from a housekeeper she rattles round that place on her own and wants company. She has a suite on the ground floor. Alice said they'd been looking for someone suitable but so far without success. Apparently Mrs Latchley has views about who she'd like to have living there.'

'She has a housekeeper?' I was making notes as we spoke.

'Ya, it's just a little woman from the village who goes in to cook and clean on an almost daily basis. I'm not sure how it all works but Alice lives close by in one of the estate properties and keeps an eye on her. I can give you Alice's number.'

'Thank you.' I wrote the number down wondering what Helena meant by the term "estate properties". I needed to do a bit of research. And was Alice keeping an eye on the disparagingly described "little woman" or on the elderly Mrs Latchley? It didn't sound like something I wanted to get involved in.

The internet provided me with some background. I learned that Mrs Latchley had been Felicity Gray, an actress some sites described scathingly as a B-movies starlet. Good at playing either the seductress or the femme fatale who screams convincingly in a murder movie. She was a notable beauty with photogenic curves who'd never quite made the big time and had married the heir to the Latchley fortune before she stopped being offered roles. Her late husband Robin Latchley seemed to have been a bit of a wild boy who'd enjoyed everything money could buy and then died leaving the family to cope with death duties and debts. They'd had no children. The family had sold a sizeable portion of the estate to keep Trelerric House and the estate farm. As I read the various reports and stories I wondered if they could actually afford a live-in help. It will be drudgery, I told myself, keeping company with a mad old bat who probably stinks of pee and either has a drink problem or who wanders about in her nightie. Ah, the sweet caring nursing angel I had once been, I thought. Nursing showed you everything about life.

There were some photographs of Trelerric House taken in the summer when the house had had an open day. It was quite beautiful. Intrigued I went down to my car for the road map. Trelerric was shown as Mike had said, overlooking the River Tamar on the Cornish side. Well there's no harm in taking a look, I thought to myself. I had nothing else to do so I decided to go for a drive.

The river was like liquid milk chocolate beneath the toll bridge at Saltash and traffic was heavy on the other side of the road with people pouring into Plymouth to go to the sales or to return Christmas presents. I was a careful driver, having seen the results of too many traffic accidents when working a short period in A&E. I'd briefly had a romance with a traffic cop when I was a student nurse. He'd always advised that we should "drive to arrive" and keep an eye on the behaviour of cars ahead as drivers were easily distracted by anything from horses in a field, to trying to unwrap a sweet or arguing with a passenger. In his opinion using a mobile phone whilst driving was just shorthand for summarising how stupid the average driver was. He'd been a nice guy but as dull as ditchwater. I think I'd been more turned on by the authority of the uniform than by the man wearing it. I'd begun to suspect he suffered from a mild form of OCD when he'd made me go upstairs in the dark because he didn't like the light switches facing different ways on the double socket at the foot of the stairs. He was also a labels freak I remembered, precisely lining things up all facing the same way in the kitchen cupboards. I wasn't a sloppy organiser myself, but he'd taken it to a whole new dimension. He did verbal risk assessments for everything and I'd eventually dumped him. Briefly I wondered if I'd broken his heart, it had never occurred to me.

Following the A-road I drove for a couple of miles and then turned right into narrow lanes and lush green countryside, when an oncoming four wheel drive caused me to pull right over alongside the Cornish hedge. I swore as it splashed by me so close it almost creased my jeans. That was the only vehicle I saw, the world here was quiet and off the beaten track. There was a glimpse of the river with its muddy silted sides and I stopped briefly at a granite cobbled parking spot which looked like an old quay side. Everything was wet and the place deserted. The river made no noise, there were no buildings or bird song and not a breath of wind. It wasn't bleak or eerie, but there was a sense of waiting and of forgotten times.

I continued driving slowly, the road rising and turning ahead of me. Then I saw a battered black and cream sign with the words Trelerric House and underneath Home Farm. It didn't say private or no entry so I drove down through a wooded area and past small fields. Home Farm was on my left and looked well cared for, light glinting off window panes and old low granite buildings providing shelter in the landscape. Coming to an open set of tall metal gates with a lodge house to one side I paused, unsure about driving into the grounds of Trelerric House. I'd just bottled out and was deciding to reverse and turn round when I realised that the car which had forced me into the hedge earlier was now bearing down the road behind me rather fast and I was clearly in its way. Making an instant decision I put my Mini into gear and drove through the gates between banks of huge dripping rhododendrons and into a large open gravelled parking and turning area with an ancient circular watering trough in the centre. There was beauty in the shape of the old house with an old granite mounting block set to one side and I was about to gesture some sort of apology to the driver behind me when I realised that she had her window down and was waving at me urgently.

I stopped and put my window down and the other driver jumped out and hurried over to me.

'So sorry I'm late. I urgently needed a couple of things from the village shop, I'm Alice Marquand.' She put her hand out and smiled, a blonde blue-eyed sunflower of a smile.

I awkwardly shook her hand through the window and then opened the door and got out.

'I'm sorry, I think you were expecting someone else.' I said.

Alice was looking me up and down. I was wearing my usual black jeans with a white roll neck jumper and a black gilet. 'Oh. You're not the nurse. I was expecting a nurse to come to do Aunt Flick's dressing. She's very late. You didn't see another car did you?'

I shook my head. 'No.'

Are you lost then?'

'Yes. Well no, not really. I was just taking a look around.' I paused for a moment under her level gaze with the exquisite backdrop of the building behind her. 'Sorry if that sounded cheeky. Actually, Helena Fox-Harvey told a friend of mine that there was a position here I might be interested in. Working for Mrs Latchley. I'm Lucy Huccaby.'

'Oh well come on in then Lucy and we can talk. It's warmer inside and you can keep me company until the nurse arrives.'

TWO

I followed Alice in through a low arched door with a carved stone door frame worn by centuries of weather. There were trefoils carved into the spandrels either side of the arches instead of escutcheons. The family had no family crest or coat of arms then.

'This is the tradesman's entrance. We don't use the front except on special occasions.' Alice said, leading the way through an internal panelled hall and into a large well fitted and warm kitchen.

'I'll make us all tea, do you drink tea? Flick likes to have a cup about now. The housekeeper usually sees to it but she's having a couple of days off as it's New Year so I'm in charge until Flick's visitors arrive later.'

Saying that I was happy to drink tea I watched Alice as she moved about. Laying a tray with pretty china she handed me a jug.

'There's milk in that fridge. Flick likes things done properly.'

The fridge was a huge American thing, stuffed with food. I obliged and then held doors open as indicated and Alice carried the tray through yet another hallway with stairs rising and then into a suite of rooms which made me gasp. There were Chinese rugs on the pale green carpet and what looked like raw silk curtains in emerald green at the long windows. A green velvet sofa was strewn with Chinese yellow cushions and there was a small dining table. Oriental looking side tables were crammed with objects and framed photographs. The walls were papered in what had to be original hand painted chinoiserie wallpaper and hung with ornate gilded mirrors. The whole impression was sybaritic, like being inside a jewellery box. We continued through into a larger room and this time the colours were slightly more restful, predominantly in shades of teal with touches of black and cream. I noticed red cushions on a turquoise sofa. There was no sign of the sick room I'd been expecting to see.

An elegant slender woman with long artfully waved red hair and wearing full make up was relaxing on a chaise longue. She was wearing a colourful garment with a high collar and long full sleeves with buttoned cuffs over dark silky trousers. I couldn't call it a dressing gown and certainly not a housecoat. The effect was stunning. She put her magazine down and leaning over to a table at her side switched the radio off, regarding us both with interest. I could feel her gauging her moment, as though the director had called action and the cameras had started to roll.

'Thank you Alice. And who is this?' She drew her beautiful hands together in a slow theatrical movement, folding them to show her perfect pale coral nail varnish.

I felt drab in my casual clothes. Like a magpie next to a bird of paradise.

'This is Lucy. Lucy might be interested in helping you Aunt Flick. Lucy, this is my aunt, Mrs Latchley.'

'Sit down here where I can see you properly.' There was a pretty boudoir chair upholstered in turquoise and cream chenille. 'I always think of Lucy as being a name for a fair haired woman but you're dark. And what are your credentials Lucy? You can drive I take it.' She was straight in.

Alice sighed. 'Be nice Aunt Flick. Of course Lucy can drive, how else would she have got here?'

Alice started pouring tea whilst Aunt Flick stared at me. She was sitting with her back to the light and it was difficult to guess her age. I stared right back. I wasn't going to be intimidated that easily. I'd dealt with the desperate, the drunk and the demented in my time. Aunt Flick surprised me by giving me a lovely smile. It was like being dazzled by searchlights but at the same time I could see that she was watching me to see what effect she was having. She gracefully accepted her tea from Alice and spoke to me.

'Don't get old Lucy. It's a complete and utter bitch. My mind is fine but my leg is not at the moment and I have a bad hip. The doctor won't let me smoke any more and apparently I'm bordering on being diabetic. Does that frighten you?'

'No it doesn't Mrs Latchley.'

'And do you smoke?'

I shook my head. 'I run and swim. Smoking wouldn't help my lung capacity, never mind my health.'

Mrs Latchley looked slightly horrified. 'I've never done exercise darling, willpower keeps me slim.'

I didn't want to talk about health, blood pressure and so on. I suspected that she wouldn't be interested so I remained silent.

'Why do you want the job?'

I didn't know what to say. I wasn't sure that I did want the job, I'd come out on an impulse without preparation or even dressing nicely and found myself thrown into an unexpected situation. I realised that Mrs Latchley was getting impatient. It was extraordinary, she wasn't moving or speaking but somehow she was projecting tension into the room. Of course, she was an actress.

'I used to be a nurse Mrs Latchley. Then I stopped nursing and started a business doing something else with a friend. Things went wrong and I'm living with my sister in Plymouth at the moment. She's getting married and selling her flat so I need to find a job and somewhere to live in the next couple of months.' I spoke baldly and almost without thinking because I didn't really care. There was complete and utter silence. I took a sip of my tea.

'And were you married? I see you wear no rings.'

The question surprised me and I felt my hackles rising, it was far too personal but then I realised this wasn't a formal interview in a typical HR setting. This was a discussion about me and whether I would fit into someone's home.

'No. I was engaged once. But it didn't happen.' I remained calm.

Once again there was silence but I could feel sympathy from Alice.

'Do you like music? Did you recognise what was on the radio just now?'

I shook my head. 'I didn't hear it Mrs Latchley.'

'Beethoven's seventh. Marvellous piece. I play of course. Not classical, mostly dance music or old songs.' She indicated a small baby grand I hadn't noticed. 'Do you play?'

Again I shook my head. I remembered how Mike had been horrified by our lack of musical education.

'What do you read?'

'Sorry?' Shit, I thought, is this how interviews normally go?

Mrs Latchley spoke again. 'What do you read, what sort of books or newspapers? Tabloids or broadsheets? Are you a fiction or a non-fiction person? Romance or crime? That sort of thing. Heaven forbid you read science fiction.'

The bloody woman was trying to wind me up. I quite liked sci-fi although I wasn't a Star Wars fan.

'Oh, er,' I cast about desperately, recently I'd been looking at wedding magazines with Megan and at the bumper edition of the Christmas Radio Times, but I found an answer. 'Contemporary fiction, history - I like history. And I read autobiographies sometimes.' I dried up and looked at her helplessly.

'And references. Do you have references?'

Of course I bloody didn't. I'd been self-employed, hadn't she heard me say my business had gone down the pan. I decided the situation was hopeless and stood up

'I'm so sorry Mrs Latchley, Alice. I realise I wasn't prepared for this meeting and I've wasted your time. I think I'd better go now.'

'Not so fast. Sit down Lucy.' Her voice was suddenly filled with strength and purpose. The actress had spoken.

I was so surprised that I sat down. Mrs Latchley was looking at me intently. She had sweeping pencilled eyebrows and full lips. Under smokey eye make-up her eyes were pale silvery grey and clear. She was a very handsome woman.

'I need someone who can stimulate me. I need someone who has had a bit of a life and has opinions. I need to get out once in a while and go to places with someone who knows how to use a knife and fork and drive a car. And just occasionally I might need a little personal or intimate help when my hip goes stiff. I get the nurse in only when necessary and there's Mrs Palfrey from the village who comes almost every day. She cooks and cleans. And of course there's dear Alice, on whom I place far too many demands.'

There was a moment's pause while we all lifted our teacups and politely sipped our tea. I smiled into my teacup, it felt choreographed and faintly absurd.

'When can you move in?'

I looked at Mrs Latchley in surprise. 'Sorry?' I said.

'I'd like you to move in. You're about to be homeless aren't you? You may as well live here and we'll see if we can get to like each other.'

Alice sighed again. 'I asked you not to be rude Aunt Flick.' Alice rolled her eyes and Flick looked amused.

There was a noise and something moved in a basket at the side of the chaise longue. A small head appeared and two huge dark eyes blinked at me. Mrs Latchley leaned over and scooped a tiny blonde body out from beneath a blanket. It was a long haired chihuahua. At that point a doorbell rang and Alice excused herself and hurried off.

'Do you like dogs Lucy? This is Coco. She needs a little walk around the terrace now. Just pop out with her - would you mind?'

Mrs Latchley didn't wait for my answer. Instead she handed me a narrow dog lead plaited in scarlet leather and studded with small brilliant faux gems. I clipped it to Coco's matching collar and obediently followed instructions to go out through the French windows into a small bare courtyard.

I was glad to get outside to give myself a moment to think. At one end there was a gated opening and beyond that a long wide paved and cobbled terrace with low stone walls and large flower urns. running alongside the front of the old house. The view down to the river was lovely as I walked the tiny dog up and down. Inevitably she did what she needed to do but I noticed there were other little piles dotted about. Not very nice, I thought to myself. We didn't have pets as children and I'd never wanted a dog. Life was too short to pick up dog poo.

It was cool outside so I went back to the French windows and let myself in. The visiting nurse was dressing a small wound on Mrs Latchley's foot and Alice beckoned to me.

'Will you take the job Lucy?' She whispered. 'You're the first person she's asked.'

I was still uncertain and took a deep breath wondering what I was going to say.

'Oh but how silly of me,' Alice said. 'I've not shown you your part of the house. Let Coco off the lead and come and have a look and then please tell me yes.'

I followed Alice back to the first hall where a flight of stairs rose in an area I guessed was a link between the Tudor house and the Georgian part. It was carpeted in plain cream and didn't have a backstairs feel. On the first floor the wide landing revealed a graceful space under an ornate skylight, with three doors. Alice went to the door on the right.

'This is yours Lucy. It's the quietest on open days because it looks out over the orchards. Most visitors prefer the formal gardens and they look at the old bit of the house which no-one lives in any more.'

I was speechless. The first room was a pretty sitting room with two sash windows, dark blue sofas facing each other over a modern light wood coffee table and with a flat screen television to the side of a small fireplace. There were occasional tables, a little glass fronted bookcase and an old framed map of Cornwall. Alice told me that the electric fire was modern, safe and legal but that the central heating was usually sufficient to keep the rooms warm. There was an internal hallway with a spacious bedroom off to one side, a beautifully done bathroom and a small fitted kitchen. I looked about with a sense of homecoming.

'It's absolutely lovely. Who designed this?' I asked Alice.

'Flick did it I expect. She used to have lots of house parties and her guests were the sort that expected comfort. What's now the kitchen used to be the dressing room. It is nice though. She has amazing taste. She was married to my uncle, and we're all very fond of her. It's just that with my own family responsibilities and helping mum with the hens I'm a bit busy and can't meet her needs.'

I'd noticed she wore a wedding band. 'Do you have children Alice?' And then I remembered the birthday party Helena had catered for. 'Of course you do, Helena said so.' I spoke before she could answer but she was nodding anyway.

'Two. Thomas is three and Grace is six. Flick adores them.'

We went back downstairs and I got the orientation fixed in my head, locating the ground floor kitchen and the route to Mrs Latchley's rooms. The nurse was just leaving as we went in. Mrs Latchley beckoned me over. She looked a bit tired I thought.

'Please tell me that you're coming to stay Lucy.' She smiled that dazzling smile again.

'Yes. I think I will Mrs Latchley.' I said, realising I'd been seduced by the accommodation provided.

'Wonderful. In that case you may call me Flick.' And she held out her hand to me.

Stopping off at a supermarket I bought a huge bunch of flowers before driving back to Megan's flat feeling slightly bemused and wondering what the hell I'd got myself into. She received the news and the flowers with interest.

'Wow, these are lovely.' She kissed my cheek. 'How much are they paying you?'

'I haven't a clue Meg.'

'What? Have you lost your marbles Luce?' Megan looked at me with some concern. She was the only person who abbreviated my already short name.

'I honestly don't know. I have free board and lodging, no bills to pay. It's quiet and there are wonderful views. I get to walk something small which thinks it might be a dog and I have to spend time with the owner who is not an invalid. I met Alice who seems quite lovely and Mrs Latchley, Flick, is quite a character. There's a daily housekeeper and a visiting nurse. And you should see the interior decor. It's incredible.'

'And when do you start this unpaid voluntary work?' Megan asked.

'Flick wants me to move in as soon as possible, so I thought I'd move my stuff at the weekend. That way you can have the spare room all tidy and nice for the estate agent's photographs next week.

Megan nodded thoughtfully. 'Okay. If you've decided then we'll make it happen. Shall we get Mike's van to move your things?'

'I've not got enough to fill a van, even Mike's transit van.' I said.

'But with a van I can come and pretend to be helping you and I can see what you're letting yourself in for.' Megan's logic was impeccable. 'And why is she called Flick? Is it because she was in the flicks once?'

'It's her pet name, short for Felicity. She was the actress Felicity Gray before she married Robin Latchley.'

The next couple of days passed quickly as I sorted all my things out. I discovered I'd got more than I'd remembered; there were boxes of stuff under the bed and some boxes of catering equipment in Megan's garage. We half filled Mike's transit van and he drove the three of us to Trelerric House at the weekend. I'd phoned Alice beforehand to make sure that I could get in. Mrs Latchley was out. She'd been taken out to lunch by an old male friend. Alice had indiscreetly described him as a "disreputable old lounge lizard, one of Robin's old friends who just wouldn't give up".

While Mike carried boxes, grumbling in his good natured way that "once a roadie always a roadie" Megan helped me with my clothes, not sufficient to fill one of the two wardrobes, and walked about admiring the setup.

'It's very pretty here isn't it. And you've got a little kitchen of your own.'

'There's a big kitchen downstairs as well. And a laundry. Clothes are not put outside to dry here I gather.' I was feeling quite excited. Without Mrs Latchley being there I didn't feel able to go into her private rooms even though I would have loved to show Megan.

Megan was quite happily poking about upstairs as the other two rooms weren't locked. 'Pretty views from this side. Yours just looks out onto that scruffy orchard.'

'Alice said it was quieter and more private during open days. And mine is bigger, the only one with a sitting room.'

We went back into my rooms where Mike had just delivered the final box. 'Phew. Nice place Lucy. Oh you've even got a landline.' He was looking at a phone in a charging dock.

'No, that connects to Mrs Latchley's rooms. So she can call me if she needs assistance.'

'Oh. Let's hope that's not the downside.' Mike said. 'Bum wiping at midnight and so on.'

'I don't think she's at that stage Mike.' I said, but it was a sobering thought.

He drove the three of us back to Plymouth. I was spending one last night there and moving to Trelerric House tomorrow. We got a Thai takeaway to celebrate my new start.

On my arrival at Trelerric House the following morning I was let in by the housekeeper, Mrs Palfrey. She immediately asked me to called her Maggie.

'Sorry I missed you yesterday but I always have Sunday off. I've got family of my own to look after as well. Alice has got you a key cut, we only really use this one door. All the post and deliveries come here. And Mrs Latchley's visitors. Not like the days when they used to drive round to the front. Although I don't remember that of course because it was before my time.'

Maggie was younger than I had imagined, chatty and with a quick way of doing things.

'Does Mrs Latchley get a lot of visitors?' I asked her.

'Some days, them that's survived from the old party days and the films. Not as many as she used to. They're beginning to start dropping off the end I suppose. They do tell some stories though. I've listened at the door sometimes. It curls your hair the stuff they got up to. Proper naughty if you know what I mean.' She pulled a face.

I said I suspected I understood. Maggie suggested I should take my bag upstairs and then help her take a tray in to Mrs Latchley. 'Be good to have an extra pair of hands and legs here Lucy. I'm fit but I can't be everywhere at once even though I do try.'

I did as she said and we went through to Flick's rooms. This time Flick was dressed in some sort of lounging clothes with long wide trousers in a patterned silky material and a plain top but with the neckline finished in the same pattern. It was quite hot in her rooms. Sitting down I noticed how thin her thighs were. Of Coco there was no sign.

'Sam's taken her out. She likes Sam.' Flick said in answer to my query.

I had no idea who Sam was but didn't ask as Flick was discussing her menu with Maggie. 'Soup and then cold chicken and salad will be nice Maggie. Is that alright for you Lucy? We eat at 12.30 in the Chinese room and then I'll take a little rest. You'd normally take Coco out then but not today since she's out at the doggy parlour. She likes to be groomed and to have her hair done like all girls.'

I wondered what, exactly, I would be doing that was useful. Having lunch with my employer and walking her excuse for a dog didn't seem as though it was going to be challenging.

'What will I be doing to help Flick?' I asked as I poured her first cup of Earl Grey and as an afterthought placed a small slice of lemon into the cup.

'Oh this and that, we'll think of something. I have some fixed appointments you will take me to. My wardrobe needs some attention and there'll be some shopping to do together. Cosmetics and so on. I need a little help dressing and undressing sometimes and it will be a relief to Maggie not to have to do that. She does all the food shopping, though I think most of it gets delivered somehow. And she does the rooms out and changes my bed. I do like everything fresh and tidy. But you can do the flowers and sometimes you might read to me, on wet days and such.'

Okay, this was going to be a different experience then. Not particularly onerous and not exactly a lot of laughs. After morning tea I carried the tray back to the big kitchen where Maggie was busy. I was impressed by the fact that she was making the soup from fresh ingredients. She told me she loved cooking, and that she'd make a batch sufficient for freezing for later use. I noticed a whole cooked chicken already cooling. Maggie followed my gaze.

'Mrs Latchley eats the same sort of things every week Lucy, so I can anticipate what to do but she likes to give me instructions. Gives her something to do I suppose. I know she likes chicken on Mondays. And she'll have some in a sandwich and some fruit tomorrow for her tea. Now you're here more of it will get eaten, though Mr Sam will take it without asking if my back's turned. And Coco gets a teaspoonful as well. Then I've got salmon and lemon sole in the freezer. We have to watch Mrs Latchley's diet with the diabetes. No cakes I'm afraid.'

No problem, I thought, I've a small oven upstairs and if I want cake I'll make it myself. I shall have my cake and eat it one day.

Maggie was looking at me and I realised she was waiting for an answer to something.

'Sorry Maggie, I was miles away. What did you say?'

'I said you looked as though you could do with a good meal inside you. You don't have to restrict your intake to what Mrs Latchley eats. There's plenty here for extras, eggs and cheese and stuff. You can help yourself.'

Just as I thanked her the internal phone rang. I answered it and was summoned to join Flick. And so my first day began.

THREE

After sleeping surprisingly well I woke before the alarm went off, an old habit from my nursing years. Feeling quite at home in my new rooms I showered and dressed before eating a bowl of home made muesli, part of the provisions I'd brought with me. I liked to "knit my own" as Megan called it, toasting the oats and seeds and chopped nuts separately before amalgamating them with diced dried fruits. It tasted better than the bland stuff in the shops and I liked to think that toasting ingredients killed off a few bugs. Looking around I was ridiculously pleased to have my own little kitchen for the first time in my life.

The routine meant that I only ate lunch with Flick, but I had to be available to help her at nine with dressing as she was sometimes rather stiff in the mornings. For a few minutes I stood idly at the window looking out over the damp leafless orchard, watching a blackbird pecking at some old windfalls. The weather was quiet and misty, unlike the rest of the country which, the television informed me, was experiencing cold spells with gusts of snow. Slightly irritated by the smirking weatherman advising everyone to wrap up warm I switched the television off and as I turned to go downstairs I saw a man walk into the orchard. He was pushing a wheelbarrow and accompanied by a collie who was circling him with intent.

Apart from Flick, Alice and Maggie I'd seen no-one else here. Perhaps this was Sam who had taken Coco to the grooming parlour. I couldn't see him clearly because he was bundled up in a thick jumper, a woolly hat and chunky boots. As I watched the man he stopped under one of the apple trees and taking implements from the wheelbarrow started purposefully sawing and cutting branches which dropped to the ground. Megan had remarked that it all looked scruffy, probably because several of the trees had piles of brushwood under them. I glanced at my watch. It was time to go down.

There was no sign of Maggie so I switched the kettle on and then went through to Flick's suite, knocking politely as I did and calling her name. Flick was in the dressing room next to the bedroom, sitting at her dressing table and skilfully applying make up. The room was enormous, done out in shades of cream and with a couple of chairs upholstered in black and gold. A central circular table held a huge display of fresh flowers. The scent of lilies was almost unpleasantly strong. Flick wasn't dressed but was wearing a gorgeous dark blue silk kimono wrap. She looked at me and gave me the dazzle smile.

'Don't you ever wear make up Lucy? I can't face the day without it.'

'I do sometimes, if there's a party or something. But no, I don't wear it every day.' I said, watching her complicated procedures with blusher and eye make up.

I then got quizzed on my skin cleaning routines, advice on the best products to use, and questioned as to whether I suffered from spots.

'I must introduce you to my sister Megan. She loves all this kind of thing. We're very different but very close.' I said.

'Megan. That's a Celtic name isn't it? You said she lives in Plymouth. Are you from around here then?'

'She's slightly older than me and dad gave her his mum's name. Dad's Cornish originally, from near Looe. Mum is Irish, but they live just outside Hereford on the Welsh borders, where I grew up.' I didn't say anything about us being adopted. I wasn't embarrassed, it just wasn't necessary.

'Irish. Oh the poetry and the passion of the Irish. I love it. They write wonderful plays and make marvellous lovers. I think I may have a little Irish in me, with my colouring.' Flick paused and surveyed herself. 'Yes, that's good. I think I shall dress now. Can you move those for me Lucy?' Flick pointed at some wet towels on the dressing room floor.

I went over and picked them up and took them into the bathroom where I stopped dead. It was all done out in gold and cream, even the wall tiles were a textured gold. It was completely over the top and absolutely gorgeous. I folded the towels over an old fashioned gold-painted radiator, noticing that Flick had a seat arranged in a walk-in shower so she could sit down to wash. She obviously used a hand held shower attachment because she didn't wash her own hair and she had to keep the wound dressing on her foot dry. This woman certainly had things arranged well although the cheap white plastic seat was out of keeping with the cream fixtures and gave a hint of infirmity.

Back in the dressing room I realised that what I'd taken for pale wooden wall panelling was actually a whole wall of wardrobes behind sliding doors. I looked around, make that three walls of wardrobes. I'd never seen anything like it as I helped Flick select something to wear.

'I can see you're interested Lucy.' Flick said. 'I designed these rooms in calmer neutral colours because they should not compete with my clothes when I'm trying things on.'

Her shoes, bags, hats and accessories had most of one wall of their own; skirts, trousers, tops and dresses had another and the remaining wall seemed to be filled with underwear and the extravagant daily lounging clothes she favoured. Starting with the underwear I was overwhelmed by silk and lace, everything scented and matching in shades of peach, pale green, midnight blue and soft pink and I realised that Flick was enjoying my reactions.

'Wonderful things aren't they. I've always had the very best that other people could afford to buy me. A lot of this is Italian or Austrian and some of it is American. They know about style and quality Lucy. And they last, some of my things are thirty years old, from my acting days. And of course Robin never denied me anything. He always wanted me to have lovely things.'

Well, it was all rather different to my practical and simple wardrobe upstairs. Megan had always been amused by my capsule approach to clothes. She referred to it as sartorially feeble. I relied on plain underwear and currently possessed two pairs of black trousers, nicely cut. Two pairs of black jeans, ditto. White t-shirts with different necklines and sleeve lengths and a few white blouses, one of which had grey polkadots and a bit of a frill round the neckline. One straight black skirt and one flared black skirt, a bit dressy. A little black dress of course, a white cardigan, a black cashmere cardigan, a gilet and a jacket, both black. Today I was wearing black trousers with a long sleeved white cotton roll neck and a sleeveless v-necked black jumper. As a nurse I'd worn regulation blue and at school I'd worn grey and hideous maroon. That was the summary of my experience with colour, apart from my red Mini or making cake decorations.

Flick assessed herself in a large cheval mirror and once she was happy with her appearance asked me to ring Maggie for her breakfast. She could have done it herself but she had to give me something to do. I retired to the kitchen and had a cup of coffee with Maggie while Flick ate alone with the newspaper and a new gossipy magazine.

'Mrs Latchley always has half a grapefruit and a slice of wholemeal toast with peanut butter, Earl Grey tea with lemon and two multivitamin capsules. She likes to find out what the celebrities are doing and read the obits.' Maggie told me. 'I think she misses the good times she used to have.'

I mentioned the beautiful clothes, like nothing I'd ever seen or handled before and Maggie nodded.

'Her clothes are worth a fortune. No wonder the estate nearly went bust. Mr Latchley, that was Robin, gave her carte blanche you know. That's like a blank cheque to you or me. I reckon it was to atone for his marital misdemeanours.'

'Oh.' I thought for a moment. Don't men usually give their wives jewellery to apologise in those circumstances?'

'Do they? My husband's never strayed then.' Maggie spoke casually. 'But Mrs Latchley's only ever been interested in clothes. She was never much bothered about jewellery because her dress clothes are covered in glitter and gemstones. All fake but very impressive. She'll show you one day. It's a real treat.'

Maggie told me that Flick had fresh towels every day so I learned to put the wet towels into the laundry instead of back on the towel rail. Flick existed in a cocoon of perfection. I soon found myself taking cut flowers upstairs to my rooms rather than throw them out after four days and Maggie gave me lessons in flower arranging. Flick would tweak my arrangements to her satisfaction and was an endless source of advice regarding colour and shape.

Flick's routine meant that every Friday morning I had to drive her to the hairdresser. She thought my Mini rather cute, like Coco, but I discovered she expected me to drive her in her Jaguar which I found a bit alarming.

'I'll call Timothy.' Flick said. 'Timothy will show you how to drive it.'

She explained that Timothy was Robin Latchley's much younger brother who lived at Home Farm. He came to find me the day before I was due to drive the beast. I was exercising Coco and walking her further than I think she was used to when a man in a tweedy jacket and a mustard waistcoat with fawn cords and polished brogues came striding towards me. He stuck his hand out in a way that reminded me of Alice, and had the same fair hair under his cap.

'I'm Tim Latchley and you must be Lucy. Gather I've got to give you a driving lesson!' His hand was hard and dry and his eyes were blue. 'Alice has told us a little about you. Bloody rude of me not to come over but I've been busy with the sheep. Lots to settle in the lambing field and lots to set up in the barn in readiness. And Jane, that's my wife, is up to her neck in paperwork. But you must come over and meet us all soon.' He looked down at Coco who was sniffing his shoes which were about the same size as her. 'How do you like that thing?'

'I've never known anything like her.' I said. 'But she functions and has a character and at least she's not yappy.'

Tim clearly wanted to give me a lesson in Jaguar driving right now so we went round to the garages. There were three parking bays in a handsome old stone Coach House. One held a muddy Landrover, one held the Jaguar and the other was empty.

'The Landrover belongs to Sam. He lives in the flat above. You should use that spare space and keep your Mini under cover. Flick doesn't like cars cluttering up the courtyard.' Tim had the keys to the Jag in his hand. 'These are kept in the key cupboard in Maggie's kitchen. I'll just pull her out and then you can get in.'

I stood back with Coco as the sleek dark red car rolled out. It was a beautiful thing with a cream leather interior. Coco seemed familiar with it and of course there was a little dog bed on the back seat. Tim lifted her onto it and and fastened the seatbelt through the loop in her lead to keep her safe before shutting the door.

'In you get Lucy. Driver's side.'

Tim was patient and a good instructor. I'd been driving for years, but not anything as big as this. The car was an automatic and after going through all the sticks and knobs we went out right down to the A road and I drove further up into Cornwall as I got the hang of it. It was lovely to drive. On the way back Tim directed me round a roundabout and into an attractive set of several single-storey barn conversions around a granite cobbled courtyard.

'Private dentist, hairdresser to the film star, beauty parlour for the desperate. I don't know why Flick doesn't move here permanently, she keeps them all going. I expect you'll use them as well if she has anything to do with it.'

'I'm not desperate yet.' I responded without thinking but he laughed. I also wasn't sure that my salary would stretch that far. On my first day Flick had suggested a monthly payment which had seemed rather small, until I sat down and calculated what I would have been spending on renting an apartment, paying utility bills and buying food. Then it felt better. I still had a small sum left in the bank and in savings after closing the business with Emma, some of which had gone on rent to Megan, but even so I felt I had to be careful.

I drove us back to Trelerric House and calculated the time I needed to get Flick to her appointments. It wasn't much and I was relieved that I didn't have to drive into Plymouth as I wasn't confident about parking the Jag. Tim was obviously a mind reader.

'Right then Lucy, you'd take Flick right to the tradesman's entrance and get her back inside without getting her hair messed up or there'll be hell to pay, but then you'll have to bring the car back round here and reverse and back her up undercover. So you may as well do that bit now.'

I swore silently. It took me four attempts but I did it. Tim congratulated me.

'Nice. You're calm. You're a nurse aren't you, must have something to do with it. Steady nerves and hands. I'll have you helping with the lambing and driving a tractor next.'

I had an odd feeling that he was serious. We got out and I extracted Coco, taking my time to lift her out because my legs felt like jelly after surviving the driving lesson.

'Who cleans the car? It was spotless when we went out.' The car was a bit mud splashed now.

'Lad who's come to work in the gardens. Simon something. He's proving to be a good all rounder. Right then, got to go now, loads to do. Cheers Lucy.'

Tim strode off. He seemed to have one pace, a fast walk. I looked down at Coco who was looking up at me expectantly. She huffed through her teeth and wagged her plumy little tail. I found myself quite liking her and walked her carefully back to the house. I had a funny feeling that someone had been watching everything from the flat above the Coach House. I also wondered who owned the smart blue Honda which was parked almost out of sight to one side. It hadn't been there when we went out.

Flick kept me busy with all sorts of little jobs but I had no difficulty dealing with her requests. It was quite relaxing receiving instructions and not having to think. All my working life I'd dealt with other peoples' needs and problems and made decisions for them. When I was running a business I'd spent too much time sorting out orders and worrying over the inevitable paperwork, but I was meticulous by nature. By comparison Flick's world was in soft focus and lacking in chaos but as I worked I began to get to know her and to like her. I also discovered that she didn't just read the gossip columns and the obits, she read the financial papers as well and had a mind like an abacus together with an astonishing memory.

One day Alice came round for afternoon tea and brought the children. Flick was marvellous with them. Thomas banged around on the floor with a toy and Grace tried Flick's shoes and scarves on and traipsed about admiring herself in the mirrors. Alice said she had come to pass on an invitation to me to join the family for the annual Wassail followed by what she called Saturday supper.

'We all get together twice a month to make sure we're on track. Mum sends her apologies for not having come over to invite you, it's a busy time of year, actually it's always busy. She does most of the farm business and I help with the hens and with organising the open days here. Then we're developing the gardens side and will be increasing plant sales. Garden visitors are always taking cuttings or pinching things so now we have plants for sale when the house and gardens are open. We need to do more in the way of refreshments as well. It's manic quite honestly. Anyway you can bring Flick if that's alright.'

I was happy to accept. I was familiar with the idea of Wassail having grown up in rural Herefordshire, but had never attended one. Alice described it to me.

'We thank the orchard for its bounty and sing it a song and toast it with mulled cider. It's fun, it doesn't last very long and then we'll go inside to eat. Just make sure you dress warmly and you'll need boots for the mud.'

After they'd gone I tidied things away in Flick's rooms and then loaded the dishwasher. I was just working out the programme when the internal phone rang. It was Flick asking if I had Coco with me.

'No, she's not with me.'

'Well I can't find her anywhere. Will you come and look Lucy.'

Returning to Flick's rooms I checked around. There was no sign of her and Flick was unsettled.

'She can't have got out. She must have got into the house somehow. Lucy be a darling and search the house, she's only tiny and it's cold outside my rooms.'

Not sure where to start looking I stood outside the door to Flick's suite; the house was a rabbit warren of corridors, hallways and interconnecting rooms but most of the doors were closed because the rooms weren't in use. I knew the house didn't have a basement or cellars but I wasn't at all familiar with the layout, cold grey days didn't invite one to go exploring in a dark closed house and anyway I'd been busy learning what my tasks and role were for the first couple of weeks.

I walked back to the kitchen, checking corners and beneath the odd piece of furniture as I did so. Then I realised that a door off my familiar hallway with the stairs to my rooms was slightly open. I pushed and it swung quietly revealing a dimly lit grand entrance hall with a wide curving staircase ascending on the far side. The floor was tiled in black and white and I called Coco's name but heard nothing apart from a small echo. I shivered. There was only a little light filtering through a skylight at the top of the stairs and the window shutters were closed. I couldn't see a light switch so I hurried back to the kitchen for the torch kept there. Flick was at the door to her rooms holding Coco's lead like a talisman.

'Go back inside where it's warm Flick.' I told her. 'I'm getting a torch so that I can see where I'm going. She's probably in the big entrance hall. I won't be long I'm sure.'

Taking the dog lead I set off. The torch was powerful but there was no sign of Coco in the large hall and all the other doors leading off were closed. I guessed they had to be to comply with fire safety regulations. I looked at the staircase, it was wide and graceful with shallow risers, even a tiny dog could jump up them. Coco must be fitter than I thought, all those extra walks I'd been giving her had increased her vigour. Sweeping the torch from side to side I ascended the stairs swiftly. At the top there was a long wide carpeted corridor, part of the Georgian addition. It must have been wonderful when the house was in permanent use. Calling Coco's name I thought I heard the funny little huffing sound she made. Walking down the corridor I called her again and shook her lead, it had a tiny bell which made an irritating tinkling noise. Coco emerged from beneath an ornate padded seat. She had a cobweb over one ear and was looking pleased with herself, her little body wriggling as though she was glad to be found and that it was all a good game. I put the torch on the seat and crouched down making a fuss of her as I clipped the lead on. She had such a solid warm little body for a tiny dog. She was licking my hands.

'Good girl Coco. Come on poppet, come on let's go back downstairs where it's warm. It's like a fridge up here.' I turned to go but Coco had other ideas and with surprising strength pulled back. The bench she'd been under was almost opposite a door which was set back in a little recess. She looked up at me with expectation and gave me her most eloquent huff. As instructed I opened the door.

The light from the torch spilled into a lovely sitting room and I stepped forward sweeping the beam around, seeing a pretty side table holding photographs, a green velvet upholstered chaise longue and a small sofa with pretty matching chairs. It was very feminine, more of Flick's taste I guessed, realising there was a lot to see in this house. Suddenly all the lights went on and I nearly jumped out of my skin. I turned and there was a man standing right behind me with his hand on the light switch and looking at me curiously. I almost screamed.

'Sorry, I didn't mean to frighten you. I wondered what you were doing.'

I had an impression of height and solid strength.

'I was looking for the dog. She'd disappeared.' I looked down at Coco who was standing at the end of the lead I was holding and innocently wagging her little tail at the man.

'You obviously found her. Were you looking for anything else up here?' His voice was quite deep.

I couldn't look the man in the face. I was so embarrassed. 'No. Well, Coco seemed to want to come in here, so I opened the door. I take her for walks you see and I'm getting to know her ways.' I felt and sounded like a complete fool. And a fool who'd been caught snooping at that. The man was still looking at me and I turned away in confusion.

'Well, I'll take Coco back downstairs now. Mrs Latchley is worried about her.'

He stood back and I left him to switch the bedroom lights off and walked away, then hesitated, surely he'd be coming down the stairs with me. Who on earth was he? As if reading my mind he spoke.

'I'll switch off up here once you're through the hall. I have another way out.'

'Yes. Right, alright then. Thank you.' I picked Coco up and hurried downstairs to Flick's rooms all the while conscious of his eyes on my back.

Flick was delighted to see Coco and made a fuss of her, asking her if she'd had an adventure and feeding her with a couple of doggy treats she kept in a drawer. I said nothing about meeting the stranger but that night I made sure I locked the door to my own rooms. If he had his own way out then surely he'd be able to get in as well.

FOUR

The following morning I sat with Flick having our mid-morning tea in the Chinese room and looking out at the dreary little courtyard beyond the French windows. It was quite narrow and ran the length of the Chinese room and the day room and there were French doors from both rooms. Flick was reading snippets of gossip out of one of her favourite magazines but I wasn't really paying attention. Eventually she put the magazine down and spoke directly to me.

'You're very quiet today. Have you got something on your mind Lucy?'

'I was thinking about all the colour in this house and the way you design things. I saw one of the rooms upstairs yesterday when I was looking for Coco.' I paused, not wanting to mention the man who'd found me apparently in the act of snooping.

Flick was looking interested as I'd hoped. I thought she needed more to do than just wash and dress and read the gossip columns.

'Oh yes, I had wonderful times doing the interior design, it's a while since I've been upstairs.' Her eyes were full of memories and for a moment her expression was complicated.

'I was thinking about this courtyard here Flick. It's so dull to look out onto. It doesn't invite you to step outside. What could you imagine should be here? It should be something to compliment these rooms.'

Flick looked doubtful 'I don't know Lucy, I've never been a gardener. I love flowers of course,' she glanced over at the display on one of the tables. 'But I've never thought about outside. Have you any ideas?'

I looked around the room, seeing the excess of colour and decoration and felt the need for something simple. Then I got it.

'A Japanese courtyard. Something peaceful, low maintenance and exquisite, I think I saw something in one of your magazines.'

I went to the turquoise day room to the pile of magazines spilling over a table near Flick's chaise and found the one I was thinking of. There were photographs of a design for a small garden which had won an award at Hampton Court. The thrust of the article was that it was a garden for all seasons, lovely with frosty contours in winter and a little jewel in summer. Flick was interested.

'It's very different isn't it,' she said. 'Different in scale and very pretty with those handsome stones and that unusual path. It's not just a pile of old gravel.' She absently tapped a front tooth with a long varnished finger nail. 'I know, we need to call Sam. He's the gardener here and might be able to come up with something. Pass me my telephone would you Lucy.'

I found Flick's mobile and handed it to her. Sam, the man who took Coco to the dog parlour, the gardener. He must have been the man I'd seen pruning the apple trees in the orchard on my first morning.

Flick called a number and spoke briefly as I took the tea tray out to a side table in the outer hall. When I came back she was looking pleased and flicking through the photographs of the garden again.

'Sam's coming in this afternoon. I might not have a nap and you'll have to walk Coco a bit earlier. We'll have the tray earlier as well so that he can have tea with us. And ask Maggie if she could make a few sandwiches for us all. I think we'll just have soup for lunch in that case.'

It all seemed a lot of fuss for the gardener but it was clearly a special event for Flick. Maggie was busy with the laundry that day so I set the tea tray in readiness and made the sandwiches myself. Then I walked Coco to the gate lodge and then back round by the Coach House and across the gravel to the long terrace where I let her off the lead. She was definitely fitter and I found myself enjoying the little looks she threw over her shoulder to me as she dashed about after a twig I threw. She also came when I called her so I made a fuss and petted her before going back indoors.

I could hear voices as I opened the door. Flick was laughing, her face animated. Coco gave an uncharacteristic yap and scampered into the room as I followed. Flick looked up and gave me her most dazzling smile.

'Lucy. Come in and meet Sam. Darling this is Lucy, my companion. She's Cornish-Irish heritage.'

I walked forward, curious to meet the cause of so much pleasure to my employer. Someone stood up and turned to me, it was the man I'd seen upstairs. Unusually for me I was tongue-tied. We shook hands awkwardly, my hand cold in his warm grasp.

'Sorry, I was walking Coco and it's colder than I thought. I should have worn my gloves.' I couldn't look him in the face. 'Shall I get the tray in Flick?' I just had to get out of the room.

Flick nodded and I fled to the safety of the kitchen where I busied myself with the kettle and milk jug and unwrapped the sandwiches. There was no cake because of Flick's diabetes. I heard the door behind me and spoke.

'I'm about to go through Maggie. Can you hold the door for me?'

'My pleasure.' The voice was deep. It was Sam and he was smiling.

'These look good. There's always good things to be found in Maggie's kitchen.'

'Well I made them so don't hold your hopes up.' I responded tartly, immediately annoyed with myself.

Sam merely raised his eyebrows. 'Let me do the doors. I'm very good at opening doors and putting lights on.'

I didn't trust myself to speak but I let him help. Flick was waiting impatiently. Sam started talking about Coco and I got the feeling he was being diplomatic.

'She's looking fitter, brighter. Have you changed her biscuits or something Flick?'

I noticed he didn't call her Mrs Latchley.

'No, it's because of Lucy. Lucy pays her attention and walks her properly doesn't she my pet.' I looked up but Flick was addressing the dog directly. Sam caught my eye and grimaced slightly. I looked away and offered Flick her tea and a choice of sandwiches.

'I've made egg and cress, smoked salmon with humous and cucumber and there's chicken with Waldorf salad.'

'You made these Lucy?' Flick asked, taking one of each. I'd made sure I'd cut them daintily and set them out nicely.

'Delicious.' Sam had taken one of the chicken ones and put the whole thing in his mouth. He chewed and swallowed. 'Are these freshly caught Waldorf's then?'

'I made it,' I said, not humouring him. 'But the mayonnaise is out of a jar.'

I took a couple for myself before Sam could make serious inroads. Flick ate delicately but finished each sandwich.

'That was lovely Lucy. I liked the salmon with the humous. Normally I'd have cream cheese. You must have a word with Maggie.'

'Different.' Sam was eating a whole salmon sandwich now. 'Why humous? It's nice, I like it. Is it a Cornish-Irish speciality?'

'I just want to introduce a little variation.' I replied, trying not to scowl at him. I wasn't going to start banging on about healthy eating for the diabetic. I simply felt that Flick had a little too much dairy produce in her diet sometimes.

Sam was clearly enjoying himself but Flick was intent on getting down to business. She picked up the magazine and gestured to the courtyard outside.

'We had a thought about all this out here. It's very dull for us on a cold winter day. There's nothing to look at. Lucy thinks we should have a Japanese courtyard garden to brighten things up.'

Sam glanced at me and then took the magazine from Flick.

'Oh not another woman with ideas,' he said lightly. 'What with you and Alice I'm run off my feet as it is.'

I took the opportunity to look at him. His hair was thick and light brown, the sort that would go fairer in the sunshine. Even in winter his skin was lightly tanned. He looked up at me and I noticed his eyes were a sort of honey coloured hazel.

'Interesting idea.' He turned his attention to Flick. 'I need to remind myself about how much light actually comes in here and do some measurements. The hard landscaping will be easy enough. Maybe a big pot for a specimen acer, that would be a bit Chinese not Japanese but with this room as inspiration it would fit.' Sam was looking around at the wallpaper and the rugs. 'I went to some lectures on oriental garden design when I was a student at Writtle. I've still got all my notes in folders somewhere. I'll have a look and a think.'

'You can do something then Sam?' Flick asked.

'Of course I can. I can't promise when exactly but I'll get Simon to help.'

To Flick's regret the little meeting came to an end. Sam had things to do and I didn't want to hang about so I made an excuse and escaped up to my room for a few minutes. When I returned to collect the tray he'd gone and Flick was watching television in her day room. I knew she'd doze a bit.

On Friday morning I took Flick to her hairdresser. She insisted I went in with her and was received like royalty by Jason the owner. It gave her immense enjoyment. I stood back as she was settled in to have her roots touched up but Flick turned her attention to me.

'We have to do something about your hair Lucy. It just won't do the way you wear it. Jason, have you someone here who could do Lucy please?'

Jason handed me over to a tiny girl with an eyebrow piercing and artfully cut blonde wispy hair with blue and lilac tips. The effect was rather dramatic with her brown eyes. She introduced herself as Sunny although she was anything but as she combed my hair about and frowned.

'When did you last have it cut and styled? Is it your natural colour? What do you want me to do with it?'

I cringed. Honestly I'd rather go to the dentist. All I could say was 'Ages ago. Yes. I've no idea.'

Sunny stomped over to the basins in clumpy flat boots and washed my hair harder than I liked and then smothered it in conditioner before half drowning me to wash it all out. Then she wrapped my head in a towel and ordered me back to the seats where she proceeded to comb sections of my hair in different directions and flash her scissors about. I hate blades near my face so I shut my eyes and hoped for the best.

All I managed to whimper was 'Not too much off please, I like to tie it back sometimes.' Eventually I chanced a look. Instead of hanging straight down my back my hair was now shoulder length. The centre parting had gone and she'd shaped my hair off the hair line at my forehead where it grew strongly.

'Layers?' Sunny barked at me.

'No thank you.' I answered.

'You need something to help it to move. I'll just give it some texture then.'

Her scissors flashed again. What on earth was she talking about I thought irritably. Hair doesn't need help to move and it already has texture. I have never been able to do stylist-speak, unlike Megan who could change her looks as quickly as she changed her clothes. Sunny plugged in the hairdryer and proceeded to deafen me as she gave me the fastest blow-dry I've ever had.

I watched as my hair took on a casual curve around my face. It fell in a shiny dark curtain but even I could see that it wasn't chopped straight and flat. Sunny combed it and moved it about and snipped a few imaginary stray hairs. I was fascinated, it was like watching a disobedient pet behaving nicely for someone.

'There. I like that.' Sunny stopped and surveyed her work. Then she broke into a delighted grin which transformed her and almost did a pirouette as she reached for a mirror to show me the results. 'Lovely isn't it. I really enjoyed getting stuck into that. You've got thick straight hair and it's fabulous to cut.'

I had to agree that it looked lovely. 'Is that really me?' I couldn't help saying, turning my head and watching my hair swish and fall back into place. 'Wow.'

Flick and Jason both made admiring comments and when Flick was finished she refused to let me pay.

'You're a nice looking girl Lucy. Your face is what we used to call heart shaped and you've got good bones and eyes. If you put your mind to it you could turn a few heads you know.' Flick was chatting as I drove us home.

All I could think was that I couldn't wait to show Megan my new look. I was seeing her on Sunday.

Saturday was one of those early spring days in Cornwall that offer delight at every changing hour. I walked Coco and noticed snowdrops emerging in a sheltered corner, one of my favourite flowers. There were buds swelling on things I didn't recognise and the air was soft and sweet. I gave a bit of a skip and threw a small stick for Coco, who went as fast as her short legs could move her and exuberantly retrieved it for me. She really was a cute little thing.

Back at the house I helped Flick look through her wardrobe to find something to wear that evening.

'Something simple. It's just a plain supper and a family chat. At least we don't eat late.'

'What about dressing for Wassail?'

'Oh I shan't do that. But you must. I shall stay inside at Home Farm while all that nonsense is going on. It doesn't last long.'

She eventually settled on something she called harem pants which she wore with a full sleeved fitted sparkly blue top and a plain bolero jacket. Her foot was much better and she selected a pair of soft blue leather pumps to complete her look.

'What are you wearing tonight Lucy?'

'Well I can't match your style Flick.' I said.

Flick sighed. 'Not many people can.'

I dressed in jeans, the dressier of my blouses and the black cashmere cardigan, adding a thermal vest and black boots. I thought my new hairstyle added something. I'd washed it that morning and it had fallen effortlessly into place when I'd dried it. I really liked the rich bitch look it gave me. Flick wasn't so sure about my look though when I presented myself in her rooms but there was nothing she could do as it was time to go. She was also unimpressed about travelling in my car.

'It's only to the farm Flick, we don't need the Jag to go half a mile. And it's your family, they want to see you, they don't care about your wheels.'

She allowed me to boss her about a little but I hadn't appreciated it was about the discomfort in her leg and hip.

We were greeted at the door by Timothy who kissed Flick and shook my hand.

'Hairdresser has been busy then,' he commented drily, giving me a knowing look. 'You both look very nice. Keep your jacket on Lucy, we'll be going outside shortly.'

I followed them through into a big farmhouse sitting room, finding the furnishings and decoration to my taste. There was a fire flickering in a wood stove and well stocked bookshelves on one wall. Flick graciously accepted a glass of sherry and then gave a theatrical cry as Alice walked in accompanied by a chunky looking man and an older woman. Kisses were exchanged as though they hadn't seen each other for months. In comparison to the rest of us she looked like a peacock in a hen house.

'Alice darling, and Jonathan. And Jane my dear.'

Alice introduced me to her husband and mother. Jane took both my hands in hers.

'You're very welcome here Lucy. I've heard about you from Alice and Tim, and you're quite as pretty as they described you. I hope you're going to be alright stuck in Trelerric House with our mad relative.'

Flick snorted with amusement and I didn't know what to say so concentrated on thanking her for the invitation. Jane was a slim woman about my height. Her hair was thick and brown and she wore a rusty coloured gold embroidered blouse tucked into brown trousers with a plaited orange leather belt, which I admired. It emphasised her small waist.

'It was a birthday present from Flick last year.' Her hazel eyes were large, expressive and looked vaguely familiar.

'Have you got some wellingtons handy Lucy? It might be a bit too muddy out for those nice city boots.' Jane had noticed my little black boots. I shook my head. She put her foot alongside mine. 'You're a size five. I can lend you a pair of mine if you don't mind.'

Jonathan interrupted us and shook my hand energetically.

'Lovely to meet you Lucy. You're a nurse I gather. I was in estate management but then I switched to finding estate properties for clients. Keeps me busy and outside a bit which I like.' He had curly sandy coloured hair and very blue eyes and reminded me of a huggable teddy bear.

There was a buzz of conversation as Tim handed drinks around. I chose a spicy tomato juice, I didn't want to get smashed on my first visit and anyway I had to drive back even it was on what were effectively private estate roads. Jane vanished into the kitchen, followed by Alice.

'I expect we're dining in the kitchen Timothy.' Flick spoke as though she was pursuing a time worn argument.

'You know we are Flick. It's warmer than the dining room.'

I turned back to Jonathan and asked him if he was local.

'Just over the border, or "up country" as they say around here. Devonshire born and bred for generations. We've got a dairy farm but dad and my older brother run it. I met Alice through the young farmers setup and ended up moving here.'

I was wondering what to say next when a handsome tricoloured collie ran into the room, scanned us with a questioning look and ran out again.

'Sam's arrived then. Jane won't be pleased about having Mitch in here. She prefers dogs in the boot room when they're indoors.' Jonathan said.

'Sam?' I said, thinking Sam the gardener, Sam who took Coco to the doggy parlour.

'Sam.' A deep voice spoke behind my shoulder and I jumped. 'I seem to be good at startling you Lucy. You remember me, we met when I switched the lights on. I'm Alice's brother.'

'You're Sam Latchley?' I felt a bit of an idiot but then no-one had ever said his surname so how could I have made a connection? This man was teasing me but I was spared having to say anything by Alice calling us all to order. 'Outside everyone. Not you Aunt Flick obviously. We won't be long.'

Jane gave me a pair of wellies to wear and a dark red knitted pull on hat. Flick waved us off. Sam flashed a torch around outside as we all trooped out. His dog was running backwards and forwards as though rounding us up and Sam called him to his side. It was a short walk past some handsome old buildings and up a short track into what Alice said was the Mother Orchard.

'This is the old original cider orchard.' Alice told me. 'Sam started another one a few years ago with some different apple varieties on the other side of this one. You can see it from your rooms. Apple trees are one of his passions, he studied horticulture at Writtle but he really got the bug when he did a short placement at Brogdale, the place in Kent with all the fruit trees. Thankfully dad refused to let uncle Robin rip this out years ago.'

Once inside the orchard we all stopped while Sam stepped forward and fiddled with something. Then coloured lights illuminated one venerable leaning apple tree, surrounding it with red, blue and yellow lights glowing in the night. I was enchanted.

'The wonders of battery technology have reached twenty-first century Cornwall folks.' Sam said.

Tim lit a fire laid ready in an old doorless woodstove with a short piece of chimney still attached and Jane and Alice took a flask from a bag and proceeded to pour hot mulled cider into paper cups. Sam handed me a cup and I felt his presence strongly but his face was in shadow. The heat was welcoming in my cold hands and there was something about the smell of the wood smoke and the scent of hot spices which made my senses tingle.

Jonathan spoke next to me. 'Any virgins here tonight? We should make a sacrifice.'

Alice giggled. 'No takers there then.'

To my surprise Sam handed me his cup and took charge of the proceedings.

'I want you all to approach the tree and make as much noise as you can to wake the sleeping spirits.'

He sounded completely serious and started banging a stick on an battered old metal dustbin lid, Jonathan was knocking two sticks together and yelling and Tim joined in whilst hitting a dented old watering can. I joined Jane and Alice wailing and whooping, whilst trying to pretend that this was all perfectly normal and wondering if they were all going to go druid on me.

Sam then sang a short song to the tree, calling us to "drink to the root, the bud, the blossom and the fruit", and gave a short speech of thanks for the trees and our small community. He had a lovely singing voice and I watched him, fascinated as the firelight from the open woodstove played across his face. Then the men took their drinks back from us and we toasted each other and drank the warm spicy cider. Finally Sam took pieces of toasted bread soaked in cider from a carrier bag and placed them in the branches before pouring a libation of cider around the roots, calling out that he was honouring the old and celebrating the new, at which point they all chanted together.

"Old apple tree we wassail thee
and hope that you will bear, hatfuls,
capfuls three bushel bagfuls
and little heaps all under the stairs."

I was able to join in with the hip hip hoorah and Jane topped up our paper cups. Sam turned to me and touched his cup to mine, our fingers momentarily touching.

'Welcome to Trelerric, Lucy Huccaby.' He spoke softly and raised his cup to me, took a sip and then turned and threw the remains into the tree. It was as though he was making a wish.

'On the table. While it's hot!'

With Flick at my side we all went through to the kitchen together, a large L-shaped beamed room with the dining table set round a corner away from the range. There was a cream enamelled woodstove burning in a wide old fireplace with logs stacked to the sides and a comfortable blue sofa flanked by side tables holding farming periodicals. It was warm and welcoming and the food smelled fantastic. The table was big enough to seat ten people and there were heated serving dishes steaming on an old carved wooden side table. Tim seated Flick in what was obviously her usual place and Jane put a bowl of soup in front of her before everyone else casually helped themselves. I held back for a moment, enjoying the feeling of generosity the food suggested. I'd eaten dinner with Peter's family once, his mother had been an indifferent cook and his father had seen food purely as fuel not as pleasure. I'd gone to bed hungry that night.

Sam turned to me, holding the soup ladle.

'One of mum's seasonal specialities, chestnut and parsnip. Can I interest you? It's a bit dark here so I can serve you if you like.'

I shot him a look which my Irish mother would have described as a paint stripper before nodding and smiling. Sam sat next to me and engaged his father in conversation about the orchard. The soup was delicious and I said so to Jane.

'I always start by caramelising an onion Lucy, and you have to balance the seasoning otherwise the ingredients can be too sweet. Do you cook?'

'She makes great sandwiches.' Sam spoke before I could reply.

'Lucy had a food business after she was a nurse.' Flick commented.

All eyes turned to me. 'I ran a celebration cakes business. But I do enjoy cooking.' I added.

'What's a celebration cake? Would I recognise one if I met it?' Tim asked, offering and pouring wine. Sam took the bottle from him and poured some into my empty wine glass.

'Can you see that alright?' He asked me quietly.

I ignored Sam and answered Tim. 'Cakes for weddings, anniversaries and birthdays.'

'Of course, that's how you know Helena. Did you work together? She did a lovely tea party for Grace's birthday.' Alice said, and then she looked over the table at Sam. 'Wasn't that Helena's car I saw the other day outside the Coach House Sam?'

'News to me if it was.' Sam said. I got the feeling he was hiding something.

'Is that the horsey girl?' Flick asked Alice.

'Horsey? What do you mean Flick?' Alice replied.

'I mean horsey as in big teeth. She has big teeth when she smiles.' Flick said.

Alice shook her head in disbelief. She didn't like Flick's habit of being personal about people. Again she asked me if I knew Helena well.

'I don't actually know her at all. She knows my sister and her fiancé. They all met via work through some sort of corporate event. My sister is a freelance events organiser.' I changed the subject. 'Who looks after your children on supper night?'

'Maggie's daughter comes up. Clare, she's a nice girl. Crazy about animals. She's a pretty handy veterinary nurse.'

'Is that why she looks after your two? Because they're animals?' Sam said.

Alice made a face and stuck her tongue out at Sam.

Jonathan laughed. 'Well I can see who my offspring take after. My darling wife!'

The conversation turned to the family business and I sat listening to discussion and lively debate and learning a bit about the diverse operations employed to keep the estate going. It was an interesting evening and I watched Flick enjoying herself. She liked these people and she especially liked Sam. He helped Flick get her main course and joked with her. I was quite conscious of Sam sitting eating quietly next to me and was suddenly reminded of the annoying way Peter used to stab his food around on his plate. Jonathan ate heartily and Alice prodded his stomach affectionately. Tim kissed Jane's cheek when he helped bring out cheese and quince jelly. It was like being an episode of The Walton's. Jane asked me if I had family.

'My sister Megan who's getting married this year. And mum and dad fostered for a while as well so there was always a house full.'

Jane was about to ask more when Flick joined us. 'Jane darling I'm getting a bit tired now. Would you mind if Lucy took me back?'

I'd been enjoying the company and was a bit sorry to be going. Tim found our coats and Sam appeared with a torch. 'Just to help you find the car Lucy.'

I could have kicked him.

FIVE

The following day I was free and went to see Megan as arranged. Megan admired my new haircut and I admired the flat. It was extremely tidy and there were flowers in vases.

'I cheated and got a professional cleaning company in.' Megan said. 'They washed the carpets and polished everything. I hardly dare walk about. It looks great on the estate agents photographs.' Megan wanted a sale and she knew all about presentation and how to hook a client.

There was a bit of post for me and we caught up with news and then Megan asked me about Trelerric House.

'What's it like then Luce? Are there bats in the attic and a gothic cobweb covered Mrs Faversham moaning in the bedroom?'

I smiled. 'Sorry to disappoint. It's nothing like what I'm used to but actually,' I thought for a moment. 'I could get used to it. I like Flick, we get on alright and Maggie, she's the housekeeper, is lovely. And I went to what they call Saturday supper at the Home Farm last night and met all the family at the annual Wassail. I enjoyed it. Jane Latchley is a decent cook.' I thought about the family all sitting together and eating and talking. 'It reminded me of being at home with mum and dad.'

We'd moved into the little kitchen to keep off the newly washed carpets and were making a drink. I'd opted for hot chocolate but Megan was having what she called a weed bag, a calorie free herbal thing. It smelled like scented bathwater but then she was on her pre-wedding diet now so she had to suffer. Not that she needed to diet.

Megan nodded. 'We had nice times with mum and dad didn't we. And most of the Fosters turned out okay.' That was how we referred to the foster children that our big hearted little Irish mum took in over several years. We were still in touch with a few of them.

'Meg, do you ever think about who your real mother was? I mean especially now that you're getting married. I know I did when I was making my arrangements. I wondered if she thought about me.'

But I'd also been worried because Peter had voiced some discomfort about not knowing who my real family were. He'd asked if there were any inherited illness we should be worried about if we wanted to start a family. I'd never said a word to anyone but he'd made me feel unclean somehow. Peter had grown up in a medical family, his father was an obstetrician. I told myself he didn't mean to be unkind, he was brought up knowing about these things even though he hadn't gone into medicine himself. Then I remembered his mother with her picky little ways. When I'd first gone to visit I'd bought a new pair of natural sheepskin mules since Peter had advised they lived in a cold old vicarage and that his mother was terrifyingly house proud. She had eyed my newly shod feet that evening and asked if I'd like to put them in the washing machine since she was doing a load before bedtime. She'd mistaken the natural greyish fleece for "soiling" as she called it. I'd met catty women before but she couldn't have made it clearer that she didn't think I was good enough for her son. I realised Megan was speaking and pulled myself back to the present.

'Yes and no. Sometimes. Not really. I'm conflicted about it Luce. And I think I prefer to look ahead rather than to a past over which I had no influence. And there's mum, I couldn't hurt mum's feelings.'

I changed the subject and told Megan all about the driving lesson with Tim Latchley. And then I told her everything else, about being caught snooping when I wasn't, and about realising that Sam the gardener was actually Sam Latchley when he turned up for the Saturday supper.

'Wow, the man himself! What's he like? Is he single?'

'He's a pain. And I think he's seeing Helena. But he has a lovely singing voice.' I described the Wassail.

'Mmmm. Sounds a bit romantic Luce. And he really said "Welcome to Trelerric" to you? Wow.'

We moved on to wedding plans and arrangements, made lunch and went to the cinema in the afternoon to see the latest chick flick, giggling as we remembered how mum always loved films where beautiful actresses dressed as nuns renounced everything including the undying love of an impossibly handsome man. Thoroughly satisfied with our time together, we hugged as I got ready to leave.

'Lovely day. Come over to Trelerric House next time and I'll show you around.'

'You sound like the lady of the house already Luce. Imagine, Lucy Latchley at home to her guests.'

I snorted with laughter. 'Stop it. It sounds like "loose elastic".'

I was still laughing as I drove away.

The following morning Flick was on good form. She'd had a day out with some friends and Coco had misbehaved on their best Aubusson which for reasons of her own she found hugely satisfying.

'Well honestly she was nervous, Booboo and Henry have boisterous spaniels and Coco felt intimidated. And the rug is all patterned, it's not as though a little mishap shows. When I think of the mess those two made of my bedsheets before they were married. They were quite shameless.'

Flick had decided she wanted to see her clothes. I thought that meant getting things out of the dressing room wardrobes.

'Oh no.' Flick said. 'We're going upstairs. I'm feeling quite well. I seem to be doing more now that you're here Lucy. I might be cold though so give me a pashmina.'

I handed Flick a soft colourful cashmere thing she was pointing to which I'd assumed was a sort of blanket to put over your legs and watched as she draped it around herself. As always with Flick the result was good. Accompanied by Coco and with the lights all blazing in the grand hallway we proceeded upstairs to the recessed door I'd opened on my previous visit upstairs.

Flick looked around appreciatively as we walked through the sitting room and into a bedroom with a four poster bed. 'A lovely room this one. I didn't often sleep in that bed though, only if I was unwell or sexually unavailable. Robin and I preferred his bedroom.'

The bedrooms were connected by a large bathroom and a dressing room which Flick said were hers.

'Robin has his own gentleman's arrangements on the other side.'

Noticing she spoke of Robin in the present tense I said nothing but switched a fan heater on as she pulled a white cotton cover off an upholstered chair and sat down facing the wardrobes.

'We'll start with that one on the left Lucy.'

With something like anticipation I opened the doors, expecting the same sensory experience I'd had with her wardrobes downstairs, but I was disappointed. Then I realised I was looking at protective clothes bags. Everything was zipped and sealed against dust and moths. Flick instructed me to pull forward a mobile dressing rail from the corner.

'As you take things out hang them on that and then remove the covers and put them on the table.'

One by one I lifted garments out in the manner advised and unzipped covers, revealing dresses and outfits I'd never imagined. To say I was stunned was an understatement.

'Schiaparelli.' Flick said casually as I uncovered a midnight blue fitted jacket embroidered with signs of the zodiac. 'I only wore that once I think.'

I said the name meant nothing to me and spent a couple of hours listening to her talk about haute couture, examining dresses and outfits with beads, feathers and faux gems attached. The items were suited to Flick's colouring.

'I've never seen such beautiful and amazing clothes.' I said, letting something beaded and slinky slither over my fingers and wondering what she had put away in the other wardrobes.

'That's Yves St Laurent, I danced at Monaco in that. That dark blue creation with the lace is Gucci and of course there's some Chanel. One of her suits in there, the black one with the beaded jacket, would look good on you since you like to wear that colour. Dear Coco's clothes will never age. They have timeless style.'

Flick made me hold the black suit up against me. 'I'd like to see you try some of these things on one day Lucy, you might be surprised at how you look. That little red hat that Jane gave you to wear the other evening really suited your colouring. I wasn't the only person who noticed. You have lovely dark hair and very fine grey eyes but you do need to wear mascara.'

I didn't mind her personal chatter, it was like being with Megan and Flick was so animated it was a pleasure to watch her.

'Those drawers below the wardrobes contain photographs of me wearing these clothes. Some were taken by the film studio, others by society photographers. They show the fun we had then. Such fun. The studio was supposed to keep the clothes but they were made for me. I always slept with the directors and promised I wouldn't tell their wives if they would let me keep the clothes. I asked nicely of course. And if you give a man a good time in bed they invariably agree to your requests.' She looked at me shrewdly. 'Are you shocked?'

I shook my head, she'd clearly never heard young nurses talking amongst themselves. Opening a drawer I looked inside, seeing what appeared to be albums. I looked at Flick enquiringly.

'After the accident I couldn't move very easily. To keep myself occupied I had Timothy buy me albums and I spent months cataloguing everything. It helped me to retreat into a happier past I suppose.'

'Accident?' I asked.

'Robin and I were in a car crash. He was killed. I broke my leg and my hip. Ten years ago. I still miss him. There's been no-one else.'

I vaguely remembered something I'd read when I was researching Trelerric House online.

'It happened in France didn't it Flick?'

She nodded, her eyes unfocussed. 'We'd taken a villa on the coast and Robin hired a sports car. He forgot which side of the road he was supposed to be driving on. I never told the police that. The sun was dazzling when we came round a bend. There was an animal in the road. Robin loved animals. He swerved and we went down a bank and hit a tree so hard I was thrown out. They said he was killed immediately. Thank god nobody else was involved.'

We were interrupted by a deep voice calling our names and Sam appeared in the doorway.

'In your lair Flick?' He crossed over and kissed her on the cheek. Flick looked at him adoringly.

'Down memory lane Sam.' Flick sighed. 'But I've had enough now. Can you put everything back please Lucy. Will you help me back downstairs darling?' She put her arm in Sam's.

They left me to it and I carefully enclosed, zipped and sealed things away. I seemed to be shutting away laughter and fun as I did so, it was as though the clothes held atmosphere in their fibres. Her life had been so vibrant. As I closed the wardrobe doors Sam said my name behind me and I jumped.

'Please stop doing that. Creeping up on me. It's, it's just so ...' I was going to say peculiar but I settled for 'odd.'

'It's unintentional Lucy. You seem a bit tense and sometimes preoccupied. I don't mean any harm, it would be nice to see you relax and laugh.' Sam was looking down at me. 'I just wanted to say thanks for the way you've perked Flick up. She wouldn't show you these things unless she liked you. Did she show you the other rooms?'

'What other rooms?'

Sam opened a door. 'Robin's rooms. Let me switch the lights on for you.'

I ignored the little dig and looked around. There was a rosewood sleigh bed and handsome matching furniture, then Robin's dressing room and bathroom. I watched as Sam opened a few doors and drawers allowing me to glance at things before he closed them again.

'Everything is still here for him. She's thrown nothing away.' Sam said. 'Maggie comes up once a week to hoover and dust everything.'

It was like being in someone else's dream. There were silver framed photographs of Flick and Robin in various locations together, laughing and without a care in the world. I felt a lump in my throat. How quickly things could change.

'She really loved him didn't she.' I said, examining a photograph. Then I looked up at Sam. 'You look a lot like him, like Robin I mean.'

'There's a family resemblance, yes I think so. But I've got mum's eyes.'

I found myself gazing up into his eyes, greeny-gold hazel honey coloured eyes with thick lashes which gazed back at me, his expression kind.

I forced myself to look away. 'Do these rooms get shown to visitors on open days?'

'Oh god no. Upstairs is private. Only for the family, and for special friends.'

Sam switched the lights off and closed the doors and I returned to Flick for lunch. She was looking at a magazine.

'What's your star sign Lucy?'

'Libra. I was born in October.' I told her.

'It says you'll be meeting someone significant. Whereas I am to expect changes ahead. I'm not sure I like the sound of that.'

'Change can be good. But you don't believe in that rubbish do you Flick?'

'Oh I do, absolutely. Not this in the papers, but if you have a proper birth chart drawn up it can be very revealing. You need to know the time of day you were born. It's a complicated and individual process. Have you never had a chart done?'

'No. Anyway I don't know what time of day I was born.'

'Well that's easy, ask your mother.'

'She doesn't know either.' I'd spoken without thinking.

Flick put her magazine down and looked at me. 'Why's that? Was she anaesthetised? Were you a caesarian birth?'

For a split second I thought about brushing the comment away and telling a white lie. Then I thought of Sam's comment upstairs. Flick had shared something very personal with me and anyway I had nothing to be ashamed of. I sat down opposite her at the little table where we ate together.

'I'm adopted. I don't know those little details or who my parents are.'

Flick took a mouthful of pea and mint soup and was quiet. Then she said, 'Does that bother you?'

'Yes and no. Like my sister Megan I'm conflicted.' I told Flick about Megan and about our conversation the previous day and as we ate I told her that I'd had a lovely childhood and loved my mum and dad. 'But sometimes I wonder Flick, I mean I can describe who I am in terms of my upbringing and qualifications and experiences, but, oh, how can I explain it? For me it's about what's not there, I mean unanswered questions. I wonder where my talent for baking comes from, which parent I inherited my eyes and colouring from, whether they were sporty types.' I paused and gazed blindly into the back of my soup spoon. 'And there was a moment at the Saturday supper when I felt as though I was sailing under false colours. Everyone knew each other and the Latchley's have a pedigree going back to Adam and Eve. Even Jonathan has deep local roots.' I realised that there was genuine passion in my voice and tried to lighten up. 'So yes, part of me is curious about where I came from as I get older. And I do wonder if my real mother ever wonders about me. I'm not

Cornish-Irish. I don't know what I am. Maybe one of those DNA kits that are on the market might give me some clues.' I gave a forced laugh.

Flick was silent and I thought that perhaps I'd embarrassed her by over sharing.

'I'm sorry Flick. To be honest it's not something I think about very often. I mean I don't have a hang up or anything.'

'I did.' Flick's pale silvery eyes were watering. 'I did Lucy. I shall tell you something few people know. I reinvented myself as soon I got out of the orphanage. I was beautiful and I could sing and dance. I had natural talent and a hell of a lot of ambition. I did some things I'm not proud of but I personally created Felicity Gray. She's the product of my imagination. And at the height of my fame I met Robin, my dearest love. Sam reminds me of him every time I see him.'

We sat there just looking at each other, both aware that by revealing our secrets we'd shared something unexpected and in doing so cemented our friendship.

Over the next few days I kept myself busy helping Maggie and finding things to do for Flick. She wanted to go shopping and once again I found myself on the receiving end of her generosity as she bought me some cosmetics and skin creams after a lengthy visit to one of the pampering counters as she called them.

One afternoon Tim came into the kitchen as Maggie and I were cooking. He sniffed.

'Smells good. Maybe we should have Saturday supper here and give Jane a break. Be good to use the dining hall here when the weather warms up. Talking of food Lucy, I want to ask you a favour.'

'Ask away.' I replied. I was making a starter of salmon mousse with tiny brown prawns for Flick's evening meal. It went well with oat crackers which were good for her.

'You mentioned cakes the other night. Fancy ones. I wondered whether you could make a cake for Jane's birthday, it's at the end of February. As a surprise. I shall pay you of course.'

I smiled at him. 'Absolutely not, payment I mean. I'm in your debt for that excellent driving lesson. What does Jane like?'

Tim looked confused.

'Is she a fruit cake?' I started laughing helplessly at my mistake and Tim and Maggie joined in.

The kitchen door opened and Alice came in followed by Flick who was holding Grace's hand. Coco raced in past them wagging her tail and huffing excitedly.

'We could hear merriment. What's the joke?'

Maggie explained and we all laughed again, apart from little Grace who looked at us all in bewilderment.

'What a great idea dad. I think mum likes sponge cakes best. She likes chocolate and then there's coffee and walnut. That's a nice combination.' Alice said helpfully.

'Is there anything Jane doesn't like? Coconut for example?'

I was assured that Jane ate most things. I said that all I needed was the date and how many people I was catering for.

'I'd love to do that.' I smiled at Tim. 'Let me show you what I can do.'

SIX

Driving back from Flick's hair appointment the next Friday I realised I was following the blue Honda down the estate road. Flick had also noticed and leaned forward in her seat.

'Now then, will that car stop at The Lodge or is she on her way to the Coach House. She pretends to be Alice's friend but I was watching her at Grace's birthday party and I believe she's setting her cap at Sam.'

I feigned ignorance. 'Who are you talking about Flick?'

'The horsey woman. The one with the buttocks.'

'Oh, you mean Helena Fox-Harvey. She's acquainted with my sister Megan. I don't know her but I spoke to her on the phone once, about this job working for you. I owe her a thank you.'

Flick pulled a face but didn't reply. I saw her indoors where Maggie told me I had time to put the Jag away before lunch. It only took me a few minutes now, so I drove round to the Coach House and reversed into the space. I'd noticed that Sam's Landrover was parked but that wasn't unusual because he often used a horribly noisy quad-bike on the estate. I was getting out when a handsome blonde girl appeared, jabbing furiously at her mobile phone. Her long glossy hair was caught up with clips and she was doing the whole county set thing right down to the string of pearls over a twisted scarf and glossy brown boots over too tight blue jeans. She was wearing a lot of make up. All she needed was a riding crop and a labrador at heel. As I closed the Jag door and clicked the remote lock she looked up. I was quite clearly not the person she was hoping to see and she didn't look friendly.

'Hello. Are you looking for someone?' I couldn't think of what else to say.

'I was hoping to catch Sam. Is he around? I'm Helena.'

I acted surprised and interested. 'I think you helped me get the job here. I'm Lucy, Megan Huccaby's sister. You are Helena Fox-Harvey aren't you?'

'Yes, ya I am. Oh how marvellous to meet you.' I could tell she didn't mean that and she was looking me up and down as though sizing up an opponent. 'What's it like being on the staff?' She spoke dismissively, drawling the "a" sounds. Then she gave a high pitched false laugh, showing a lot of teeth and throwing her head back so her hair tossed about. It sounded like a neigh.

I didn't rise to the put down, being bitchy just wasn't worth it.

'I'm enjoying being here,' I said mildly. As I turned I noticed a figure crouching silently in the shadows at the back of the parking bays. Someone was hiding. 'Did you have an appointment to see Sam?' I asked provocatively, keeping my expression disinterested. Two can play at wind-ups.

Helena looked at me in momentary surprise and annoyance. I was guessing that she was unsure about how to place me, as an equal or as an employee. She decided to treat me as an employee. Big mistake.

'Oh dear girl I don't need an appointment to see Sam,' she said. 'We're close friends. Very close. But either he can't get a signal or he's very busy somewhere and can't hear his phone. It's not a problem, I've left him a message. But if you see him tell him I called round would you. I'll pop in to see dear Alice instead.'

We both knew that as Alice's car hadn't been parked at The Lodge that she was out but I didn't mention that. Instead I suggested that Sam might be at Home Farm helping with the lambing. Helena glanced at me dismissively and frowned at Sam's Landrover. Then she made her mind up and turning on her heel she marched back to her car without saying goodbye. She liked to park it just round the corner of the Coach House, almost out of sight. I made a point of standing still and waving her off with a big smile. Once the car had disappeared I spoke.

'Come out, come out whoever you are. It's safe now.'

There was a snort of laughter and Sam appeared followed by a younger brown haired man with blunt features and bright blue eyes, a kind face. Both were grinning broadly.

'Something funny?' I couldn't help smiling back at them.

'That woman is stalking me. Thanks for not giving us away Lucy. This is Simon by the way, we were just on our way to catch Flick when I spotted the Honda in the nick of time.'

I said hello to Simon and offered a hand but he shook his head and held both hands out palms up.

'Put my hands in something mucky crouching back there, sorry ma'am.'

'I'm Lucy.'

'Yes ma'am.'

I turned to Sam. He was still smiling and something about that smile lifted my spirits. He did have lovely eyes and rather nicely shaped lips. 'Flick and I are just about to have lunch, can you come after that?'

'Better than that, we'll come and see what Maggie can let us have. Come on Simon.'

Sam fell into step at my side and Simon followed. We didn't speak but at the house Sam stepped forward and opened the door for me. It was a quaint old fashioned gesture and curiously pleasant. It was as though he'd said he cared but without using any words.

After lunch Maggie ushered Sam and Simon in while I fetched tea and coffee for us all. Maggie was giggling about how much the boys had eaten.

'Soup, quiche, cold chicken, cheese. It's being outside, gives them a healthy appetite. I don't often feed them of course, it's not my job. But I can't say no to Sam and that young Simon.'

I reckoned young Simon was in his early twenties but his fresh colouring made him seem younger. Flick was holding court and I noticed that Simon now had clean hands and was holding some drawings. I looked over his shoulder at lovely colour washed sketches.

'What are these?' I asked.

'Simon has done a few drawings of what your oriental courtyard might look like.' Sam said as Simon seemed incapable of speech in Flick's magnificent presence.

'Wow. They're good.' I looked at Simon with respect and he smiled back. 'You're a garden designer then?' I couldn't make him out. I thought he was just the lad who washed the cars and helped in the garden.

'I did a course. Just a year. They taught us to use a computer design package but I like drawing best. I'm not much good at anything else.'

Flick was looking at him in surprise. 'Well I think they're delightful. What do you think Sam?'

'Brilliant. I handed over my course notes and photos from college and Simon went online and found loads of information. He just ran with it.'

'There's a society. They do Japanese garden design. They've won medals at Hampton Court and Chelsea but they work all over England, they're amateurs, enthusiasts and professionals. Sam and me did some measurements. Not much will grow out here because of the wall and part shade but I reckon this dry garden might be something we could kick around.' Simon gave me a shy smile.

'Do you like them Lucy?' Flick was asking me.

'I do. I like the paths and having somewhere to sit, and the rocks with a small acer planted between them is magical.'

'The rocks sometimes have meaning,' Sam was speaking and Simon was nodding. 'We shall investigate that a bit more before we place anything. And they have to be chosen carefully.'

'That's agreed then,' Flick was pleased. 'Something like that would be very acceptable Sam. And thank you Simon, you're a gifted young man.'

As they left I noticed that it was still light. The days were beginning to get longer. I didn't say anything to Flick about Sam hiding from Helena.

One afternoon as I was walking Coco and enjoying the fresh air in the gardens a large BMW swept in a stately way into the gravelled parking area and a very satisfied looking tall dark haired man got out. He was pulling a tan cashmere coat casually around his shoulders when he saw me with Coco and waved, walking over with a jaunty air.

'Hallo. You must be Lucy,' he said, looking at me curiously. 'I'm Hugh Flinton, an old friend of Flick's. Thought I'd pop by and see how the dear girl is. Usually see her on Sundays when we're both at a loose end. Is she up and about?' His vowels sounded as they had been dipped in melted chocolate.

He'd taken my hand in both of his and squeezed it as he was talking. I was happy for him to let go.

'Hello. Yes, it's nearly tea time. Won't you come in Mr Flinton.'

'It's Hugh to someone as pretty as you my dear. Tell me, have we met before? Only you seem familiar.'

What a crappy chat up line I thought uncharitably. 'I don't think so.' I replied as I lead the way back through the door near the kitchen rather than go to the French doors. I didn't want to surprise Flick if she wasn't expecting him.

Maggie had the tea tray ready and seemed a bit flustered.

'I thought I saw your car Sir Hugh.'

Oh, it was *Sir* Hugh then. I noticed she coloured slightly as Sir Hugh went over to her, took her hand and kissed it gallantly. What a creep I thought to myself, but he engaged Maggie in conversation while I took Coco through to Flick and told her she had a visitor. As usual her make up and clothes were faultless but I had to switch on a few lamps to set the stage as she put it.

'Will you have your tea with Maggie please Lucy. I'll see Sir Hugh alone.'

I showed him through although he clearly knew the way. I wasn't impressed by the way he slid his hand right down my back to my bottom at the doorway before walking forward to greet Flick. Back in the kitchen I shuddered. Remembering something Alice had said I asked Maggie about Sir Hugh. Maggie made sure the kitchen door was closed. She seemed a bit jumpy.

'A lounge lizard? That's a funny expression Lucy. It's just his way, his people are gentry and he never forgets his manners. He really knows how to treat a lady. And I think he's kind.'

I thought Maggie seemed defensive.

'I just don't like the old wandering hands routine. When I was nursing we used to get a bit of trouble sometimes from the old guys. It was a combination of wearing a uniform and having unrestricted access to their bodies that turned them on. Fortunately I did a course in self-defence so I could take care of myself.'

Maggie was all ears and started laughing.

'He dyes his hair as well.' I went on. 'I noticed it outside. He's carefully left a little bit of grey around his ears.'

'Who dyes his hair?'

Maggie and I both jumped. We'd been so companionable that we hadn't heard the kitchen door open. It was Tim.

'Oh, an actor we're talking about.' I said blandly.

Tim wasn't interested. 'Lucy, the date for the cake is the twenty-first, a week after Valentine's Day. Alice is going to do Saturday supper at The Lodge that evening to give her mum a treat and the night off. Maggie, Alice won't need Clare to come that night if that's okay?'

Both Maggie and I were nodding but I spoke. 'Fine. That's no problem, I'll have it done.' I had an idea. 'Will Alice want a hand with the supper?'

Tim thought she might and suggested I should speak to Alice myself. After he'd gone Maggie asked me about the cakes I used to make so I fetched a book from my rooms. I'd had photographs of my work consolidated into a hardback internet publication. The result was rather good and Maggie was impressed as she turned the pages.

'For someone who doesn't wear colours these are amazing Lucy.'

Maggie was looking at the examples of my wedding and anniversary cakes, all dressed with sugar work. I could make flowers and pearls, ribbons and lace which all looked realistic. I explained that there were gadgets on the market which helped to create the effects, but dexterity and an ability to make delicate things was essential. I'd always been able to do it. Some women could sew and embroider, I could make and decorate special cakes. Maggie said she'd like to watch me work when I did it because she might learn something. I didn't mind at all.

A few days later Sam appeared while I was walking Coco. I'd started taking her to an uncultivated grassy bank in the new orchard because she could do her business without messing up the terrace. Sam thanked me for being considerate.

'Simon's swept all the poo up and I want to keep that terrace clean if possible. One less thing to do. But actually I've come to ask if you'd like to come down to a garden place with me near St Mawgan.'

'Oh.' I was surprised at the tingle in my tummy. 'I'm not sure how that would fit with Flick.'

'You could come straight after lunch when she watches television and has a rest. We'll take Coco with us. My dog Mitch will stay here with the others. Do you mind going in the Landrover or would you prefer the Jag milady?'

'Oh.' I said again. 'The Landrover is okay. Is it special this garden centre?'

'You'll see. I shall tell Flick. We're going tomorrow.'

'Oh.' I said for the third time. 'Okay.'

Sam smiled briefly at me. 'Good. We'll leave at half past one from the Coach House. See you there.'

He strode away, so like his father in that mannerism and I watched him as he walked, he was clicking the thumb and fingers of his right hand together, preoccupied and busy. There was something about him that I liked.

Flick didn't say much other than to acknowledge that Sam was taking me to a garden centre.

'He has his reasons Lucy. I'm pleased for you.'

What she meant by that I didn't know. Anyway she had something else on her mind.

'I've been reading about tracing family in this magazine. There's a company which can handle it all for you. What do you think?'

'I think I can't possibly afford it.' My reply was immediate and honest.

'But you don't even know what their fees are.'

'I'm afraid to ask.'

'Well you should read this article and then we'll talk about it again.'

By now I knew Flick well enough to know that she wasn't going to give up easily.

SEVEN

I tried not to think about how slowly time passed the next morning but if I hadn't admitted to myself that I was excited about the mystery trip with Sam I would have been in denial. For the first time in a year I looked at my wardrobe with something like dissatisfaction. And when I went downstairs to Flick I said as much.

'Well I wondered when you might like to come out of your Diane de Poitiers phase.' Flick said as we sat in her dressing room.

'Diane who?' I asked.

'She was a French courtesan, stole the heart of the French king. She only ever wore black and white but he was mad about her. She probably knew some extraordinary sexual tricks. Now, I don't suppose I can get you to wear foundation and such but what about a touch of mascara and then I think perhaps a scarf to throw a little colour onto your skin since it's a grey day.'

I giggled and allowed Flick to fuss about, it was rather nice, like being back with Megan only I used to watch Megan doing miraculous things to herself. This time I was sitting at the dressing table while Flick was holding scarves against my shoulder as she assessed their effect.

'I guess you will be wearing that black quilted jacket since you don't seem to have anything else?'

Flick had selected a multicoloured silk which she folded and twisted deftly around my neck.

'Like this, with the ends hanging down, then wear your jacket over it. It has black in it but the dark reds and blues look good with your hair and skin tone.'

It was like being back at the hairdresser, watching some subtle change take place. I smiled with delight and Flick looked at me in the mirror.

'Smile like that Lucy and Sam won't know what's hit him. Anyway I'd rather you were the focus of his interest than that fat-arsed horse-toothed social climber.'

I kept mulling that comment round in my mind but stayed calm throughout lunch and then collected Coco. It was such a long time since I'd gone out to meet a man that I was really glad she was there for support. As I rounded the corner to the Coach House I saw that the Landrover was already out, and unusually clean.

'Hi.' Sam was standing in the parking bay wiping his hands on a cloth. He was wearing clean dark jeans with a red, green and white checked shirt and a dark green chunky jumper. His eyes went up and down me swiftly and he was smiling. 'You look nice. Your hair suits you like that. Is that one of Flick's scarves?'

'Yes, she thought I'd be cold and insisted I should wear it.' I was lying and I could feel the colour rising in my cheeks. I needed to take his attention off me quickly. 'The Landrover looks very clean.'

'It needed a birthday. Simon helped me. I told him to go and get a sandwich off Maggie but he wouldn't, he's nervous when I'm not there, but he does like her daughter. Have you met Clare yet? She's a pretty girl. She's got the same colour hair as you.' He didn't wait for an answer. 'Coco can go in the back behind you, I've put a blanket in for her.'

Coco was huffing and wagging her tail in a frenzy at the sight of Sam. He bent down and took hold of her in both hands. I couldn't help thinking what nice hands he had. He was asking Coco if she'd been a good girl and done her business as he didn't want a nasty dirty dog in his clean machine. Coco was wriggling in excitement and pleasure and started licking his fingers. Looking down at his thick hair and the exposed skin on the back of his neck lust swooped over me and I had a strong urge to put my hands on his shoulders and bend down and kiss it. It was such a powerfully erotic moment that I had to suppress a groan.

Sam stood up. 'You alright Lucy? You've gone pale.'

'Oh it's nothing, I'm fine.' My insides were melting like a newly emerging volcano but I couldn't tell him that. 'Let's go on this magical mystery tour then.'

'Okay, hop in and let's go.'

It was even worse inside the cab. I could smell his soap and kept staring at his hands on the wheel and the length of his muscular thigh so close to mine. I wriggled in my seat. He asked me if I was uncomfortable but I said I wasn't, I'd just got the fidgets. He smiled and drove, at ease with the vehicle and intent on where he was going.

'There are some mints in the front there Lucy, could you pass me one?'

I learned forward and located them.

'Can you see them alright?'

'Oh stop it Sam. You don't need to remind me of that day.' I held the mints out.

'Can't touch them, Coco licked my fingers and anyway I'm driving. Hands on the wheel.'

I extracted a mint and holding it very carefully reached over to put it to his lips.

'Closer.' He was smiling.

As I held it closer we went over a pothole and I almost smacked him in the face. The mint shot into the back of the Landrover much to Coco's interest. She picked it up and then spat it out and whined.

'Oh bugger.' I reached into the back and retrieving the mint I wrapped it in a tissue and put it in my pocket. 'Sorry Coco, nasty mint. I'll try again Sam, please co-operate.'

'Well I hope your hands are clean. Coco washes her arse with that tongue and I don't want dog lick on my mint.' That quite effectively cooled my unexpected passion and I deftly flicked a mint into his mouth and took one for myself. At least it would stop me panting as though I was on heat.

We drove down the A30, past Launceston which Sam told me should be pronounced to rhyme with dancing, but with a long 'a', like the town in West Sussex.

'Only proper Cornish folk can say the names. Folk from up country can't get it right.'

Past Bodmin we took a turning toward Newquay and into some lanes and then down into a car park. There was a sign announcing a Japanese Garden.

'Oh what a brilliant idea! Did you tell Flick about this?'

'I did. I said I needed you to help me with my research. She agreed with me.'

'Flick would probably agree to anything you asked,' I commented. 'But really shouldn't Simon be sitting here in my seat since he's doing a lot of the work?'

Sam said he'd make it up to him and paid for us to go in. Even though it was late winter the place was fascinating. Sam took photographs of particular features he liked and talked about *karesansui*, describing a dry rock garden, using raked gravel to represent waves or water. I was delighted by the miniaturisation of landscape by the way rocks and bushes were composed.

'It's not low maintenance, people shouldn't get the wrong impression,' he told me. 'I remember when I was studying at Writtle the tutor there told us a story about the Japanese tradition of employing old women and young children to do the weeding and tidying, because they would leave a leaf on the ground which would encapsulate the season with a simple example.'

'Flick would be great at that then.' I giggled.

Sam made enquiries about various granite items to help him get the right look. He was particularly interested in a small snow viewing lantern. I wandered off to look at the shop and the books and when I returned he was paying for some items.

'We don't need to buy stones because Trelerric has plenty of granite boulders lying around and a collapsed wall which might provide something appropriate. I'll be back next week then to collect that.'

'That's the benefit of living in Cornwall, plenty of granite and the right growing conditions if you live near the moor.' The man behind the counter was enthusiastic.

Sam said we'd get on our way and once again he held a door open for me so that I could slip under his raised arm. I brushed past, quite close to his body and once again felt that lively tendril of lust tingling in my veins.

'I'll bring Simon down with the trailer next week to collect that stuff. He can take a look at the garden as well then.' Sam told me as we got back into the Landrover. 'Fancy a quick walk on the beach?'

He drove us into Newquay and the walk was brief, the light already fading and the place had a damp down at heel midwinter atmosphere. I was concerned that it would be too cold for Coco as she didn't have a dog coat. The sea was pounding with a rhythmic thumping noise and the wind was getting up. We were almost blown back to the Landrover and the now familiar intimacy of the interior.

'I could really do with a cup of tea and a comfort stop Sam. But I don't suppose there are any tea shops open at this time of year.'

'Well let's find a pub then. Somewhere Coco friendly where she's not force-fed mints.'

We smiled at each other. This guy's so kind, I thought. I could imagine telling Megan about our little trip out. Sam's mobile started chirping and he fished it out of a pocket and looked at it, frowned and shoved it back. Saying nothing he started the engine and drove up the coast towards Padstow.

'Bound to be something available in Padstein. It never closes.'

We parked by the harbour and what I could see of the town looked pretty in the streetlights. Within minutes we were inside a suitable hostelry, warm and cosy. As soon as we saw the specials board we both had the same idea. This was turning out to be a lovely trip.

'Okay to have the dog in here?' Sam asked the barman.

'That's a dog? Thought it was the lady's handbag.' The barman joked. 'But for sure it is. We're not busy tonight.'

It was easy being with Sam. I loved how considerate he was to Coco who was now under the table between our feet. And there was loads to talk about. As we shared a plate of whitebait I told him about the secret cake I was going to make for his mother's birthday and the idea I'd had about using violets to decorate it with.

'Why violets?' He slipped Coco a tiny piece of whitebait.

'Her birthday is February and the violet is the birth flower for the month. It's probably all victorian legend crap but it's great marketing.'

He looked at me thoughtfully. I was really getting to like looking into his eyes, big honey hazel eyes. 'You've had quite some experience haven't you, running a business and dealing with people.'

I said that I had.

'What would you do with Trelerric if it was yours?'

I was taken aback and stared at him for moment, hearing Megan calling me Lucy Latchley. I swallowed hard and spoke.

'Lie awake at night worrying first of all. I mean Home Farm is okay from what I gather, but at Saturday supper I got the impression that Trelerric House is going to need some ideas and imagination.'

Sam nodded. 'Yes. Have you got any?'

'Well, Alice mentioned the open days, garden plant sales and refreshments, but they're a bit obvious aren't they and not that frequent at five weekends a year.'

The waitress came with our mains, we'd both chosen locally caught fish with posh chips and salad. I was faintly amused, not really needing to know the provenance of my fish, but Sam gave a hungry moan.

'I love chips with salad, something about mayonnaise and red onion with salty chips is fantastic.'

We started eating and the food was delicious. Ideas which had been forming in the back of my mind over the past few weeks began to shape themselves into something coherent. As I finished I scooped Coco up onto the seat next to me and fed her a little bit of fish I'd cooled and taken the batter off.

'I really enjoyed the Wassail that night. How about making that a short event and getting people in. It was wonderfully atmospheric. Maybe you could sell the cider, and you could link it to other things to do with orchard management, tree pruning lessons and apple identification days. Maybe you could sell cooked apple products, like apple pie and apple chutney. They do things like that up in Herefordshire where I grew up. But you have to run any food plans past Environmental Health. I met them when I started my business.'

Sam was nodding, looking at me thoughtfully. 'That's the lines I've been thinking along although I might have to find someone to make apple products. Mum and Alice are busy enough as it is. I shall count on you to give me support next Saturday. I just need to convince dad. And mum needs to get her head round the insurance and visitor safety side of things.'

We talked some more and I declined a pudding but got my longed-for tea. Sam ordered lemon meringue pie and at his insistence I tasted a bit. He'd put some of the filling on my teaspoon and leaned over the table to feed it to me. I was intensely conscious of his focus and closeness, I could feel him looking at my mouth.

'How do they get it that lemony in restaurants?' He asked.

'It's easy.' I answered without thinking, picking up my paper napkin and carefully wiping my lips. 'You need to include a lot of the zest. From unwaxed lemons of course. That's where the real flavour is, it's lemon oil.'

Then we got talking about the scent of flowers and garden design, which lead to the Japanese garden and his course at horticultural college.

'Mum gave me some sunflower seeds to plant when I was at infant school. My passion was bordering on obsession, I measured them every day, I've still got my notebooks. How sad is that? But it taught me maths and patience. I've never looked back, I'm not a farmer, I'll help with the animals but I'm a gardener and probably a source of deep despair to my landed ancestors.'

Sam was gazing at me and I felt my insides starting to melt again. He really did make me feel randy.

'I like the way that you know about things Lucy Huccaby, like violets being the February birthday flower. They're old fashioned ideas but they suit Trelerric. We should use that sort of idea to improve sales, but I'm not sure how.'

I stopped imagining what he'd be like to kiss and pulled myself together with an effort. 'Maybe you could commission a local artist or an illustrator to design something with Trelerric on it and the month and the appropriate flower. Something attractive, not naff. I don't know, maybe come to some sort of arrangement on the sales, not just pictures, but mugs and tea towels and birthday cards, all the sorts of things that appeal to mums and grannies. They'd be unique to Trelerric. And what about a craft outlet at open days, get local makers in to sell their goods and make a small charge for a stall.' I paused and looked at him. 'I'm just bouncing ideas around.'

I'd heard Megan doing this sort of thing over the years and on impulse followed her impish line of thought. 'Or maybe a line in Trelerric bikini beachwear since we're down in Cornwall.'

Sam exploded with laughter.

Coco whined and wagged her little tail, looking up at us questioningly. The time had flown by and it was getting late.

'Time to go home I suppose. And Coco needs a drink and a pee. I've got a bowl and water in the Landrover. I always carry it for Mitch when we go out.'

I insisted on paying my half of the meal, after all this wasn't a date even though I had to acknowledge I was definitely attracted to Sam. He didn't make a fuss but he hardly spoke on the way back to Trelerric. He dropped us right outside the tradesman's entrance.

'Lovely day Sam, thanks, I've really enjoyed it.'

'Me too. See you at Saturday supper then.'

And he was gone.

EIGHT

I was concentrating hard. It was the day before Valentine's Day and just a week until Jane's birthday.

'Goodness me, I hadn't realised you'd be using real flowers Lucy.'

'Some flowers like rose petals, calendula petals, borage and violets are edible. The first Elizabethans were big on using flowers to decorate their elaborate sugar and almond creations. The Victorians liked using them as well.'

Flick and Maggie were watching as I'd mixed dried pasteurized egg white with cooled boiled water to make a thin paste. I'd managed to collect a handful of violets from beneath a hedgerow spotted when out walking Coco, and carefully cleaned them by dropping them into water so that any insects or debris would float off. I could remember mum saying you had to eat a peck of muck before you died, but I'd argued that some muck was best avoided. Especially muck which had legs or which might include pesticides or herbicides. Never get two nurses discussing hygiene in the same kitchen, I'd learned.

I'd dried the flowers off on clean kitchen paper before shaking them onto clean baking parchment. As a child I'd always called it 'goose-proof' paper. Taking a tiny paint brush which I kept solely for this purpose I painted each flower with a thin glaze, using the tip of a cocktail stick to hold them in place.

Flick was turning the pages in my book of cake photographs. 'These are marvellous Lucy, absolutely beautiful. You really are clever. Everything is so lifelike.'

'Well it helps if you can use something real like this, but I can make convincing roses and orchids out of sugar.' By now I was sifting tiny amounts of icing sugar over the flowers using a sieve I'd found in a craft shop. Apparently jewellers who worked with enamels used them.

'Right, that's all there is to that part. They need to be left to dry overnight in a warm undisturbed place. Then they just go into an airtight tin for safekeeping. I'll make and decorate the cake next week. I'm going to make some sugar ribbons as well but I'll do that on the day.'

I was really just talking to myself, it was a tried and true method of making sure that all the steps of the process were in place, but I was loving doing it again. Flick still had her head in the photographs and Maggie was making us tea.

'Lucy these colours are gorgeous. I just can't understand how someone with such a restricted wardrobe can see and combine colours like this.'

Maggie poured tea, we'd never all sat around in the kitchen before and it felt friendly although Flick looked a little out of place in one of her colourful lounging suits.

'Well I think Lucy looks good in black and white with her colouring. Who did you get your grey eyes from Lucy, was it your mum or your dad?' Maggie asked. 'You've got eyes the colour of Cornish Delabole slate, grey with a bit of gold in them.'

Flick was looking at me, her expression carefully neutral.

'I don't know, they must have skipped a generation.' Maggie didn't know that I was adopted.

I turned to Flick. 'I can see colours when it comes to designing things like this Flick. I can see the pale coffee icing enhancing the purple and lilac tones of the violets. I'll do a very simple pale ribbon and a bow to put around the sides. It will look beautiful. It's just a pity you can't eat it.'

'Oh don't worry about me, I've never really had a sweet tooth. Now tell me again, your sister is coming here on Sunday for lunch? I'm looking forward to meeting her.'

The day after the trip out with Sam I'd phoned Megan for a chat. We'd dissected the whole trip in proper girl talk and I'd confessed I found him so attractive he made me ache. I also mentioned Flick's catty comments about Helena including the arse and teeth.

'But I don't want to rush in and make a fool of myself Meg. I wasn't sure if he was being friendly or flirty. I can't remember how it all works. It wasn't a date anyway.'

Megan had advised caution and coolness. 'Don't make a prat of yourself Luce, just get to know him a bit better, you seem to have opportunities to meet but it's early days yet. Let him do the running. And find out about his past if you can, he must've had girlfriends before. Is there a dark secret?'

I agreed, she was absolutely right, but I didn't think I could ask Alice or Jane. That was uncool. The main reason I'd called Megan was about Flick's dresses and outfits. After talking to Sam about ways of putting Trelerric on the map I'd had the germ of an idea about Flick's wardrobe and had tentatively put it to Flick the day after Saturday supper. She'd agreed to meet Megan and talk about it.

I thought back to Saturday supper. Sam had talked about the apple events we'd discussed as another publicity option and for the most part the family had been interested and supportive. Sam had acknowledged my suggestions and had been friendly, but he hadn't sat next to me and neither had he teased me. I'd been left feeling a bit disappointed and let down.

'It's a good idea Sam.' Alice had said. 'But for Trelerric we need something more. Something really interesting that other places haven't got. I just wish I could come up with something.'

Well, I'd had an idea but I needed Flick's and Megan's support first before it could be announced.

The conversation had then moved on to the farming side of things. Tim farmed rare breed sheep and free range hens. He'd moved into organic farming almost before it had become fashionable and one of the benefits was that local restaurants were queuing up to use Cornish produce. Chefs liked to tell their customers where they sourced their food and the happier the animal the happier the client. For Tim though it was about treating the animals and the land respectfully and he was passionate about it.

Flick decided she'd spent enough time in the kitchen and after I'd tidied up I went to her rooms and invited Coco for her walk. She really was a cute little thing and I didn't need to fake my affection for her, which wasn't lost on Flick. Feeling a little bit unsure about how to speak to Sam if I met him I avoided the Coach House and took Coco round the back of the house. I really liked exploring with a dog to walk, it gave me the perfect opportunity to nose about. A dog gives you permission to go places and do things.

The original driveway, once used by carriages, had approached the Tudor entrance, but when the Georgian extension had been built the driveway had been moved to the new entrance and a new Coach House built. The building was eventually altered to house the chauffeur and the cars in the 1930s and these changes resulted in an unused triangular patch of ground which had been planted with maples and evergreen shrubs like camellia and azalea. Someone long ago had placed a couple of curved stone benches there with some heavy rustic slate paving and a lichen encrusted figure of the god Pan. It was very pretty and a perfect place for a lovers tryst and I wondered, not for the first time, about the wild parties which used to held at Trelerric.

While Coco sniffed about I stood idly and gazed at the Tudor building. It was lovely with small paned windows between thick stone mullions, a huge studded door and aged stonework. A secret place, it rested quiet and dreaming in the pale sunshine. I realised I didn't know anything about the first Latchley's, how they came to Trelerric or how they got their money. The Tudor house wasn't very big, but even so it must have taken a fair number of people to service its needs. I knew that the old dairy was now incorporated into Maggie's laundry room and held a new oil fired boiler, but the Tudor kitchen, buttery and dining hall, long gallery and bedrooms were all still there. And there was the chapel, cosily built into the side of the house. I still hadn't been into these parts.

I was about to move on when I heard voices one of which was Sam's so I stayed still, hidden by the glossy evergreen leaves of Camellia as he came into view. He was talking to Helena Fox-Harvey and carrying a spade over his shoulder.

'Well I'm very busy too Sam, I do run a business you know, but that doesn't have to stop us from having some private time together does it? If we work hard all day then surely we deserve some fun time at night. And we did have fun that night after Grace's party didn't we? You seemed to enjoy yourself and I know I did.'

She was having to walk fast to keep up with him and I thought she sounded a touch desperate but I had to admit she was looking good, she'd taken a lot of effort with her appearance.

Sam murmured a response and I heard Helena's quacking tones say something about an "intimate dinner chez moi". Of course, it was nearly Valentine's Day, but what was it Sam had said that day? "She's stalking me." Well she really was trying very hard to invite him out.

I couldn't hear Sam's answer as they walked on by. So they had been together. I felt a bit flat, although his body language just now wasn't saying anything special. He'd been gripping his spade with both hands and I had the sudden mad hope that he'd wanted to brain her with it and then use it to dig a hole and bury her. Coco was looking up at me, ready to move. I was glad she wasn't a yappy dog, I would have hated to have revealed myself just now.

'Good girl Coco.' I said softly. 'You're a very good girl. You shall have a nice walk and a special biscuit when we get back.'

We walked slowly around the side of the Tudor building while I peered in through the windows, not seeing much because of the angle of the sunlight and the dark within. Then I was right by the chapel. It was tiny, jutting out at an angle from the building and with a small arched doorway set in a pretty porch. Unaccountably I shivered and moved on round the corner and stopped and caught my breath. A whole carpet of snowdrops spread across a bank to a low stone wall which curved around the small building. It was a beautiful sight and I just stood there gazing and lost in pleasure. There were a few early purple and lilac crocuses as well, their flowers giving just the right accent of colour to accentuate the snowdrops. I don't know how long I stood there admiring the view but I was vaguely aware of a door slamming and then I realised I'd better get Coco back indoors, she'd been outside long enough.

Unusually that evening I sat with Flick and shared half a bottle of Viognier while we talked about her clothes and the idea that I was developing. I wanted to have something tangible to put to Megan and I couldn't do it without having Flick on board.

'We'd have to look at security as well Flick. Those dresses must be worth an awful lot.' I said.

'Oh Jane will have a view on that. I'm sure she'll come up with something.'

We said our goodnights and I made sure things were all set ready for the morning. I'd taken a few tasks off Maggie to her relief. I was smiling as I switched the hall lights on to go upstairs. I really was enjoying myself, things were becoming familiar and pleasant and I felt almost contended. At the top of the stairs I turned to my door and stopped in surprise. Carefully placed on the carpet outside the door was a small white glass vase filled with snowdrops. Around the neck of the vase was a narrow red ribbon tied into a bow.

Megan and Flick took to each other immediately, they had a lot in common with their love of personal adornment and their sound financial brains. I'd made us a good lunch with Flick's favourite salmon mousse followed by a chicken casserole. Megan ate well despite her wedding diet. Flick looked at her appraisingly.

'You're as slim as a wand. You'll look marvellous on the day. When is it?'

'Easter Saturday. Easter is late this year.'

They talked in great detail about the wedding dress and fabrics. I could see that Flick was assessing Megan's appreciation of clothes. Then we went upstairs where I'd opened the shutters and left the fan heater on to warm the room up. We took a bottle of cold white wine and some glasses upstairs with us. Flick was excited.

'It's like going to a couture house for a fitting!'

Megan was amazed and didn't contain her enthusiasm as the clothes were revealed in all their exquisite beauty. I saw things I hadn't seen before.

'People would pay to see these. You've got a story and original photographs and some of the photos are with famous people. It's got everything, glamour, history, society and beauty. And of course you Mrs Latchley. You're a legend in your lifetime.'

'Oh please do call me Flick, but spare me the crap.' Flick was bright eyed and enjoying her wine.

Megan was in full flow though. 'And you've got enough to change the exhibition, so people could come back and pay again to see more. Wow. The shoes alone are fantastic. And hats. The magazines would go bonkers to be able to photograph these. I'm thinking free publicity but with a fee to you. I'm thinking Royal College of Needlework to add gravitas. There could be a coffee table book, mostly photographs but with some contextual narrative.'

'People would come, wouldn't they.' I said. 'It would put Trelerric on the map. No-one else has got anything like this down here.'

Megan had ideas and contacts and organisational skills. We put everything away again and saw Flick downstairs, with the wine and the excitement she wanted to put her feet up. Megan came up to my rooms.

'It's even prettier than I remembered now there's a few of your own things in it. You've fallen on your feet here Luce.'

Megan didn't ask me anything about Sam Latchley because her mind was full of ideas about Flick's clothes and she wanted to see the Tudor hall in daylight to see if it would make a good exhibition space. That meant another visit. And of course Flick and I had to put the idea to the family.

The day of Jane's birthday was anything but spring-like. There was a mean easterly wind blowing and short hissy squalls of hailstones were bouncing off the car as I drove the short distance to The Lodge, not wanting to risk carrying the cake. Alice had decorated their dining room with birthday bunting and balloons, more for the sake of little Grace who was thrilled to bits. She'd made grandma a special card covered in strips of scrunched up coloured tissue and coated with glitter. I thought it would have suited Flick rather better than grandma Jane.

'It's very clever Grace.' I said, admiring her efforts. 'I love abstract and it's quite beautiful. Grandma Jane is going to love it.'

I helped Alice with the food prep for dinner. We were having a vegetable consommé into which I stirred a splash of sherry, followed by beef wellington with creamed celeriac and a medley of tiny coloured vegetables. Thinking of Sam I made a lemon tart which people could have with cream if they didn't want a slice of birthday cake. Finally Alice put a vase of daffodils in the sitting room and thanked me for my help. We sat down together for a much needed cup of tea, we'd worked well together and she clearly had her mum's cooking skills.

'It's great having another useful pair of hands here Lucy.'

We chatted about cooking and nursing and about my cake making business. Alice was a sympathetic listener.

'And your best friend went off with your fiancé? That must have been crap. But on the positive side your business didn't fail, it was the circumstances that changed. You've nothing to be ashamed of. And now we've got the benefit of having you here. That's a win for us.'

I couldn't help it, I asked her how long she'd known Helena Fox-Harvey.

'Oh her family live further up the old Liskeard road. I first met her when we were both riding at events. Nothing posh, just the local village gymkhana, although we were very competitive. I seem to remember whacking her with my riding crop once. Her father's something in London but her mother's local.'

'Have they always run a catering business?' I asked.

Alice shook her head. 'Oh no. It's all Helena's idea. At school she was thick but her folks sent her to a finishing school where she found she could cook. And she cooks like a dream. She did ski chalet catering for a while but then she came home and set up here. Why do you ask?'

I mumbled something about her knowing my sister via business and then said I'd better get back to wash and change and get Flick ready for the party.

Flick and I had gone down to Truro to shop and I'd bought Jane a pair of earrings with a small amethyst stone, explaining that it was the February birthstone. Flick had been amused.

'Do you believe in that Lucy? I thought you were anti-horoscopes and that rubbish.'

'I don't but I do, if that makes any sense. We seem to have lost the meaning of things lately. Beautiful things sometimes need explanations as to why we find them beautiful.' I gave up. I wasn't even making sense to myself. 'But I just think they'll suit her.'

'They will, I like them.' Flick was generous. 'I shall buy her the matching necklace. Alice is getting perfume and I expect Sam will give her something garden related since that's his passion.'

I was suddenly reminded of the little white vase of perfect snowdrops and my heart skipped a beat.

NINE

That evening I dressed with care. Flick had insisted on me buying a new dress in Truro.

'It's a birthday party,' she'd said. 'You can't wear black and you certainly can't wear trousers.'

I'd found a scooped necked winter dress in a soft light blue-grey silky material. My eyes had watered at the price but it was ages since I'd felt I deserved anything. Flick had insisted that I should accessorise with a chunky modern resin necklace in shades of lilac and purple with something gold and glittery in the resin.

'It wouldn't suit me of course but you have a different look. A very different style. The dress brings out the grey of your eyes and the necklace deepens the tone. But you simply must wear mascara Lucy.'

I'd bought some new lacy underwear as well in shades of silver grey and peach. I was learning a lot from Flick.

'You never know when you might get lucky, and you don't want to put him off by wearing those sexless sports underthings.'

I couldn't imagine Flick going into the laundry but I wondered if she'd seen my knickers drying.

Flick was looking fantastic in a long emerald ensemble with a shorter floaty cinnamon coloured top embroidered with delicate gold flowers. I'd left my car right by the tradesman's entrance and the weather had turned cold and dry by the time we left for The Lodge. Tim and Jane arrived after everyone else but there was no sign of Sam.

'Mitch has cut his paw quite badly. Sam's at the duty vet. He'll try to join us later.' Jane explained. 'Some fool left broken glass up in the woods. Tim's furious.'

Jane was delighted with her presents and made a fuss of Grace for making her such an amazing card. As I had suspected even Flick was impressed with it.

'What talent Grace has. I think we must be related.' She said fondly to Alice as Jonathan took Grace upstairs to bed.

The meal was lovely but I was achingly conscious of the empty seat opposite me. All this dressing up hadn't been for Jane's benefit I realised. Alice and Jonathan cleared the remains of the main meal away while the rest of us sat chatting. Tim had taken Jane out for the day. They'd had lunch in Tavistock.

'I don't think I can eat any more,' Jane said. 'I've eaten like a horse today. I do hope Alice hasn't made anything too fancy.'

At that moment the lights went off apart from the fairy lights Grace had insisted on having and a voice started singing Happy Birthday to You. My skin tingled, I knew that voice. The door opened and Sam came in carrying the birthday cake I had made. Alice had placed a single candle on it for Jane.

'There wasn't enough room for a hundred candles mum so you'll have to make do with just the one.' Sam laughed. He put the cake down on the sideboard and stepped back so that we could all see it. He looked over at me and our eyes locked. He smiled and nodded. I felt congratulated and almost overwhelmed with happiness.

I was pleased with the cake. The violets were bunched together centrally with a fine sugar ribbon looped, folded and entwined with tiny sugar pearls, the shades of the violets delicately offset by the light coffee icing. I'd done a pale sugar lace wrap over the coffee iced sides and placed just a few caramelised walnut halves in sticky clumps around the dish. Jane got up to look followed by Tim. Flick had already seen it of course but she leaned over and squeezed my hand.

'Well done. That's a thing of beauty you've made.'

Tim kissed me on the cheek and then Jane did. She wanted to know how on earth I'd done it but I shrugged and said it was the fairies.

'But it's too beautiful to cut.' Jane said.

'Looks like mud, probably tastes like mud too.' I said, thinking of the fun we used to have round the table when I was little.

Everyone was busy then getting themselves a small slice of lemon tart. Jane cut into the cake but not until it had been photographed with us all grouped around it so that Jane could email a picture to her sister. Sam came in and sat down opposite me, his plate heaped with beef wellington and vegetables.

'Is Mitch going to be okay?' I asked.

Sam nodded, his mouth full. I could see he was famished.

'Good job you had that candle lit so you could see to come in.' I said with a giggle. I couldn't resist it.

Afterwards, in the sitting room, Flick made the announcement about her couture collection as she had decided to call it. She competently sketched out Megan's ideas but then gestured to me.

'But I'm not taking any credit for this. It's all Lucy's idea. Lucy thinks we can put Trelerric on the map and her sister Megan is happy to handle arrangements and publicity. You'll have to meet her of course Jane.

There was a buzz of interest and questions and answers were bounced around. By now Sam was standing just inside the door eating a slice of lemon tart and listening. Flick said she'd really like to try just a tiny piece.

'I think I can smell the lemon, unless it's air freshener,' she said. 'Is that a cooking additive of some sort Lucy?'

'You just need to use the zest.' Sam replied before I could answer. 'It's where the flavour is, in the lemon oil. I know about these things. An expert told me once.'

'Oh dear,' Flick murmured to me as I got up to fetch her a little piece. 'I do hope it wasn't the horsey woman.'

Sam followed me into the dining room.

'Great cake. Good ideas too. You've made mum's day.' And leaning forward he kissed me on the cheek.

'Nice legs too.' He said cheekily, following me out. 'I mean, nice dress.'

I was glad he couldn't see my face or hear how hard my heart was beating.

When I finally got into bed that night I felt as though I'd turned a corner. I was happy, I felt appreciated and accepted but more than that I felt a sense of belonging. I'd settled down very quickly and easily into life at Trelerric House and I could see myself playing a part in its future.

The article about tracing your family that Flick had given me to read a while ago was still on my bedside table. A couple of times I'd meant to throw it away but now I read it carefully. At the back of my mind I could hear Alice describing Helena and her local connections. Finishing school, huh, so what, I said to myself. But she knew who she was. I didn't. I realised that I needed to talk to mum and dad.

The opportunity arose quickly as they were driving down to see Megan about the wedding plans the following weekend. We were also all meeting Mike's best man for the first time and Mike was able to put mum and dad up at his place since he had loads of room. He lived in an old house up on the edge of Dartmoor with outbuildings which were perfect for his music business. The only problem in mum's eyes was that he'd spent too much money on converting and doing up his music studio and offices and not enough on the house. She liked things modern, magnolia and mundane. Old fashioned plumbing, trendy sanded floorboards and an irritable heating system weren't her cup of tea.

'What's wrong with underlay and nice fitted carpet?' She said incredulously to Megan, eyeing some vibrant framed posters of Mike's various successful protégées in the hall.

'It doesn't suit the house mum.' Megan replied.

'And keeping warm? What about that? This house is on a moor, not the south of France. When the babies start coming Megan you'll not be wanting to be catching your deaths in a cold house. It's just not practical.'

Megan gave an inscrutable smile. 'Don't worry mum. I'm sure I'll find ways and means of making things a little more comfortable in due course.'

I knew that once Megan's flat was sold she intended making a few changes.

Megan and I had been busy with mum all day doing the mother of the bride stuff. I was Megan's matron-of-honour and had a simple rather Grecian-style dress already made. Mum hadn't wanted to wear what she'd bought for my wedding because she felt it was unlucky so a shopping trip had been arranged.

I looked at mum now, we were all together in the sitting room after dinner. Mum was as close to the woodstove as possible. Dad was nursing a brandy which he'd said he needed quite badly after the stress of the day. He'd spent the day at Mike's, reading the paper and helping to assemble the meal which Megan had left prepared. Mike was quite competent in the kitchen and dad had been well trained by mum over the years. He'd had to be helpful, with a house full of children for so many years.

'What do you mean your day was stressful?' Mum said to dad.

'It was the stress of thinking about how much you were spending on dresses.'

Mum rolled her eyes and turned to me, desperate to get some after dinner conversation going. 'And what about you now Lucy?'

'What about me?' I smiled at her, hoping she wasn't going to refer to Peter. It came to me that I hadn't thought about Peter for weeks. He'd been the wrong shape for the space I'd been trying to fit him into, like a child's puzzle. I just hadn't seen it at the time. But I didn't want to be obtuse.

'I'm fine mum. I'm really happy at Trelerric House, the people there are lovely. In fact I wanted to ask you something in connection with all that. But it'll keep till later, before I go.' I didn't want to ask about my past in front of Mike's best man, his closest friend Matt.

Mum fixed me with her no-nonsense stare but failed to detect anything wrong with me. We used to call it mum's radar. Dad cleared his throat and sipped his brandy and Matt asked me if he could get me another drink. He'd been attentive all evening. Megan had told me that he was getting divorced and that he saw his children at alternate weekends. I declined another drink since I had to drive in an hour or so and smiled at him. He was shorter than Mike and stocky, well muscled. We'd discovered a common interest in running and he enjoyed various sports. He'd asked me if I fancied entering the Lanhydrock half marathon but I wasn't sure I was fit enough, I hadn't been running for a few weeks.

'It's a punishing course, a lot uphill. I've done it once before.' Matt said, with the air of someone who always completes what he sets out to do. He certainly wasn't a lame duck.

Eventually the evening drew to a close and Matt said he'd be off. I stayed behind in the sitting room with mum and took a deep breath.

'I was wondering if you'd mind if I tried to find out about my birth mother.' I said, holding both her hands in mine.

Mum looked into my eyes. 'Well I'm surprised it's taken you until now to ask. Of course I don't mind, how could I? You've been my girl all these years and you'll be my girl whatever happens. But what's prompted it, dare I ask?' Her Irish lilt was pronounced, always a sign of her feelings.

I told her about Trelerric and how everyone knew who they were.

'They all fit in and belong.' I said. 'Mrs Latchley understands, she grew up in an orphanage. She gave me an article about ways of finding your birth family. There are various pros and cons and I understand that not everyone ends up with the ideal sort of story about their origins. I've given it a lot of thought and, well, now I think I'd like some questions answered. So I'm going to register with the Adoption Contact Centre. I think I do it via the Register Office website and I might need your help filling in the application form.'

Mum nodded, looking thoughtful. 'All we knew was that your mother was very young and that her family were not forthcoming with details. When we got you your mother's tears hadn't dried I think. But you're over 18 so you have the right to ask. We have a simple birth certificate with your adoption papers.' She paused thoughtfully. 'They'll want to know where the adoption was arranged of course. We were still living in London then, it was before daddy decided he wanted to teach engineering rather than do it. It meant that he had more regular hours and time to spend with us all in summer as a family.'

I realised she was telling me things I hadn't really been aware of.

'And are you going to be taking counselling Lucy? It's wise to if it's offered. People can find some unwanted surprises when they do this.'

I said I didn't know at this point.

'I've never seen my birth certificate.'

'Well there's no reason why you shouldn't have it. Shall I send it down to you.'

I nodded and there was a moment of quiet between us.

'And you have feelings for Trelerric did you say, or for someone there?' Mum said, shrewdly changing the subject. Typical mum, nothing escaped her.

I was saved from answering by everyone coming back into the room. But I had a special secret, when Sam had complimented me and kissed my cheek a week ago I had been staggered by the rush of emotion I'd felt.

Megan didn't waste time in putting an action plan together and sending Flick a copy of her draft proposal with a copy for Jane. Megan came to meet Jane and take a look at the Tudor Hall and the long gallery with a view to finding exhibition space. There was so much to organise; insurance, security, parking, refreshments, dressmakers' dummies, lighting. The list was endless. Megan was also planning a press release, interviews with the Sunday papers, Visit Cornwall and local magazines. It was decided to launch the event in time for the school summer holidays. Flick and Alice joined us with the children in tow after she'd collected Grace from school.

'I've been thinking,' Alice said. 'Parking might be a problem. We can't cope if three hundred people turn up at once. We haven't got space and we certainly couldn't run to refreshments for that many. Sorry to be a pain, I'm not meaning to be negative because it's a fantastic idea.'

'No that's okay Alice,' Megan said. 'We need to be realistic.'

I spoke up for the first time. 'How about a ticketed event? Advertise with a price payable in advance which includes a simple morning or afternoon tea. No lunches. That way we can control numbers and the catering burden.'

Alice agreed. 'We can serve Cornish saffron cakes and a cream tea, maybe with a choice of sandwiches. Groups in from nine till twelve and two till five. A few might hang about to look at the gardens but Sam should be able to manage that.'

'And that will help with the security and insurance side of things.' Jane said.

'And makes it more exclusive, more special.' Megan added.

'It's got legs hasn't it?' Flick said excitedly. 'I was talking to Sir Hugh at lunch on Sunday, we always do our financial planning over lunch. He's suggested selling posters of the clothes, cards and maybe books too. He knows a few publishers.'

I knew that Flick's main interest was in the merchandising because she'd proposed a split on the income. Any profits from the exhibition would go to the estate and any profits from merchandising would be hers. She paid my wages, Maggie's wages and the utility bills for our living accommodation, so it made sense to enhance her portfolio as she described it.

Alice and I spent several days working on plans. We would be the room stewards in the hall and upstairs in the gallery. Sam would be in charge of the plant sales and would perfect the gardens with Simon's help. Simon and Tim would be the main men in charge of ticket collections and the parking arrangements, but Jonathan would help at weekends. Maggie had a friend who usually came to assist on open days and her daughter Clare was happy to earn extra cash on her days off from the vets. Jane would help as relief wherever she could and Flick would put in appearances and be her charming self. And we decided not to open on Mondays. We had a couple of months in which to prepare and still had to incorporate the set fixtures of opening at Easter and Mothering Sunday and the May Bank Holidays.

By the time Saturday supper came round Sam surprised me at the Coach House. He was getting the Jag out.

'Thought I would drive you and Flick over to Home Farm tonight. That way you can let your hair down and have a drink if you like.'

'Oh. I thought maybe Flick might like to have a go on your quad bike.' I said pointlessly. Since that kiss on the cheek I'd had the feeling he was avoiding me and I'd seen Helena's car again when I'd gone out for a run one afternoon.

'No need to be defensive Lucy.'

'I'm not.' But I knew I was. I just didn't want to go where my heart would be hurt again. I made an attempt at a joke. 'I could just see her in sequinned gauntlets and an Isadora Duncan scarf.' I stopped, suddenly remembering that dancer's tragic death. 'No that's not a good image is it.'

Sam was looking at me seriously but he just gave me a curt nod. 'I'll collect you both at the usual time then. Now I need to go and wash.'

Flick of course, was thrilled, but she was less thrilled that I was back in my black and white. I apologised, explaining that I felt pre-menstrual and bit grouchy.

That evening Jane took me to one side.

'Lucy, I have to thank you for this, although how we'll all feel after six weeks goodness knows because we've never done anything like it. But my dear, you're taking on a lot. You're here to look after Flick, we don't expect you to slave on the estate like the rest of us.'

'I am looking after Flick,' I said. 'She's part of it and passionate about it. And I've never been afraid of hard work.'

'Well I think you're amazing. And I'm not the only one.' And she patted my hand.

TEN

The great thing for me was that Megan could legitimately pay visits to Trelerric House so I got to see quite a lot of her. One day we were walking Coco together on the route past the Tudor chapel and I told her about seeing Sam walking with Helena, and about the snowdrops outside my room that night.

'And were they from him?'

'No idea. He's never said anything. He continues to tease me and I give as good as I get when I can. And he comes into the kitchen regularly. The other day Maggie said we seemed to be seeing a lot more of him. Apparently he mostly used to go to Home Farm to eat but now he cadges off her.'

'And do you still see Helena's car around?'

'It's been there a couple of times when I've come back from an outing with Flick. Flick doesn't like her, I don't know why. She's from a good local family I gather.' I felt myself droop at the thought of Helena, I just couldn't work out what was going on between her and Sam and didn't want to pursue the conversation any further.

Megan gave me a quick look. 'And have you contacted the adoption agency thingy?'

'I'm still researching the options, it's complicated. I could approach these people and they'll do the necessary research to discover the identity of my birth mother, or I could just register my details for a small fee with the General Register Office, and if she's done the same they'll match us up and let us both know. But they don't do tracing. If she's registered with them I gather it would be up to me to make contact. I kind of prefer it that way. Mum's sending me my birth certificate so that I can fill out an application form.'

We stopped walking while Coco investigated something, her tail wagging. Megan looked at the Tudor building and chapel.

'It's so beautiful here Lucy. Is the chapel in use?'

'I think the local vicar does a service at Easter and at Christmas.'

'Do they have weddings here?'

'I gather Alice and Jonathan were married here. Why? Oh you're thinking of business opportunities aren't you.' I said. 'I can almost hear your brain-cogs clicking.'

'Hmm, I think I could design an attractive package. At the very least it would make a great venue for a wedding fayre.'

I groaned. That's like saying olde worlde.' I emphasised the letter 'e' in my pronunciation. 'It's naff.'

I gave her a friendly shove and she shoved me back.

'I know my job.' Megan said, 'I know what people like and how to sell it. And this is a cracking venue the Latchley's have.

I understood her intuition about the assets of the property but something in me didn't want hoards of people intent on acquisition and lifestyle opportunities treading the ancient grounds. It seemed lightweight and almost dishonest.

'Matt likes you Lucy.' Megan said, changing the subject. 'Mike said he was asking about you. Matt's a nice guy, he runs his own printing and design business and it's doing well. He employs staff you know and handles all Mike's promotional materials. He's quite soluble.'

'You mean solvent Meg.' I was amused by her word play. 'I guess we could approach him about doing stuff for Flick.' I deliberately ignored the information about him liking me.

'Well you could ask him yourself. Mike has suggested that the four of us have dinner out together this week. There's a place in Royal William Yard in Plymouth that we fancy trying tomorrow night. You could dress up a bit for a change.'

I felt as though I was being manoeuvred but couldn't think of an excuse not to go.

The next day Simon started work preparing the courtyard for the new Japanese style garden. He lifted all the old slabs and methodically stacked them for removal and I took him a mid-morning mug of tea and a hot bacon sandwich.

'That's hard heavy work Simon,' I said. 'Are you okay doing this alone?'

'Not a problem ma'am.' Simon spoke through a cheek bulging with bacon and paused while he finished eating. 'Done this sort of work before at an old place beyond Minions. Up on the moor near Liskeard.' He explained, noticing my blank look.

'I've not been there.'

'It's nice, the moor is lovely. I was working for Mr Pencraddoc, have you heard of him?'

I shook my head.

'Millionaire. Super bloke. It was his lady who encouraged me into doing the computer course on garden design and drawing a couple of years ago. She's an artist. She's beautiful.'

The words "his lady" resonated in my mind. It sounded quaintly old fashioned.

I took his mug and plate when he finished. 'Maggie's making a lasagne for lunch Simon. You're to eat in the kitchen, Maggie's orders.' I informed him. Actually it was Flick's orders.

Simon's face lit up. 'I love Maggie's cooking. That's ideal.'

Flick and I were having the same but with a side salad and served in the Chinese Room. When we had finished eating I carried things back through to the kitchen and found it full. Maggie, her daughter Clare, Simon and Sam were all sitting eating and talking. Simon was gazing at Clare with devotion, his feelings for her easy to read. She was a pretty girl, with dark hair like mine and very neat features. Absently I wondered what Maggie's husband looked like; Maggie had chestnut curls and witchy green eyes. I switched the kettle on and watched them, it was so obvious when people liked each other that way. Others could see it often before they themselves had acknowledged it. Then I wondered if anyone had noticed me making sheep's eyes at Sam during Saturday supper. Realising I was blushing I had to turn back to the kettle, feeling like a complete idiot.

Sam got up and came over to me. 'Let me help you with the doors and the lights Lucy.'

Unaccountably I felt too down to respond with anything more than a single word. 'Thanks.'

We went through into the inner hall. Sam took the tray from me and indicated that I should open the next door.

'Can you see it?' He asked.

'See what?' I said crossly, not in the mood for his special line in teasing me. I wanted an awful lot more than a private joke. I was so frustrated I could scream.

'Young love.'

I stopped dead in my tracks. For a moment I thought he was talking about us and my hopes, withheld and suppressed for weeks, soared into the heavens and exploded into stars, comets and planets with rings round them.

'Simon and Clare.' Sam said, but he was looking at me peculiarly. The atmosphere between us was so static it was almost crackling.

I couldn't speak. I was speechless with emotion and embarrassment and my eyes filled with tears.

'Lucy. Oh Lucy.' Sam put the tray down on the hall table and his arms went round me. His lips found mine and I kissed him with every ounce of pent up longing that had been smouldering for weeks. I was on fire, all I could feel was his solid strength and his mouth and then the slight rasp against my cheek of his. He was breathing hard and his eyes had an unfocussed expression.

'Lucy,' he said again. 'I wasn't sure.' And he kissed me again.

Then the door to Flick's suite opened and she was standing there surveying us.

'Well, thank heaven you've both finally come to your senses. Tea when you're ready then. In your own time.' And she closed the door.

I stayed in Sam's arms and he was looking down at me with an expression of confused wonder, his honey coloured eyes glowing.

'Lucy. I think we need to talk. Shall we go out to a pub tonight.' He kissed the tip of my nose.

I was about to say that I'd love to when I realised that I already had a date of sorts.

'I can't. I'm having dinner in Plymouth with my sister and Mike and his best man. It's a pre-wedding thing. I can't get out of it.'

'Okay. Well, not okay. I'm busy all day tomorrow, I've got a company here erecting a new gazebo in the old orchard. It's got to be completed before I move the bees in, they don't like disturbance from power tools. The vibration upsets them. Maybe tomorrow evening then.'

It was my turn to say okay. He could have been talking in tongues for all I knew. Vaguely I heard him mention something about an erection but all I cared about was the feel of his arms round me.

We let go of each other reluctantly.

I took the tray into Flick's suite and carried it through to the day room. She put her magazine down and looked at me searchingly.

'Well?'

'Well what Flick?'

'Well I could see that you liked each other, Jane and Alice have noticed as well. Has he asked you out?'

Flick was so matter of fact and straightforward that I had to smile. And she was interested in my welfare. 'Sort of.' I poured the tea. She had to be content with that but I was twitchy and distracted and glad to be able to take Coco out for her afternoon exercise. I kept turning the events over in my mind but mostly it was the feel of his lips on mine that I kept returning to.

That evening I arrived at Megan's flat before Mike and Matt.

'You're early Luce. Did I give you the wrong time?' Lucy let me in with a towel round her and her hair wet. She looked me up and down, recognising the dressier of my black skirts but she admired the coloured scarf I was wearing.

'That's nice. Where did you get it?'

'Flick gave it to me to wear when Sam took me down to see the Japanese garden. She didn't want it back.'

Just saying Sam's name gave me a thrill. Megan was looking at me in her dressing table mirror.

'You look lit up Lucy. What news?'

I couldn't contain myself. 'Sam kissed me this afternoon. A proper kiss.'

Megan turned round on her seat and looked at me. 'I wondered why your eyes were sparkling. Matt will be disappointed.' She looked thoughtful. 'Luce. Keep your options open. Eggs and baskets you know.'

Later that night Megan and I retreated to the ladies loo, the scene of so much female plotting.

'It's not fair Megan. Matt's really nice, but he's not floating my boat. I can't lead him on or go on a date, it would be unkind.'

Megan was checking her appearance in the mirror. 'I know, awful isn't it. Men are like buses, none for twelve months and then two come along at once.' She turned away from her lovely reflection and looked at me. 'But Lucy, don't get taken in by one kiss from the heir apparent. He might be practising his droit de seigneur, history tells us that the lord of the manor did it all the time.'

'His what?' I asked.

'His right as the lord to deflower a virgin, usually on her wedding night admittedly. But don't be his casual fuck. Don't get your heart broken again.'

I knew that Megan had my welfare at heart, she'd seen me through a devastatingly awful period in my life. But she had me worried, the glistening golden treasure of Sam's kiss might turn out to be tarnished brass after all. I resolved to take a closer look at Matt.

That evening I'd spoken to Matt about advising Flick on costs for merchandising and marketing and he'd said he would be delighted to come along and talk to her. Matt had trained as a graphic designer before starting his own business, and he knew his business well. He asked me for my mobile number and when I hesitated he smiled at me and I noticed that the skin crinkled attractively around his eyes.

'I'm not a stalker Lucy,' he said jokily, touching my arm. 'I haven't met Mrs Latchley so rather than phone her out of the blue it's perhaps best if I call you to make arrangements to meet her. That's okay isn't it?'

The next day I was away with the fairies. Maggie asked me if I was alright.

'You've put the teapot in the dishwasher with a teabag inside it Lucy. Something on your mind?'

'Oh I'm just woolgathering Maggie, I didn't sleep well last night. So many things juggling about in my mind right now. So much to organise and arrange.'

Actually I'd lain awake with my hands behind my head thinking about kissing Sam and wondering what he'd meant when he'd said we needed to talk. My initial reaction had been one of optimism, now I could feel doubts and fears creeping in. What if he wanted to say that it was all a mistake, that there was no way he'd get involved with someone of no background, someone on the staff. I'd also been thinking about sorting out the adoption paperwork.

Maggie however was calmly taking everything in her stride. 'Things will work out. They've had a bit of practice handling the public, the family I mean. And Clare is thrilled to get some extra paid work. She's takes holiday or lieu days off from the vet's to work here. She's a good saver is Clare, she understands money.'

I was reminded of the way Simon looked at Clare yesterday. 'Has she got a boyfriend?' I asked. 'She's a very pretty girl Maggie. She takes after her dad I suppose?'

Maggie looked distinctly uncomfortable. 'Well I'd better be getting on Lucy,' she said, not answering my question. 'Got the laundry to finish and Mrs Latchley's bed to change.'

I was dismissed. At that moment my mobile started ringing. It was Matt.

'Lucy hi,' Matt said. 'Is this a good time? Only I'm driving back from Launceston and could call in at Trelerric if that's convenient for Mrs Latchley. Megan said last night that things were quite urgent given the timescale.'

I wondered why he was talking to me as though I was a business associate he was trying to impress, but then I thought maybe he was a bit shy and taking refuge in professional talk. I'd already told Flick about Matt while we were in her dressing room before breakfast and she was quite keen to set the ball rolling, so I walked through to her and waved my phone. Flick was at the piano and she paused in her playing.

'Matt Ashton is wondering if he could call in shortly? He's quite nearby apparently.'

She confirmed that was convenient. Flick loved receiving visitors.

I went upstairs and looked at myself in the bathroom mirror. I don't know what I was expecting to see. My grey eyes looked back at me, not giving away any secrets. I combed my hair and went to the sitting room window overlooking the orchard. Sam was by the wall in the far corner in consultation with a group of men. The gazebo was obviously on track. I gazed at him but I couldn't see his expression or hear his voice so I went back downstairs, wondering if I was on his mind as much as he was on mine.

Almost immediately the doorbell sounded and I answered the door before Maggie. Matt was standing there, smartly dressed in chinos and a blazer, with expensive looking loafers, a trendy shirt and tie. He looked every inch the successful businessman and his this year's plate Audi parked outside backed that up. When he phoned he must have been about five minutes away.

'Lucy. How lucky am I? Seeing you twice in two days.'

He leaned forward and kissed me on both cheeks. I didn't kiss back but made an embarrassed noise of welcome. Maggie was standing in the kitchen doorway, her eyes huge with interest.

'Maggie, this is Matthew Ashton, he's come to see Mrs Latchley. I'll just take him through.'

Flick received him gracefully, not getting up from her chaise longue. He actually bent over her hand once I'd made the introductions. I tried not to feel cynical but I felt his charm was effortless since money was involved.

Maggie already had the kettle on, she was accustomed to doing refreshments for Flick's visitors.

'Matt drinks coffee, Flick would like peppermint tea. I'll see to it Maggie.' I said.

'Good looking man. A friend of yours?' Maggie asked.

'He's going to be best man at the wedding. I've only met him twice, once was last night.'

I was wondering why he made me feel uncomfortable and then I realised. He was a toucher. At any opportunity he'd put a hand on my arm. He was a too-much too-soon kind of person. Uncharitably I felt that if he'd been a dog he'd be humping my leg at every opportunity. Flick, however, seemed quite taken with him and invited him to stay for lunch. Well, there was a lot to talk about but at least I was able to leave them to it while I set the table for three and reorganised a few things in the kitchen.

To be fair Matt was good company, at ease and charming, full of anecdotes and quite witty. He was just too smooth and pleasing for my taste. After we'd finished lunch he stood up to go and promised Flick he'd be in touch as quickly as possible. I walked him to the door and he turned to me.

'Lovely to see you again sweet Lucy. Something tells me we'll be seeing quite a lot of each other over the coming weeks, for obvious reasons of course.'

Matt's voice sounded intimate, as though we shared a secret. He'd taken my hand and pulled me closer as he spoke and then swooped forward to kiss my cheek. It was then I realised that the kitchen door was half open and that Sam was standing there watching us.

ELEVEN

'Goodbye Matt.' I finally extricated my hand from his, waved him off and shut the door behind him. Full of anticipation I turned to Sam. He wasn't there. I went into the kitchen where Maggie was clearing up.

'Did I see Sam just now?' I asked her.

'Yes, he came in to grab a sandwich but he's working on the hoof today. Busy with a gazebo he said. I had to ask him what that meant, apparently it's a posh word for a sort of summer house without sides, which seems a bit pointless to me. Anyway he wants it for his bees.'

I wasn't really listening, and what I did hear didn't make much sense anyway. I fetched my jacket and went to find Coco. Flick had already retired for a doze. Slipping my new wellingtons on I hastened outside and in the direction of the orchard where I could hear power tools and work in progress. Coco didn't like the sounds and pulled back, her big eyes anxious.

'Come on Coco, it's okay, nothing's going to hurt you poppet.'

I bent down and patted her reassuringly but she wasn't having any of it. I got her as far as the orchard entrance and no further but at least I was clearly visible to the men Sam was standing with. I hoped he would come over to speak to me, I knew he'd seen me, but he didn't even wave.

'Going about your obligatory duties?' A posh voice quacked behind me. It was Helena Fox-Harvey. Before I could think of a reply she'd spotted Sam. 'Ah there he is. I've come to remind him about my drinks and nibbles party tonight. Just a few close friends of ours. Very cosy.'

She strode off across the orchard as though she owned the place, her curvaceous bottom concealed by a well cut flared skirt, but she still walked like a duck in her fashionable flat designer-label boots. I couldn't help it, I stayed there and watched them. She kissed his cheek in a familiar way and made plenty of extravagant gestures for the benefit of all those watching. I could hear her high pitched neighing laughter.

'Shit.' I said. 'Shit and bloody sod it.'

So that was that. I couldn't eat and spent the first part of the evening pacing around my rooms, Sam didn't appear. Finally I couldn't stand it and put my running things on. The nights were drawing out and there was enough twilight for me to see to run to the estate entrance and back, past Home Farm. There was no sign of his Landrover and there were no lights on in the Coach House.

I stared moodily out of my window at the daffodils making a show in the orchard. Sam had cleared all the pruned apple tree branches and mowed meandering paths through the trees. After the winter bleakness it looked charming. I noticed evidence of his skills everywhere as I walked Coco, the terraced garden at the front of the old house had clumps of wine red and snow white hellebores in flower, accompanied by snakes head fritillary. Near the old stables, where the summer tea rooms were I saw primroses and blue grape hyacinth beneath venerable magnolia trees unveiling their fantastic blossoms. It was a magical place and I often just stood and stared, half expecting to see an Edwardian lady in an afternoon tea dress taking her pleasance on the old paths, not that the current planting would have been recognisable to someone of that period. A low hedge of scented evergreen daphne grew below the kitchen windows by the tradesmen's entrance. I'd never noticed it before until the scent stopped me in my tracks; it was heavenly.

Unable to confront Sam I threw myself into working with Maggie making batches of cakes, starting with a variety of fruit cakes for the freezer in readiness for the opening days, Mother's Day was just a few days away now. We made Dundee cake, Cornish saffron loaf and Farmhouse fruit cake and I practised an idea I'd had for making tiny Cornish pasties filled with spiced fruit, something like an Eccles cake but with a dab of icing. Some cakes had cherries, others had dried fruit soaked in fruit juice and spices. We avoided using nuts in the cakes but planned on making Madeira sponges and cupcakes nearer the day using almonds and coconut in some. Selling food to the public these days was fraught with difficulty. And of course for the Easter opening there would be the ubiquitous chocolate creations incorporating mini Easter eggs and pastel decorations.

All these delights would be served in the old stables, appropriately named the Stables Tea Room, where the stalls and loose boxes had been turned into intimate booths named after the working horses they used to house; Duke, Prince, Violet and Clover. Someone had hung enlarged sepia-tinted photographs of them standing outside in the courtyard with the farm labourers of the time, lithe hard men with steady eyes and too much facial hair. Chunky circular wooden picnic tables were already set outside on the cobbles amongst half barrels and old granite troughs planted with flowering hebe, variegated ivy, hyacinth and heather. Alice said that Sam had stopped using alpines because people pinched them.

Meanwhile I was occupied making Megan's wedding cake, a task which filled my evenings. Her wedding was growing closer, she already had a buyer for her flat and was working all hours on Flick's clothing exhibition, now tentatively named Trelerric Vintage. And Matt was becoming a frequent visitor as he needed Flick to see his ideas for posters, cards and other merchandising proposals. Both he and Megan spent a day at the house pouring over Flick's albums as their ideas took shape and there were yet more visitors as photographers and magazine reporters turned up to design their articles.

'We usually know about events like this a year in advance, not less than six months. We can put it on the website and say something in the editorial but I don't know if we can drop planned copy.' Grumbled one harassed looking woman when she came into the kitchen searching for a socket to charge something. I had to shoo her out.

'Sorry, no strangers, it's a commercial food prep area right now.' I waved a spoonful of cake mix at her.

I was run off my feet but so was everyone else. Alice stopped by for a cup of tea one morning and devoured one of my tiny Cornish pastie cakes.

'Delicious Lucy, I like the sweet flaky pastry. What shall we call them? How about Piskie Cakes, unique to Trelerric.'

'Pissed off cakes more like.' I said, collapsing into a chair opposite her. 'I'm shattered.'

'It's all the standing up,' Maggie agreed, sitting down and kicking her shoes off. 'I'm sure my feet have gone flat.'

Alice told us that everyone felt the same. 'Dad and Sam have had a few nights with late lambs, dad's like the walking dead this morning. Sam's been sleeping in his old room at Home Farm for the past week. He and mum have been slaving all hours over bedding plants and cuttings in the greenhouses as well. And this is only March.'

I cautiously welcomed the sense of relief Alice's words gave me. I'd been running again and noticed that there were still no lights in the Coach House. Naturally I'd suspected the worst, imaging him cosily cosseted with toothy Helena and her bouncy arse. It wasn't the only thing she had which bounced, I'd noticed.

'Okay for Saturday supper Lucy?' Alice said as she got up to leave.

I had my answer ready. I wasn't prepared to face Sam after several days of uncertainty.

'I'm going to have to give it a miss Alice, I meant to call Jane today. Flick is having a weekend away with her friends Booboo and Harry at what she describes as a hideous house party, so she won't be there and I'm away at Megan's for a couple of nights. More wedding talk.' I added as though needing a significant reason for my absence.

Alice was unconcerned. 'Oh well, have a lovely weekend. Where's the wedding taking place?'

I named some place on the side of Dartmoor which was all part of Megan's extraordinary network of local gems and promised to call Jane to reduce the numbers for dinner by two.

Megan and I had an evening alone together and talked about everything. Once again she gave her warning against misinterpreting one single kiss. Then we filled out the form from the General Register Office. Megan sat holding my birth certificate.

'Is that it? It's so small.'

All I'd got was a pink certificate with my name, date of birth, sex and place of birth on it. Lucy Wingfield.

'I know mum and dad kept your name. You were lucky. My given name was Marigold. You can't imagine how that feels.'

'Sounds like the cleaning lady.'

'Are you calling me a scrubber or something?!'

We pushed each other about a bit.

On Saturday morning I woke in my old bed at her flat sobbing. Megan came in and shushed me, a handful of tissues ready to dry my tears.

'What was it Luce? The old dream?'

I nodded, blowing my nose and wiping my eyes. There was a vague memory of corridors, the claustrophobia of a small room and the sense of overwhelming sorrow.

'Still no idea what the dream is about?' Megan asked.

'No idea,' I blew my nose again. 'It's just so sad. There's something I want badly, but it's not there.'

We went for an early run together and then did girly shopping in Plymouth where I was persuaded to buy a pair of cut off fashionably frayed skinny jeans with embroidery on the pockets. In black, naturally. Megan insisted they'd look good with heels and she matched them with a black silky top which had a floppy droopy neckline.

'You've got the sort of skin which tans in the time it takes you to walk from the front door to the car Lucy. This is a killer outfit for a smart pub evening once your legs are tanned and the neckline will disguise the fact that you aren't very heavy on the top.'

'You mean a date don't you. And I resent your reference to my bust.' I said as I drove us up to Mike's place for the evening. 'Are you trying to set me up for a date with Matt?'

Megan just shrugged but once again Matt was in close attendance. This time I endured a full frontal embrace and a small hug. It left me cold. How could this man completely fail to notice my physical indifference, I wondered. And what on earth was wrong with me, he was a nice looking, witty, intelligent and successful man. But I still kept getting the doggy image, he looked at me as though he wanted me to throw him a ball or, vile thought, tickle his tummy.

Dinner was described as a simple pizza and salad, but Mike had made the topping himself with roasted and skinned red peppers cooked with onion, garlic and sliced mushrooms in a rich tomato sauce, spread on toasted French bread and then grilled with a Gruyere topping. It was simple and gorgeous and I asked him how he did it.

'I can taste basil but there's something else, a low note beneath the garlic. What is it?'

'The trick is to use anchovy, a teaspoon of the oil in the cooking and a couple of filets in the sauce. They dissolve into salty gloriousness. Just don't get it on your clothes because it won't come off. Gloria taught me the recipe years ago.'

I glanced at Megan at the mention of Travis's mother, but she was unconcerned. She liked Travis, everyone did, and Mike's relationship with his son's mother was one of old friends. They'd never married although they'd tried living together when Travis came along. Now they hadn't seen each other for years since she'd moved to New York to manage a music studio, having begun an interesting life as a singer from Tiger Bay in Cardiff.

'Thinking of Travis, when does he arrive?' I asked.

'Three days before the wedding, then he's going to Cardiff to see relatives before going back to New York. I hate to think what his carbon footprint is at his age.' Mike replied.

Matt got his phone out and showed me a few photos of his two children, two girls called Lily and Laura clutching a puppy. Dutifully I admired their gap-toothed grins whilst thinking that they were going to need braces before long. The puppy definitely had the edge on looks, but it was obvious that Matt loved his kids. I still hadn't a clue why he and his wife had split up.

After a pleasant evening I gathered my things together in readiness to drive back to Trelerric House. Megan was staying the night at Mike's. I was dawdling in the bathroom waiting to be sure that Matt had left when I heard Megan scream. Hurrying downstairs I saw the two of them standing in the kitchen staring at the television. Mike had switched it on to see the late evening news while he loaded the dishwasher. Megan had her hands over her mouth.

'What is it? What's happened?' I asked.

'It's our wedding venue on the local news slot.' Megan replied.

'Or rather what's left of it.' Mike said grimly. 'It's gone up in smoke. Fortunately we took out wedding insurance but I really didn't expect to have to use it.'

'Fuck.' Was the only thing I could think of saying.

I could see that Megan was shocked and I sat her down at the table.

'Alternative venues, any ideas?' I said, plonking myself down opposite her.

Megan grabbed her tote bag and pulling out her notepad starting flicking through it. I loved the way that she relied on pen and paper but she was a very visual creature, liking coloured inks and using mind-maps to pursue options.

'Batshit, hell and crap. It's the last thing I need right now. Obviously I shall have to start making phone calls in the morning and it would be Sunday wouldn't it! Fortunately it's not a huge wedding.' She spoke lightly but I could see that she was deeply worried.

Because of the way the bank holidays had fallen this year, friends had already booked their early holidays so Megan and Mike had organised an intimate ceremony with a wedding breakfast and were having a party a month later at home after their honeymoon in the Florida Keys.

Mike came over and stood behind her, his hands on her slim shoulders. Bending down he kissed the top of her head. 'We'll find something, even if I have to obtain a wedding licence for this place.'

At that moment an idea blossomed in my head.

'I wonder. Megan, you know you asked me if the chapel at Trelerric was still consecrated and I said that Alice and Jonathan had got married there -'

'And that the vicar still held Easter and Christmas services every year.' Megan finished my sentence.

'I wonder if you could get married there instead?'

'Wow. That would be a bit special wouldn't it?' Megan's eyes were huge and hopeful.

My mind was racing. The house was going to be open for Easter so there was already a lot on, but I would throw myself into making this work.

'Leave it with me. I'll go and see Jane and Tim first thing in the morning.'

Sam opened the door at Home Farm when I knocked early the next morning. For a second he looked almost shocked to see me and for an idiotic moment I thought he was going to hug me.

'Lucy! This is a surprise, come in.'

Jane appeared at the kitchen door and glanced from me to Sam. 'Lucy, we missed you yesterday evening. What a nice surprise, we're just having coffee, come and join us.'

I had the weird feeling they'd been talking about me. The kitchen was warm and cosy, it was a relaxed family scene with breakfast things still on the table and I noticed Mitch lying on the rug near the woodstove which held a damped down glowing fire. He still had a dressing covering his injured paw but thumped his tail in greeting.

'Don't get up Mitch.' Tim said, standing up and kissing me on the cheek. 'I swear this dog is just using this injury to get special treatment. But to what do we owe this pleasure Lucy? Do you want me to build you a running track round the sheep pasture or something?' He said with his easy charm.

I sat on one of the kitchen chairs opposite Tim. Jane poured me a cup of coffee and Sam took up a neutral position standing with his back to the woodstove. He bent down and fondled Mitch's ears.

'I'm not sure where to start.' I began.

All eyes were on me and Jane said she'd better sit down then.

'My sister Megan, you know she's getting married at Easter? I don't know if you've seen the local news? Her wedding venue burnt down last night.'

I wasn't sure if I was imagining it but for a moment there was a sense of relief in the air. It was Tim who clarified the situation.

'You're not leaving us then?'

'Sorry?' I was confused. 'Leaving you, why would I do that?'

I saw Tim glance at Sam but it was Jane who took over.

'What a silly joke Tim,' she said calmly. 'Lucy's clearly worried for her sister. Now then, what can we do to help?'

'I wondered if Megan and Mike could get married in Trelerric chapel instead? It's still consecrated isn't it?'

Sam let out a huge sigh and there was a moment when I could feel everyone going into thinking and planning mode as they called it at their Saturday supper sessions.

'What about the vicar?' Tim asked.

'He's doing the Easter service isn't he, could we persuade him to do a wedding ceremony as well?' Sam asked.

'What day and how many guests?' Jane said, taking another line of thought.

'Easter Saturday. It's only a small event,' I said. 'About twenty or so very close family and friends. They're having a party a month later at Mike's place. If they have a finger buffet instead of a sit down meal we could use the Georgian salon on the ground floor next to Flick's suite.'

'Parking space; the usual problem since we're open at Easter.' Tim spoke.

'Dad,' Sam spoke up. 'Lucy said it's only about twenty people. Assuming that's not twenty cars we could park most of them outside the Coach House.'

I'd been thinking along the same lines.

After some more discussion it was agreed. Jane was happy because she'd already met Megan and felt she could reciprocate in some way for the work Megan was doing with the Trelerric Vintage exhibition. Megan was getting paid for her work but I thought that was sweet of Jane.

'Call her this instant Lucy. Tell her yes. And I shall need to know about her insurance cover and her catering and flowers arrangements and I'd like to meet Mike, is that his name? They could come for lunch today if they're free. I'm sure I can cobble something extra together. And I'll call the vicar and ask how this can be done.'

I called Megan giving her the good news and everyone in the kitchen could hear Megan's cries of relief. The offer of lunch at Home Farm was accepted and Jane went into organisational overdrive, accepting my offer to stay and help prepare the vegetables. Tim and Sam went off to look at the lambs and the chickens.

Megan and Mike turned up at Home Farm and thrust the biggest bouquet I'd ever seen into Jane's arms.

'You've saved the day. Literally saved "The Day",' Megan spoke with emphasis, hugging Jane. 'I don't know how to thank you.' Her chin was wobbling and she finished the sentence with a tearful squeak.

Tim served pre-lunch drinks and everyone clinked glasses. At that moment Sam walked in. He'd obviously showered and changed his clothes after helping with the animals and his hair was a bit damp at the back. I longed to touch it and to cover my feelings I took a large mouthful of white wine and started coughing. Sam pulled a large clean handkerchief from his pocket and handed it to me as my eyes were streaming. At the same time he took my glass from me and put it down before turning to Mike and Megan and introducing himself.

Through watering eyes I noticed Megan looking at Sam with interest. He was wearing an olive green button down shirt which suited his hazel gold eyes, tucked into grey jeans with a tan plaited leather belt. His shoulders looked so broad against Mike's more slender frame and he was taller than Tim. I was so physically conscious of him I couldn't compose myself so I slipped away to the kitchen on the pretext of getting myself a glass of water. Jane was already putting the flowers into a vase and I stayed to help her with the vegetables.

Lunch was a simple roast chicken, fragrant and reared on the farm. Megan complimented Jane's cooking.

'It's good because it's had the sun on its back all its life and a field to forage in.' Tim said. 'But my wife knows how to cook.'

Jane asked about the wedding catering. It was Mike who replied.

'We've had to rethink that since the catering was part of the package at the now burned out venue. The only person we could think of who might be able to help at such short notice is Helena Fox-Harvey. She's worked for both of us before.'

I had a mental image of myself asking Helena what was it like being on the staff, remembering her subtle put down of me when I first met her. I glanced at Sam sitting opposite me but his expression was neutral.

Mike spoke again. 'So I called Helena this morning. She's flat out for Easter but says that since it's Trelerric she'll pull out all the stops. She said that Trelerric held a special place in her heart.'

He seemed a bit surprised that his contribution was received with silence. 'I thought I'd call her to start the ball rolling since you'd got such a lot on your mind. Did I do the right thing?' Mike said to Megan, putting his hand on her thigh.

Megan covered his hand with her own, the engagement ring flashing. 'Of course darling.'

I avoided everyone's eyes and sipped my wine. Sam slipped Mitch a piece of chicken and got told off by Tim.

'Please Sam, not from the table. In his bowl if you must.'

At least that cleared the atmosphere. I think that was why Sam did it.

Megan and Mike came back to my rooms with me. Megan was thoughtful.

'So that's Sam Latchley then,' she said. 'He certainly puts the Cor into Cornwall doesn't he!'

Trelerric House was deserted, Flick wasn't due to return until the early evening. We looked at Maggie's kitchen in terms of catering space and then went and looked at the Georgian salon. The heating wasn't on so it was cold but the big green and white and gold room was graceful. I suggested that we could serve the finger buffet in the big black and white hall and dress the salon with extra chairs and lots of flowers. Megan could see it working and her blue eyes sparkled. Then we walked round to the chapel, Jane had given me the big key. Inside it was compact but the proportions were pretty. There was still a family box pew for the comfort of the head of the household and ancient wall plaques listed the virtues of various Latchley's and sometimes their wives. I noticed the tiny old glass window panes with their wavy blurred surfaces, some with a hint of blue or green.

Mike was enthusiastic. 'It's a gem.' He clapped his hands experimentally. 'Great acoustics. It'll be lovely Megan. It's so kind of them, it's almost like Lucy was meant to be here so that she could save the day.'

TWELVE

Flick was sorry that she'd missed all the excitement and demanded that I should tell her everything. We were sitting in the day room, as she insisted on calling her sitting room, and watching Simon labouring outside in the courtyard. I told her everything about the altered wedding arrangements and she was thrilled that she was going to represent the family and see the wedding.

'And why haven't you gone out with Sam yet?' she asked bluntly, catching me off guard.

'I don't know. Well, I do know, I think.' I took a deep breath. 'He misinterpreted an overly familiar kiss on the cheek from Matt, and I saw Helena kiss him on the cheek in the orchard when she went to invite him out that evening. The evening we were going to go out to a pub together to talk. And now I think he's avoiding me.' It sounded foolish as I told her.

Flick sat back and considered me closely. 'Lucy, for intelligent adults with some experience of life you are both remarkably dim. I have little hope for the future of Trelerric if you are both going to behave in this way. I don't want to interfere but I shall if I have to.'

'Please don't Flick. I don't know what to do yet but I'm not throwing myself at him, I've made that mistake before in my life. And if I made a fool of myself over Sam then how could I go on working and living here? I couldn't bear it.'

I remembered the odd comment Tim had made on Sunday morning. "You're not leaving us then?" It was as though they'd been discussing the situation with Sam. Had they been talking about me?

The situation kept buzzing round my head like a demented bee. Thinking of bees I took Coco into the orchard for her afternoon walk and wandered through the mown grass paths amongst the daffodils. Some of them had a distinctive and powerful scent, better outdoors than in a room I thought, liking the pale narcissi better than the yellow daffodils. There was no sign of Sam's bee hives. I stepped up onto the new gazebo and looked around, someone had fixed three strong hooks into the overhead beams. I considered them for a moment, they didn't seem right for a swing because they were spaced irregularly.

The nearby drystone wall was built higher and thicker in one part and there were unusual niches constructed within the wall. I hadn't a clue what I was looking at but it made me think of medieval monks. I'd started reading a history of the buildings at Trelerric which Flick had loaned me and was finding it fascinating. The resourceful self-sufficiency of people in previous ages was particularly impressive. I'd thought I was working hard, but at least I could buy all the ingredients I needed and didn't have to thresh the wheat to make the flour to make the cakes. Or pound almonds in a mortar and pestle to make marzipan. I preferred the old word, marchpane. Women must have had highly toned upper arms in those days I thought.

Alice had pointed out the buttery off the great hall one day and I'd said nothing at the time, assuming they kept the butter there ready for the high table. Now I'd learned that the buttery was nothing to do with the dairy activities, it was where the butts of wine and other alcohol were stored. That was why my mind-bee was buzzing about I thought, linking the uses of the garden flowers to the house and buildings. Bees made wax and honey from the flowers, people made candles and took honey to eat and to make mead, a drink which they would store in the buttery.

I was so pleased with myself that I started giggling, I've got bees in my buttery, not bats in my belfry. Engrossed in my mind games I didn't hear the engine until the ride-on lawnmower was almost upon me. Coco gave a shrill yip of alarm.

Sam stopped the engine and took his ear defenders off.

We regarded each other not exactly defensively, but my barriers were up. He didn't get down from the seat. Sam spoke first.

'Lucy.' He gave me a nod. 'Glad it's all coming together for your sister. It'll be good to have a wedding here.'

I couldn't think of what to say so I just nodded back at him.

Breaking the silence he spoke again, gently. 'I'm pleased you're here, I'm bringing in the bees.'

For the first time I realised that the ride on mower had a small trailer attached. It was holding two hives. I knew nothing about bees.

'I know nothing about bees.' I said.

Sam looked at me gravely. 'First of all, the bees have to know you Lucy. Then I shall teach you what you need to know about them.'

Our eyes locked for what seemed like an age. If I was reading the situation correctly he expected me to be around to learn this information. My skin tingled and my heart gave an exploratory skip. But what he said next dashed my hopes.

'But it's best not to have Coco here, she might get upset. I've three new skeps to bring over. I'll introduce you to them once they're all in place.'

'Is that a date?' The words were out of my mouth before I could stop them.

'I shall make a bee-line for you Lucy, and bring you here.' He smiled.

I was about to make a flippant comment about that being the bees-knees but something stopped me, Sam didn't look as though he was joking.

'Okay. Um, that's okay, I think.' I didn't know what else to say. This was a man who sang to his apple trees and talked to his bees. Well, he was certainly different, not weird but somehow connected and sympathetically in touch with his surroundings. He must have inherited something from his father, I thought as I gazed at him. I knew that Tim was dedicated to the care and husbandry of the land and his animals and he farmed the estate as though it was a garden.

'I'm going to start unloading now, Simon's coming to help me.' Sam stopped looking at me and glanced over my shoulder.

I looked around, Simon was just coming into the orchard.

'I'll get off then, take Coco away I mean.' I felt a bit dizzy from the intensity of everything that hadn't been said. There was definitely something there between us in the atmosphere, a vital electrical current, a feeling and on my part, a longing to get to know this unusual man better.

That night I worked alone in the big kitchen completing another stage of Megan's wedding cake. I needed solitude to create the perfection I was capable of and it was almost midnight before I was satisfied and ready to drag myself upstairs to bed. Outside my door I stopped and smiled. Someone had left me a distinctive little pot. Reaching down I picked it up and smiled, a hand written label in neat black calligraphy script told me it was Apple Blossom Honey.

It was a good job that Easter was late this year because March had been an unusually poor month, grey drizzle and sea fog rolling up the Tamar valley for days at a time, almost flattening the daffodils with moisture and browning the white blossoms on camellias. Visitor numbers had been down on Mothering Sunday as a result, but the upside of that was that Maggie and I still had a good amount of home-made cakes in stock. Which was fortunate because when I wasn't running around after Flick I was carrying things through to the Georgian salon and helping to clean, rearrange and decorate the room. My fingernails were not going to be my finest asset on Megan's wedding day.

Mike and Megan came over for a day and Tim and Sam mucked in to help. Flick was delightedly making suggestions and I left them to it on the excuse of getting us all a drink. I was dressed in jeans and a distinctly grubby tea-shirt and Maggie had just gleefully told me I had a dirty mark across my forehead when I heard a tap at the kitchen door and Helena put her perfectly groomed head round the door.

'Oh hi, it's me.' Helena glanced at me and ignored Maggie. 'Megan said she'd be here. I'm meeting her to finalise the wedding buffet. I gather this is to be my kitchen for the day?' She came in smelling of perfume and looking glamorous in a simple golden cashmere v-neck and a spotless white shirt under with the collar turned up. A blue necklace and a pretty gold, white and blue silky scarf completed her look, along with tight cream trousers. I felt like Cinderella standing next to the overdressed ugly sister, except that she wasn't overdressed and actually she wasn't ugly.

Maggie stiffened at the side of me. 'This is my kitchen. I'm Mrs Palfrey. I work for Mrs Latchley.'

Helena gave her braying laugh. 'Oh ya, Alice has told me all about you, she says you're an absolute treasure and a godsend in times of crisis. So delighted to meet you.' She held out a neatly manicured hand to Maggie who took it, looking slightly less guarded.

'Megan and Mike are in the salon with everyone.' I said. 'We were just going to have a hot drink.'

'Oh lovely.' Helena gushed. 'Let me help. What shall I carry?'

From that moment Helena took charge. Maggie handed her a couple of plates of nibbles she'd thrown together and opened the doors while I handled the tray and brought up the rear, my position in the pecking order complete. My biceps were improving daily with the amount of carrying I was doing. Helena swanned into the salon like a high priestess carrying gifts to a deity and greeted everyone with confident familiarity bestowing kisses and giving little shrieks. Flick assumed a watchful pose and folded her arms with her hands clasping her elbows in a curiously elegant manner. Helena carefully avoided her as though she had a force field in place.

I dutifully poured tea and coffee and kept myself occupied, trying not to feel concerned that Helena had plonked herself next to Sam, touching his arm and laughing gaily up at him, flicking her thick blonde hair back in a carefree and charming manner.

After a moment he disengaged himself and walked over to me where I was standing next to the table with the tea pot still in my hand.

'More tea?' I asked, avoiding his eyes.

Sam didn't reply. He put his mug down, took a small plate and put a mini sausage roll and a dainty cheese sandwich on it. Turning to me he took the teapot off me and put the plate into my hands.

'You need to eat something Lucy', he said quietly. 'You've been working hard for days and you look all in.'

I looked up at him, surprised and grateful. He had his back to the others so only I could see the kindness in his eyes.

'Quite right Sam.' Flick spoke. 'Lucy never stops, I don't know where we'd be without her resourcefulness.'

Helena immediately praised the food. 'Who made these?' She was holding up a sausage roll with sesame seeds in the pastry, desperate to call attention back to herself.

'Oh that's Maggie,' Tim said. 'Maggie's a dab hand with delicacies and a light hand with pastry.'

Maggie blushed appreciatively.

'And will you be helping me produce the wedding buffet for this happy couple Maggie?'

Maggie looked uncomfortable. 'Well, I could I suppose if Mrs Latchley doesn't mind. But I haven't been asked.'

Megan took control. 'Helena is here to help me sort all these things out. Sorry folks, the problem is that Helena's staff are fully committed since it's Easter, she's doing Mike and me a huge favour. The thing is, I was wondering if I could ask for your help Lucy, and Maggie too if that would be possible?'

We retired to the kitchen and left the guys completing the salon layout with Flick happily giving orders and directions since she'd held many a party there. Megan delicately deferred to Maggie and made Maggie feel as though she was in control. Helena made suggestions of her own and I simply agreed to work hard to help make a superb wedding buffet for my sister. Fortunately the cake was almost ready for final assembly.

That afternoon after everyone had gone I pretended to collapse in Flick's rooms after I'd walked Coco. We sat together companionably and ticked things off on our fingers. Flick had decided in her generous way that, since there was room, Megan and our parents should have use of the rooms next to mine before the wedding so that they could be on the spot. It was very kind of her but I added refreshing, airing and making up those rooms to all my other jobs. Flick however had other ideas.

'You're doing far too much Lucy. It will spoil your looks. I'm getting a local person in, she runs a cleaning company and looks after some holiday lets and is very reliable. You and your mother and Megan are coming with me for a day spa. I've cleared it with your sister and it will be a surprise for your mother. Jason and Sunny are coming here to do everyone's hair on the morning of the wedding. And you can stop fretting about the salon and the chapel, Megan's florists have all that in hand now. I haven't had so much fun for ages.' Flick's eyes were sparkling.

'So there's just the buffet arrangements to finish.' I said.

'Will that be a complete bitch for you Lucy? You stayed very calm when Megan dropped that bombshell I must say.'

'To be honest I think I'd seen it coming. Mike had already told us that Helena was stretched. And it's only a finger buffet for twenty plus.' I sighed. 'It's just lots of fiddling about but Helena knows what she's doing and at least Maggie knows how the ovens work.'

'Not my sphere of knowledge I'm afraid, my strengths always lay elsewhere.' Flick smirked. 'Some women are born to the kitchen, others have kitchens thrust upon them. Women like me never set foot inside them darling.'

'Mum!' I fell into her embrace as she got out of the car. Dad got out and sidled up to me playfully.

'Any chance of a hug for me as well maid?'

I let go of mum and hugged dad. 'You found Trelerric okay then.' I said pointlessly, grinning broadly and feeling unaccountably proud of welcoming them to the house.

'Well it must be so or we wouldn't be standing here. Isn't that a fact my girl?' Mum responded. 'And this is the grand place my Megan is getting married from.' She was looking about. 'And is herself the bride here yet?'

'She'll be here soon. You're to come in and meet Flick, my employer, Mrs Latchley. We're all having tea together. And we're eating at Home Farm tonight, not Mike obviously, he's out with his mates and Travis tonight. He won't see Megan now until the wedding day.'

I ushered them indoors, a shame since it was a glorious late afternoon. March had left like the proverbial lion, growling wind and roaring skies, and April had slipped in with buttery warmth and scented breezes. There was some fuss about clothes which needed hanging up immediately and mum wanted to see where they would be sleeping for the next few nights. She was pleasantly surprised.

'And you are in here next door and with a kitchen of your own, so it's a cup of tea I can be making for daddy and me without having to cover up my shimmy. Well that's nice. So I'd better be thanking the lady who has made it so. Where will she be?'

I took my slightly agitated and exuberant mum back downstairs, followed by dad and we bumped into Maggie. I made more introductions and Maggie said tea was waiting for us in Flick's rooms.

'And will you be joining us Maggie Palfrey?' Mum asked.

'Oh no, it's Lucy who keeps Mrs Latchley company, not me.'

Mum raised her eyebrows but took Maggie's hand and patted it. 'Well we'll have a cup of tea to ourselves in your room later then and you can fill me in with what my Lucy has been up to.'

Maggie giggled and looked from mum to me. I pulled a comical face.

'She means every word Maggie. You'd better believe it.'

I took them into Flick's suite and paused while mum gasped.

'Holy St Patrick, what's this place? It's fit for peacocks!'

Flick appeared, striking an elegant pose at the door between the day room and the Chinese room, resplendent in one of her exotic lounging outfits. 'I shall take that as a compliment,' she drawled. 'You must be Mrs Huccaby?, and Mr Huccaby I presume?' She held out a hand invitingly.

Mum advanced in her neat Irish-green skirt suit, her legs shapely in unaccustomed heeled shoes and took Flick's hands. 'Lady Latchley, it's a great kindness you are doing for us.'

Flick smiled warmly, hugely entertained. 'At this point I'm delighted to have the opportunity to say, and I quote, "I'm no lady." It's plain Mrs Latchley, but please call me Flick.'

'And I'm Moira. And this is my husband.'

Dad stepped forward. 'I do have a tongue in my head Mrs Latchley, I'm Mark Huccaby.'

I quietly enjoyed the moment. Mum was still a petite and attractive Irish colleen, dad was tall and with a good head of thick grey hair. He was distinctly amused by the whole situation. As Megan and I often agreed, they scrubbed up pretty well.

I'd previously noticed Flick loved having visitors and she was charming and welcoming so I poured tea and joined in with the chatter and laughter and then Megan arrived. Flick greeted her like an old friend and there were more cries and shrieks and hugs and kisses. I saw dad noticing Coco in her basket, her little tail wagging as her dark eyes looked from face to face. He put his hand out and she licked it. Dad loved anything small with a heart beating in it.

'Sounds like a barnyard in here. Dare I come in?' A deep voice spoke from the doorway.

'Sam my darling, come in and meet Lucy's family.' Flick made the introductions.

'We're having ourselves a tea party,' dad said to Sam. 'I've a horrible feeling it's about to become a hen party and I'm feeling out of place so I'm very glad to meet you.' They shook hands.

'And is this your son?' Mum was looking up at Sam with something like admiration.

'Alas no, this is my nephew.' Flick took Sam's hand in hers. 'My very special nephew.'

Phew, I thought, the level of excitement is becoming quite unnecessary. Fortunately Sam had come on business. He suggested helping dad with the rest of the baggage and then said he'd show him where to put the cars. Megan threw dad her car keys.

'We'll need to keep the area out front here clear for the wedding cars on Saturday and the florist tomorrow.' Sam explained.

They left to sort things out and the four of us sat back and smiled like conspirators. Mum couldn't thank Flick enough and of course she wanted to see the salon. Flick was honest though.

'It's Jane and Tim you really need to thank Moira, Trelerric belongs to all the family, it's held in a sort of Trust now for safekeeping, but they have the final say over the use of the estate since they do most of the work. You'll meet them this evening. They are Sam's parents.'

'And the vicar,' Megan added. 'He's coming to dinner at Home Farm as well. Mike and I saw him yesterday. We drank sherry together! I felt as though I was in a Victorian novel, I mean, bloody sherry? But he plays guitar so he and Mike talked more about music than about the wedding.'

While mum and Flick talked nineteen to the dozen Megan quietly thanked me for spending most of the day working with Helena.

'Honestly Luce, I owe you big time. Was she a mare?'

I thought for a minute, trying to find a balance between the truth and being diplomatic and gave up. 'Well she farts through silk and she's a bossy bitch but she is a competent professional and having Maggie with us diluted the atmosphere. We all got along just fine.'

I wasn't going to mention Helena's huge curiosity about my past and the probing questions about where I'd grown up and about my family. I'd had my deflector shields at full capacity all day, it had been exhausting.

'So you're not actually from around here? You're so different, you and Megan. In looks I mean. She's so fair.'

'And I'm dark. Genetics are fascinating aren't they? I didn't study midwifery in depth when I was nursing but I've always found Mendelian genetics and his work on peas fascinating, haven't you?' I'd been a bit short with her, remembering that Alice had once said that Helena was thick.

Helena had not pursued the topic, clearly out of her depth. Instead she'd coyly asked Maggie about the frequency of weddings at Trelerric. I really got the impression she had her own wedding plans in mind.

That evening Sam collected Flick while I drove the four of us over to Home Farm. Jonathan was up country on business and Alice couldn't be there because Thomas was feverish. The vicar was drinking beer and he kissed Megan heartily on the cheek as she introduced us all. Mum got a bit emotional and hugged Jane and kissed Tim on the cheek. I think she would have kissed the vicar as well if dad hadn't put a restraining hand on her shoulder.

'And this is before she has a glass in her hand.' Megan muttered to me.

'Oh but it's a pleasure Mrs Huccaby', the vicar was saying. 'It doesn't conflict with my other services on Good Friday and Easter Sunday and at least the little place will have a full congregation with a wedding on Saturday. It's good for it to get some use.'

Mum was in full flow though. She'd learned that we were going to a spa tomorrow and was a bit anxious about having someone laying hands on her, as she put it.

Dad looked at Tim and Sam. 'Help.' He said faintly.

'Laying on hands?' The vicar said jovially, accepting another glass of beer from Tim. 'Isn't that how miracles happen if I'm right Mrs Huccaby?'

Mum looked shocked for a second and then burst out laughing. 'And it's miracles I'll be needing from this spa if I'm to look the part for my girl here.'

Sam sitting opposite me took in my family, tears of laughter in his eyes. 'I thought the Latchley's were a voluble lot, but the Huccaby's win on points I think Lucy.'

'Is he saying we're talkative Lucy?' Mum said, her eyes dancing. 'Ah but we're just a normal chatty friendly family.' And she was off, advising the vicar about their years of fostering and how real conversation at table was good for family bonding. 'I was a nurse you see, I've always loved to have the care of people. Like my Lucy here, she was a nurse as well.'

The talking carried on back in my room long after we'd left Home Farm. Dad left us to it.

In the morning I drove the hens, as dad insisted on calling us, to the spa for Flick's spontaneous wedding present to us all. Mum and Megan were thrilled with the Jag. Dad was spending the day with Sam and Tim. He was relieved that he could do something out of doors and was going to help fit a field gate. 'Proper job for a Cornishman,' he told me. 'Once an engineer always an engineer.'

At the spa the girl signing us in assumed that we were a family bunch. 'Is this grandmother, mother and daughter and maid of honour? How lovely.'

Mum was a bit nonplussed but Flick was enjoying the silliness. 'Well you could be my daughter Moira, we have similar colouring.'

'Ah but you're far too glamorous. Though you do look as though you have some Irish in you. Where were you born?'

I winced but Flick didn't bat an eyelid. 'I was actually born in Liverpool.'

'Oh,' mum said, 'that's the capital of Ireland in Britain isn't it? So you must have Irish blood.'

We were saved from any more by being whisked away for our treatments. I went from the shower to the sauna, followed by a massage and facial. It was fantastic after the work I'd put in during recent days. We reconvened on squishy sofas with herbal teas and freshly squeezed fruit drinks before lunch.

'I've been boiled, steamed and pummelled.' I said lazily cocooned in a towelling dressing gown. 'I feel so clean.'

'Marvellous.' Megan yawned, stretching out her legs and admiring her pedicured toes.

Even mum was unusually quiet and lost for words.

Megan and Flick talked about makeup and I reassured mum about the hairdresser tomorrow.

'I feel like I'm in a film Lucy. Is this how you live at the castle?' She whispered.

'No, and it's not a castle. It's all quite ordinary really.' But as I spoke I thought, it's not ordinary at all. Life at Trelerric is completely unlike anything I've ever experienced and I love it.

Mum and I got up early in the morning and she came with me to move the wedding cake into position in the salon. It had pride of place on a suitably decorated regency table with a huge gilded mirror behind it so the cake was visible from all angles. Megan had wanted something simple yet traditional so I'd dressed each tier with sprays of handmade white roses, some in bud and placed on sugar lace with my trademark twisted ribbons and pearls. Mum got a bit weepy.

'You can't tell them apart from the florist's own decorations Lucy. They look so real.' She said, looking around at the flower-dressed green, white and gold room with its intimate clusters of little tables and chairs. 'And this is so lovely, it's been so beautifully dressed. It's a palace.'

I hoped she wasn't working up to a motherly weep and was relieved when Maggie appeared with Clare, her daughter. Finally we were satisfied that we'd got things together and under control. One of Helena's assistants was also coming along to help because Maggie and Clare had to move on to work in the Stables Tea Room. I'd thought that Helena herself would be in charge of laying out the buffet but Megan had put me straight the previous evening, just before we all retired to bed.

'She's gate-crashed the wedding Luce. Because she's done us a favour and because of what she calls her "special relationship with the Latchley's", she's decided she's going to, as she put it, "pop in later". Which means she's honouring us by coming to the reception.'

I was gobsmacked. 'Special relationship? Does she think she's the prime minister or something?' I couldn't believe the cheek of it. 'But she's not invited herself to the chapel then?'

'Well, no, she's not coming to the ceremony, even she had the wit to realise that's personal invitations only. But we'll have the pleasure of her company at the wedding reception afterwards.'

So she won't be turning up wearing an apron then, I thought crossly. With an effort I didn't explode, after all it was Megan's wedding day.

Later I submitted myself to Sunny's ministrations for what she called a wash and wedding style in Flick's rooms. She was a bit in awe at being in Trelerric House and was quietly efficient.

'You look fab,' she said once she'd finished. 'Elegant.'

'Make-up Lucy.' Flick called as I went off to dress. 'Don't forget what I've taught you.'

Just as I was ready mum hurried in to say the car had arrived to take me, her and Flick round to the chapel. She stopped dead in her tracks.

'My darling girl. What a transformation.'

Sunny had put my hair up in a soft loose style and I was wearing a simple grecian design dress in ivory with pearl studs in my ears and a plain gold necklace. Megan had chosen white bud roses with gypsophila and delicate green fern for me to carry. It was a classic and stunning combination.

'You don't look so bad yourself. Is the bride okay?' I asked.

'Come and see.'

Megan was standing in her room with dad and sipping something for her pre-wedding nerves, although she looked anything but nervous. She looked fabulous and raised her glass to me.

'To infinity.'

'In a cupcake.' I responded, and knocked back the small glass of sherry dad handed me.

'Stop it the both of you. You'll be having me in tears so you will.' Mum was trying to be cross but failing completely.

'Out.' Dad said, kissing us both skilfully without touching our make-up. 'Be off now both of you. I want a word with my daughter here.'

We went downstairs where Flick was ready and waiting in a beautifully cut turquoise trouser suit and a Quentin Crisp floppy hat. She had a narrow creamy silk scarf with a gold thread folded like a cravat around her throat. Her silver eyes glittered as she looked me up and down and nodded. 'You'll do nicely sweetheart,' she turned to mum. 'As for you Moira Huccaby, you're a show-stopper.'

'I don't look like a sofa do I?' Mum said anxiously, already deferring to Flick's superior knowledge of clothes. She was wearing a lovely soft floaty dress in pastel greens and blues with a plain blue fitted jacket. Her shoes and bag and hat all matched.

'The three of you look amazing. I'm welling up here.' Maggie said, standing at the kitchen door with Clare peering wide-eyed over her shoulder. 'We're on duty over at the tea rooms later but relax, everything is under control here.'

It was weird being driven round to the chapel since it was only three minutes walk away, but we couldn't soil our shoes. I waited outside shivering slightly in the Spring sunshine in my sleeveless thin dress while mum and Flick went in. A small crowd of Easter visitors was gathering to watch and some were taking pictures on their mobile phones. I glanced inside the open chapel door and saw Mike standing there with Travis and Matt. Travis appeared to be wearing a jacket made out of some sort of crushed raspberry coloured fabric which suited his golden skin and tiny dreadlocks. After what seemed like ages I heard the crunch of wheels and Megan's car drove slowly towards the chapel. Dad helped her out carefully as the driver went to the chapel door and I saw him nodding to someone inside. There was a pause and music started.

FOURTEEN

Megan was on dad's arm, utterly beautiful in a slender ivory satin creation with panels of lace, her light veil a wisp of silk and lace matching some detail on her long sleeves. Dad handed her the bouquet of white bud roses and freesia and she took a deep breath. We exchanged a look and I followed them into the little chapel, scented by white freesia and filled with love.

Dad was talking to me at the wedding reception. I was already on my second glass of wine and glad to be standing near a radiator.

'Nice family Lucy, the Latchley's I mean. Had a good day with Tim and Sam yesterday, a right laugh they are. Tim was telling me about how he coped when he was giving Alice away at her wedding here. He said he concentrated on images of fixing the tractor to stop himself from crying. I tried it myself and it worked.' He laughed pleasurably. 'We hung a gate and I met some sheep and saw the hens. Jane gave us all a hefty sandwich and Sam walked me all around the grounds afterwards so I saw the chapel being made ready.'

For dad that was a big speech.

'We had a good long talk. I like Sam. He's solid I reckon.'

Was it my imagination or was dad trying to tell me something?

'Are we doing alright?' Megan was at my side, her eyes sparkling.

'I think we are Mrs Bartlett. It's nice, this intimate gathering. It's not false. I love the way everyone can just circulate and enjoy themselves.' I said looking around.

Mum was talking to Jane and Tim who had just arrived. Only Flick had attended the wedding ceremony. Mike's son Travis was being closely attended by some of Megan's close friends from our schooldays who were all admiring his New York accent and good looks. Mike and Matt were talking to Anne and Tina who were a couple of the Fosters we'd stayed close friends with. Matt was looking quite handsome and eyeing Tina who was a cute brunette. I remembered her when she was all hurt eyes and self-harming, now she was a confident officer cadet undergoing training. Flick was holding court in a corner with Mike's parents who remembered seeing some of her films.

We'd had photographs taken at the chapel and out on the terrace in front of the Tudor building. Sam and Simon had thoughtfully planted the stone urns with cascades of white flowers. More photos were taken indoors in the salon and by the cake. Matt had stuck to my side like glue throughout, it was only when I'd said I had to oversee something to do with the buffet that I'd managed to dislodge him. It was like getting chewing gum off my shoe.

Jane joined us. 'It's all lovely Megan. And you look absolutely wonderful. I shall write an entry in the Latchley Book.'

'What's that?' Megan asked.

'It's a register of events at Trelerric. There's always been a tradition of recording the details of weddings, births and deaths on the estate and it's a great resource for people doing their family history. Over the years we've had enquiries from all around the world from people who have traced their families back to the ancient Trelerric lands and want to know more.'

'Wow, that's interesting. How far back does it go?' I asked, seeing an idea for a book and another way of making sales.

'We've got records starting in the early seventeenth century, so we're unusual and fortunate.' Jane replied. 'But we also have a separate book which is a little bit earlier, the Latchley Chronicle, recording the Latchley family fortunes. And their misfortunes too.' She added, taking a mouthful of wine. 'Goodness I'd better eat something or I shall get squiffy.'

I said I was feeling a bit the same and asked Megan if I could get her something. She shook her head.

'In this dress? I've been poured into it, there's no room for food. I'm living on love and alcohol.'

I told Jane I'd join her at the buffet table and was just turning to leave Megan with dad when Alice and Jonathan arrived at the salon doorway. They came straight over to Megan to give their congratulations and I was standing back a little, smiling, when Helena walked in followed by Sam. Helena was looking very pleased with herself in a bold blue and white flower patterned dress with a little blue jacket and a small blue hat. For some reason she'd teamed the outfit with white heels but she looked highly polished, confident and made a point of standing still at the entrance as she looked around beaming at everyone with an air of belonging. I had a strong suspicion that she'd spent the morning at the hairdresser's and with the beautician, so much for being flat out with her business. The way she stood, with Sam just behind her, made them look every inch the couple.

It seemed as though the dynamics in the room changed at that point, as though someone had called time for change in a dance. I realised that Matt was walking towards me with a determined expression and he reached out and touched my arm. I'd lost count of the number of times he'd touched me; a hand under my elbow, and hand on my shoulder.

'You've been avoiding me Lucy.' He gave me a smouldering look.

I glanced at him. 'I haven't Matt, you've barely left my side, you've been quite, er,' I really wanted to say "clingy" but I settled for 'attentive.'

'The prerogative of the best man for the very beautiful maid of honour. And the best man would like to ask the MoH out for dinner tonight, just the two of us.' He twinkled his eyes at me and raised my hand to his lips.

It nearly freaked me out. Did he really just speak in abbreviated capitals? What a plonker. I glanced around looking for an escape and saw mum looking at the two of us with interest. By now Helena and Sam were walking towards us all, Helena intent on gushing all over Megan. I took a deep breath. The congratulations were high octane and I felt decidedly light headed on the periphery of it all. With an effort I forced a smile, playing my part but deliberately not answering Matt's question. I looked up and straight into Sam's eyes. His expression was impossible to read.

Turning to Matt I spoke quickly. 'I must eat something now, immediately. I'm going to faint otherwise. Please excuse me for a moment.'

Matt looked briefly irritated but I just had to move away. Ducking round the group containing Megan at the centre I headed for the door and mum joined me.

'Lucy, you look as though you've seen a ghost. Are you alright?'

'I'm fine mum, nothing in my stomach since the breakfast slice of toast, I've had too much wine. I need some carbs.'

'Was he hitting on you?'

I was surprised by her grasp of the situation but pretended not to hear.

Mum followed me out into the great hall where the buffet was set up in attractive and colourful mounds of things. It was cool enough not to need to refrigerate anything out there. I filled a plate with a selection of tiny morsels, tasty little bites of cheese, chicken, prawns, salmon and egg in all sorts of combinations. At Megan's request we'd avoided dips and slaws and stuff you could slop down your front. Megan had been set on what she called "retro food".

'I've had some disgusting things at events and parties, I want food you can eat in one bite and that will get eaten. Just make it tiny and attractive.' She had pleaded.

I stood with Jane and mum as we ate. Jane was particularly enjoying a minuscule chicken tartlet with a sticky spicy glaze. 'Yours or Helena's?' Jane quizzed.

'Mine.' I confirmed, 'The same glaze is on the salmon tartlets. Helena made the quail scotch eggs and some of the little cheesy things. Maggie did the tempura prawns this morning while we were at the wedding ceremony.'

Once sated mum and I slipped away up to my rooms. I needed the loo and wanted to check my make-up and make sure I didn't have sesame seeds between my teeth. We both flopped on the sofa for a few minutes, mum took a shoe off and rubbed her foot between both hands.

'Funny how one foot is a bit bigger than the other and never quite fits the shoe, even though it's always perfect in the shop.' She grimaced as she squeezed her aching foot with both hands. 'Now tell me, is there something between you and Matt? He likes the idea of you on his arm that's plain for the world to see.'

'He's a pain mum. I'd rather gnaw my own arm off than go out with him.'

'He's decent looking.'

'He's split up with his wife and has two children. And a dog, which he misses.' I told her.

'Baggage. The pity of it.' Mum said, 'Split up or divorced did you say? I wouldn't want you to be the groundsheet for a married man with issues.'

Goodness, this woman astonished me. I looked at her in amazement.

'Don't think I don't know a thing or three about life my girl. Nothing surprises me.' Mum smiled. 'And the other one, the nephew. What about him now. He's a good fellow. Your daddy liked him yesterday he said.'

I shook my head. 'Don't even go there mum.'

I got mum's radar look but I wasn't giving in to pressure.

'And one last thing. Any news from the adoption people?'

I shook my head. 'Nothing yet.'

Suitably refreshed we went back downstairs. You could tell the wine was having an effect as the noise levels and the laughter had gone up a few decibels. I decided to take a leaf out of Mike's book and got myself a wine glass filled with tonic water and went to find him. He was with Travis and Tim.

'Cheers brother-in-law.' I raised my glass. 'I'm having one of your specials.'

Mike bent across to me and kissed me on the cheek. 'Cheers Lucy. Have I told you how very stunningly lovely you look and that my gift suits you.'

Mike had given me the necklace and Megan had given me the pearl earrings. She was fond of pearls.

Travis groaned. '*Ma-an* that's a slime-ball comment. Just tell my new cousin Lucy she looks hot.'

Tim and Mike burst out laughing.

'You look pretty hot yourself Travis Landis Bartlett. Love the dreads and the jacket.' I said. At seventeen he was ageless, tall and quite beautiful with his toffee coloured skin and lovely dark eyes.

'Working on my image. I'm going for "millennial troubadour with a bad ass attitude". Think it works?'

It was my turn to laugh. 'You've got style Travis, I'll say that. And talent if your dad is to be believed.'

Flick beckoned me over to her, she was standing at one of the long windows on her own.

'Anything I can do for you Flick? Something to eat yet?' I asked.

Flick shook her head. 'That horsey woman. Why on earth is she wearing white shoes? She looks like Minnie Mouse in them. Anyway I've just hit her with a five star charm offensive and told her that Matt ought to do some advertising for her for a book of recipes or something. I told her that he's talented and loaded and that he's the man to help a woman as fabulous as her.'

I stared at her, amazed for the second time in an hour. First mum and now Flick.

'I've watched them independently Lucy and I think they're a match made in heaven. She's shallow and he's needy. They both want the same things. He could never make you happy.'

'Fine. Thanks, er thank you Flick.' I didn't know what else to say.

'I've done the right thing Lucy, believe me. Ah, now's here's Sam. He went to get me something from the buffet.'

I looked up to see Sam coming through the room straight towards us. He looked good enough to eat, his shoulders wonderfully broad in a pale grey suit with a contrasting red waistcoat.

'Thank you darling.' Flick put her glass down and took the plate. 'And I'm so pleased you've finally found an occasion to wear that tie I bought you.'

With an effort I tore my eyes away from his face and looked at Sam's tie. It was expensive woven silk in shades of green shot through with a scarlet thread.

'Yes, that is nice. It suits you.' I said, thinking how different he looked in formal clothes.

'Thanks, I did the best I could but it's my only suit. The waistcoat belonged to Robin. I had to let those fastenings they have at the back out fully. Guess I'm just a fat boy.'

I couldn't help giggling and then we stood there with our backs to the room looking at each other while Flick delicately ate something and dabbed her lips.

'I feel like a gooseberry children. Why don't you go some place secluded and talk to each other. Sort things out. It's time don't you think?'

The sound of a fork being tapped against a glass sounded through the room. It was Mike, ready to make some thank you noises with Megan at his side.

'On behalf of Mrs Bartlett here,' he began and paused to allow the whistles and a whoop from Travis.

'Can we get away?' Sam's voice was in my ear.

'I'm not allowed yet, I have duties to the bride I think.' I replied.

I felt rather than heard Sam groan. 'Okay. But I'm not giving up this time.'

A warm glow started in my stomach, like a pilot light going on. and I'm not even an old boiler yet I thought, stifling the strong desire to laugh out loud.

Mike was talking about the unexpected change in wedding venue and how wonderfully things had all turned out. 'This wouldn't have happened without the help and extraordinary kindness of the Latchley family, to whom we are forever indebted, and to Helena Fox-Harvey for stepping in to help with the catering despite her own punishing schedule.' He looked over to Helena and acknowledged her with a little nod, to which she responded with a toothy smile and an "aw shucks that's just sweet little old me" shrug of her shoulders. 'But I especially want to thank my sister-in-law Lucy for her loving and practical support from the moment when it all looked as though it was going to go badly downhill. I'm not going to embarrass her any further, but Megan and I would like you all to raise your glasses to Lucy.'

All eyes were on me and I was painfully aware of Sam standing at my side murmuring my name and lifting his glass to his lips. I caught a glimpse of Helena looking poisonous, mum and dad beaming at me and then my eyes met Megan's. She raised her glass and I saw her lips form the words "To infinity". I smiled back at her, tears pricking my eyelids. She knew that everything I'd done was to thank her for taking care of me last year. Several people were taking photos on their mobiles, including mum. I knew she'd be busy with what she called her "face-ache page" later. Mum was an active user of social media, something I couldn't be bothered with.

'And one more thing,' Mike hadn't finished yet. 'I know this is an informal sort of wedding thing, but there's one thing we have to do according to tradition.'

Oh shit, I thought, Megan's going to throw her bouquet.

'We have to cut Lucy's fantastic cake. I know, it's sacrilege because it's so beautiful, but it has to be done.'

'I have to help with this part. They want to save the bottom tier for the party next month.' I said to Sam reluctantly.

'Okay.' He sighed theatrically but smiled at me and turned back to Flick as I walked away.

Mum and I assisted with the cake. Megan had refused the tradition of saving the small top tier for a christening.

'Honestly mum, I don't believe in all that tripe and anyway it won't keep, this one's a sponge cake for those who don't like the fruit cake section. It's for eating now and Lucy can always make another if it's needed.'

We busied ourselves cutting and plating up and then I began circulating and handing out cake to those who wanted it. To my surprise Matt started helping so I decided to see if anyone in the hall at the buffet table wanted any. I stopped just outside the salon doorway, Helena had cornered Sam and was standing with her back to me.

'So, do you fancy coming over to my place after this? They aren't even having a proper party so it's all going to fall rather flat.' She said, drawling the "a" in rather.

I stood frozen to the spot waiting for Sam's reply.

'Sorry I can't Helena, we have the Huccaby family to look after this evening.'

'What?' Helena sounded cross. 'What on earth for? Can't Lucy look after her own family this evening?'

'She deserves some support. The wedding wouldn't have happened if it hadn't been for her. She's worked her socks off, from helping with the chapel and the salon to cooking. And she made that amazing cake in her time off.' Sam said gently.

'Oh yah I agree, she's all very girl guide I'm sure, but who is she? She's very *vin ordinaire* if you ask me.' Helena tossed her head irritably.

I almost stopped breathing, conscious of an overwhelming desire to dump a lump of wedding cake on her perfectly glossy head.

Sam was looking down at her with a complicated expression. 'Okay Helena, there's no need to be nasty and no easy way for me to say this but I have to say it anyway. I don't actually want to spend time with you. We have nothing in common. So please stop coming round because it's going nowhere. I'm sorry.'

I backed into the salon to avoid Helena's reaction.

'Lucy, can't you find any takers for those?' Matt was at my side and touching my arm caressingly.

'No, not out there, I'll um, I'll put them back on the cake table, people can help themselves if they want.'

'Are you going to put a piece under your pillow tonight?' Matt asked archly, standing far too close for my personal comfort. I could hear the air whistling down his nose as he breathed out. 'Don't you girls find out who you'll marry that way?'

I looked into his eager moist eyes and came to an immediate decision.

'It probably wouldn't work since I made it Matt.' I said a little too jovially, then I lowered my voice. 'And in answer to your kind offer earlier, do you mind if I don't accept your invitation to dinner. I'm sorry, but I just don't think we have anything in common.'

The smile went from his face and I felt awful.

'Sorry Matt, I feel awful, but -.'

'No it's fine, really. Better to know now than to be disappointed later.' Matt said. 'Excuse me.' He walked out of the salon with the attitude of a man who had to be somewhere else.

FIFTEEN

People were gradually drifting away, some clutching their little bits of boxed wedding cake. The Latchley's still had open day duties to attend to and Megan's school friends and the Fosters bore Travis away with them. Mike watched indulgently.

'Travis is about to find out what life is all about I think.'

Mum had been watching as well. 'Do you think he's still a virgin then Mike?'

Dad clapped a hand to his head. 'Behave yourself Moira,' he said in mock alarm, 'Mike's only just become our son-in-law.'

I giggled. This day was full of surprises. Thinking of surprises I looked around, there was no sign of Helena or Matt and I asked Megan if she'd seen them.

'Yep. They came and said goodbye together. Helena said something about needing to discuss a business proposal with Matt over dinner together. He had his hand on her arm.' Megan added significantly.

Sam came over and told me he was going to change and help close things up after the Easter visitors. There was lots to do.

'After that I shall be back here to collect you, so don't disappear.'

'Oh, are you going to help me look after my folks this evening?' I couldn't help saying it but I did manage to keep my voice neutral even though the atmosphere was charged between us.

Sam didn't blink an eyelid. 'I can if you like, but first there's something we must do.'

Feeling a bit of a tingle in the pit of my stomach I went upstairs with Megan and mum and we all changed out of our wedding clothes. It was such a relief to put my jeans on and flat shoes on. Leaving my hair all pinned up I went through to mum and Megan, who was pulling a soft blue leather jacket on over white jeans and a blue and white striped top. She looked down at her left hand and splayed her fingers to admire her rings.

'Well that was my wedding day. Married at Trelerric chapel and buffeted to bits in a Georgian salon thanks to you Luce. It's been a fantastic day, probably because I didn't plan it.' We hugged briefly. 'Have you any tupperware downstairs? I'm going to fill us a doggy bag from the buffet before we go, I'm famished.' Mike and Megan were simply going back to his place, they weren't flying to Florida until after Easter Monday, once Travis had left for Cardiff.

Mum had the same idea. 'Your dad and I can eat from there as well. I'm nearly ready to put my feet up and do nothing in front of your telly.'

We all trooped downstairs and found Mike and dad already eating in the salon with plates balanced on their knees so we joined them. Mum found glasses and wine.

'We may as well enjoy ourselves, it's all paid for.'

It was lovely, just sitting there being family. While we were all chatting Maggie and Clare put their heads round the door to say hello and cheerio.

'Leave it all Lucy, there's hardly anything left and the dishwasher can do its business tomorrow. Trelerric isn't open in the morning so there's no rush.' They were both earning overtime since it was Easter.

Megan and Mike decided they would be off and we ceremoniously waved them away, taking photos on our phones. Someone had fixed a 'Just Married' sign to the back of Mike's car and added a horseshoe and streamers, I suspected Travis had done it. Mum was shattered and said she needed to go for a lie down and dad said he could do with a bit of quiet. I avoided making a quip about not spending time in the same room as mum then and wandered off into the kitchen to find a bin liner. At least I could bag up the few bits of uneaten food. I was scraping things off a plate and playing the day through in my head when a voice behind me spoke.

'You never stop do you Cinders.'

I jumped out of my skin as two strong hands took me by the shoulders. Sam was right behind me. 'Your hair looks nice up like that.'

I felt his breath on my skin and his lips grazing the back of my neck. Shuddering with delight I bent my head forward as he very gently bit the side of my neck. I felt my back arch and my spine turning to liquid as his hands tightened, then he turned me round and kissed me, a long, slow, sensitive kiss.

'Lovely Lucy.' Sam's eyes had turned the colour of honey. He put his face against mine in a way that our foreheads and noses touched. It was expressively tender. 'We have to go now or it will be too late.'

I was mystified as his eyes left mine and glanced over to the buffet table.

'Ah, just what we need.'

Sam took a piece of the unclaimed sponge cake and carefully peeled the icing away, which he then pulled into little pieces. Placing them into a paper napkin he licked a bit of icing off one finger and then put another finger suggestively to my lips. I couldn't resist, I touched his finger with my tongue and then as he applied a little pressure I bit his finger gently.

'Tastes sweet. Like you.' He smiled at me. 'Come on.'

Outside it was cool and still and he put an arm protectively around my shoulders and pulled me close.

'This way.'

I loved the way we walked in step without speaking, his hip against mine, his arm warm and strong. There was purpose in the way he lead me and I felt utterly secure and as though everything was right in my world. We walked up past the Coach House and through to the orchard I could see from my windows. A few late narcissi were pale in the twilight and the gazebo's light wooden structure loomed at the end of a mown path. The bee hives were all in place, two placed well apart on the gazebo floor and three hanging from the hooks and made out of some woven natural material. Everything was quiet, the bees had done their work for the day.

'I'm trying out a new system, the hanging skeps reflect the way bees like to build their nests at height. It's thought it will help their health and survival rates. The gazebo is to give them some protection from the weather, like the ancient bee-boles in the old stone wall there.'

I looked over to where he was gesturing, so that's what those niches were in the wall. Enclosures to hold bee hives.

By now Sam had opened the napkin and was holding it out to me.

'Lucy, please take the offering you made and place a piece at the entrance to each of the hives.'

He sounded almost formal and his voice was calm and serious but there was a look in his eyes which caught me by surprise. He looked both pleased and proud and like a man who had made his mind up about something. As I went to do his bidding he spoke.

'Madam queens and worker bees of Trelerric orchard, this is an offering to you all from the hands of Lucy Huccaby. Lucy made this for her sister's wedding in the chapel today and she would like to share it with you because she lives here now. Lucy is gifted in sugar work and understands the sweetness of things, as do you all.'

For a moment I hesitated, respectful of the fact that I knew nothing about bees and wasn't wearing any safety clothing. But there was a sense of trust and understanding radiating from Sam so I moved quietly, gently placing the small pieces of icing at each hive, instinctively pressing them down to make them stick. Then I felt, rather than heard, a swell of energy from the hives and looked round at Sam in surprise. He was leaning against a post, watching me and smiling.

'Message received and understood I'd say.' He held both hands out to me and I walked forward and into his arms.

The Coach House was a surprise. The whole room was painted white, an open plan living area with a double futon bed behind a Japanese screen printed in an autumn design of leaves changing colour and falling. The only enclosed part was the bathroom at one end. Apart from the red, green and gold colours on the screen Sam's taste was simple, uncluttered and plain. He'd furnished it with some thick red and white rugs, two old red upholstered Ercol chairs and a footstool, a huge red corduroy bean bag and a low coffee table made out of aged wooden planks scarfed together and fastened to an old packing crate. I could see the remains of stencilling advertising Tamar Valley Strawberries. An identical crate had been smoothed a little and turned into a bookshelf. Ornaments consisted of a piece of weather bleached twisted wood, some large chunks of white quartz and a rustic stoneware pot with the words Trelerric Dairy glazed on it. He had a kettle and a microwave oven, some mugs, plates and glasses and very little else on a small hand built kitchen unit housing a white ceramic sink.

'Simple basics, purely functional.' Sam waved a hand indicating the room. 'I pinched the screen from Flick. But I do have a sandwich toaster in the cupboard for when I have guests.'

For a moment I jealously imagined Helena in here, intimately sharing a toasted sandwich, but banished the thought. It didn't seem her style although I wouldn't put it past her to slum it for a while if she thought the end game was worth it.

There was a small woodstove standing on a thick slab of slate with a basket of logs to one side. Sam lit some large candles and then turned his attention to the fire while I stood looking around, noticing a very modern computer and a pile of books. There was no television but he did have a radio. And I noticed a handsome telescope on a stand near the side window.

'I don't think I need a toasted sandwich right now.' I smiled, admiring his broad muscular back and looking at his tight bum. 'I'm full of carbohydrate.' And all I could taste was his kisses.

'This is the only heating I have apart from the power shower, the place is dry and weather proof and the floor is insulated and fire proofed, but it can get very cold until the wood stove kicks in. Then it gets so hot I sit around in my pants because it turns into a sauna.' Sam laughed. 'At least I have my own space when I want it.'

'I like it. Has Flick seen it?'

'Once.' He pulled a face. 'She described it as "very bachelor and not even attractively bohemian darling" but she agreed that since I would inherit just about every damned stick of furniture on the estate one day that I could get by with a few simple bits and pieces.'

There were a few windows, two overlooked the parking area at the front and one at the end looked towards the old drive to the Tudor house. I looked out but it was dark now. Sam pulled the blinds down to the front windows and came over to me.

'Nothing but stars out there now Lucy. I look at them through the telescope some nights.' Sam spoke behind me and wrapped his arms around and across me. My heart was banging around my ribcage and there was that moment when you know you're about to do something which could seriously change your life. I closed my eyes and felt the pressure of his body against mine. He kissed the back of my neck again. 'I can understand why the Japanese find this part of a woman's body erotic.' His lips against my skin were sending tingles down my spine. 'If you only knew how I've hoped for this moment Lucy. I stood here once and watched you standing amongst the snowdrops, not long after you arrived. You were a girl in a trance, like you'd woken from a long and not very pleasant dream and found yourself someplace unexpected.'

I turned in his arms. 'The snowdrops outside my door the night before Valentine's?' I said. 'It was you then?'

'Yes. Snowdrops are like light at the end of winter. They show the way ahead.'

'I did wonder, but then I thought you'd gone to Helena's.' Damn my big mouth.

150

For a moment he looked uncomfortable. 'Yes I did. Only for a couple of hours to eat, only because, well. Let me be honest. I first met her when she came and did Grace's birthday party. I was being best uncle in the world and Helena wouldn't leave me alone. After the party I helped her pack all her catering stuff up and ended up going back to her place. To cut a long story short I stayed the night and from that moment I couldn't shake her off. Remember this was all before you came along. I tried not answering my phone and not being available. At one point I even asked mum and dad what to do about her, and about you. How pathetic is that?' He looked down at me, his eyes honest and his expression serious. 'But once she got involved in your sister's wedding I couldn't tell her there was nothing between us because I didn't want her to throw her dolly out of the pram and let you all down.' He took a deep breath.

My relief was huge, I put my arms up around his neck, my fingertips touching his skin and his hair. 'You once said she was stalking you.' I could feel his warmth.

'I did. I was trying to make a point, after Simon and I hid from her that day I thought you'd got it. I was going to tell you all this after we first kissed and then I saw you with Matt. Or I saw his expression when he was looking at you and I heard what he said. I thought there was something going on between you and I didn't want to make a fool of myself.'

Flick was right, we'd both been complete idiots. Sam pulled me closer and looking into his eyes I could see the unspoken question.

'He did ask me out for a meal but I refused. I only ever saw him with Mike and Megan. There's nothing between us. I told him so this afternoon, after the cake had been cut.' Then I remembered Flick's intervention. 'And Flick told Helena that Matt was the answer to her dreams, or words to that effect.'

I could feel the heat from his body and couldn't help stroking his hair. Sam gave a great sigh.

'So it's just me and you then?' He said.

'Yes, just the two of us.' And I kissed him. Oh how I kissed him.

We woke at dawn, a blackbird singing outside. Sam was lying curved around me, one arm over my waist with his hand folded between my breasts. I moved and turned to look at him and got a drowsy smile.

'Magic. You're still here. You didn't vanish at midnight.'

'Yikes.' I sat up in alarm. 'My parents. Oh god I forgot all about them. I've got to do breakfast. I must get washed.'

Bloody hell, I was thinking, I didn't even take my make up off last night. I must look like a clown. Sam had unpinned my hair and undressed me and at some point had fetched us both a glass of water. My stomach rumbled.

'Okay.' Sam rolled over and sat up. 'Shower's all yours, I'll make us some tea. I haven't got any coffee. Or any milk come to think of it.'

I showered and used his shampoo and his towels and then his comb to fix my hair. He handed me a mug of black sugarless tea which I gulped while dressing. He'd sweetened his with a spoonful of honey and sucked the spoon afterwards. For some reason we were both grinning.

'When do they leave?'

'Late morning I think. Flick's having her day with Sir Hugh since it's Sunday.'

'Oh hell, we're open this afternoon. I was going to ask you to spend the day with me, we could go to a pub.'

'Pointless, everything'll be booked solid since it's Easter in Cornwall.' I replied, thinking fast. 'Toasted sandwiches tonight?'

'Be my guest.' Sam kissed me. 'Have you got any bread and cheese available then?'

I was making tea in the flat when there was a knock at the door and mum wandered in wearing her dressing gown. She sat down at the little table and looked me up and down, an amused look on her face.

'Well you're looking spruce for a young lady who didn't come home last night.'

You couldn't get anything past this woman, she didn't miss a trick.

'Do you have a problem with that Mrs Huccaby?' I said lightly as I placed a cup of tea in front of her. Mum didn't recognise mugs as valid drinking vessels.

'Well that depends on the circumstances in my way of thinking.' She looked at me shrewdly. 'Is he special Lucy? You wouldn't answer me yesterday when I asked about the nephew.'

'How on earth did you know? Can you see through walls or something with your radar vision?'

'Daddy saw the both of you leaving the house last evening, him with his arm close around you. He said you made a picture. And I looked at my photographs last night when I was doing the face-ache. There's a good one of you with him, all ivory and grey standing together, looking every bit like a couple.'

'I'd like to see that one.' I sat down opposite her. 'Yes, he's special mum. It all came together last night for the first time. He's wonderful. He got under my skin the day I met him. He's given me snowdrops and honey.' It sounded so romantic as I said that. I looked at her sweet kind face. 'You don't seem surprised?'

'Well no, not with the happiness spilling out of you like a fountain. The fact of the matter is that he asked daddy all about you while we were having the works done to us at the spa the other day.'

I was astonished and sat there with my mouth half open. 'What?'

'He asked nicely, daddy said. Apparently his sister, what's her name now, Mary is it? No Alice. Alice had told him about your cancelled engagement. You must have told her about it.'

I realised I'd been holding my breath so I breathed out heavily. 'Yes I did. Anything else?'

'Daddy didn't say. But he's a fine young man, I told you daddy said he liked him. Just be careful my pet. I don't want you broken hearted again.'

'Mum, I'm sorry I abandoned you last night.'

She reached over and took my hand. 'We got together with Lady Latchley later on. I found some soup and heated it up and we had ourselves a grand time. We all ate in the big kitchen. She's very fond of you.'

I tried to imagine Flick eating in the kitchen and failed. While mum went off with a cup of tea for dad I assembled a hearty breakfast for the three of us and made them sandwiches for the journey, raiding the big kitchen downstairs shamelessly. After we'd eaten I was just going to help dad with the bags when I heard a call from the hall below. My heart gave an extra beat at the sound of that deep voice.

'Ahoy, anyone still home?' Sam called again.

Mum went out and looked down the stairs. 'Sam hello there. Come up and say hello before we leave.'

'I came to say goodbye and safe journey from all of us.' Sam spoke as he walked into the room. 'Mum and dad send their best wishes, they're busy opening up and I've got parking duties and plant sales to attend to for a few hours. But I can help you with the bags Mark.'

I was pleased by Sam's familiar use of dad's name and delighted by his appearance. I'd seen his olive green shirt and grey jeans before but I was looking at him with new eyes. This gorgeous man was my, my what, lover?, boyfriend? With an effort I dragged my eyes away from him. Mum was almost smirking.

'Well it's lovely manners you have Sam. We've had a wonderful time and it's been a real pleasure to meet you and your family. You've welcomed us like friends.' She handed him a bag. 'That's not heavy, it's my hat and shoes and handbag.'

'Let me take that then mum. Sam can help dad with your cases. You packed enough for a month.' Sam's fingers touched mine as he handed the bag over and he and dad went downstairs. Mum waited for a few minutes, quite clearly listening for the door to close downstairs.

'Well would you look at that. He has stars in his eyes when he looks at you Lucy Huccaby.'

SIXTEEN

'You've changed darling.' Flick said. 'You don't look closed up and defensive any more. I remember when Robin first brought me to Trelerric, the terrace is so romantic in the moonlight.'

'Were you married then?' I asked her. We were walking together outside on the terrace with Coco. The sunshine was warm and everything was quiet now that Easter was over and we had Trelerric to ourselves again.

'Goodness no. I was a famous socialite and actress and Robin was the most wanted bachelor of the decade in the County set. But we became lovers here and he asked me to marry him on the little stone seat next to the statue of Pan. You must have found that by now?'

I nodded. I'd been hiding there that day when Sam had walked by with Helena desperately asking him out to dinner at her place. It seemed like ages ago now.

'Did you get married here?'

'No, I was living in Ealing. We married up in London and went to Paris for our honeymoon.'

'Flick, can I ask you something personal?'

Flick stopped to admire a clump of tulips. 'I reserve the right not to answer. But yes, you can ask.'

I stared at the tulips, Sam had planted casual arrangements of yellow ones with others which had bloomed a bruised purple so dark they were almost black. They were growing through carpets of white flowering saxifrage and blue forget-me-nots. It was a heavenly combination. I was aware of Flick projecting her attention onto me in her actressy manner and I chose my words carefully.

'You didn't have children. But I've seen you with little Grace and Thomas, you're good with them. And you're not putting on an act for Alice's benefit. I just wondered why you and Robin hadn't had any of your own, that's all.'

'Well I wasn't expecting that question.' Flick glanced at me, her eyes unreadable behind her sunglasses. 'Let's sit over there, that bench in the dappled shade.'

I let Coco off the leash and she scampered about in her funny little hopping style, keeping us under observation as we sat down. I waited quietly while Flick composed herself.

'There are three sides to every story Lucy, mine, yours and the truth. It's a question I can supply several answers to. I never intended to have children. After growing up in the orphanage the idea of imposing childhood on another being was abhorrent to me. Childhood was all about lack of control over one's destiny. It was all about emotional and physical deprivation and loneliness.'

I made no movement, not wishing to distract her from deeply personal memories.

'Sometimes the past is a secret even to those who have lived it. There are memories we deny, things we have no wish to recall or are unable to cope with.' Flick sighed heavily. 'Of course one could argue that I could have given a child everything I didn't have, but then one has to cope with the consequences of spoiling the child.'

Coco came bouncing up to us, huffing and wanting a game. I found an appropriately Coco-sized ball in my pocket and threw it for her.

'I've been lucky Lucy. There has been love in my life, there still is. Even for that little beast.' Her eyes were following Coco affectionately as she ran about.

'And of course children smell, they're disruptive, noisy, objectionable parasites when they're not being adorable. They didn't fit in with the life I wanted. I had a good twenty years in my profession unencumbered by such responsibilities. 'And look at me Lucy, do I look like a mother? My hips are too slender.'

I smiled but I still didn't say anything. After a while Flick gave an irritable gesture and blew a raspberry. 'You're not buying any of it are you Lucy?' She said.

'Well you've given me several answers, which is how you started the conversation. Do you want me to pick one and pretend to believe it's the truth?' I shook my head. 'You're a warm and caring woman Flick. I'm guessing you've not gone anywhere near the real reason. But I'm out of order here. It's none of my business.'

'Exactly. And as I said, I reserve the right not to answer. But let me ask you the same question. Do you want to have children?'

'Touché.' I replied.

A magic carpet of childhood memories unfolded in my mind. Being tucked up in bed and kissed goodnight. Megan and I each sitting on mum and dad's knees being lulled before bedtime while they played a silly game sayings things like, my dolly is quieter than yours, look, my dolly's eyes close when I tip her head back like this, my dolly sleeps longer than yours. Books, stories and board games and getting our paints out on wet winter weekends. Being encouraged to share. The car journey to the seaside at Looe for summer holidays. Being helped, advised and sometimes disciplined by mum. Blimey, she'd done an amazing job as well as working part time in a nursing home and fostering other lost girls. For the first time in ages I remembered my dreams of having a baby with Peter. But I'd never been able to imagine who the baby would take after and now I could barely remember what Peter looked like.

'Earth to Lucy?'

Sam was standing in front of me and I came out of my dreams with a bump. Coco was snuffling round his feet and desperately hoping for a pat. I felt pretty much like doing the same, I was delighted to see him even though I'd been in his arms only a few hours ago.

Flick gave a snort of laughter. 'We were having a serious conversation Sam.'

'Well I thought you were both asleep. Two biddies dozing on a bench.'

He was laughing down at us, so vibrantly solidly alive and happy in his garden, standing with his feet apart and dressed in working clothes with his hair tousled and the sun kissing his skin. I noticed his eyes were the colour of cider when the sun shines through the glass.

'Simon and I are going to get on with your Japanese courtyard. It's muscle power today ladies.'

'In that case we had better arrange refreshments for you both.' Flick held out her hand to him so that he could pull her up.

'Do you want to have something later in the kitchen then Flick, all of us together? I heard you slummed it in there with mum and dad after the wedding.' I teased her.

'I will if I must.' Flick replied lightly, taking my arm for companionship as much as for support.

We'd decided to go through the Trelerric Vintage documents which were piling up on the table as there were things to talk through with Jane later. Flick was also sharing the ideas with her friend Sir Hugh. She said she'd trust him with her life and that it was he who had introduced her to Robin at one of his house parties. Sir Hugh had property all over the place but when he was visiting Cornwall he often slept on his boat. Apparently there were numerous marinas and moorings which he frequented although Falmouth was one of his favourites.

'Dear Hugh, he's the Worcestershire Flinton's, there's another branch established somewhere in Dorset. If it hadn't been for him the family would have gone under. He made a fortunate marriage and he has a brilliant financial mind. His import/export business is very successful.'

As well as being a *bon viveur* and with an eye for the girls, I thought.

There was a tap at the door and Maggie came in with the post. 'Sorry, I would've brought it in earlier but you'd both gone outside. This is yours Mrs Latchley, and there's a postcard for you Lucy and a letter.'

I turned the postcard over, it was from Megan, sent from the airport. "Killing time before the flight. Don't expect one from honeymoon, we shall be too busy enjoying ourselves!" I smiled and picked the letter up. There was something formal looking about it. Tearing it open my eyes fell on the words Registrar General. I scanned the letter rapidly. There were dignified words about a match having been established, a name and address of a woman and something about confirmation of this person having been advised according to procedures. I gasped and read it again.

'They've found my real mother,' I said faintly. 'She lives in Great Malvern. I can write to her and make contact if I want to.' I read the letter again, it meant that she had also registered her contact details and was open to the idea of finding me. It wasn't a one-way street.

'Lucy. Lucy. Are you pleased sweetheart?' Flick had reached over the table and was patting my hand. I'd already told her that I'd simply registered with the Adoption Contact Register rather than pay an agency to do all the work. 'What's her name?'

'Sorry. What did you say Flick?'

'I asked what her name is.'

'It's Mrs Jennifer K. Blythe. Her name is Jennifer.'

I was trying, and failing, to comprehend that my mother was called Jennifer.

'And where does she live?' Flick was speaking again.

I looked at the letter again. 'She lives at Great Malvern, in Worcestershire. My god, she lives in striking distance of where I grew up. About thirty or so miles away. I've been to Malvern, there's a theatre there and I went to a flower show once with mum and dad. How weird is that?' My heart seemed to have stopped beating.

Flick didn't seem to be paying attention. 'Malvern, that's Hugh's ancestral stamping ground. Flinton Hall was where I met Robin for the first time.'

All our good intentions of working on the Trelerric Vintage papers were now forgotten. I wanted to find a map and the only one I had was in my car which was parked up at the Coach House. Flick agreed I should fetch it. As I was hurrying to the car I met Sam and Simon negotiating a sack truck over the gravel with difficulty. On it was balanced a large lump of mossy granite.

'It keeps getting stuck.' Sam said by way of greeting.

'Get a plank or something,' I said absently. 'The wheels need purchase.'

'That's what I told him ma'am, I mean Lucy.' Simon grinned at me, his earlier shyness fast receding. 'But he wouldn't listen to the likes of me.'

'It's as clear as daylight to us Simon. We can both see it.' I couldn't help remembering the way Sam used to tease me in the early days.

Sam sighed. 'Okay, I'll get a board from the Coach House. I know when I'm beaten.'

'You know when you're being a plonker you mean.' I giggled as he made a playful lunge at me. Simon looked at us, knowledge bright in his eyes. 'Not in the way here am I?'

'Cheeky sod. Just for that you can come and help carry boards.' Sam replied.

I was grateful for Simon's presence. I didn't feel ready to share my news with Sam, I'd not told him I was adopted although anyone with an eye could work out that Megan and I weren't related. Part of me was rapidly processing information and had gone back to the conversation I'd had with mum before Megan's wedding. The night we'd met Matt for the first time. Mum had said I'd been adopted when they were still living in London. Dad's teaching job at the technical college and the move to Herefordshire hadn't been on the cards then. It was surely a coincidence that I'd grown up not all that far from Malvern in the neighbouring county. Of course, I reasoned, Mrs Jennifer K. Blythe could also have moved there as changes occurred in her own life. People moved all the time for all sorts of reasons.

Flick and I looked at the road map together and she pointed to a spot with an elegant coral coloured fingernail. 'There I think.

Flinton Hall is about there and your Mrs Blythe is somewhere here. Not far away.'

'I can look at her address on google maps.' I said. 'But if you want to see you'll have to come upstairs to my computer.'

Flick declined, distracted by a thump and an oath in the courtyard outside. She craned her neck to see what what happening.

'I do hope that rock isn't going to come crashing through the French windows.' she said. 'I prefer rocks of the right size and kind on my finger or in a glass of G&T.'

I desperately needed to think and to Sam's disappointment pleaded fatigue and asked for an evening on my own, saying I wasn't getting enough sleep. Somewhere out there was a woman who knew that I existed. I'd looked at her address on Google maps and seen a hedge with a glimpse of a pretty white painted cottage behind it. I wondered who she shared it with, what she was thinking and why she'd registered herself as contactable. What was she hoping for? Was she lying awake remembering something painful in her past and wishing that I would get in touch and make things better for her?

It's like climbing the Helter Skelter at the funfair, I thought. Once you're at the top there's only one way to go and that's down. It's fast and your stomach knots and then you land with a bump. I spent hours debating with myself and finally made a list.

Should I make contact now as the ball was in my court?

Should I let bygones by bygones?

What did I want to know or achieve?

Did I want to find out if I had siblings?

Would I like them - and would they like me? (Did it matter?)

Did I want closure or was I hoping to start a relationship with the woman who had given me away?

Would it be painful to learn the truth of the circumstances at the time of my birth?

Would there be things it would be better not to know? (Pandora's box/can of worms).

I thought back to the comment mum had made about counselling. For me it wasn't a legal requirement, but I had to think sensibly about whether to pursue it. I spent the evening on my computer searching for information, answers and looking at other people's experiences. Finally I came to the conclusion that I shouldn't expect an easy journey and I began to doubt my earlier reasons for pursuing the matter, which had been largely based on that comment Peter had made so long ago now about not knowing my origins. I was no further forward really.

I thought again about mum and dad and the love I had for them. They were the significant adults in my life and I wasn't going to do anything to hurt them. I told myself I was lucky and healthy, knowing my talents and capabilities. Mostly I was comfortable with myself. And that was down to Moira and Mark Huccaby.

I really needed to speak to them in person, I realised. I can't do anything without them, and Megan too.

SEVENTEEN

At Saturday supper the Easter weekend had been declared a success and there'd been much friendly talk about the wedding. I very lightly dropped the idea of offering Trelerric as a wedding venue into the conversation, suggesting a package for an intimate event along the lines of Megan's successful day.

'It's a niche opportunity isn't it,' I said. 'Rather than the whole bun fight with hundreds of guests and a party half the night and all that bother, we could accommodate little events like second marriages or renewals of the vows. Just a half day event with a buffet and taxis off the estate after five or six hours.'

'Renewals?' Jonathan sounded horrified. 'You mean people go through it all again? And with the same person? Blimey I couldn't do that, I was bricking it the first time.' He received an odd look from Alice. 'Darling,' he said quickly. 'Whatever floats other people's boats is up to them, I meant every word I said the day you married me, it's staying that way, believe me.'

I watched the amused glances passing between Tim and Jane.

'Thirty love I think.' Sam muttered. 'New balls anyone?'

Alice tried to kick him under the table.

After supper Tim took Flick back and Sam and I walked Mitch all around the orchards. They were just coming into blossom and it was exquisite.

'This is the best time of year, you can feel the life racing through the ground and up into the plants.' Sam was saying. 'And today I found a blackbird's nest with three chicks hatched.'

I smiled to myself as he talked, we were holding hands and walking in step. Then he stopped and pulled me in front of him, placing his hands on my shoulders.

'Lovely Lucy, there's something on your mind. What is it?'

I was startled. 'Nothing. I was just thinking you sounded like a little kid, I can see the little boy in you finding frogspawn and bird's nests and stuff.'

'Frogspawn is February around here. It's nearly the end of April, so there'll be tadpoles now.' He looked into my eyes, serious and kind. 'I'm going to ask you once more, is there something on your mind? Because I want the sort of relationship that's open and honest. I want to be able to solve problems before they turn into raging horned monsters with huge teeth and spoil things.'

I was fascinated, gazing into his eyes and feeling the intensity of his words. 'Like those things that hide under the bed at night and make you too scared to put a leg out?' I said.

Sam started laughing. 'Night monsters you mean? No they're a different problem. And they don't fit under my futon, it's too near the ground.' He smiled at me and kissed the tip of my nose. 'I just want things right between us.'

I put my arms around his neck and kissed him back. 'So do I. And no scary monsters. The only horned monster in the bed is you.'

But I was thinking how on earth can I tell him about this new knowledge? I'm not who he thinks I am. And what would he make of Mrs Jennifer K. Blythe after meeting Mrs Moira Huccaby?

We took Mitch back to the kennels where he slipped into his bed alongside Tim's two dogs with much tail thumping. Sam had said he rarely let him sleep at the Coach House because he objected to finding Mitch on the futon with him. 'He's male, he's hairy and his breath smells. Not my preferred choice of bed partner. I like sweetly scented smooth curvy females, exactly like you in fact.'

That weekend was blissful. Flick went off on Sunday morning with Booboo and Henry, whom I'd never met, to spend a few days away with friends in Bath. I gathered that they'd be meeting up with a couple called Jumbo and Fizz. Flick had a peculiar habit of telling me about people she knew as though I knew them too. In this case I wasn't sure whether she was describing a menagerie or a circus troupe, but it meant that I had free time and that Maggie had time off in lieu of Easter.

'I could walk around Trelerric House naked and no-one would know.' I said to Sam as we snuggled together on the bean bag.

Sam was keenly interested in the idea. 'Would that be the Tudor part or would madam prefer to disport herself in the Georgian wing?' He murmured, breathing tiny kisses onto my neck.

'How many bare bums do you think Trelerric has seen over the centuries?' I giggled, wriggling in his arms because his kisses were tickling me.

Sam fell off the beanbag and athletically rolled over and up onto his knees at my side. 'Dozens I expect. The Latchley Book describes some wild festivities during Christmas and at harvest, the usual times of revelry and feasting. And my late uncle Robin used to throw some rather bohemian bashes I gather.'

I told him I'd heard the rumours and that Maggie had mentioned listening in to some of Flick's conversations with old friends. Sam gave me an odd look.

'Why did you just give me that odd look?' I challenged him, smiling. 'Was it because I'm gossiping?'

Sam knelt quietly, a pensive look in his eyes. 'All I can say is that Maggie's a very pretty woman, she was a bit of a head turner twenty years ago according to my dad.'

'Oh.' The information sunk in. 'Did Maggie get, er, involved in Flick and Robin's parties then?'

Sam didn't answer. He raised his arms like a grizzly bear and flopped onto me growling and pretending to bite. I shrieked and we tussled while he held me down, laughing at my attempts to fight him. Then he grew serious and started kissing me until I forgot about everything but him.

That evening we ate together in Maggie's kitchen, I found cheese and teamed it with olives and tomatoes and crusty bread, a good bottle of red wine open on the table between us. Sam found some salted almonds and added those.

'I love simple stuff,' Sam said, tearing the bread into chunks. 'Fresh, tasty, uncomplicated.'

I was mixing balsamic vinegar with virgin olive oil to dip the bread into. 'I think it helps who you're eating with. Some people enhance food for others by their own enjoyment.'

Sam ate quietly, regarding me with a thoughtful expression. He swallowed and took a sip of wine, savouring the combination of flavours.

'Lucy,' he said, reaching over the table and taking my hand. 'Lucy you've had a whole life I know nothing about. All that nursing and general busyness with the business and everything. Until now you've always lived where there's some action. I've imagined you at parties and pubs. Don't you find Trelerric a bit tame and dull after all that?'

I was genuinely surprised. 'Trelerric, tame?' There's not been a dull moment here since I walked through that door in January.' That was four full months ago I realised as I tapped the months onto the table almost unconsciously with the fingers of my other hand. And now I'm sitting here with my lover, the heir to the Latchley estate. It was surreal.

Sam was looking at me thoughtfully and sipping his wine. It occurred to me for the first time that he might be feeling uncertain about my intentions here. Was he seeking some reassurance?

'I'm loving being here. Your family are great, Flick is amazing, there's so much to do and to learn here. I want to know about the Latchley's, who they were and where they came from. And ...' I stopped speaking. What was I going to say, and there's you Sam, you knocked me sideways the moment I met you and I wasn't in the market for a man. I gazed at him helplessly, not wanting to let my mouth and my feelings run away with me.

'Only I was thinking,' he said, letting go of my hand and picking up another chunk of bread. 'There's a good little cinema over at Wadebridge. We could go out one night.'

Flick returned late one afternoon and I finally got to meet Booboo and Henry, who were nothing like I'd imagined. I'd mentally seen them as a world-weary slightly sozzled deb and a heartily avuncular and pompous bloke with a belly and a double chin. In fact Booboo was a slim stylish woman with neat short grey hair and fine ankles and Henry was a fit looking man with a patrician English face. They greeted me pleasantly and insisted I should join them in Flick's rooms for tea before they went on their way.

'Our youngest has the dogs and we've got to collect them.' Booboo was telling me. 'He's a struggling artist, lives with a delightful teacher who supports him in more ways than one. He's never going to amount to anything but he's a very sweet young man. Do you paint or draw? I've heard about your cakes so I know you're talented artistically.'

She was the sort of woman who liked to draw people out but she did it gracefully and kindly and I didn't mind talking to her. But I couldn't help remembering Flick's comment about the state she and Henry had left the sheets in before they were married. Funny but I couldn't imagine Henry in the throes of animal passion. I smiled to myself, wondering what Jumbo and Fizz looked like, probably not circus performers I suspected.

'So we're all meeting again next month up at Flinton Hall.' Flick was saying, checking her diary. 'Are you getting anything for Hugh?'

'What on earth do you get for a man of his age and who has everything?' Booboo said.

'A Tuscan villa maybe.' Henry growled. 'He hasn't got one of those.'

'Neither have we darling.' Booboo said absently.

'Is is Sir Hugh's birthday then?' I asked politely.

Flick nodded. 'He's throwing a long weekend party. There'll be loads of us.'

'Those who are left standing or who are still living that is.' Henry commented.

'Well if he's got everything, how about getting him a packet of wine gums and a saucy magazine, give him something to occupy himself with in the evenings.' I suggested cheekily. 'Good quality gums and all nicely wrapped of course.'

Flick and Booboo stared at me in amazement and Henry shouted with laughter. 'Bloody marvellous idea.' He extracted a snowy handkerchief from his pocket and wiped his eyes. 'Can see why you get along with this girl Flick. Boo, make a note. That's exactly what I'd like for my birthday! And for Christmas too come to think of it!'

Flick was looking at me with approval. 'Yes, Lucy has brains, beauty, talent and wit. She fits in at Trelerric quite perfectly.'

The sound of sobbing woke me. Tears were cascading down my cheek and soaking the pillow. A bedside lamp went on and Sam gathered me into his arms, a handful of tissues in one hand as he wiped my eyes.

'Lucy, what on earth was it? A scary monster from under the bed? I'll get rid of it for you.' He looked really concerned.

We were in my rooms in the house. I hadn't had that dream for weeks.

'I don't know.' My breathing was ragged and I knew I looked a fright. 'I need to splash my face.'

I got up and went into the bathroom. A glance in the mirror confirmed the worst, red eyes, a red nose and mad hair. I soaked a face flannel in cold water to cool my cheeks and soothe my eyes, then I put a comb through my hair and blew my nose. There was only a marginal improvement.

Sam was sitting up in bed. 'Three hours till getting up time. Do you want to tell me what that was all about?'

'Nothing to tell. I've had it all my life and never known what it means. I'm just lonely and terribly unhappy and I cry. There's some awful loss but I've no idea what it is or what it means.'

'Well come here. I'll cuddle you better and see if we can get a bit more sleep.'

Sam was so gentle and comforting. He switched the lamp off and I relaxed against him. He didn't speak, just kissed the top of my head a few times. I lay and listened to his soft breathing as it became regular and slow. It was a while before sleep claimed me again.

I told Flick that I needed to see my folks and that I had to talk to them about Jennifer Blythe. A plan was forming in my mind and I shared it with her.

'If I decide to contact Mrs Blythe I'm going to ask mum and dad if I can use their address, rather than this one. If we do decide to meet, I think it would be better if we did it someplace between Great Malvern and Hereford. That way I'm near emotional support from people who matter to me.

'And you can expect your adopted parents to provide this level of support Lucy?'

'Yes I'm sure I can. And I wouldn't meet this lady behind their backs or without their knowledge. It's not an easy thing to ask of them and I need to reassure them about my feelings.

'Well I'm away next weekend at Flinton Hall. Why don't you go home that weekend. And I've an idea, you could come over to Flinton Hall and bring me back here, it would save Booboo and Henry having to make the detour to drop me off.'

'It means you'll have to travel in the Mini.'

'No darling, I wouldn't be comfortable and my luggage won't fit into that shoebox you drive. You'll have to take the Jag.'

I texted Megan with the brief details and she replied "*Just do it. You won't rest until you've got this bee out of your bonnet.*"

The mention of bees made me think of Sam. Trelerric was all about Sam. Everywhere I walked I saw the evidence of his presence, his designing hands in the garden terraces, the cupped shapes of the blossoming apple trees, the warm happy hum of the hives. And now of course he and Simon were putting the finishing touches to the Japanese dry garden in Flick's little courtyard. It was a beautiful piece of work. The lumps of granite they'd laboured to bring over the gravel were now placed in a way which suggested mountains, one had a vein of quartz running down through it which looked like a mountain stream cascading from height. They'd spent hours positioning them, talking about place and something they described as "right feel", struggling to move one a quarter turn here or there, standing back and crouching down, constantly assessing form, shape, angle, impact.

'They tell you when they're right, Lucy.' Simon had explained. 'Rocks talk when you work with them like this. You don't hear it in your ears, you feel it in your ...' He'd placed one hand on his heart. 'Here, your belly, heart, I'm not sure.'

Then Simon had worked for days selecting and placing slate paddle stones overlapping one by one to imitate a river curving from around the mountains and eventually down to what looked like a lake. The sense of scale and perspective was extraordinary. There was an island in the lake, a carefully chosen flattish piece of Trelerric granite with moss growing on it. One end had a raised point and as I gazed at it I got the impression of a boat.

'It looks like a boat from this angle Simon.'

'That's right, you've got it just right.' Simon replied looking pleased. 'It's symbolic.' He didn't explain any further.

Finally they'd worked on the path leading from the French windows through the courtyard and up to the little private gate which separated Flick's rooms from the public terrace, before putting in a couple of small bronze-leaved trees, another group of three rocks, the small snow viewing lantern and a sympathetically designed bench. The courtyard was transformed from a forgotten place to a special space.

'I'll have to put a new "private no entry" sign on that gate Flick and renew the lock'. Sam said. 'Anyone looking over will want to come in and see all this. Before you know it they'll be indoors and rummaging through your smalls.'

'Those little feathery leaved trees are gorgeous Sam, what are they?'

'*Acer palmatum* Dissectum Atropurpureum'

'Bless you.' Flick snorted. 'Wish I'd never asked.' She said sideways to me. 'Do you have any idea what he's talking about?'

'No, but I love it when he talks dirty.' I replied.

Sam smiled politely at us. 'I've heard it all before ladies.'

Sam had watched Simon working and his liking and respect had grown. 'This boy's got something,' he informed us. 'I'm thinking of us both doing a Japanese inspired stroll garden area over near the Stables Tea Rooms where the public can see it. Japanese gardens were very popular in country houses at the turn of the last century so it wouldn't be out of place. And if we do that I'm putting Simon's name on it in the guide book.'

'That's a lovely idea. But why do you describe Simon as a boy. He's only a couple of years younger than you I think.' I said.

'I'm twenty-three,' Simon spoke up, unconcerned at being discussed. 'Not as old as the boss.' He indicated Sam, who was grinning at him. 'I've got my mum's looks, and she looks ten years younger than she is. Bloody embarrassing it is. People think I'm out with an old bride when I go out anywhere with her.'

That evening I told Sam that I'd be going up country to visit mum and dad for a couple of days.

'I'll miss you lovely Lucy. Is it a special occasion?'

'What do you mean?' We were lounging on one of my sofas, facing each other with our legs entwined. Sam was stroking my feet and idly pressing his thumbs into the sides of my instep and heel, it was wonderful.

'I meant is it a birthday or something, I haven't seen you making a cake.'

'Oh no, nothing special like that.' Unaccountably I felt some relief that he didn't know my secret. 'I just need to sort something out up there, and then I'm driving to Flinton Hall which is about thirty miles away to collect Flick and bring her home.'

'I like the way you refer to Trelerric as home.'

I just smiled. Trelerric felt more and more like home to me.

EIGHTEEN

Mum was quite excited when I turned up driving the Jag. 'It's every inch the lady you're looking in that car, and with your swanky hair. And is that a bit of makeup Lucy? It's very subtle, you look so well, it suits your eyes.'

On and on she prattled, you wouldn't think we'd seen each other only a few weeks previously at the wedding. But there was something about that car which made me want to dress up. Simon had washed it down and Sam had held me close and kissed me before I'd left. He'd insisted on having my mum's telephone number as well as their address.

'And please text me when you get there. Let me know everything is okay.'

That afternoon I showed mum and dad the letter from the General Register Office.

'Her name was Jennifer.' Mum was rubbing the letter between her thumb and index finger as though she could learn more that way.

'You didn't know her name?'

Dad shook his head. 'We weren't given any information other than your birth mother was very young.' He sighed.

I looked at them both. 'Is this very hard for you? I won't go any further if it's causing you pain. You both matter more to me than this. I haven't made any contact with Mrs Blythe.'

It was dad who spoke first. 'Obviously we've talked about you wanting to find out about things Lucy. You must do what's right for you maid, but we can support you every step of the way, if that's what you wish. Unlike with Megan,' he paused and looked at mum, 'we had no details about your circumstances.' He sighed again and took mum's hand in his. 'We don't know what to expect or what to prepare you for.'

'That's why I was talking about the counselling Lucy.' Mum said. 'You really should have professional support from the adoption society.'

'I don't know if it's on offer mum, I don't know if I should ask in London where you adopted me, or Cornwall where I live, or Hereford where you live and I grew up. In fact I've not really done my homework properly. All I did was register directly and they came back with a match.'

'And this lady now knows you've made enquiries but she doesn't know where you live. Is that right?' Mum asked. 'And she's registered to say she's open for business. In that case she must be in a proper state of worry so she must.'

I noticed mum's accent strengthening as it usually did in moments of feeling. After a respectful pause I outlined my idea about using their address. 'And if I was to meet with her then I'd do it somewhere up here, not from Cornwall. I'd want to be near to you both, if you can bear it.' I felt near to tears.

'If I'd had to give up my baby then I'd want to meet her if she came calling.' Mum said. 'It's a terrible terrible thing to lose a child. You wonder about them every day.'

Now we were all emotional. I knew that mum couldn't have children because she'd had a catastrophic ectopic pregnancy followed by complications after surgery. She'd nearly died, indeed she claimed she'd had an out of body experience which had confirmed her belief and trust in the church.

It was decided then. I would make contact. Dad went out to buy us all fish and chips and I showed mum a brief and factual letter I'd already drafted, explaining I was using my parent's address for contact and not my current home address. Together we tweaked it a bit; mum thought I was being a bit cold and she found a recent photograph of me from her face-ache collection.

'You're so lovely Lucy. We've been blessed with you. You were meant to be with us I think.'

'I think so too mum. Nothing will ever change that.'

Poor dad got home to find us both sobbing on each other's shoulders.

The following day mum and I went into Hereford where I posted the letter. Then we did some therapeutic shopping together with Megan and Mike's party in mind. I surprised myself by choosing a figure hugging sleeveless dress patterned with poppies and teaming it with chunky red beads and a pair of sexy red shoes. I wondered what Megan would make of it, but then I was dressing for Sam. We'd texted several times and his texts were affectionate and funny.

Mum on the other hand was going in fitted trousers and flat shoes. 'I'm not suffering foot pain again. And I doubt we'll get a wink of sleep since the party is in that barn of a place they live in now. There'll be loud music and intoxicated people falling about all over the furniture.'

I realised she had pretty dim expectations of the event even though Megan had said that the party would be held in the rooms next to the studios. By rooms she was barely describing the old beamed barn that Mike had had carefully restored for events like parties in mind.

'Stay at Trelerric then. I don't think Flick will object. In fact I'm sure she'd like to see you both again.'

'Really? Well that might be a blessing. I'll speak to daddy and ask Megan what she thinks.'

We mooched about and had lunch in the cafe at the side of the Cathedral. It was such a beautiful building. I could barely recall my feelings that day Peter had dumped me on the walk over the Cathedral green. I told mum about it.

'I don't feel anything at all. In fact I think I wish them well. It's nearly eighteen months now and I'm a different person.

'Well I'm glad. He wasn't the one for you, my heart sank when you got engaged. He never put the light in your eyes that you have now.'

'Is it that obvious mum?'

'It is to me. You've met someone very, very special. And it's not just because he's loaded.'

I burst out laughing. 'I don't think the Latchley's are loaded. Everything's tied up in a Trust and various complicated protective business arrangements. They are secure now I gather, but loaded with disposable cash? I think not.'

Mum was having none of it. As far as she was concerned they virtually lived in baronial splendour and were landed gentry. I made a mental note to get on with learning about the Trelerric lands and the origins of the Latchley family.

The morning I was due to leave and drive over to Flinton Hall to collect Flick I woke with temptation sitting like a lump on my chest. I knew from looking at the map that Jennifer Blythe's address wasn't far off my route. It wouldn't hurt to look at her house for a moment would it, I kept telling myself. After breakfast I put my bag in the boot and set the satnav. They waved me off with smiles and messages of best wishes to Flick; we'd all be together again in just over a week.

Gentle farming countryside paled into insignificance against the Malvern Hills rising ahead of me. It was such an unmistakable feature in the landscape. As I followed the verbal directions I had a weird feeling, it was almost as though the satnav was giving me permission to take a peek at my birth mother's address. Then as the roads narrowed I began to wish I hadn't made such a foolish decision, I wasn't one hundred percent confident about driving the Jag on anything but A-roads with plenty of space. Luckily the traffic was light and glancing at the screen I could see the little chequered flag announcing my arrival at the destination.

I slowed the car to a stop and sat there at a loss as to my intentions. A short drive lead up to a double garage and a large parking place and I could see part of a well tended garden with a group of potted flowering plants. There were no cars visible but someone had put some washing out on a rotary line and a window was open upstairs. While I was sitting there a post office van drove round me and parked outside the house so I occupied myself by looking busy and fiddling with the satnav to set it for

Flinton Hall. The postwoman walked up the drive to the cottage and I had the uncomfortable feeling that I'd just witnessed my own letter being delivered. It made me feel like a voyeur and it wasn't pleasant. What if Jennifer was at this moment retrieving my letter from the mat and opening it as I sat outside. I imagined distress and excitement, fear and tears. It wasn't a good feeling and for a mad moment I toyed with the idea of going and knocking on the door and apologising. Then a tap on my side window brought me to earth with a shock. It was the postwoman.

'Not lost are you? Can I help?'

'No, thank you I'm not lost. I was just setting the satnav for Flinton Hall.'

'Oh yes, I know that place. About five miles as the crow flies but a bit more by car. Best to turn round,' she was pointing back the way I came. 'But the magic voice will no doubt tell you that. Although you can't always believe what they say can you!' She smiled and tapped the bonnet approvingly and went on her way.

Now I had an image of her in my mind giving a description of me to the police.

"Such a normal pleasant looking person, you wouldn't have guessed she had any intentions ..."

'Oh for god's sake pull yourself together Lucy. You're just wondering what Jennifer looks like, you don't want to kill her.' I said out loud and started to manoeuvre the car. I could see a possible turning place ahead, no way was I going to back the Jag into Jennifer's drive.

I calmed down as I drove to Flinton Hall. It was a very nice looking Queen Anne house. There was a large and rather posh looking new garden room built to one side and set back a little from the front of the house. I could see people in there as I parked. Sir Hugh came straight out to meet me and welcomed me pleasantly. He played the part of gentleman of the residence with impeccable manners and didn't try to cop a squeeze.

'Lucy, you found us, how delightful. Come into the garden room, we're all having a very relaxed time of it and putting the world to rights. And those who don't like today's world are happily reminiscing about the old days. I hope it won't be too much of a bore. Ah look, there's Flick. Looks marvellous doesn't she?'

In answer to my question Sir Hugh answered that he'd had a perfectly nice party thank you, and indicated a side table set with hot drinks and small pastries.

'Tea, coffee, anything you want just help yourself. I always use this room in the mornings because the light is so appealing. Best thing I ever did having it built. Got rid of a useless sunken garden put in by my late mother. She was a thoroughly nasty old trout and the gardener always hated it. And her.'

I couldn't help it, I giggled and he looked pleased.

'Funny thing Lucy, from a certain angle you remind me of my mother, in her youth she was considered a very handsome woman. There's a portrait of her in the music room if you're interested.'

I really wasn't in the mood for a bit of bottom patting so I said some other time perhaps. Flick was wandering over looking languid and lovely in one of her floaty silky lounging outfits.

'Lucy.' She kissed me on the cheek. 'Darling girl. You've met Booboo and Henry, you won't get a word out of Henry because he's not a morning person.' Henry raised a finger from his teacup and nodded at me before turning his attention back to the newspaper he was reading. 'You haven't met Fizz and Jumbo though.'

At last, I thought, the circus troupe. Of course they weren't what I'd been expecting. Fizz was a bright eyed woman with a strong handshake, smartly dressed in navy and white with red and white scarf. She instantly reminded me of an air hostess. Jumbo was a skinny bald headed man with arresting dark eyes and plummy vowels.

'Bewildering isn't it Lucy?' Fizz said to me. 'I originally got the nickname because I love drinking Champagne. I'm not going to tell you my real name.'

'And Booboo?' I asked politely, smiling across the room at her.

'Her childhood name,' Fizz answered. 'She couldn't say Rebecca. We were professional dancers together. I expect Flick told you?'

I shook my head. 'Actually Flick's told me nothing about any of you.'

'Flick always was the soul of discretion.' Jumbo butted in. 'I'm actually James Blackham. Unlike my wife here I'm not going to divulge the reason for my soubriquet.' He gave me a brief thin-lipped smile and his eyes twinkled.

I didn't know whether to nod or smile back so I concentrated on looking interested, I hadn't a clue what this man was talking about. Fortunately Henry beckoned to him so I was left with Fizz. She pulled me down onto a sofa next to her. Flick was deep in conversation with Sir Hugh over the financial papers.

'Is there a ...' I hesitated, unsure about whether I should say Mrs Flinton or Lady Flinton. 'Sir Hugh's wife?' I settled for lamely, remembering that Flick had said something about a fortunate marriage.

'Caro? Poor darling she died two years ago. Very sudden. Don't think Hugh's over it yet. Did you know the Bransden's?'

'No.'

'Local family, old money. Not many of them left now. Funny how families can suddenly become depleted. Their old house has been turned into a ghastly Country Hotel with a spa. I think a Russian owns it now. Fortunately Caro got some nice pieces before the place was sold off. They sit well with the items Hugh's mother inherited. And her family is all but disappeared now, I can't remember their family name. Didn't Flick say you were from hereabouts?' Fizz was chatty, very much a morning person.

'The Welsh borders, on the Herefordshire side.'

'Oh very pretty.' Fizz said vaguely. 'Hay-on-Wye and all that. We're in Cheltenham of course.'

I could tell she hadn't a clue. This was very much a city girl. Sir Hugh came over and asked me which way I was driving back and laughed when I told him it was really up to the satnav. He advised that with his business interests he did a lot of driving around the south and west. Without his lounge lizard persona in place I began to warm to him, he was pleasant and personable. Eventually Flick asked me to help her pack up her things. She closed the door to her room and turned to me with a wicked smile.

'To answer the question you're dying to ask, Jumbo is so called because he's lavishly deployed in the trouser department. So rumour has it anyway, I've never tested the theory myself.'

I let her enjoy the moment. 'And what about Fizz? What's her first name?'

'Don't know if she ever told us. Like me she reinvented herself but unlike me she abandoned her family, they weren't up to the standards she wished to acquire. I gather her father was handy with his belt on a Friday night after the pub.'

'Fizz talked about Sir Hugh's family but she said nothing about hers.' I said over my shoulder to Flick who was sitting at the dressing table and checking her lipstick.

'Fizz and I go back a long way. She was a professional dancer, a very good one. Lots of pretty girls who were in the demi-monde or like myself in the film industry made the most of their opportunities and made successful marriages to wealthy men in my day.'

'She was very interested in furniture.'

'That's because Jumbo has a successful antiques business. He's also an auctioneer with his own rooms. But she comes from a family who bought their furniture whereas the likes of Jumbo and Sir Hugh inherited theirs.'

I was reminded of Sam's comment. "I shall inherit just about every damn stick of furniture one day." It was a very different world to the one I'd grown up in.

Flick's baggage was quite light, in fact her make-up case weighed more. Henry very kindly took her things to the car for us and I lingered in the bathroom before looking for the way back to the garden room to find Flick and say our goodbyes. She was just inside the door in conversation with Jumbo and I heard his fruity tones as I walked silently down the thickly carpeted hall towards them.

'Nice looking gel Flick. Found her down in your neck of the woods eh? Is she one of Hugh's leavings on some pretty Cornish maid of the village?'

NINETEEN

Flick had said that she'd be delighted to have mum and dad stay and Megan didn't object to having one less thing to do.

'I love them both but the party arrangements and the work I've got to catch up on aren't giving me a moment spare.' She told me over the phone. 'If they'd rather stay with Lady Latchley that's fine by me. Will you be driving them over to us then?'

'Sam will. He's bringing the four of us.'

'Ooh-ooh. Wow get you. It's happened then?'

I confirmed that we were an item. Megan was pleased.

'I am so looking forward to seeing you both together. Do mum and dad know?'

'Yep. Likewise delighted. Apparently dad and Sam had quite a bonding moment hanging a field gate that day we were at the spa with Flick.'

Sam had been openly pleased to see me back. He'd been in Maggie's kitchen when we arrived and came out to help with Flick's bags and pretended to look the Jag over as Coco jumped around greeting us.

'No knocks, dents, dings or scratches then? Unbelievable.' He dodged as I made to punch his arm, deftly catching my wrist and pulling me to him, his hazel gold eyes dancing with fun. 'Welcome back Lucy Huccaby. I've missed you.' He kissed the tip of my nose.

I could see Maggie staring out at us. She waved and grinned. I was overwhelmed by my feelings, Sam wasn't keeping anything a secret so I hugged him hard.

'I've missed you. Shall we have nice times and treats tonight?' I whispered in his ear.

'Can't wait.'

The week flew by and I was carried along in a state of positive happiness. Flick and I were busy with the Trelerric Vintage arrangements now and had decided to stick with the name. The Tudor Hall and first floor gallery were being fitted out as display areas with mannequins for the clothes and secure display cases all lit by what looked like old film-set lights on tripods. Flick gave them her seal of approval.

'Sets the scene for the era quite perfectly. Your sister is a very clever girl Lucy.'

'Apparently it was a nightmare finding them Flick. Because the building is listed Megan couldn't have lighting installed any other way than via cables. It works though doesn't it.' I was really pleased with the way things were beginning to take shape.

Jane and I had the tummy flutters over it all though. 'What if nobody comes?' She had her head in her hands. 'It's very expensive making all these arrangements.'

Alice was surprisingly calm. 'We're hitting it with social media, national magazines have it in their June or July issues, there's going to be at least one good Sunday newspaper supplement, and there'll be a local television interview as well. Visit Cornwall have it on their website, it's on ours and it's in our new leaflets which have gone out to all the local hotels and so on.' She was ticking things off on her fingers. 'We just need to stay calm and focussed and work like slaves until the end of August.' She gave a short laugh. 'No problem, my children are perfectly behaved and never get ill and my husband never intended to take us away on holiday anyway.'

Jane looked anxious.

'I'm kidding mum. We knew it was going to be like this. Granny and Gramps Marquand are taking my little darlings over to Polzeath for a week to give me a break. And they've also volunteered themselves to help us out one day a week. And Jon is making noises about a night away in a posh hotel in Devon on our own. We'll be fine.'

'I just hope people buy tickets.' Jane said. 'Hopefully any shortfall will be filled by holiday people who can fill any vacancies.'

Jane was quite pleased that she was going to have a night off from Saturday supper that weekend because of Megan's party. 'I shall put my feet up while you party. We'll have Sunday lunch together instead. Your parents are invited of course Lucy.'

Mum and dad arrived on the Saturday afternoon and went straight outside for tea on the terrace with Flick. Sam had fixed a large sunshade for her because she didn't like too much sun, it was too ageing she complained. I unsuccessfully argued for the health benefits of twenty minutes sunshine so that she'd get her vitamin D.

'We don't all have skins which tan quickly like yours Lucy and anyway, I don't have skin, I have a complexion. And I don't want to end up looking like an old leather handbag.' Flick commented.

'Or an old shoe.' Mum added.

'Old boots more like.' Dad murmured, enjoying the expected uproar.

Naturally the topic of conversation was the Vintage summer event and mum was fascinated.

'I hope we can come and see it Lady Latchley.'

Flick had given up telling mum to stop calling her by the title. She had an idea though.

'Maybe you could come and stay a few days and help out. It's all hands on deck for about six weeks. Everyone's going to be exhausted.'

Finally I suggested we should be getting ready and we all went indoors. I'd shown Flick my new dress and red accessories earlier and she'd been impressed.

'Well it's a start. And don't forget to wear attractive underwear. A girl feels her best and ready for anything when dressed in her finest. Are you wearing stockings?'

I told her to mind her own business.

Sam thought I looked great. 'I like your moonlight look, but now the sun's getting a look in.' He'd taken my hand and was twirling me round slowly, looking me up and down appreciatively and I was basking in his admiration.

'That's very poetic.'

'I'm quoting more or less what your dad said once. He said you and Megan were his moonlight and sunlight when you were little girls.'

I stopped twirling. 'Dad said that? Really?' Well what a soft soaper.

Sam drove us the back way through Tavistock and up onto Dartmoor. We weren't the first to arrive and I was delighted not to have had anything to do with the cooking. I felt light hearted and carefree and absolutely determined to enjoy myself.

'Luce you are lit up from inside!' Megan said, laughing at me and giving me a kiss. 'You look like you've just had the honeymoon, not me.'

Mum went off to interrogate Megan's old school friends and the Fosters about what happened to Travis after the wedding and Mike took dad off to get some beer. Megan went to greet some more new arrivals. Sam and I were left looking at each other.

'I can barely keep my eyes off you,' he said, holding both my hands. 'You're beautiful and gorgeous and you're with me, which is the best bit.'

We went and investigated the party arrangements. There was enough food and drink for a siege. Dad joined us.

'Looks like enough for an all-nighter,' he said. 'Once upon a time the thought of staying up all night was a fabulous idea, now I'm an old git and it fills me with horror. Will you want us to get a taxi back when we're done?'

Sam shook his head. 'Farm duties call early in the morning I'm afraid, so I shall be conjuring the white mice and the homeward bound pumpkin for us all by midnight.'

Dad spotted mum talking to Anne and Tina and wandered over to be received with hugs.

'And you won't have to disappear leaving your glass slipper behind Cinders. You're with me now.' Sam pulled me close for a moment and kissed my nose. It was one of the special little things he did.

We were ready to enjoy ourselves. The whole thing was informal, Mike had said no speeches, just eat, drink, dance and be merry. The barn was hung with silver and white bunting and fairy lights and the music made your feet twitch. Sam surprised me by being a good dancer and I complimented him.

'Ah you've not even scratched the surface of my talents and abilities Lucy Huccaby. And all this on one glass of beer.'

We left the dance floor out of breath and went to find something non-alcoholic and thirst quenching. There was plenty of tonic water but Sam wanted a glass of plain water so we headed over to the house hand in hand, laughing about my dad's gyrations with a female music celebrity. A couple were just coming out of the house and walking in our direction, guided by the fairy lights and lanterns Megan's team of party planners had put out. We all stopped, facing each other.

'Helena, Matt,' I said. 'Good to see you both. Isn't it great not to be responsible for any of the work for a change? We can just relax and enjoy ourselves.'

Recalling how we'd all parted without even polite goodbyes after the wedding I wondered for a moment which way this meeting was going to go. For once Helena wasn't trying to impress and we were spared the neighing and head tossing. She moved closer to Matt and he put his arm possessively around her waist. She was looking good in a blue dress with a very low neck and a flared skirt. Unfortunately she was also wearing little fringed ankle boots which did nothing for the shape of her legs and made her feet look like pig's trotters.

'I don't think we're staying long,' he said, looking smug. 'We have a different agenda don't we darling.' He squeezed Helena who gave us a defiant smile but didn't speak.

'Well have a great evening, both of you. I'm gasping for some water. This woman is a diva on the dance floor and has exhausted me.' Sam said, and he firmly propelled me in the direction of the house. 'That went well,' he commented wryly once we got inside. 'Do we have an agenda for tonight Lucy?'

'Agenda?' I snorted. 'What kind of a stuffed shirt remark was that? And it's like Matt's got her on a tight rein. A martingale or something. Do you think he's been riding her over the jumps yet?'

Sam looked at me in astonishment and started laughing. 'I'd no idea you could be such a naughty girl.'

We all enjoyed ourselves. Mum was laughing in the car on the way back to Trelerric, she'd got some gossip from the girls and great photographs for her face-ache page.

'Fancy that, your daddy dancing with that famous singer. Michael knows some amazing people.' She'd taken to calling Mike by his full name, I think it was a sign of approval.

Sam drove us down to a junction on the A38 and we entered Cornwall over the Tamar Bridge, friendly lights reflecting a welcome on the great old river. I was reminded of my solitary journey at New Year, I'd had no idea that just five months later I'd be doing the trip again in a car full of people I loved. The thought jolted me in my seat. Sam briefly put his left hand on my thigh.

'Okay?'

I covered it with mine for second before he put his hand back on the wheel.

'Yes. Very okay.'

Back at Trelerric mum and dad went in while Sam held me close outside. He'd already told me that he and Tim were on early duties and that because mum and dad were here he'd stay over at Home Farm.

'So I'll see you for lunch lovely Lucy. And tomorrow afternoon and evening and all night are ours. I'm having thoughts about what sort of jumps I might need to put you over.'

Mum and dad joined me for sourdough toast and a poached Home Farm egg at breakfast.

'And who looks after Lady Latchley on a Sunday?'

'Flick sometimes visits Alice and the children on Sunday mornings, when she's not away seeing friends. She's here this weekend so she'll join us for lunch at Home Farm.' I'd explained the rituals and habits of life at Trelerric House several times but mum hadn't quite got her head around it. This morning she had something else on her mind, I could tell.

'So we've got the morning to ourselves then,' she said, finishing her egg. 'That's fortunate, I wanted you to myself because I have something for you.'

Something about the way mum looked at me, not quite her radar look, focussed my attention. As she reached into her handbag I knew with immediate foresight what she'd got.

'You've received a letter.'

'Yes. It came on Thursday. I didn't want to spoil Megan's party or have any kind of upset, so I've kept it until now. Daddy agreed.' She looked to dad for support and he obligingly nodded.

I took the letter from her, glad I was sitting down. The handwriting was large, well formed and sloping forwards, addressed to Lucy Huccaby at my parent's address, my old childhood home.

I had a distinct feeling that the writer had looked at the map, just as I had, and calculated the distance between us. But it wan't a distance of miles, it was a distance of a lifetime.

'You haven't opened it.' I said.

'The idea!' Mum looked shocked. 'It's addressed to you.'

I could hear my heart beating as I took a clean knife and slit the envelope open.

TWENTY

Unlike my typed letter, this one was handwritten.

Dear Lucy

I've started this letter several times and can't seem to find the words I need to express myself, so I've decided to keep it all short and simple. When I registered with the Adoption Contact Centre a year ago I felt as though I was lighting a single candle in the darkness.

Recently learning that you had also made an enquiry was the most wonderful and extraordinary thing and I'm not ashamed to say that I cried.

To receive a letter and a recent photograph from you lifted my spirits even further. Better still was reading that you had a very happy childhood and have a loving and caring family.

I stopped reading and looked at mum and dad, unable to speak. I'd worded my own letter carefully, deliberately giving nothing away about my private life; she would have no idea as to whether I was married or had children of my own. She didn't even know where I really lived. I wondered if I'd been over-cautious and somehow mean by withholding information.

'What's she saying?' dad asked.

I shook my head and looked back at the letter.

I'm really hoping that you would like to meet me. I've enclosed my personal mobile number and my email, but I'm willing to meet you at your choice of place or venue wherever that may be. I'm self-employed and able to travel to wherever you live if that's preferable to your circumstances.

Thank you so much for writing and for sending me a photograph. I didn't know if we would ever find each other and this moment is so precious. To see me all you need to do is look at my website, I own and run a florist in Great Malvern ...

She hoped we could meet before too long.

The letter finished with a signature written with a flourish. *Jenny Blythe.*

I handed it to mum and dad and went and fired up the computer. The florist was called Gillyflowers. The first picture on the website was of a woman sitting sideways on a black chair with her legs elegantly crossed. She was surrounded by posh buckets of long stemmed pale pink and white roses, architectural lilies and white carnations. They'd been placed on stands and trestles in a way that framed her. She was holding a couple of carnations in one hand, her arm resting on her crossed thigh. It was captioned "Welcome to Gillyflowers, Florist for all Occasions" and there was a menu of options. The camera had caught her face three-quarters on in an expression of pleasure, as though she had just turned her head to see a dear friend.

I sat and stared at her face. Her hair was in a light brown shoulder length bob and looked expensively streaked with blonde highlights. She didn't have my colouring but the shape of our faces and noses were similar. My lips were fuller. She was dressed in cream, wearing a simple plain top and trousers with high heeled navy shoes sporting a pink heel. A short pink and navy scarf was knotted around her neck.

'Is that her Lucy?' mum's voice spoke softly at my shoulder.

I nodded.

'And she's a florist then. I'll bet she doesn't wear those shoes if she's on her feet all day.'

I clicked on the menu options, choosing the one titled "About Gillyflowers".

'Named after her dead twin sister Gillian. She's suffered loss then the poor woman.' Mum was reading out loud for dad's benefit.

Jennifer was holding two carnations because they were the same family as clove pinks, once known as gillyflowers. I enjoyed the play on words with her late twin's name but I still didn't know what to say or what to feel. This was the woman who, for unknown reasons, had given up on me. She looked happy and as though she'd got a good life. But what did I expect, a woman dressed in sackcloth and ashes and with an expression of sorrow and penitence? I clicked back to the photograph. She was wearing a wedding ring and pale pink nail polish. I wondered what Mr Blythe did for a living.

'Well, there you have it.' I spoke flatly, finally finding my voice. 'That's the person who apparently gave birth to me twenty-eight years ago. That makes her around her mid to late forties I suppose.'

'She wrote you a nice letter Lucy.' Dad put his hand on my shoulder.

'And she'd like to meet you.' Mum whispered and burst into tears.

There was commotion and I was immediately contrite. I felt as though I'd done something awful and we all ended up in a group hug. Dad went and put the kettle on and made more tea and mum and I sat back down together at the kitchen table. It was cozy and more intimate in the kitchen. Mum dried her tears on paper kitchen towel.

'I'm happy for her Lucy. Really I am. She's thrilled that you made contact. Don't make any judgements until you know her story.'

'You think I have to see this through then?' I asked them both, already knowing the answer.

Dad looked at me sympathetically but when he spoke he sounded quite stern. I realised he was having to control his own emotions. 'You've started something Lucy. The consequences could bring you great joy. The reverse could also be true. But there's a lady full of precious hope waiting to hear from you. If you want us there at your side ...'

I shook my head. 'Dad, mum, that's lovely. I'll have to think hard about what's best. At the moment I'm not sure.' I stopped speaking, being fully on the end of mum's radar look. She knew that I'd already thought things through so I sat forward and put my hands flat on the table. 'Okay. This is how I see it. She knows by now that you live about thirty or so miles away from her own address. She'd like to meet me. I think it should be on neutral ground. Shall I suggest meeting at Hereford Cathedral? That way I could stay up here with you and tell you everything that happened on the day it happens.'

'We can support you, and each other that way.' Dad said, nodding at mum. 'We don't want you to go through this alone.'

Dad loaded up their car and drove the three of us up to Home Farm. It was a relief to be surrounded by the family, mum was immediately enchanted by Grace and little Tom, but it was dad who Thomas took to. Dad got down on the floor and started talking engineering as he explained what Tom's toy crane and toy digger could do.

'They're really seeing eye to eye in all senses of the word.' Jonathan was charmed. 'I'm seeing something in my son which I'd not appreciated before. He's asking questions and stringing sentences together. Do we have any engineers in the family Alice?'

'Not in the Latchley Chronicle, what about your family mum?'

'I think I had an uncle in the Royal Engineers or something.' Jane said vaguely. 'Didn't they just blow things up though?'

'It's a bit more complicated than that Jane. I could tell you all about it if you like.' Dad said, smiling up at her. Military history was one of his hobbies.

'Please don't. My head is already full of useless facts.'

I could hear noises in the hallway and Tim and Sam came in. Sam was fresh from the shower, I could always tell because he left his hair damp. Grace was in his arms with her face pressed against his shoulder.

'Look at this. The prettiest and best behaved little girl on the Trelerric lands came to meet her Uncle Sam.'

They made such a picture that I felt my heart ping and I immediately saw images in my mind of Sam as a father. Mum was looking at me knowingly and I pulled a face at her. She giggled. Then Sam came over to me, still carrying Grace and kissed me on the cheek, an action which made me blush while everyone behaved as though what he done was perfectly normal and usual in the circumstances. Putting Grace down he greeted my parents and made small talk while I bathed in the pleasure of watching him. Flick of course had observed everything with enormous enjoyment. I realised I was looking forward to telling her about my letter.

Lunch wasn't a prolonged event and after waving mum and dad off Flick decided she felt fit enough to actually walk back to Trelerric House. Sam made noises of amazement and pretended to go weak at the knees.

'You sure I can't give you a lift on the quad bike?'

'It's not a form of transport used by a lady as well you know. Any more than baked beans can be considered a sensible vegetable at the breakfast table.' She said inconsequently. 'But if you wouldn't mind walking with me, both of you, I'd appreciate it. After that I won't take up any more of your time alone together.'

Flick linked arms with us and chatted about Trelerric Vintage. Plans were all well in hand and she was looking forward to the publicity. All her friends would be coming of course, the whole circus troupe and menagerie including several I'd never met. She missed her house party days.

After we'd seen her indoors I turned to Sam. 'So then you heart-breaker. Grace is the prettiest and best behaved little girl on the Trelerric lands is she?' I pretended to look cross.

'Oh mirror mirror on the wall, who is the fairest of them all?' Sam took my hand and started twirling me round across the black and white hall, the one where the wedding buffet had been set up.

There was a kind of time shift in my head, all the balls and parties this place had ever hosted seemed to echo from a distance and for a moment I saw candlelight reflecting softly on jewels and soft skin. There was the secret murmur of voices making assignations, the movement of a fan and sounds of laughter. Sam deftly stopped twirling me in our private dance and caught me round the waist with his other arm, bending me backwards for a kiss. He really was a good dancer.

'Did you feel that?' I looked up at Sam.

'What, the earth moved already then? I'm such a mover and a kisser you lucky girl.'

'No, I mean candlelight and distant party noises. I got goosebumps.' I rubbed my arms.

Sam wasn't surprised. 'I didn't, not this time. But sometimes when I'm prowling about I feel as though another life is going on in the place, just behind a veil, or a few rooms away. We haven't got wailing banshees or things that go bump in the night, no walled up pregnant housemaids either that we know of, but sometimes there are, how can I describe it, impressions of activity, odours even.'

'Odours? What sort of odours?'

'Well there's a scent mum describes as being like of attar of roses on the private stairs up to the old Tudor chamber, the one where generations of Latchley man slept with their wives. And a distinct pong of male sweat in the corner of the Tudor kitchen, near the old fireplace.'

'You're joking!'

'Not joking. This is where I grew up and played and explored. I had no preconceptions. I just accepted what I felt or saw. There was nothing weird or scary. You get weird pongs in places, a dead rodent or rot or damp can do funny things. But Trelerric's a happy place, it shares itself with people who can access the right wavelength. It's why I could understand Simon when he was explaining how the stones felt in the Japanese garden.

Atmosphere builds up in certain places and our animal senses can detect them. I've seen the dogs react sometimes.'

I was fascinated. 'Are those smells always there?'

Sam shook his head. 'Nope. They get you when you least expect it. Come on, I'll walk you through the ancestral pile. I like to do regular checks anyway. And I'll show you my secret doorway, or two of them. I'm sure there must be more into other Trelerric dimensions, probably through the back of a wardrobe.'

Sam took my hand and walked us straight towards the panelling behind the sweeping staircase, the one I'd gone up looking for Coco all those weeks ago. There was a door concealed there, I never would have noticed it.

'Do we need a torch? Will we be able to see?' I teased him.

The side of his face was illuminated as he reached in and clicked a switch. His obvious pleasure in the private joke between us made my tummy flip.

'Come on down the rabbit hole.'

I followed Sam into a narrow corridor, one side was stone, the other side rough plaster. I could feel a cold draught around my ankles.

'The stone side is original, it was an outdoor wall once. The other is where they built what we call the Georgian part onto the building. Some clever sod had the idea of making a service passage, the servants could slip in and out of the rooms and deliver or remove things without disturbing the family or their guests.'

'Anything from chamber pots behind screens to firewood or coal.' I said, having done my homework on the book Flick had lent me.

'And the rest. You've heard of backstairs I suppose. There's a narrow staircase down at the end which emerges opposite Robin's old room. Great for smuggling up a willing wench for a restoration romp.' Sam raised his eyebrows in a suggestive manner but I was having none of it.

'Restoration England was post-Cromwell. You're a century or more out if it's Georgian.' I told him.

We didn't go upstairs, instead Sam lead me halfway along the passage to another door and opened it. This was a real door, not disguised in any way and made from sturdy timber planks, braced nailed and latched, discoloured with age and worn smooth on the side by decades of handling.

'Oak. As old as the original house I guess.' Sam touched it affectionately.

We were now standing in the buttery at the side of the Great Hall. The slate floor was well worn under my feet and a large heavy plank and board constructed working table still stood in there, scored and marked with years of use. There was a similar low bench to one side. I wondered if these floors had been strewn with rushes and herbs to keep them sweet when they were in use. I was already becoming familiar with the Great Hall and the long gallery upstairs so Sam took me down a couple of steps into a small set of rooms behind the hall. He referred to them as chambers.

'It's not known exactly when these chambers were constructed, they have fireplaces though and that's when the Tudor building spree really took off. There's the private access here into a room which connects the chapel that you already know about, heavily locked of course.' Sam paused to admire the combination of modern locks, bolts and an old wooden bar slotted through metal frames which had in turn been fitted into the granite wall in earlier times.

A small stone fireplace was still fitted with a fire grate. 'Must have been much cosier in here on a winter night. And through here in the small chamber next to this is where I reckon they kept the Latchley Book and the Chronicle. I've always had the feeling they did the accounts and the estate records here and used it like an office or a study. It's south facing and on the other side of this interior wall, about sixty centimetres through the stone is the kitchen fireplace so it must have been warm by the standards of the day.'

I followed him through an old doorway, noticing initials and dates carved or scratched in the door, possibly made by generations of small Latchley boys. Vandalism which was now precious evidence of lives and times past. There were little leaded windows quite high up and the claustrophobic feeling of enclosure which I hated. Sam didn't notice, he was opening a sizeable built in cupboard at the side of the fireplace which backed onto the one in the first room.

'To the casual observer this was used for storage,' Sam said. 'There are old hooks to hang things on. But look here.' He was pointing upwards into the cupboard.

I looked but couldn't see anything. 'What am I looking at?'

'There's a small trapdoor hidden in the ceiling part of the cupboard.'

'Is that a priest-hole?' I asked.

'Reckon so. Fairly warm too. I could get into it when I was thirteen, you need a ladder, now I can only get my head though. But it gets better, look here, the side panel of the cupboard opens as well.'

The whole construction was something that a magician would have been proud of. The side of the cupboard folded outwards on oiled hinges and revealed a tiny space, just large enough for a modern door mat. A solid windowless low door was beyond that which Sam unlocked. I noticed he used a modern key on his own keyring and the door opened outwards soundlessly onto a small path. Outside all I could see was vegetation, the entrance was concealed by metal railings against which grew high neatly clipped evergreens. I was enchanted, a secret door into a secret world.

Sam had to stoop to go outside and so did I. There were old granite cobbles set underfoot and the tiny narrow path, protected by the railings, connected with a little cobbled area at the rear of the chapel. I'd walked by with Coco many times and never really noticed it, probably because there was nothing to excite or draw the eye. Sam kept a couple of wheelbarrows there, casually placed to deter explorers.

'I'm the keeper of the key.' Sam said, his eyes glittering with amusement. 'It's my private way to raiding Maggie's kitchen or to sneak up on naughty girls.'

'Snoopers you mean.' I smiled.

We went back indoors and Sam closed everything up. Trelerric seemed satisfied at sharing its secrets and the place was calm. Later we ended up going over to the Coach House. Once indoors Sam tripped me onto the bean bag and dropped astride me. Taking hold of my wrists he raised my arms up over my head and held me down.

'Now let's see who is the best behaved girl on the Trelerric lands.'

TWENTY ONE

We were sitting in Flick's day room and I had my family research folder open on the coffee table. Flick read the letter from Jennifer with interest. 'And you're going to meet her.' It wasn't a question.

'I've got to make contact with her and make some arrangements. I need to find a date or two to suggest and I'm thinking of meeting her outside Hereford Cathedral. Significant moments of my life seem to happen on or around the green. There's a good cafe we can use, and some decent pubs very close by if alcohol is required.'

'And what's this?' With an elegant finger Flick was touching the small birth certificate mum had sent down to me.

I explained what it was and she picked it up.

'Lucy Wingfield. A pretty name. And Mark and Moira kept your name. So am I right in thinking your mother was Jennifer Wingfield?' Flick's voice was light and neutral. She was looking at me over her reading glasses, her silver eyes keen and bright.

'Guess so.' I replied.

'Well I'm pleased. And it will be good to get a few answers to a few questions.' Flick was lost in thought.

'Penny for them Flick?' I said.

'Oh, just some regrets. Perhaps I should have looked into my own beginnings, not that I believe there was anything to learn. All I know is that I was a bastard. A beautiful bastard though, and once upon a time I was curious about where my looks and talents came from.'

'Is there no way of finding out?'

'Oh I can't be bothered now Lucy, and the orphan girl I once was no longer exists. I'm fortunate in that I've had a fulfilling life. But I am very interested to know what your Mrs Blythe will have to say about herself. Now, because I'm feeling so well these days I've decided to accept an invitation to stay up in London for a few days next week with Sir Hugh, so I suggest you make your plans to meet Mrs Blythe at once. Are you going to telephone her or use your email?'

I opted for email and carefully typed my suggestion that we might meet in Hereford one lunchtime, saying Thursday or Sunday were good days. I provided the dates and said I preferred the Thursday and sat with my fingers hovering over the keyboard. The message was brief and businesslike. Finally I clicked Send.

When I checked my emails later, after walking Coco, there was a reply. Jennifer had replied to say that she was thrilled and delighted. Thursday it was then.

That evening I told Sam who looked a bit down when I said I would be going back up to Herefordshire to see my parents next week.

'What, again? So soon? They aren't ill or anything are they?'

'Well you see yours all the time.' I sounded a bit sharp, but I was agonising over telling him the truth.

'Yeah but we all live here and work together. I don't have any choice, I'm nearly thirty and I still live at home. But, okay. There's no reason why I should get the grumps except that I like knowing you're here. I love it when I see you walking in the garden or out and about on the Trelerric lands, especially when I'm not expecting to see you. Life's very good with Lucy in it.'

I looked at him, he was so honest and straightforward and I felt deceitful and unkind. My eyes filled with tears.

'Hey, crap, what did I say?' Sam looked bewildered.

'You said something very sweet and it caught me by surprise. That's all.'

Sam took me in his arms. We were up in the Coach House again in our private little retreat.

'I've never pried into your private life Lucy. If you want to tell me about what happened between you and your previous fella then I'm happy to listen. I know you were badly hurt. Can I just ask one thing, are you going up there to resolve things with him? I need to know.'

My relief was huge. 'No, absolutely not. That all ended ages ago, eighteen months ago.' I paused, remembering a snippet of gossip that mum had told me. 'And Peter and Emma, my ex fiancé and my one time business partner and best friend have got married now. Mum knows because Emma's parents still live in the same village. Emma and I were school friends.' Funny how Emma and I had always sworn we would be at each other's weddings since we were schoolgirls together. Well, that would never happen now.

I was grateful to Flick for keeping me fully occupied with her routines and requirements. In spare moments Maggie and I cooked, cleaned and organised things between us. We were a good team. Megan came over to supervise an interview Flick had to give and afterwards we went to my rooms. She surprised me by saying that she intended being at mum and dad's when my meeting with Jennifer Blythe took place.

'I'll keep them occupied and be there for you when you get back.' She told me firmly.

'Sam's not too chuffed that I'm going to be away again.'

'Treat 'em mean and keep 'em keen.' Megan said lightly. 'Does he know why you're going?'

'No. But now I can say you're going up as well, it might make him feel better if he thinks it's just a family gathering. And I'll probably come back here on Friday.'

I didn't have to tell Sam, he saw me waving Megan off as he came down the drive from the Coach House.

'See you Wednesday night.' She made a point of calling out as she waved through the car window, and seeing Sam she blew him a kiss before driving off.

I smiled, 'That's nice, Megan's coming up as well.'

'Great. Shall we go to the cinema this evening and behave like normal people, or do you need ravishing right now?'

I wasn't in ravishing mode. 'Cinema would be good.'

'Whatever takes madam's fancy. Fish and chips or pizza?'

'God, you Latchley men know how to treat a girl.'

Before I left he'd lounged on the bed watching me pack my overnight case; jeans, tops, underwear.

'Nothing fancy to wear out?'

'We're not going out. It's just family time. I'll text you when I get there.'

He'd cuddled me before I left. 'Have a nice time lovely Lucy. My best to your folks.'

As I drove away I checked my rear view mirror and saw him waving. I wondered what it would be like to take him home with me. It strengthened my resolve to get this mystery about my past resolved so that I could tell him all about me. But first I needed to find out just who I was.

This time I woke up before the dream took hold. There was still that sense of desolation but I hadn't been crying. Switching the bedside lamp on I cursed. It wasn't even dawn yet and I'd had difficulty getting to sleep. I crept downstairs, my feet remembering the number of steps and the twist at the bottom of the staircase from my childhood days. Mum still left a nightlight plugged in by the telephone so it was easy to see my way into the kitchen. I closed the door softly and put the kettle on to boil.

'You can't sleep either?' Dad said quietly as he let himself in.

'I'd got off in the small hours, then I started with the dream so I woke up. Slept about two hours I think.' I lifted another mug down for him.

'Have you thought about what you'll say to Mrs Blythe?' Dad asked. By some unspoken agreement we'd not discussed my reason for being there the previous evening.

'Not in specific words.' I sat down at the kitchen table with him. 'I suppose it all boils down to something like "who?" and "how?" and "why?" and finishes with "and what happened next?"

I took a sip of the calming herbal concoction I'd selected from the cupboard. It wasn't very satisfying. Dad had sensibly opted for a glass of milk.

'Well maid, it's not a crisis, it's an occasion. And whatever happens it's something a close family can deal with. Sweet of Megan to say she'll be here this afternoon. That's good for Moira.'

'And what's good for Moira?' Mum said. I hadn't heard the door open. She gave us her radar look, it looked even more scary than usual when combined with tousled hair.

I decided to take my drink back up to bed and we all retired for what was left of the night. I doubt any of us got much sleep and later, at breakfast, I could only manage half a slice of toast and honey. That of course reminded me of Sam so I told mum and dad about the little jar he'd left outside my room that night.

'Apple Blossom Honey. It's pale gold and fragrant. Sam puts the bees in the apple orchard in Spring and the first lot of honey is taken from their time with the apple blossom. They keep it for family use only, it's rare and special. And he writes a fancy label in a medieval looking black script, with proper ink. He taught himself after learning to read the Latchley family books.'

'He's a gifted young man Lucy.' Mum said.

'He's very special.' I replied.

I dressed in my usual black and white but added Flick's colourful scarf and wore it the way she'd shown me. That scarf was becoming a talisman of good luck. Mum hugged me and dad hugged us both.

'Good luck Lucy'. Mum whispered.

On the familiar roads into Hereford I felt oddly numb. It was the same feeling you get when you're going to the dentist for some invasive work. Parking the Mini was easy and I checked my watch. After paying to park for the day I was half an hour early for the meeting so I strolled casually through High Town and up Church Street. I'd always loved the paved narrow shopping lane and dawdled a little, killing time before the appointed hour. A new craft shop had opened so I popped inside to see what the clever locals were making. Walking past a jewellery display case my eye was caught by a set of cufflinks in the shape of lightbulbs.

'Good aren't they. He's new, we've not shown his work before. They're enamelled silver. Want a closer look?' The shop assistant had noticed my interest.

'Please.'

She got them out and I examined them closely, there was even a little filament in the bulb. I smiled, thinking of Sam. I'd no idea if he wore cufflinks but the private joke between us was clear and his birthday was in July.

'I'll take them please.'

Back outside I couldn't help looking at people's faces as I walked, were they just going about their daily routines or were they on their way to a meeting which could be life changing. News can change a life in an instant and we're rarely prepared when it happens. Would I be the same person in a few hours time, or a new, different person?

Ahead of me the Cathedral green enfolded the beautiful building. A city guide was standing with a group of people and giving some animated spiel about history and Nell Gwynne's connection with the city. His group were smiling, hanging on his words, enjoying their day. I stopped and looked across the green. There was a woman sitting on a bench and she looked a little bit familiar. My heart started banging around as though my chest cavity was an empty drum and my legs felt weak. I started walking.

All I could hear was the sound of my own breathing. As I drew closer the woman's attention focussed on me and she half rose from the seat.

'Is it you? Lucy?' She said.

Calmer than I felt I held out my hand and she grabbed it and held it hard. We both plonked rather than sat on the bench. My legs wouldn't have held me up for much longer anyway. I stared at her, she was a bit shorter than me even in her heels, and much fairer.

'Lucy.' she said again, not letting go of my hand, her expression anxious and serious. 'They didn't change your name. You're beautiful. My god you look like my twin sister.' And her face split with emotion and what I thought for a moment was grief, and she started crying.

Dad had slipped me a couple of packets of tissues before I left. 'Just in case, if my experience of living with you women is anything to go by.'

I reached into my bag but Jennifer was already fishing in hers and had also come prepared.

'I'm so sorry,' she said, sniffing. 'Forgive me. I didn't know what to expect. I'll pull myself together and be British in a minute. I'm a Wingfield after all.'

'I thought your name was Blythe now.' The first sentence I'd said to my real mother.

'Yes, my husband is Miles Blythe. I'm making a silly joke.'

We looked at each other again, searching for something. The website photograph hadn't misled me, I certainly resembled her in face shape and features if not in colouring. Questions were building in my mind but common sense and courtesy were important.

'Should we go to the pub or would you prefer the cafe here?' I asked.

'Oh I need tea. Life giving tea. And some sugar, I couldn't eat breakfast this morning.'

I smiled at her. 'I know the feeling. I couldn't sleep last night.'

'Me neither. I must look a wreck.'

She actually looked pretty good although her mascara had smudged slightly.

'Well let's go into the Cathedral cafe then. Get tea and buns. Very British.' I sounded hearty and jolly hockey stick and not like me at all. My mind flashed to Helena describing me dismissively as "very girl guide". And then Sam, saying he liked the way that I knew about things. I realised that my mind bee was buzzing around in my skull furiously. I was unsettled but I wasn't nervous. 'Come on then, in this door and through here. It's nice.' I couldn't say Jennifer's name and I didn't call her Mrs Blythe. I hadn't a clue what the protocol was for meeting your mother for the first time.

Jennifer insisted on paying. 'I've never given you anything. Let me at least start with this.' She said, making a feeble attempt at a joke.

The words formed in my head, "you gave me life, that's gift enough". But I said nothing as we went about the safe ritual of asking for tea and selecting a pastry and choosing a table in a far corner away from prying ears.

TWENTY TWO

'So where do we start?' I asked Jennifer. 'I'm Lucy, I'm twenty-nine in October. But you already know that.' As I spoke I thought I sounded hard. 'Sorry, I'm accustomed to dealing with straight facts, I was a nurse for a time. I'm not being bitchy.'

Jennifer's eyes hadn't left my face. 'Actually I was thinking you sounded like a Wingfield. They were a plain speaking bunch.'

Her second and not very complementary reference to the Wingfield's I noticed.

'Your family.' I said. 'I've so much to learn, so much to ask. And of course there's the point about who my father was if we can go that far today. If you can bear it. So do we start with my story or with yours, which is also mine if you see what I mean.'

'Tell me about yours Lucy. You're beautiful and you look, ...' Jennifer searched for the word she wanted. 'You look good, happy, successful.'

I saw her glance at my hand. She could see that I wasn't married.

'Yes, I'm happy and ...' Was I going to say, successful? What did that mean exactly? 'I actually live and work in Cornwall. I'm up here staying at my parents' house, with my sister Megan. She lives in Devon. She got married last month.' I stopped speaking and took a mouthful of tea. It was too hot and my eyes watered.

Jennifer was looking at me sympathetically. 'This is hard isn't it. I realise that I want to be your friend, but friendship is something which is based on trust. How can you trust me when I gave you away?'

I was surprised by her honesty. 'So, why did you?' I ventured and she winced. 'My parents told me that you were very young.' I added in an attempt to soften my words.

'Yes. I was pregnant at fifteen, under age obviously, though only just. I had you when I was sixteen. Legally still a minor, under the rule and thumb of my parents and my father's family. The Wingfield's. They weren't best pleased I can tell you. The decision was made that I couldn't keep you because you would ruin my life. Ruin theirs more like.'

'That must have been tough.'

'They were tough people. Not brutal or deliberately unkind, it's just the way they'd been brought up to think. The integrity of the family name was important to them and that meant no family member could step out of line. I actually had a privileged upbringing and with a lot of material comfort.' She paused, remembering something. 'But breeding outside the accepted time was frowned upon. An unplanned pregnancy without provenance of the sire just wasn't the done thing, not just inconvenient but absolutely bloody unacceptable.'

'What?' I spluttered. 'What on earth are you saying?' Her choice of words shocked me.

'I'm more or less quoting my great aunt. She was the family matriarch and my father looked up to her and admired her strong moral standards. I thought she was a cold hearted opinionated bitch. I think father hoped to inherit lots of nice things really so he made a lot of time for her in his life. My mother was a sweet hearted lightweight, the original beautiful little fool and did whatever she was told. But then she never really got over losing my twin, Gillian. Neither have I really.'

I remembered mum saying that this woman had suffered loss and for the first time I felt sympathy. Reaching out I put a hand over hers and squeezed it. Jennifer looked startled and then grateful.

'I'm so sorry. Tell me about you. Tell me your story Jennifer.'

Jennifer told me about growing up in a lovely house near Pershore in Worcestershire. She and Gillian had belonged to the pony club and done all the nice things girls of her class did. Dancing and ballet, tennis and swimming, private school and prosperity. Gillian, I learned, was the older twin. They weren't identical but Gillian had been dominant and daring, she got the breast while Jennifer got the bottle; Gillian was the swan whilst

Jennifer had been the duck but Jennifer had adored her. When they were ten there'd been a hot summer and Gillian had decided they should swim in the lake because there was no-one available to take them to the local swimming baths. Rather than splash about from the jetty with Jennifer, Gillian had taken their father's rowing boat out and had jumped into the centre of the lake. She'd got into difficulties and drowned.

'Looking back no-one seemed to care or realise that I witnessed the whole damn thing and that I was in grief too. She was my twin and we did everything together. That was my heart being stopped. I wasn't blamed for her death but it altered everything. My mother was devastated, understandably. I was sent to a boarding school as planned but alone, without my sister, and mum and dad went off travelling without me. Our relationship was never the same, there was distance between us. I was rubbish at school, apart from sports, and the only really pleasant thing I ever shared with my parents after that was the annual half term ski-ing trip.'

Jennifer paused and absently tore her Danish pastry into small pieces. Our tea had gone cold so I decanted the remains of the pot into our cups to warm it up.

'We always went to the same place, near Villars in Switzerland. It's very pretty and you can see Mont Blanc. When I was fifteen some friends of my parents came out with us, I didn't care for them much and anyway I'd got friendly with some kids my own age and we used to go out during the evening. A couple of the ski instructors always joined us. They were just boys really although they seemed so sophisticated and grown up. There was one I liked, he was about eighteen I think but a marvellous skier, they grow up wearing skis over there. He'd spent quite some time with me on the slopes over the days and had been coaching me. I wasn't a beginner so we were often away from the others.'

I sat very still, watching the distant memories on her face.

'I was pretty. He was sexy and good looking. You've got his eyes.' She stopped speaking and looked at me wistfully. 'They have such lovely accents when they speak English. On our last night we all drank some ghastly spirit they have. Someone had brought a whole bottle and we passed it round and fooled about. He started kissing me, it wasn't our first kiss. I liked kissing him, he made me feel funny inside and that night I was more than squiffy. We ended up in an unlocked linen room. It was my first time. Three months later I noticed I was getting fat.'

She stared across the table at me, her eyes full of misery.

'I didn't realise what was happening. I didn't know you could get pregnant your first time.'

'What was his name.' I asked, my voice barely audible.

'Yann-Luca, it's like Ian Luke. I never knew his surname or even where he lived.' She looked slightly ashamed.

'Did you or your parents ever try to find him?'

Jennifer shook her head. 'My father was incandescent with rage. He said there was no point, he didn't want a penniless ski instructor in the family and he suggested that I probably couldn't be sure who the father was since I'd been drinking. He asked me if I'd slept with the waiters as well. He wasn't very nice to me.'

'He sounds a complete bastard.' I said. 'Do you still see much of your parents?'

'Dad passed on a few years ago. When he died I began thinking about how cold he'd been with me and I started thinking about you. I realised I wanted to find out what had happened to you. Mum's still alive, she's in her late sixties and pretty fit. She lives in Portugal with her second husband.'

I drank my tea and went and bought us a second pot. Back at the table Jennifer had eaten her bits of Danish pastry. She was lost in thought and I waited for a while before resuming the conversation.

'What happened next?'

'What? Oh, let's see. You were conceived in February ...'

'In a linen closet.' I smiled, making light of the fact.

'Yes, sorry about that. It was May when I began to realise that things weren't right. I'd been anxious about the end of term exams and thought they were screwing up my system. But the exams came and went and my periods didn't appear. I failed everything except art and biology. They'd taught us lots about plants and frogs but sweet nothing about human biology. Once the pregnancy was confirmed I was kept in seclusion at home and then dad shipped me off to a clinic in London, out of the way and very discrete. I had you in October.'

'How did you feel?' I asked her.

'Poorly. Things didn't go well so you were born by caesarian and I was out cold. I never saw you because it was agreed that you were going straight for adoption. I wasn't allowed a say in the matter. My father said he knew what was best for me and for my future. But I told the nurses that if you were a boy your name should be Ian or Luke. If you were a girl you should be called Lucy. The nurses smiled and I thought they were humouring me. But you got your name and I'm so grateful to your parents for keeping it.'

The expression on Jennifer's face made my heart turn over with sympathy.

'And what then? How did you feel after all that?'

'Horrible. I didn't understand my body and I think I had to take tablets to stop the milk. I felt ill with sorrow and I suppose my hormones were crashing about all over the place. Looking back I think I must have suffered post natal depression for quite a while. I used to go to sleep crying and wake up crying. I cried a river.'

That last expression was so like something my mum would have said that I was jolted by surprise.

'It must have been hell for you.'

'It wasn't a picnic, I'd known from pretty early on that I, or rather my family, weren't keeping you. But the sense of loss was terrible. And I was pretty much told to pull myself together and get on with life.'

Jennifer went off to the ladies and I sat there in the cafe letting all the information sink in. Those anguished descriptions of sorrow and loss meant something to me. Perhaps there was some weird sort of connection between us and I still felt it in my recurring dream. She returned looking fresher and brighter, with her lipstick re-applied and the mascara smudge removed.

'I've dumped a lot on you Lucy. But I guess there's no protocol for these things is there. And now with all the emotion of it I'm starving, do you fancy a sandwich?'

The cafe was doing well out of us and the sandwiches were fresh and tasty.

'And you Lucy, you said in your letter that you'd had a happy childhood. I'm so glad. Did you ever go ski-ing?'

'No, I don't suppose we could afford things like that.'

'Miles and I go every year, but not to Villars. He prefers the Bavarian mountains. He went to an international school out there because his father worked in Munich for several years. We like cross-country ski-ing, it's very different. I told him about you when we fell in love. He knows everything.'

She was chatting a bit nervously I thought, so I talked about mum and dad and told her about Megan and the Fosters and summer holidays in Cornwall. Then I told her about nursing and the celebration cake business and the awful year I'd had.

'And now I'm working in Cornwall, living about twenty miles away from my sister. I look after an elderly lady, but it's more complicated than that.'

'But are you happy?'

I smiled at her. 'Yes, very happy.'

I was wondering how much more to share with her whilst noticing it was getting late. At that point my mobile pinged and a moment later so did hers. We checked our phones. Megan said she'd arrived and hoped I was okay. Jennifer looked up at me.

'The business. We've a huge order to deal with, a massive wedding in two days time and two funerals to service. And my husband is wondering how I am, bless him.'

'Shall we call it a day then? I'm shattered after not sleeping much last night.' I suggested. By mutual agreement we got up and walked back outside. It was strange to see people still going about their ordinary business when our worlds had turned at a different pace.

'Lucy,' Jennifer said. 'It's been amazing meeting you and learning about you. If I'd just met you for the first time without knowing that we were related,' she paused and then continued delicately, 'I get the impression that you're someone I'd very much like to know. To become friends with.'

It was nicely said and I looked down into her face, noticing that her eyes were pale blue and thinking that Flick would have approved of the skill with which she'd applied her makeup.

'Thank you Jennifer. I'm a bit stunned by it all, but thank you for telling me all those things. I need a few days to get my head round some of it, but yes, I think we'll have to have another get together.'

We kissed each other awkwardly on one cheek.

'Let's not leave it twenty nine years.' She said.

Mum had clearly been doing a lot of cleaning and polishing to keep herself occupied while I was out. Dad had also been busy, there were stripes on the lawn and you could have cut yourself on the edges. Neither of them were in. Megan was at the kitchen table, her laptop open as she'd been working. I sat down opposite her.

'Where's mum and dad?' I asked, unwinding Flick's scarf. I stretched and yawned hard. 'God, am I bushed.'

'Dad's taken mum for a walk round the block to cool off. She'd got up quite a head of steam and I think I saw it coming out of her ears. How'd it go then?'

'Okay. She's - Jennifer, is okay. It was rough on her.'

'On you too. You look done in.' Megan got up. 'Tea?'

'Shit no, I've had enough for one day. Something stronger, lots stronger.'

Megan was pouring us both a glass of wine when we heard the front door. Mum appeared looking a bit wild, dad close behind her.

'Lucy? Your car's outside.'

I stood up and gave her a cuddle. 'It's alright mum. That's because I'm here, inside. You can pinch me if you like, I'm real and everything's okay.' I smiled at dad over her shoulder. It was going to take a while telling them Jennifer's story. Even though mum had a kitchen full of food dad was once again dispatched to get us all fish and chips.

There's something comforting about fish and chips to the British. It's the ultimate feel good food. You want it the day you move house or the moment you arrive at the seaside. It's the thing you turn to when nothing else feels right. Mum even allowed dad to have tomato ketchup, a product not usually seen on the table in our home. She and Flick definitely had a view about processed tomato products, not a view I shared.

'So she felt wanted and approved of when she went with this fella then.' Mum was summing up the story. 'Probably for the first time in her life since she'd lost her twin. What a time she had of it. The poor lamb.' Her eyes were full of compassion.

Megan was fascinated by the news of my father. 'So you're half Swiss, or Italian, or French? And it was a holiday romance.'

'Barely even a romance.' I said. 'They hardly knew each other, and she never knew his family name or exactly where he came from. It was more a seduction fuelled by schnapps and teenage hormones. And the Swiss aren't usually known for their physical philandering and passion are they?' I said.

Dad had got the atlas out. 'I can't seem to find Villars on the map.'

Megan tapped rapidly on her laptop. 'Villars-sur-Ollon. North of Chamonix. '

Mum was watching me. 'Lucy, do you feel any different?' She asked.

I'd thought about it in the car driving back from Hereford. 'Not really. It's weird but I don't. And I can't relate to her family at all, the way they treated her. In fact I'm amazed she seems to have turned into such a normal person.'

'Does she have any children with Mr Blythe?' Megan asked. 'Have you got any half-brothers or sisters?'

I turned to her, shocked. 'Bloody hell, I never even asked. But we had so much to talk about I suppose that's something to ask when we next meet.'

Driving down the M5 I was really pleased with myself and the way things had gone. Well, perhaps pleased was tempered by relieved. No-one had been hurt or upset, the milk hadn't been spilt and the apple-cart was intact. I enjoyed my mental metaphors and was feeling so much more optimistic and in control of my life but I couldn't help mulling over the things Jennifer had told me. She'd said she preferred to be called Jenny, only her mother still used the full name. There was still so much to discover and to this I added the question, would she, could she, tell her own mother that we had been reunited. I'd the feeling that it would be difficult in view of the way the Wingfield's had refused to accept me, their flesh and blood offspring. Mum had been surprised that Jennifer, Jenny as I was trying to think of her, hadn't brought any family photographs to show me.

'Maybe she's estranged from them after what happened.' Megan had commented. 'Maybe she doesn't have any family snaps anyway since they buggered off travelling on their own while she went to boarding school.'

'I don't think so, but I got the impression that with her father dead and her mother living abroad that there isn't much family to speak of.' I'd said. 'And no grandparents were mentioned so maybe there's no family around to keep such things.'

Mum had been horrified by the idea since she was the undisputed keeper of the family photographs.

Roadworks and heavy traffic made the journey longer than I'd expected and the estate was quiet when I got back. I put the Mini in its space under the Coach House, noticing that Sam's Landrover was there, and took my things indoors. Sam wasn't expecting me until tomorrow and I'd hoped to surprise him. While everything was quiet I put a wash load into the laundry and looked inside Maggie's fridge. With Flick away and Maggie having a couple of days off herself, fresh stores were depleted. Fortunately I hadn't come back empty-handed and was planning a feast. I was standing idly staring out at the courtyard, admiring the way a purple wisteria cascaded down the wall with a foreground of contrasting yellow flowered scented azalea when I heard footsteps crunching on the gravel and Sam appeared. He was unaware of my presence and I gazed at him, my heart beating double time and my stomach doing backward flips. I saw him turn and call and watched as Coco and Mitch appeared. It was a perfect cameo of loyalty and affection. I hadn't grown up with dogs but now I realised I'd hate to be without them. My vision blurred with tears and I was overcome with emotion, a mixture of pleasure, pride and love. Without a second thought I dashed to the door and was across the hall and outside faster than I could think.

'Sam!'

Mitch barked and Sam turned as Coco came scurrying over the gravel towards me with her little body heaving and wriggling.

'I'm home.' I said, 'And I want pats and cuddles and walkies too.'

We all collided, Sam laughing and Mitch barking, Coco was in my arms huffing and trying to lick my face. Sam grabbed my hand and managed to kiss my nose whilst fighting the dogs off with the other.

'That's the best thing I've heard. My lovely Lucy saying she's home. I thought it was tomorrow, when did you get back?'

'Less than an hour ago.'

'I'm so bloody pleased to see you.'

We just stood there staring at each other and smiling.

'Fancy a toasted sandwich?' Sam said after what seemed like ages.

'We can do better than that.' I said. 'I've bought us some treats.'

'So how did it all go then Lucy? Tell me everything.' Flick was sitting comfortably on her chaise longue after breakfast on her first morning back. She'd had a very satisfactory trip to London, seen a show or two, done some totally unnecessary shopping and been spotted at dinner in someplace fashionable where the rich, fabulous or merely wealthy liked to go.

'Good. She's okay. She had a tough time but as the story unfolded I found myself quite liking her.' I was more or less paraphrasing the words I'd used to mum and dad.

Flick asked some sensible, and sensitive, questions and nothing I said seemed to surprise her.

'How very unpleasant for the poor child.' Flick summed it all up. 'And what next, when are you next meeting up? There's still lots to learn obviously.'

'I don't know Flick. I'm down here working and she runs a business. Oh, I did a screen shot and printed her photograph, here.' I extracted Jennifer's website picture from my family folder and handed it to her.

Flick studied the photo for a while. 'So this is little Jenny Wingfield then.' I thought the way Flick said it sounded odd, as though she knew her but then she looked at me appraisingly. 'Quite definitely a family resemblance.'

'Yes, but I obviously get my colouring from my father. She said I have his eyes.'

'And she can remember that clearly can she? I'm not sure I can remember the exact eye colour of a lover I may have had briefly thirty years ago.'

'Flick, that sounds a bit unkind.'

'And now you are starting to sound like Alice, telling me off for what are quite honest thoughts. Where are we on Trelerric Vintage?'

And so we went back to work. We were well into May now and the exhibition was scheduled to start at the end of July, just as the main holiday season kicked in. It seemed like ages away. Alice had suggested that we should visit some of the other houses which were open in Cornwall to get a more up to date feel of how they were running things so Flick and I had a day out as visitors. The one we chose had a school party visiting and Flick was both fascinated and appalled.

'All that work, designing activity sheets and then having them tramping all over everything. It's all admirable of course but I don't want that. It's my home, I want it all decent, grown up and well behaved.'

'Well it will be, it's a ticketed event and the visitors won't be having to search for clues or learn things. They'll just be standing around adoring your clothes and buying a few small items as mementoes. But I've had a thought, maybe we should put you in a booth, something stylish like a medieval jousting tent and charge them to have their pictures taken with you.' I kept my face straight. 'I think Alice and Jane would approve of the idea.'

For a moment Flick looked at me in horror and then started laughing.

'Do you play poker Lucy? If not maybe you should have been on stage. You can certainly carry a line. But you know, I really should start looking at what I'm going to be wearing, do you think I need a different outfit for each set of visitors or would one for the whole day be sufficient?'

'Definitely just the one please. Just don't overload Maggie and me with extra laundry Flick. We're going to be run off our feet as it is.'

Megan invited Sam and me over to her new home one Sunday and since Flick wasn't away she was included in the invitation.

'I don't want to be in the way of all you love-birds, but of course I'm delighted.' Flick responded, being terribly brave about the idea of eating lunch in yet another kitchen. I relayed Flick's reservations to Megan who'd promised to find a tablecloth to put on the table and to dress it prettily.

Meeting up gave Mike an opportunity to talk about music to us.

'Megan has told me a fair bit about your plans and arrangements for Trelerric Vintage, and obviously I've seen the exhibition space. I wondered what sort of music you might have in mind to help set the scene for the exhibition, or for the mood in the cafe.

'It hadn't occurred to us, music hasn't been mentioned.' I said.

Mike gave me a pained look. Life without music wasn't worth living.

'I don't think we want popular music Mike.' Flick said. 'And great big speakers would look awful.' She'd seen some of the boy band posters in the music studio when she'd had the tour of Bartlett Towers as Mike jokingly called his home. I'd been impressed with Flick's appreciation of the recording studio, but anything to do with media on that level was of interest to her.

'I agree.' Mike said. 'But I can fix a music system the size of a paperback book that nobody would even see. And pop wouldn't suit either the Tudor building or the clothes from what I've seen of the photos in Megan's office. I'm thinking of your era, there's more than a twenty year span of fantastic dance music and the crooners of the day are unparalleled and timeless. I'm imagining Sinatra, Billie Holiday, even our own Robbie Williams did a fine version of the old songs with him dressed in a tux.'

I could see that Mike had rehearsed the idea with Megan but I agreed that it enhanced the vision.

'Again it's something different,' I said. 'Something the other open houses don't have. As long as it's subtle. And I guess there are those musician royalty fee things to sort out.'

'Not another job for poor mum.' Sam said. 'That will make her day complete I'm sure.'

'Oh sure, but I can sort that.' Mike responded with a dismissive gesture. 'And there's a lot a psychology in the use of music in places, if you want the visitors to move along a little faster you put something on with an up tempo, that applies to eating as well. But it also helps fix memories. It makes you feel good. They'll associate the music with the exhibition and tell their friends.'

'Or we could use Dowland. He's bang on the money for the Tudor period.' Flick knew her music, and of course she tinkled the old ivories herself.

'In the cafe maybe, but I don't think he fits with the clothes.' I said.

'Can you suggest anything I could play to stop them nicking my plants?' Sam asked.

We all got a bit silly after that.

'Trelerric doesn't have a coat of arms, I mean, the Latchley's haven't got one have they? There's nothing over the doors or the chimney breast in the Tudor hall. How come there's an ancient family seat but no crest.' I asked Jane at Saturday supper.

'The original Latchley was Johannes de Lachele. He was a merchant who came over from the low countries during the latter part of the reign of Henry VIII. His exact place of origin isn't recorded. Thomas Cromwell encouraged trade during that period. Apparently the first de Lachele bought the Trelerric lands because of their proximity to Plymouth, the trading routes along the south coast of England, and probably because of the climate.' Jane said. 'He traded hides, wool and seasonal crops like cherries amongst other things. The banks of the River Tamar eventually became famous for their market gardens and of course when the railways were introduced in the nineteenth century the Latchley's, as they were by then, made a lot of money sending flowers and fruit up to Bristol and London.'

'So as a merchant trader he was just an aspiring middle class chap, an entrepreneur, nothing to do with being landed gentry or receiving benefits from the Crown.' Tim said. 'Jane,' he added, 'we really do need to get the Latchley Chronicle translated into modern English. There've been several attempts by well meaning scholars over the past one hundred years but we really should get a proper job done.'

'Don't look at me, I've got enough on my plate.' Jane replied. 'But it has crossed my mind.'

'It's the sort of thing you do when you're recovering from illness or injury.' Flick spoke up. 'I did so much cataloguing and sorting of my personnel effects when I was recovering from the accident and now look where it's got us. I never expected that something positive like Trelerric Vintage would be the result.'

'Okay, so who wants their leg broken so that they can be nominated for the task of transcribing the Chronicles?' Sam asked.

'One break or two?' Alice laughed at him and the general level of merriment rose in the room.

'You don't list reading old English language amongst your talents do you Lucy?' Jonathan asked.

I shook my head. 'No I don't, but I'm really interested to learn about the history. Jane,' I said, turning to her, 'you once said something about a Latchley Book, when Megan and Mike got married.'

'Yes, the estate births, marriages and deaths. I've entered their marriage and the reason why it took place on the estate. What's your interest there?'

'I'm just toying with ideas about family research and history. You said that you sometimes got enquiries, even from abroad. I'm beginning to wonder if there's a need for a simple story about the origins of the Trelerric estate. One which includes family names, with their duties and occupations. Something a bit more than a pamphlet. But there isn't a family crest to put on the cover so we'd have to find something else.'

The family started kicking the idea around and Alice came up with the idea of doing a chapter for each century. 'You know, with a timeline, a short introduction stating the names of the monarchs, significant inventions, wars, all that sort of thing. Then we could list the names and match the occupations from the estate records.'

'We've got old photographs and some engravings which would make good illustrations.' Jane said.

'And I could dress up in period clothes,' Sam said. 'You could photograph me as Latchley down the ages, with gardening tools appropriate to the times. We've always managed the land, I could have a fork and a Cornish spade in each photograph and just change my trousers. Easy.'

'And a straw in your mouth too.' Tim laughed.

After supper we took Flick back to the house and then went for a stroll alone outside with Coco. It was a beautiful still evening with lots of stars and a new sickle shaped moon. I'd once read that you should make a wish when you saw the new moon for the first time, but that it was unlucky to see it through glass. Scent from the various bushes and flowers that Sam loved so much hung in the air and there were a few bats swooping after insects along the terrace below us.

'It's so lovely here.' I said. 'You're right, Trelerric is a happy place, it has a happy atmosphere.'

'Probably because the Latchley's have always been simple folk and have never really been involved in anything beyond the level of local magistrate. As mum and dad said, we're originally trade, then farmers and land managers and market gardeners. We're not posh.'

'But as landowners did your ancestors never marry up, a wealthy heiress or something.'

'I think the Latchley men mostly have a penchant for marrying for love. Younger daughters with dowries or pretty widows with assets helped pull some money in over the centuries, but no titles.'

'And how big was the estate originally? We had stopped at the end of the terrace and I could hear something rustling in the undergrowth.

'Big enough. We owned the village, the village pub, which obviously isn't called The Latchley Arms since we don't have any, three farms and the land including and beyond the old quayside. Now we just have Home Farm, the main house and the various outbuildings, two orchards, some woodland and the gardens. That's enough isn't it?'

Sam paused and kissed the top of my head absently.

'And then there's the old market garden on the southerly slope, which is currently an acre of overgrown scrub partly enclosed by walls. It's not been used since dad was a little boy and the only way of clearing it now would be to put pigs in for a year. Along the top of the old market garden is where the original cherry orchard used to be, I've looked at the old hand drawn and coloured estate maps which show it all. They're beautiful. There's a tumble-down cottage there as well.' Sam kissed the tip of my nose, his arm round my shoulders. 'You'll be coming up with ideas of turning it into a holiday cottage next won't you.'

I snuggled against his side, enjoying the hard warm muscularity of his body against mine.

'I think I agree with your mum, I've got enough on my plate without taking on more cleaning and organising.'

'That's a relief, because I've got that cottage marked down for my own future.'

'How do you mean?' I was puzzled.

Sam didn't answer. Coco had come scampering over to us huffing and sniffing. 'Time you were indoors young lady. And I mean both of you.' He said.

TWENTY FOUR

Jennifer and I, or Jenny as she preferred to be called, exchanged several emails. I asked her about family photographs and she apologised for not having brought any with her to our first meeting.

"I just didn't think Lucy." I read. "I was so caught up in the excitement of meeting you at last that I didn't really have a clue what I was doing. Miles and I are going out to Portugal to see mum soon and I'll ask her what she's got. Hope we'll meet up when I get back."

So she must have decided to tell her mother that we'd found each other after all. I thought that was brave of Jenny but I didn't say anything. It was best if she found her own way of dealing with the situation. I told her about my job at Trelerric House and about the forthcoming preparations for Trelerric Vintage. She responded saying it all sounded very interesting and that she and Miles might get down to Cornwall in the summer to see the exhibition.

Meanwhile I thought about telling Sam about what I'd discovered but I just couldn't seem to find a way to approach it. Our relationship was comfortable and I couldn't remember when I'd last been so happy. I didn't want to spoil anything. The family seemed to have accepted us as a couple without comment but although we both lived and worked on the estate we were so busy with our day jobs that we didn't actually spend much daytime together. Now that it was summer I'd got into the habit of going for an early run before starting the day and Sam never hung about because if he wasn't organising things that he and Simon were doing, he had jobs to do helping with the animals at Home Farm before getting on with his own work. Flick and I were busy with her needs and her visitors, and I often helped Maggie. By the time the evening came and we'd eaten we sometimes just wanted to flop onto the beanbag and cuddle.

The month of June flashed by and my focus for early July was Sam's birthday. I'd looked up symbols for Cancer the Crab and July birthdays but didn't see him as a larkspur and ruby kind of man. I'd had a better idea and Maggie had to ban him from entering her kitchen so that I could make his cake. This time I simplified things by making cup cakes adapted from a Dutch honey cake recipe, and topping them with pale lemon icing. My special touch was the extremely fiddly creation of little sugar bees. Rather than put them on flowers, which I'd decided was too girly, I used the piping bag with a tiny nozzle and drew honeycomb shapes onto the lemon icing using a darker colour. Maggie watched, intrigued.

'You must like him a lot, going to all that trouble.' Maggie said, watching me work.

'It's no trouble, I like doing things like this for people who will enjoy them.' I wasn't going to enter into a discussion about my feelings for Sam. We'd only been together since Easter, it was too early to be making statements about our relationship. 'How's things between Clare and Simon?' I asked, changing the subject.

'He's taken her for a picnic walk on the moor up Minions way near where he lives with his mum, and she's met his mother for tea. Apparently she's very nice. He doesn't have a dad, he did a runner when Simon was born. Couldn't handle the idea of family commitment I gather. I think his mum's done a nice job bringing him up on her own. He has a granny and grandad in the village though so they've been around.'

'He's a good bloke. I like him. Sam likes him as well, he says Simon has potential as a designer, and he's certainly not afraid of hard work.'

'Typical Cornishman Lucy, the Cornish are grafters. They see a job and sort it. The saying goes that if you look down any mine anywhere in the world you'll find a Cornishman down it.'

For some reason the idea of a man digging himself a deep hole made me want to giggle.

There was a moment of quiet while I fiddled about. Maggie sighed.

'What's up Maggie?' I murmured, hardly daring to breathe on a tiny sugar wing I was attaching with a minuscule drop of warm sugar.

'Oh, nothing. Well, it's just that I worry how the kids will cope these days. Clare works at the vets and when she's not needed there she comes here and helps me or goes to help with the children at The Lodge. And Simon works here and does odd jobs in his time off, he has some clients via a builder he's worked with. But they don't earn enough to start a life these days. I pray for them, I really do. I hope something will come along to help them, but I don't know what.'

Once again little Grace had been instrumental in influencing the decorations. For her uncle Sam's birthday lunch, which was being held at The Lodge, Grace had chosen a pirate theme. The dining room was festooned with skull and crossbones bunting and the same motif was on paper napkins. Black and white balloons were strewn about and I made Alice laugh when I said I'd better not sit amongst them or I'd disappear. I was wearing the cropped frayed skinny black jeans and the black silky top Megan had chosen for me to wear weeks ago. Thomas was thrilled to bits because he'd got an eyepatch and pirate hat to wear and Alice had fastened a soft toy duck to his shoulder. Jonathan, when he saw it, went into hysterics.

'What's that?' he spluttered.

'It's a carrot.' Thomas advised him, seriously.

Jonathan went down on his knees, crying with laughter and Thomas jumped on his back.

'A carrot! A carrot!' He shouted excitedly, not knowing the reason for his father's mirth but enjoying the fun.

'A special pirate carrot.' Jonathan managed to say before collapsing helpless with laughter and setting us all off.

Alice and I had just finished laying the party food out when everyone arrived. Flick had walked up to The Lodge with Sam and was looking her best in an elegant long sleeved cream linen tunic over cream trousers. The tunic had a high neckline embroidered with tiny coloured beads. I hadn't seen that before. She was also carrying a parasol to protect her complexion from the sun.

'We can eat on the terrace if you like, there's a sun umbrella up Flick.'

Flick declined. 'Not for me darling thank you. I don't enjoy engaging with the local entomology and anyway it's nearly the horsefly season. I react very badly to bites.'

'That's 'cos the old grey mare ain't what she used ta be.' Jonathan was laughing immoderately and parodying a bumpkin accent. I began to suspect he'd already had a glass or two of something convivial.

Grace gave Sam a card she'd made and a present wrapped heavily in sellotape. Sam sat down with her at his knee. 'Is this all for me?' He smiled at her.

'I made the card. And that's a present.' Grace was twisting from side to side in excitement.

'Wow. It's fantastic.' Sam opened the card, which had barely fitted the envelope and revealed another of Grace's speciality scrunched tissue paper creations. This time it was black tissue with white bits stuck to it and the inevitable glitter. 'Wow.' Sam said again, turning it around in his hands. 'I think I'm a bit scared!'

'You should be Sam.' Alice said. 'Can you tell what it is?'

'It's a skull!' shrieked Thomas. 'Grace made a skull with teeth!'

'Wicked. It's awesome Grace. And you made it all by yourself? You're a very clever girl.'

Grace was delighted. 'And there's a present.'

'Yes, I'm having some difficulty opening it.'

Alice handed Sam some scissors. 'Try these.'

Grace had given Sam a large packet of her favourite gummy sweets in various colours and animal shapes.

'They're made using organic natural vegetable colours Sam.' Alice took the scissors from him.

'What, all these for me? Will you be able to help me eat some of them Grace because there are an awful lot.' Sam said, giving Grace a hug and a kiss. 'You are the sweetest little girl on the Trelerric lands.'

At that point he looked over Grace's head at me and winked. I giggled. I could guess what might be coming later when we were on our own.

Jane gave Sam a new leather belt, Flick gave him an expensive casual shirt from a London outfitter. Alice said providing a birthday tea was enough and Jonathan gave Sam a bottle of whisky.

'Talisker. I bought that one on Skye at the distillery with you in mind, it's special. I know you like that peaty smokey flavour on a cold Cornish evening.'

'Sure do Jon. I likes gulping liquor better 'n I likes rubbing liquor. Thanks mate.'

Tim shook Sam's hand. 'Son,' he said, 'in view of my appreciation for everything you do here I'm giving you the rest of the day off. And a small bonus.' He handed Sam a brown envelope. 'Pocket that and say nothing.'

Finally I gave Sam my tiny package and an envelope. Sam held the package in his hand as though reluctant to open it.

'You can open the envelope first if you like.' I said, feeling a bit excited. It was a gift voucher for a helicopter flight for two from an airfield near Saltash.

Sam opened it and read it out, clearly surprised.

'I got the idea when you said you'd looked at the old hand drawn and coloured maps of the estate. I thought it might be nice to see Trelerric from above and maybe take some photographs.'

'That's brilliant Lucy. I love it. And it's for two? You're coming with me then?' I nodded. 'That makes it perfect.'

'Fantastic idea Lucy.' Tim said. 'You can kill two birds with one stone and check the roof when you fly over, see what needs mending next before winter. And don't scare the livestock.'

In the laughter Sam slipped my small present into his pocket, unopened.

'Oh dear, is it a bad idea then?' I said to Tim.

'No Lucy, I'm joking. We get the Ministry of Defence roaring over plus Coastguard, Search and Rescue and various private flights. The animals are used to it, as long as you don't fly too low.'

Everyone got something from the party food table and my honeybee and lemon cupcakes were much admired. Grace was worried. 'There's bees on the food mummy!' She exclaimed.

'All that for me?' Sam said seriously. 'Well, I'm blown away by the detail and the thought that's gone into it. Thank you Lucy.' He showed Grace my work. 'Look, Lucy made these out of sugar. You can eat them. They're quite safe. Just like the gummy animals you've given me.'

Grace wasn't sure and wouldn't try her cake until uncle Sam bit into his.

That evening the two of us went to a pub called The Wheal. We drove up onto Bodmin moor and I recognised a place name.

'I think Simon lives near here.' I said.

'Simon recommended the pub. It's his local, I've never been.'

'It looks nice.'

'I thought we should check it out and maybe use it as a bolthole during the Vintage exhibition.'

There was a couple with children sitting outside at a picnic table. The woman was striking, with amazing mahogany coloured hair flowing over her shoulders. A little girl with the same colouring was sitting next to her and chattering nineteen to the dozen. The man sitting opposite them had a tiny baby cradled in his arms and look of wonder on his face. It made a pretty scene and I couldn't help smiling at them. The red haired woman caught my eye and smiled back.

Sam ordered us a half pint of bitter shandy each and we shared a basket of salty freshly cut and cooked potato chips. For a second Sam looked annoyed. 'What am I thinking, it's my birthday and you look amazing in those sexy jeans and then I bring you out to a pub for chips. I've got no style. We should have gone to Tavistock or Plymouth.'

'Don't be daft.' I said. 'We're just having fun. Just the two of us and no pressure. And you haven't opened your other present yet.'

Sam fished in his pocket and taking the little package out he placed it on the table between us. 'I didn't want to open the first thing you've ever given me until we were alone. Is that silly?'

'No.' I glanced around and dropped my voice. 'Nobody is watching so you can open it now.'

Sam tore the wrapping and opened the little box and I melted inside as his face lit up in a delighted smile. I'd written a tiny card which he picked up and read.

'It says "To help you see the way to me." Oh Lucy, that so special. I love them.'

'I didn't know if you ever wore cufflinks, but I just liked the private joke. You don't have to wear them, they're a novelty thing but they were made as a one-off by a craft designer.' I was babbling nervously.

Sam put a finger to my lips.

'We'll find an occasion I think.' He leaned across the corner of the table and gave me a salty kiss. 'Time to go home and find out just who is the sweetest girl on the Trelerric lands I think.'

TWENTY FIVE

'So it all went well then?' Flick was asking about the helicopter flight we'd taken the week after Sam's birthday.

'He had a lovely day although I wished I hadn't had the complimentary glass of champagne. I felt a bit nauseous after we took off. The views were amazing though. Trelerric looked so different from above.'

Sam had pointed out various features including the old market garden and the tumble down cottage. I'd never noticed it before because it was set beyond the sheep fields opposite Home Farm and down what I'd only seen as a rustic farm track. When I went out running I stayed on the smoother tarmac lanes where injury was less likely, and it wasn't on Coco's walk route.

'Well congratulations for being so imaginative. I wonder what he'll do for your birthday in October.'

The idea that Sam might be part of my future and could be planning for something months ahead filled me with pleasure but I kept a neutral expression.

'That's ages away Flick, we've got Trelerric Vintage to get through first. And that reminds me, we need to phone "Life in the Country" magazine, they want to come and do an article on the house and gardens. You can probably get yourself some more publicity although the article won't be run until next summer because they plan months ahead. But we should have a glossy book to sell about you and your clothes by then and we'll get them to mention it somehow.'

Flick had been working on the book idea with advice from one of Sir Hugh's contacts. She'd only used Matt for posters, fliers and cards but even so he'd benefited from a sizeable order.

'I still need a good photographer, someone I can relate to.' True to her way of summing people up in an instant Flick had turned away a couple of people Megan had suggested.

Requests had started coming in for tickets and I'd taken the job off Jane. Flick had surprised me by becoming a willing helper and was proving reliable at keeping an accurate tally on visitor numbers and already some dates were booked solid. The website was being updated continually which meant I had to go over to Home Farm a couple of times a day. Flick was thrilled with the interest being shown. She'd also got a coterie of friends coming but had refused to make them pay.

'The very idea is ridiculous. We shall have lunch together in my rooms and I shall show them around personally. None of you will need to do anything.'

It wasn't worth arguing or pointing out that it wasn't the fairies who did all the work when she had friends in. Meanwhile the local television station were coming in to do an interview with Flick. They'd already had a cameraman in filming Megan's work and shots of the garden and were going to put the interview out as a pre-recorded filler on a day when news was slow.

But all the planning and effort was proving effective. The only battle I'd had was with Maggie who had wanted to put on a "proper decent Cornish tea" for the guests since it was included in the ticket. I'd vetoed the smoked salmon and thin ham salad sandwiches she'd wanted to do, partly because of costs, and insisted we should provide only two options, hard-boiled egg and cress bridge rolls and cheese and salad sandwiches. The visitors would have a selection of cakes to choose from as well, I reminded her.

'What, not even a bit of tomato?' Maggie had groaned.

'No, it makes the bread wet unless you let them drain for a while after slicing and that will hold preparation up. We're keeping to acceptably tasty and innocuous fillings, made and served fresh on the day and within strict time limits. We have to faff about with temperature control records and all that food safety malarky so we're keeping it as simple as possible.' I said, and scared her with stories of sick people suffering from food poisoning calling for ambulances.

'But my food has never poisoned anybody.'

'And that's the way we're going to keep it.'

But I had to concede on the Cornish cream tea option since it was a local tradition.

Everyone was commenting about the extra work and getting a bit peevish. Sam was very busy. 'Everything's growing all at once, I'm constantly weeding and dead-heading and Simon's complaining because we're having to water things on the terraces since we've not had much rainfall this year. And Flick gets pissed off when I bring the water bowser over behind the quad bike in the evening because she doesn't like the noise when she's playing the piano.'

Actually Simon was loving it all. He owned a disreputable old campervan and Jane had allowed him to camp in a private corner out of sight behind the barn and use the downstairs shower next to the boot room. It meant he was on hand for all the extra work but really it gave him and Clare the chance of some personal time together.

Then Megan turned up with a couple of helpers and spent a few days dressing mannequins and arranging the flow of the exhibition. Sam offered to help her with placing a few large decorative pots dressed with white sprayed arty looking twigs "no colour, nothing to detract from the clothes" but she dismissed him with a smile.

'They don't weigh anything.' She picked a pot almost as tall as herself up with one hand. 'Look, they're just cut foam shapes sprayed to look like stone.'

'Well it fooled me.' Sam said, standing back in admiration.

Simon who'd just turned up and missed the exchange looked on, impressed.

'Keeps herself well fit doesn't she your sister.' He said.

Finally the laminated information cards were placed in trendy woven baskets - '50p each from the pannier market in Tavistock.' Megan told me - and suddenly everything was in place, making sense and we were ready. And terrified.

The day before opening we all walked the course, as Tim put it, to check that everything was in order. Sam and Simon had put half barrel planters filled with clumps of red and white daisies at the entrance to the parking field and Tim had even replaced the battered black and cream name sign with a smart new one. But he stubbornly refused to have waste bins cluttering the place up, insisting that all waste should be contained within the cafe boundaries and that visitors could take their personal rubbish home with them. The only other rules were strictly no smoking in the buildings and eating area. Nevertheless Jane provided a few shallow earthenware dishes filled with white sand which she placed on a low wall across from the cafe.

'For fag ends. But people will still drop ends on the ground.' She said long sufferingly. 'Sam goes nuts.'

And then it started. Visitors of all sizes, shapes and ages poured through the gates. Tim and Simon were great, allowing drivers to drop any slightly infirm passengers right outside the door to the Tudor house.

'Just call me Sir Walter.' Tim said jovially to a nonplussed looking woman as he directed her and her companion. 'I haven't got my cloak to lay down but there's a bench just inside for your friend. She can wait there while you come back and park.'

Much later Alice, who was checking social media, announced that a lady had tweeted that she'd been thrilled to meet Sir Walter Latchley in person and that he was a charming man.

'I can't remember who suggested having it as a ticketed event only.' Jane said one day, 'but I'm so glad they did because it's made it all manageable. Busy but manageable. I even have ten minutes spare for a lunch break before the afternoon group.'

My role as a room steward was mainly to make sure that nothing got nicked, although small items were securely locked in display cabinets, and to tell people where the toilets and cafe were. I'd also been appointed first aider in view of my previous life. Thankfully there were no accidents other than a lady stepping backwards off a step to photograph her friend in the garden and finding herself on her bottom in some azaleas where she blamed herself for her own stupidity. The azaleas came off worst. Flick, who saw the whole thing from the terrace calmly invited the lady and her friend into her suite for a brush down and tidy up and made the whole episode seem like the best part of the visit.

Several times a day visitors asked us if Flick would consider selling things. On her regular visits to the exhibition Flick engaged in chat and banter and flattered people into believing that they, and they alone had personally made her day by coming along. Camera phones clicked and selfies were taken and Flick was the undisputed queen of the moment although Coco got a lot of attention too. Flick's ability for self promotion was phenomenal and sales of cards rocketed. Another order had to be placed with Matt.

We were all hugely relieved. The major part of the work was of course the food preparation. Boiling and shelling eggs sufficient for the day was a killer.

'I never want to see, smell or eat another egg. I even dream about them.' Maggie sighed as she deftly flipped the shells off with a teaspoon.

'Funny thing, 'Simon said as he collected another food waste bin for composting, 'I never get tired of eggs. I can eat them any time.'

'I'm beginning to realise that you can eat anything anywhere young man.' Maggie told him.

'That's because I'm clean living and hard working.' Simon replied smugly.

Mum and dad came and stayed for a few days and mucked in, relishing the experience. Mum was pretty handy in the kitchen both at the Stables Tea Room and in my flat. I told her she was a godsend when Sam and I found she'd made dinner for the four of us one night. Alice's in-laws provided relief one week and Mrs Marquand took to room stewarding like a duck to water. She was a rather regal woman and quite imposing. Maggie was terrified of her.

After four weeks I felt as though I'd never done anything different but we all adjusted and just got on with it. There were some days when we weren't completely sold out but we were busy. I was shepherding my flock one afternoon when I spotted a face I thought I recognised.

'Hello,' I said. 'I think I've seen you before. You're local aren't you?'

It was the woman with the mahogany hair, the one I'd seen sitting outside The Wheal with her family. This time she was accompanied by a woman with strawberry blonde hair.

'Ah yes, I remember you too. The smiling lady in black,' she said in a husky accented voice. 'You were with a man who was proud to be with you.'

At first I was a bit taken aback and it must have shown, then I was intrigued. The other woman spoke. 'Don't mind Fiona, she's a bit fey. She's an artist and half Scottish so she can't help it.'

The one called Fiona clearly enjoyed the teasing. 'Do you work here? The atmosphere is quite remarkable. I'd love to see more, but when people aren't here. Can I do that?' She fixed me with green eyes and I couldn't think of a single reason to say no.

'It's not my place, you'd have to ask one of the Latchley's. I work for Miss Gray, whose clothes these are. She's the widow of Robin Latchley.' I paused. 'I'm not making much sense. Why don't you phone the number on the brochure and say you were speaking to Lucy. It might help.'

'Thanks, I might do that. Now come on Su, I'm hungry and it's a rare treat to get something to eat without Flora on one arm and the baby on the other.'

I watched them go off towards the tea room and then got distracted by something else. As usual my thoughts turned to Sam, we were so busy that we weren't seeing much of each other.

'What do ordinary people do with their time Lucy?' Sam had said one day. 'I think I must have run over a vicar or something in a past life and that working for Trelerric is some kind of penance.'

One evening I checked my emails and there was a message from Jenny. She wrote that she was hoping to get away from her business and come down with her husband Miles at the end of August, but hadn't managed to find any accommodation. Tired, I went downstairs and told Flick.

'She should have realised, bank holiday anywhere is booked months in advance but especially in Cornwall. Can they stay here Flick?'

'I'd be delighted. But my lot are all coming to visit next weekend. They're staying with Booboo and Henry. Tell Mrs Blythe that if they could come next weekend instead of the bank holiday we could fit them in with my private view and join us for lunch. It won't be a problem will it?'

To her credit Flick had arranged her friends' visit to coincide with the day we were closed. I went back upstairs to offer Jenny the alternative dates and a bed for the night. Then I flopped into bed and forgot about it.

TWENTY SIX

It was hot and a lot of our visitors were pleased to be indoors. Sam and Simon found themselves having to do an emergency cash and carry run for extra cold drinks and ice cream and Jane ordered extra patio shades.

'Look on the plus side dad,' Sam said one day. 'Not having a wet summer means we haven't got a boggy car park and the weather puts the visitors in a good mood.'

'And your sun tan is remarkable this year Sam. You look like you've been on a cruise. Whereas Lucy and I are turning pale and interesting since we're stuck inside so much.' Alice said. She'd been keeping up with twitter and was reporting the comments we were getting. The words "hidden gem" and "clothes to die for" were repeated quite often, and a few people wrote complimentary things about meeting Flick. The phrase "we spoke to the actress Felicity Gray, she's divine" kept Flick happy for days.

'We're over halfway through now folks.' Jane said. 'We're on the downward slope but not yet into the final furlong.'

When we closed up on the Saturday night there were tired smiles. We'd abandoned the idea of Saturday supper and all just wanted to go our separate ways for the evening. Flick had been whisked away earlier by Henry to spend the evening away with her friends.

'I'll see you here at lunchtime tomorrow then, we'll all come over together and have a light lunch, Maggie's left something for us.' She'd told me before she left. 'And you can introduce Jennifer and her husband before we all go and look at the exhibition.'

Shit, I'd forgotten. Jenny and Miles were arriving mid-morning and I still hadn't made up their room. Thankfully mum had stripped it and used the laundry before she and dad had left but it still meant that I was rushing about getting things ready when Sam turned up. He switched the vacuum cleaner off at the wall to get my attention.

'What on earth are you up to now Cinders? I thought we'd be eating and crashing out for the evening.'

'I forgot, someone's staying here tomorrow evening.' I couldn't bring myself to explain, I still hadn't told Sam about finding my birth mother.

'Who? Oh never mind, Flick's friends I suppose.'

Without asking Sam helped me snap the fitted sheet over the mattress. Hospital corners were something my mum talked about, I certainly wasn't familiar with them. Together we put the duvet cover and pillow slips on. I'd been quite surprised when he'd first shown me his domesticated side both at the Coach House and in my rooms. He wasn't a slob. 'My mum showed me how to look after myself. My dad let her show me.' He joked.

'That'll do for now.' I said, gratefully. 'I'll pinch some of Flick's flowers in the morning and finish off before they arrive.' I managed to explain that Flick would be here with a load of her friends and that I'd have to be around to help.

'But Lucy, it's Sunday tomorrow. We hardly see each other and it's the only day we get to spend together.' Sam looked put out.

'It's just this once Sam. It's all part of the exhibition and Flick is perfectly okay about me slipping off at other times to do things, so I owe her. And they go on Monday so we'll have a bit of time to ourselves then.' Why couldn't I just come out with it and say these were special visitors and tell him who they were? Sometimes you wait in vain for the right time and moment but it never appears.

Sam gently brushed a stray hair from my cheek. 'Okay, okay. Let's eat, I'm famished. I've brought a bowl of salad leaves and some cherry tomatoes I've just picked so we can have salad and a cold pasty. I got a couple today when Simon and I went out for provisions.

I kissed him and said thanks. I was so knackered I could have eaten road kill.

I'd just finished putting the final touches to the spare room when a car crunched on the gravel outside. Downstairs I found Jenny standing looking up at the side of the house. She saw me and gave a huge smile.

'Isn't this a wonderful place? Like a fairytale. So you live and work here?' She stepped forwards with both hands held out, a neat figure in sandy coloured trousers and a navy blue and white cotton knit summer top. She looked fresh, summery and well groomed, as though she'd just attended a catalogue shoot. We exchanged polite kisses and Jenny turned to include the man standing by his car observing us.

'Lucy this is Miles, my husband. Miles this is Lucy.'

'In the flesh.' I said awkwardly, taking the hand he offered.

Miles looked at me, a searching interested look. He was tall and balding with a short greying neat beard and sharp blue eyes behind rimless glasses. 'Lucy. What a pleasure, Jenny's told me everything. And I can see a strong family resemblance. It's so kind of you to invite us to stay when we've not even met.' He gave me a lovely smile.

We made a bit of small talk about the journey. It seems they'd met Tim on the road and he'd directed them down to the house.

'He said he was Tim Latchley and I just said we were friends of yours Lucy. Is that okay? Is he your employer?' Jenny said as we took their bags indoors and upstairs.

'Yes, okay that's fine.' I said. 'His sister-in-law Flick is my employer. She'll be back soon with some friends, we're all having lunch together if you don't mind and then going over to the exhibition for a private view.'

'And it's Felicity Gray you're talking about.' Miles said. 'I used to like her films.'

They expressed pleasure in their room and then I took them through to mine where I had some refreshments ready. It was weird, I should know this woman I thought to myself, but I don't. And she doesn't feel like a mum, but then she's only sixteen years older than me.

It wasn't too long before I heard more cars arriving outside and excused myself. Flick was with Booboo and Henry who greeted me like a friend, and Jumbo and Fizz had another couple with them.

'This is Red and Black.' Flick announced, looking amused at my expression.

'Naturally.' I heard myself respond drily. 'Should I even attempt a guess?'

The woman called Red lived up to her name. Her professionally dyed dark red hair was cut in a classic short bob with a straight fringe which made the most of her even features and straight short nose giving her a gamine, French look. Her lipstick, clothes, nail varnish and shoes were all in various shades of red. She had the air of woman who had never struggled with her conscience.

'Some people describe me as a fire engine.' She said in a rich throaty voice. 'But I tend to start fires rather than put them out.' Her eyes were as dark as sloes and twinkling with mischief. She turned to her companion. 'This is Blackie.'

The man kissed the back of my hand and I smiled. This was clearly a pattern of behaviour amongst Flick's male friends. He had pale blue eyes and light eyelashes and fair almost white hair combed straight back off his forehead and which curled down over his collar. When he spoke his accent was Ayrshire Scots. 'Magnus Black.' He said. 'Ignore Red, she's been on the sauce already the little madam.'

Wow this bunch were a handful I thought as I helped usher them indoors. Flick let them go on through and turned to me. I heard Red giving cries of pleasure at the sight of the food I'd already laid out in the Chinese room.

'Your guests are here?'

I nodded. Surely she must have noticed their car. 'An hour since.'

'Are you, and they, happy to join us?'

Again I nodded. Flick smiled, a secret sort of smile and there was something in her clever grey eyes. 'Splendid darling, splendid. Come down and join us in a moment. Henry and Blackie can pour the drinks. And Lucy,' Flick paused. 'Put some mascara on.'

'It's very brave of you to submit to this.' I said to Jenny and Miles. 'I've met four of the group before but I don't know them, it's just that Flick, my employer, loves a crowd. And she's very kind.'

Miles was unruffled. 'Well I'm looking forward to meeting her.'

'People are his thing.' Jenny said enigmatically. 'And I meet new people all day long in the shop.'

I lead them downstairs and into the maelstrom. Red was laughing immoderately at something Henry was saying and Fizz was sitting on the arm of Jumbo's chair, thumbing through a magazine and unconcernedly showing a lot of leg where her dress had hitched up. The legs of a dancer, I thought.

'Steady on, calm down and behave yourselves, we have company.' Flick was using her actressy voice to good effect and the atmosphere quietened. 'Most of you have already met my companion Lucy, who is part of the brains behind my exhibition. But let me just make a few introductions.'

She pointed at people and said their names and one by one they all said hello which caused Fizz to get the giggles. 'Lucy,' Flick said finally, 'would you be so kind and introduce your guests?'

For a moment I was speechless but taking a deep breath I managed to speak. 'This is Jenny and Miles Blythe.'

There was a chorus of hello's but I noticed Fizz looking from Jenny to me with the air of someone who'd just put two and two together and made a connection totalling exactly four. Red however, was in a state of excitement.

'Did you say Miles Blythe? The photographer?'

Miles was smiling. 'I'm flattered. Yes, unless there's another of the same name in the profession, I'm Miles Blythe, jobbing photographer.'

'Jobbing my arse.' Red said. 'I saw your last exhibition. Fabulous. Your lighting is superb. I used to be in the profession myself.'

'Was that with your clothes on or off darling?' Jumbo said, accepting a drink from Henry.

Flick saw the look on my face and started laughing and then looked over my shoulder, an expression of pleasure lighting her eyes.

'Room for one more?' A man's voice sounded behind me and I turned. Sir Hugh Flinton was standing there, looking impossibly elegant in a pale linen suit with a blue striped shirt and holding a cane and a summer hat. His eyes went from face to face in friendly recognition and Jenny turned to see who it was. Their eyes met and both of them froze.

I felt the room going quiet.

Sir Hugh spoke first and his voice, full of warmth, filled the room. 'Little Jenny Wingfield, you'd quite gone off my radar. What a pleasure it is to see you again after all these years my dearest girl. And looking as pretty as you ever did.'

Everything went into slow motion. I glanced at Flick but she was looking at Jenny. Jenny was looking confused. Then I saw Jumbo looking at me. What was it I'd overheard him saying to Flick when I'd met him the first time, the morning I'd collected Flick from Flinton Hall. I had a clear recollection of his words. *"Nice looking gel Flick. Found her down in your neck of the woods eh? Is she one of Hugh's leavings on some pretty Cornish maid of the village?"*

Shit, I thought. Sir Hugh's my real father isn't he. All that talk about a ski instructor was baloney. I felt my knees going weak. Then another memory inserted itself, something about Sir Hugh saying I reminded him of his mother, *"a throughly nasty old trout"*. And what had all that been about a portrait in the music

245

room at Flinton Hall? I'd refused his invitation to view it because I hadn't been in the mood to fight off any wandering hands. I felt nauseous.

Jenny had turned pale and Miles stepped forwards and put an arm round her shoulder.

'Let's sit here on this couch shall we,' he said, guiding her to sit. He turned to Sir Hugh, 'I'm Jenny's husband, Miles Blythe.'

There was something protective and strong about Miles Blythe and everyone was looking at him admiringly. I half expected a gauntlet to be thrown down and an invitation to a dual issued. Instead Sir Hugh politely offered his hand to Miles and spoke mildly.

'Please forgive me Mr Blythe. I had absolutely no idea that our paths were going to cross. It must be all of thirty years since Jenny and I last met. Jenny and I are cousins. My mother was Beatrice Wingfield, Jenny's great aunt.'

I was staring at Sir Hugh in complete astonishment, barely able to comprehend what I'd just heard.

'Well, this is an interesting to do isn't it.' Someone in the room spoke.

'I used to play at Flinton Hall when I was a little girl.' Jenny's voice sounded as though she was speaking from another room. 'Dad was always taking us to see his precious Aunt Beatrice. But we had to be seen and not heard so Gillian and I usually went off to play somewhere. Aunt said we were a bit too wild and undisciplined and was always telling us off.'

I sat down on the nearest chair and felt a hand on my shoulder. It was Flick and she was smiling down at me, her face alight with interest.

'I had my suspicions,' she said. 'I've seen Beatrice's portrait so often when I've played the piano at Flinton Hall, and when you said your mother was Jenny Wingfield I knew I was on to something.'

Fizz was bubbling with excitement. 'So Lucy is a relative of yours Hugh?'

'So it would seem.' Sir Hugh was his urbane self again.

I gave Flick a hard look. She'd obviously been talking about me and my relationship to Jenny to her friends and I was annoyed.

'You didn't know?' Miles was looking at me.

I shook my head. 'No. No idea. I'm shocked.'

Someone put a glass of something in my hand.

'Well I do hope you're not horrified as well my dear. For my part I'm charmed and delighted to be able to claim such beautiful relatives.' Sir Hugh said.

'Let's celebrate - we should have champagne! And a party! Have you got any Flick?' Fizz was on her feet and together with Booboo they disappeared off in the direction of Maggie's kitchen, followed by Henry, then Jumbo and finally, Red. Who turned to us at the door before she left and pulled a face.

Jenny's colour had come back and she looked from me to Sir Hugh and started laughing.

I wasn't laughing. The more I thought about Flick gossiping about me the crosser I became.

'So just how far back do you and Flick go?' I asked Sir Hugh in an attempt to gain some time and space before analysing our new relationship. We were all sitting in a huddle now.

'I've known her since my early twenties. I met Flick when she was in some cabaret thing in London, before she got into films. You know I introduced her to Robin Latchley after Caro and I were married?'

It was just small talk and Jenny took over the conversation. 'Did you know that Lucy was a relative of yours Hugh?'

He shook his head. 'I did not, although I did once say to Lucy that she reminded me of my late and unlamented mother.'

'Beatrice Wingfield-Flinton was a complete and utter cow. A bitch to end all prize bitches.' Jenny spoke vehemently. 'I've never forgiven her.'

'My dear I'm not surprised. She did you a disservice. I wasn't party to the discussions at the time obviously, but I learned of their content. I suppose in her defence I might say that she was a woman of her times and not *au fait* with the changes in social mores ...'

I was looking at him uncomprehendingly and he stopped talking and shifted into a more elegant position in his chair.

'Let me make the situation clearer. My mother felt, rather strongly, that Jennifer had gone off the rails and let the family down. For reasons I've never understood Jenny's father, my first cousin Anthony Eric Oswald Wingfield, god rest his sterile soul, adored my mother. Their relationship was more mother and son than aunt and nephew. I never got on with my mother and spent as much time as possible away from home. When Jenny,' he coughed politely, 'found herself in trouble Anthony asked my mother what should be done. Beatrice was a woman with non-negotiable beliefs and she was the undisputed matriarch of the family. Jenny's fatherless child had to go in order for the Wingfield name to remain unstained.'

His words did more to clear the air and were cathartic for Jenny.

'So you weren't part of the family cabal who decided our future?' Jenny said, looking first at Sir Hugh and then at me.

'Goodness me no. Remember I was a callow young man about town and rarely to be seen at Flinton Hall. And Anthony and I, although first cousins, were born over a decade apart. He was more like a young but distant uncle to me and we had nothing in common. We did not have a particularly friendly relationship. Your, er, situation was decided by the family elders and dealt with as they saw fit and I seem to recall that your mother was not a strong person. I've no idea what her views were but I gather that losing Gillian so tragically had made her a little delicate ...' Again he stopped speaking.

'We saw mother last month. Miles and I went out to Portugal. She's remarried you know. I tried to raise the subject and she didn't want to know. She said that what's in the past should remain in the past. I said, didn't I Miles, "but you've got a beautiful and educated granddaughter and I've met her", but she still didn't want to know.' Jenny looked at me, her expression raw and passionate. 'I'm so sorry Lucy. I never had any more children so it's not as though you'd be competing for her affections.'

I sat there, gazing at Jenny. She was tougher than she looked, I thought. And life sometimes deals the cards in a way that can never be resolved but she'd learned and grown and made something of herself. And she had a strong streak of decency. I saw Miles fold her hand in his and I glanced at Sir Hugh. He was looking at Jenny with such compassion and kindness that I got a lump in my throat. I coughed to clear it and picked up the glass that someone had given me.

'They all have their past and I think we should let it die with them.' I said. 'Personally I'm more than happy to drink to our future.' I raised my glass to them, 'Jenny, Miles, cousin Hugh. Cheers.'

TWENTY SEVEN

After that the late lunch in Flick's rooms had been a very casual affair. Apart from my being astounded by just how much Fizz could drink without falling over and becoming aggressive or incoherent nothing much happened and everybody was very pleasant. It was all so British, courteous and well mannered. After lunch we all walked round to the exhibition and the clothes took Jenny's mind off things. Her pleasure and interest were genuine and Flick's friends were laughing and chatting and telling anecdotes about the parties and events they'd attended. There were cries of "Oh I remember that outfit, it was when ..." and "Flick, you wore that dress when the Earl of whatshisname propositioned you, d'you remember what you said to him, the randy old goat ..."

I noticed Flick on Sir Hugh's arm and Miles watching them with a half smile playing over his face before turning to critically assess the original photographs we'd framed as part of the display.

'Just what is it you're famous for photographing Miles?' I asked him.

'People. I photograph people. It started when I was working overseas helping to record the work of a military aid initiative. I've always been freelance. I collaborated on a book showing what people were suffering and that got me more contracts. I found myself travelling all over the world photographing everyone from the great, the so-called good, and the disadvantaged. Then the privileged started asking me to photograph them, which put butter on my bread. I've spent all my life looking but not much of it talking. I think I prefer it that way Lucy.'

There was something about Miles which relaxed me. He was a thinker, a kind man. Then I realised what it was.

'You remind me of my dad. My step-father Mark. He's an engineer, he knows about strength and tolerance, and about weakness too. He's one of the kindest men I've ever known.'

'Thank you.' Miles smiled at me briefly.

Strolling back to Flick's suite I noticed Jenny and Sir Hugh deep in conversation and wandering off together towards the terraced gardens. Flick noticed as well and came to my side and we stopped walking while her friends drifted slowly away.

'Lucy. This is all going well isn't it. But I can tell you're cross with me.'

'I just feel let down somehow. I mean, I'm happy that Sir Hugh and Jenny are reunited, but I feel manipulated. And I suspect you've been gossiping about me.'

Flick considered me for several moments. 'These are my friends and we all go back many years and we know an awful lot about each other. There's a lot of loyalty under the surface. But Fizz remembers meeting Beatrice and she's certainly seen the portrait of her at Flinton Hall many times. You must see it one day Lucy, you do look like her. Fizz isn't stupid you know, neither is she malicious. She made a connection, that's all.'

'But you had a motive for inviting Jenny and Miles this weekend Flick, and it wasn't just about the convenience of everyone seeing the exhibition. Don't you think it was unkind dumping Jenny and Sir Hugh in a room together and in front of strangers like that. Because I do.'

'You're right Lucy. I saw an opportunity to right an old wrong but yes, in retrospect I think I might have handled it differently and I accept your criticism. But I've always known that Hugh thought his family treated Jenny badly. Until recently it was just a family story, one of many, that I paid little attention to. In fact he used it as a way of offering me sympathy for my own past and origins. He's a decent man. We were lovers before he introduced me to Robin you know. Hugh had married Caro by then. He couldn't marry someone of my background, his bitch of a mother would have disinherited him. When you opened up that day about your feelings about yourself I wanted to help and I showed you that magazine article. I never for a moment imagined that this occasion would present itself, or that you were related to someone I loved.'

I stood quietly mulling that over in my mind. The world according to Flick was starting to make some sense although I would have to give it some careful thought before I could accept everything she was saying. For some reason I wanted to test her, to see what sort of person lay under the many layers which made up Flick. 'Were you unfaithful to Robin? With Sir Hugh I mean.' I asked baldly.

Flick gave me her dazzling smile. 'Never. I loved Robin, deeply and passionately. He was a wonderful, funny, handsome man and I had eyes for no-one once I'd met him. I still can't believe he's been gone ten years.'

'So what about all these wild debauched parties I've heard rumours about?'

Flick threw her head back and laughed, then she linked her arm through mine and we started walking slowly. 'There's always sex at house parties, that's what the bedrooms are for. There's nothing new in that. Everyone has lots of fun.'

'Was Robin unfaithful to you?'

'It was always our bed he was in at night.'

'That doesn't answer the question.'

'It's a question you have no right to ask Lucy. But he gave me no reason to doubt his love.'

I remembered that comment Jumbo had made. 'So just who is the pretty girl of Hugh's leaving on some pretty Cornish maid hereabouts?'

'At this point that's not for me to tell Lucy. I'm not a gossip despite what you might think. Now let's stop being grumpy my darling and go and join the others.'

And I had to be content with that.

The following morning I left Flick to Maggie's ministrations and looked after Jenny and Miles, making them a good breakfast. Jenny was so much more relaxed; after a long and personal talk with Hugh and a decent sleep - helped by the wine - she'd found the whole thing helpful.

'It was so unexpected,' she said again over her teacup. 'Hugh always was a nice man. He apologised for turning up out of the blue like that, he said he knew some of the gang as he called them were visiting Flick at the weekend, but he had no idea that I would be there. They all meet up quite regularly I gather.'

I confirmed that they did, explaining that they'd all been friends for many years. Dancing and acting their talented social climbing ways into better lives. Except that I didn't put it as cynically as that. And to be honest, after talking to Fizz and Red and Booboo the previous evening, since the visit had spontaneously carried on for many more hours than expected, I'd found myself liking them.

'So it really was just a coincidence.' Miles said blandly, buttering another slice of toast and accepting another poached egg.

'Yes.' I said. 'Flick offered you this weekend's date because she already had a few friends coming and we all knew that Bank Holiday was going to be manic here, it being the end of the exhibition and with so many things to do.'

Miles gave me an old fashioned look but left it at that. I was pretty sure he thought that Flick had set the whole thing up, but since Jenny was happy there was nothing more to discuss.

'Hugh has asked us both to lunch at Flinton Hall next weekend. I don't suppose you'll be able to come Lucy?' Jenny said.

'Not a chance. I haven't got a weekend free until September.'

I was thinking about Sam. There'd been no sign of him since we'd eaten our pasties and fallen asleep. It seemed like ages ago. I checked my phone, there wasn't even a text, but then I'd not sent him anything. Don't take him for granted I told myself. We hadn't parted on bad terms, there was always lots for him to do and he knew where I was and that, to all intents and purposes, I was working. But I could hear my voice telling mum that he was special, that he'd given me snowdrops and honey. What had I given him?, a helicopter flight, some silly cufflinks and a cupcake. I hadn't given him my trust and I'd hidden the truth from him. Had Peter really damaged me so much, I wondered.

Miles and Jenny were making noises about leaving and were offering to clean everything up but I told them to leave it for the fairies and helped Jenny downstairs with one of her bags.

'Oh, silly me I'd forgotten this.' Jenny said, handing me a small wrapped package. 'I meant to give it to you last night but everything was a bit different to what I'd expected and I forgot.'

I accepted the package from her. 'What is it?' I asked stupidly.

'Just a small thing. Open it now if you like.'

I tore the end of the paper and peeled it back. It was a photo frame, or rather two frames joined together with a silver metal hinge, all rather nice and modern in black wood and silver. I opened it and looked at the pictures.

'That's one of me with Gillian, my twin, shortly before she died. I can see you in her. It's odd to think that she would have been your aunt.' Jenny said. 'And that's Miles and me, he set up the camera and took it a few weeks ago. You don't have to put it out on display or anything, but I thought your parents and family might be interested at some point.'

To my surprise tears were pricking my eyelids. 'Sorry.' I wiped my eyes with the tips of my fingers, thankful that I wasn't wearing mascara despite Flick's frequent entreaties that I should do so. 'That's such a thoughtful and lovely thing Jenny. I'm really touched.'

This time I hugged her goodbye with some feeling and then shook hands with Miles.

'It's been a pleasure and a surprise Lucy. I hope to see you again before too long.'

I waved them off and went straight in to see Flick. She was dressed and looking well presented. The dry cleaners had obligingly delivered the outfits she was wearing during her Vintage Outings as she was calling them, and she was happily reorganising her wardrobe for the coming weeks. It was another hot day and the windows were all open.

'Only three more weeks Lucy, but I cannot allow my standards to fall. One never knows who might turn up and accordingly one must dress to impress.'

We were back into the swing of things and no mention was made of the weekend's events. I checked supplies and made sure everything was in date and correctly stored over at the Stables Tea Room and somehow I found the time to do all my share of the domestic chores and take Coco out. Despite burying myself in activity I felt twitchy. The only thing for it was to go for a run.

I really pushed myself, up and through the estate and out onto the quiet lane for another mile. I noticed that someone had been out and mown the verges leading to the entrance to Home Farm and Trelerric House. Turning back I could see sunlight glinting on water, the tide would be in, the tide which had once brought Johannes de Lachele to this shore, to the Trelerric lands wondering what sort of life it could provide. Did he buy himself a local wife or did he fall in love I wondered as I ran. I was running past the buildings his descendants had built, through the landscape he'd known and which generations of Latchley's had farmed and cared for. On impulse I slowed and turned down the track which Sam had pointed out, the one down to the overgrown market garden slopes where the ancient cherry orchard had stood. Someone had once planted wisteria against the side of the tumbledown cottage, its flowers long since finished but the graceful leaves were unmistakable. I stopped in a patch of shade the wall provided, breathing hard and sweating heavily in the heat, and took a swig from my water bottle. There was a granite cobbled and slabbed path leading from the back door to an outbuilding, once the old privy or the coal store perhaps. Peacock butterflies were soaking their wings in sunlight on a dark purple buddleia and there was the comforting murmur of bees foraging. As I listened to them words began to form in my head.

Madam queens and worker bees, I thought, I shall tell Sam the truth. There's no shame in my story, to even think it is disloyal and ridiculous. I thought I heard a swelling hum of approval.

I'd run far enough, it was too hot to continue so I walked back to the house. There was no sign of Sam, the Landrover or the quad bike so I showered and washed my hair and used the various scented conditioners and creams which Megan and Flick had suggested I should adopt over the past twelve months. I tidied my eyebrows and made sure my hair looked nice. Then I dug around in my pathetic wardrobe and gave a small scream. I wanted a cotton summer skirt or a pretty sun dress. Even shorts would have been acceptable. What planet had I been living on I wondered as I gazed irritably at my drab clothes. I realised I'd been living in some kind of self-imposed mourning. Pulling my cotton bathrobe on over my bra and pants I went downstairs to Flick.

She was at her piano playing something soft and gentle and looked up at me in surprise. We didn't normally see each other in the evenings.

'I'm fed up Flick. I've got nothing to wear in this heat.'

She gave a small shriek of laughter.

Her clothes weren't my style or taste but I ended up with a well fitting pair of what she called palazzo pants in some soft material patterned with a design of green leaves and orange berries on a white background.

'I'd loan you a matching top but it wouldn't fit since my bust is so much more generous than yours. But one of your white t-shirts will suffice. The pants are a cotton and silk mixture, quite heavy but they wear well in this heat. You really need a bracelet and something round your neck, and green or orange pumps or sandals would be nice but you're not going out. I think we shall have to go shopping Lucy. I'm going to so enjoy helping you hatch out of those dull things you've worn all year.'

Lesson over I went back upstairs, still barefoot and found a pair of black espadrilles. I could see what Flick meant. I was going to have to make some serious changes. There was still no sign of Sam so I sent him a text. Then I took Flick's clothes off and put my bathrobe back on, and made a simple meal of crudities with humous and multigrain crackers and a finger of cheddar, some cherry tomatoes and olives. I pinched a couple of cold cooked chicken legs from Maggie's kitchen and was half way down a glass of chilled white wine when Sam arrived, dusty and dirty.

'What's up? Are you okay?' You look okay and you smell fantastic. You said you had something to tell me urgently.'

'It can wait an hour. Do you want to shower and change?' I was relieved, Sam was his usual self, a hard working dusty self admittedly. But there was nothing mean or moody in this man.

'Yes. I didn't realise what the time was. I often don't when it's summer here. I'm filthy. Too mucky to even kiss you.'

Sam had started keeping a change of clean casual clothes in my flat. He said it was getting complicated having his clothes in three places since he still stayed over at Home Farm when he was helping Tim. While he was in the shower I put Flick's clothes back on and made the table look nice. Sam sat down gratefully and looked me up and down. He reached out and pulled me over so that I was standing in front of him and he placed both hands on my hips. I reached out and caressed his damp hair.

'I've missed you. But there's something different Lucy. Apart from smelling lovely and wearing clothes I've never seen you in, there's something different about you.' He frowned. 'It's not bad news is it?'

I kissed his forehead and sat down at the table. 'No. Let's eat. You must be famished.'

TWENTY EIGHT

'You still haven't told me what you wanted to tell me.' Sam sat back after eating.

'No, that's because I can't tell you here.' I sipped my wine and thought for a moment and put my other hand over his on the table. 'Sam, when you speak to the bees do you always take them a gift?'

Sam's attention was fixed on me. 'Yes I do. I think it's respectful.'

'I've made a couple of teaspoons of sugar paste in a cup, just icing sugar, nothing fancy.'

'Lucy, if you want to tell the bees something it can't be trivial or silly. You don't mess about when you tell the bees things. It has to be true and important.'

'It's both of those latter points.'

'And you want me there?'

'I can't tell them without you being there.'

'Okay. Shall we do this thing then?' Sam said.

We walked into the orchard as the sun was settling on the horizon, the sky a combination of peachy pink and orange and an odd olive green colour heralding dusk. It was so hot that we didn't hold hands but anyway I was carrying the cup. Remembering what I'd done on that first visit I quietly placed a drop of paste on each of the hive entrances, and took a deep breath. The atmosphere was always different in the orchard I'd noticed, as though it was facing a different way to the rest of the world. The hours of time moved in a pattern of their own here.

'Madam queens and worker bees, you heard my thoughts in the old market garden this afternoon. I promised you I should tell the truth. I'm called Lucy Huccaby but I was adopted when I was just a baby. I've learned that my real name was Lucy Wingfield and a few weeks ago I met my birth mother for the first time. She was called Jenny Wingfield and is cousin to Sir Hugh Flinton who visits here regularly. I only discovered that yesterday. I'm only just finding out the truth, and I wanted to share it with you.'

I stood there in the gathering dusk and there was no sign or sound of a bee. Desperately I turned to Sam.

'What's wrong, did they hear me? Have I said something wrong?'

'No Lucy, you've said nothing they don't already know, in so many words anyway.' He put his hands on my shoulders and held me very gently, looking down into my eyes in the gathering twilight. 'The bees already know you're adopted, I told them weeks ago. They're just satisfied to know that you are Lucy.'

'What?' The news shook me. 'What? How?'

'Shhhh. Shush. Come on, I'll explain, but I thought you already knew to be honest.'

'What, what did I already know that I don't know?'

Sam walked me away from the hives and back into the orchard, his arm around my shoulders. 'Your dad and I talked a lot that day before the wedding. It was when he told me that you and Megan were his moonlight and his sunlight. About how proud he was of the both of you. I've known you were adopted since then. So what. It's no big deal. But I thought he might have told you about it.'

I digested that statement for a while as we walked. 'I love my parents, but lately I was concerned, worried even, about who I was and where I came from. It was becoming a big deal for me.' I said.

'Well, let's stop it from becoming a scary monster. It isn't, and shouldn't be, for either of us.' Sam stopped and turned me to face him. 'You're my lovely Lucy. That's all that matters. And you smell gorgeous and I've bloody missed you. I'm sick of all this work and activity that's keeping us apart. For god's sake put your arms round me and cuddle me will you woman, do I have to spell it out?'

I cried a bit and kissed him, gratefully at first and then passionately. Much later, lying in each other's arms spent and tired he turned to me.

'Did I hear you right? You're related to Hugh Flinton?'

Yes. We're cousins, slightly removed but definitely related.'

'Well bugger me.' Was all Sam said before falling asleep.

I just lay there quietly, wondering why he'd already told the bees about me.

Social media was red hot, news of Trelerric Vintage travelled and Flick was becoming a celebrity once more. This time the local news did an interview about her film days and she found herself in demand for local appearances. One lunchtime during our brief meal break she showed me her post.

'Look at this, I'm invited to open a flower show in Devon, a dog show in Cornwall and the Christmas lights in Liskeard. But more importantly there's this, read it.'

I took the proffered letter and scanned it quickly, and then read bits of it again.

'Wow. Is that real?' I said, swallowing my hasty bite at a sandwich.

'It is.' Flick's grey eyes were glittering. 'A small one-off part in a locally shot television series. They want me to play a bad tempered lady of the manor who might have a nasty secret but who turns out to have a heart of gold. It's a peach. I shall love it.'

'Flick I'm so pleased, that's fantastic, it's more than fantastic.' I got up and impulsively kissed her on the cheek. 'I've got to go now, I'm back on duty.'

The week raced by and Tim took Flick to the hairdresser on the Friday. Sir Hugh was picking her up and taking her back to Flinton Hall with him for another long weekend. 'I shall be meeting Jenny and Miles again Lucy, you don't mind do you? Only I rather took to Miles, and I think he's the person I've been looking for to take some photographs of me for the book.'

I told her didn't mind at all.

'I won't gossip about you Lucy. I shall only say nice things.' She said provocatively.

I fought the desire to stick my tongue out at her. I didn't, it was beneath me.

It meant that Sam and I could have some time together at last even though we were still open for the exhibition on the Saturday. It was indefinable but something had changed since I'd talked to Sam's bees. We were completely at ease together. Sam was always sweet tempered and affectionate but there was something strong building in the relationship between us. I told mum over the phone, I'd told her everything about the Wingfield-Flinton connection obviously and she'd been fascinated, but she had her own view about me and Sam.

'It's why being honest with both yourself and the person you love is so important Lucy. It's how trust is built.'

Mum knew, even before I could admit it to myself. I loved Sam Latchley.

Sam, being a bit of an amateur astronomer, told me that August was the time of the annual Perseids meteor shower. On the Sunday evening, after a day of unaccustomed leisure we strolled on the terrace in the gathering dusk and then sat on a seat watching the sky for shooting stars. The evening air was like velvet on my skin. Sam had brought a bottle of wine out with us and we clinked glasses.

'Should I make a wish if I see a shooting star?' I asked him, leaning against his side and idly stroking his muscular bare forearm.

'Of course.' He kissed the top of my head. 'Do you know what you want to wish for?'

'Well, I can't tell you that can I. It will stop the wish from coming true. Wishes have to be private don't they?'

'Is that so?' I could hear the smile in Sam's voice and my tummy went squiggly. This man was so gorgeous.

A shooting star streaked across the sky followed by two smaller ones.

'Wow, that was good.' I was quite excited. 'There's another!'

'Let's make our wishes then.' Sam put his glass down on the floor and turned to me. Then he put his hand under my chin and tilted my face up and lightly kissed my nose, my eyelids and then my lips.

I wish, I wish to stay here forever, in this moment and with this man. I felt my wish in my heart.

"Go and catch a falling star, tell me where all times past are." He half sang the line under his breath, it sounded like a folk song. 'That's like you Lucy isn't it, wondering where your past was.'

'Is that an old song?' I asked.

'Dad's got it on an old vinyl LP. It's actually a poem by John Donne. He was an Elizabethan poet amongst other things. He would have been quite at home here, the Tudor house was built during his lifetime.'

'Goodness, there are things I don't know about you Sam.'

'I know. We're only just beginning to get to know each other. It's great isn't it.'

'Yes. It's the best thing that's ever happened to me.' The words were out of my mouth with a spontaneous honesty. Sam went very still and I held my breath.

'Do you mean that?'

'Yes. Yes I do.' I didn't think there was anything else I could say. I tried and failed to see his expression but it was too dark.

'Lucy,' Sam said. 'Lucy, I was wishing that you'd tell me your feelings, but perhaps I should be the one to start. Lucy, I love you.'

And we kissed while the shooting stars wrote their own timeless words above us.

Flick returned on Tuesday and the first I saw of her was when she put in an appearance in the long gallery. She joked and laughed with visitors and there was a radiance and gaiety about her which I hadn't seen before.

'Good weekend then Flick?' I managed to ask her when she emerged from a group of admirers.

'Marvellous darling, thoroughly lovely.' The dazzle smile was on full beam and her silver grey eyes were sparkling.

Later, back in her rooms all she told me was that Jenny and Miles had spent several hours with them and that they were very good company. Miles had agreed to do the photography Flick had in mind and she said that all contributed to her pleasure.

'You're telling me that a nice lunch and someone agreeing to take your photograph has put that light in your eye and that spring in your step?' I said. I knew how far I could push her now.

'You're being very cheeky Lucy.' Flick responded.

'It's in my job description. When you took me on you said you wanted someone who could stimulate you.'

'Did I say that? Oh I'm a terrible person aren't I? Now then, when are we going to be able to get away from this treadmill and go shopping?'

The opportunity came sooner than expected because Jane and Mrs Marquand decided that Alice and I should have a day off. I got the Jag out and took Flick down to Truro. Everything looked tired and dusty, the fields had a stripped, parched look.

'You know, we should really go to London together. We can use Hugh's flat. Shopping, lunch or afternoon tea, a show and dinner would be marvellous Lucy. Have you ever done that?'

'I've never lived that sort of life. Megan does, but not me.'

Flick was horrified but soon became happily engaged looking for better ways to dress me. She had a shop assistant running about fetching and carrying and I ended up with a scarlet and cream sun dress, a floppy woven hat with a scarlet ribbon band and a sexy pair of scarlet sandals.

'I'm beginning to look like Red. Does everything have to be scarlet?'

Flick had spotted a string of chunky beads with turquoise and scarlet splatters on a creamy grey background. 'Clever stuff this modern resin jewellery. These are perfect for the neckline and the turquoise is the perfect foil against the other colours and they all suit your colouring.'

I realised I had so much to learn. Flick supervised the purchase of some plain coloured cotton t-shirts and in another shop she found a multi-coloured casual shirt. 'Look Lucy, don't dismiss this. You can wear it open over your t-shirts, any one of them will pick up this colour, or this. And look, the shirt has a black line running through it, so it will dress up your safe old jeans and trousers and Sam will be delighted to take you up to that pub you both like so much on the moor.'

The Wheal was becoming a favourite hiding place for us, the food was good there and we could get away on our own.

Flick found something for herself and treated me to the shirt. I flinched at the price but she told me it was a thank you gift for everything I'd done over the summer. Flick preferred natural materials, she was a cotton, silk, linen and cashmere sort of woman. 'Always get the best you can afford Lucy, treat yourself to one very good item and build on that. It's advice which has never failed me.'

I wondered who'd given her that advice and asked her as I drove us back to Trelerric.

'Oh, costume designers, couture houses. People who really understand fabric. It has to allow the skin to breathe. It has to feel good when a man touches it. Manmade fabrics can be used to some effect, but not if they make you perspire or give the man kissing you a jolt of static electricity. The only jolt a man needs is the one when he realises he can't live without you.'

On the final night of August Bank Holiday, when Trelerric Vintage closed to the public, we all met at Home Farm. With the exception of mum and dad everyone who had worked to make it happen was there and Jane had put a huge buffet together.

'You did all this Mrs Latchley?' Simon appreciated food and was staring at the spread with respect on his face. He was looking sturdily attractive in a red checked summer shirt with brown jeans. He was very tanned and Clare couldn't take her eyes off him.

'Waitrose helped me out Simon, they deliver a good party meal don't they. I never want to see inside a kitchen again. And I think that when this is all eaten I shall just smash all the plates as well.'

Simon looked a bit startled but then smiled and responded in his practical, laid back way. 'Sam and me have got some potholes to fill. The crockery can all go in them, shall I tell him?'

Megan was taking in my new look. I'd gone for cropped stone coloured jeans with a dusky cinnamon t-shirt and a plain gold chain round my neck. Strappy pale leather feminine sandals with a little cluster of coloured beads in dark blue, orange and pale yellow adorning them completed my hot summer evening outfit.

'Where's the old black and white negative sister of mine gone? You've transformed yourself Luce. It works on you, it really does.' She hugged me and whispered in my ear. 'And you're lit up inside like one of those things you put candles in. You're glowing and I think I can guess who is responsible?'

Everyone was in such a state of relief that we hardly needed alcohol to get a party atmosphere going although I noticed that Jonathan wasn't holding back. Alice, coming downstairs from checking the children, noticed as well and exchanged a look with her mother-in-law. I couldn't help wondering if all was well at The Lodge.

Tim tapped a spoon on his glass and everyone quietened down. He stood and regarded us with a solemn, almost stern expression on his face whilst waiting for his moment. Finally he spoke.

'Well, that went very well didn't it!' He said casually and gave a huge grin as laughter broke out but he raised a hand. 'Seriously, I think we can say Trelerric is on the map and is currently very much in profit. People know that we're here now and have something to offer, but from talking to you all individually over the weeks I think I can say the consensus is that we won't do this again. Not like this anyway, and not for this time period. The time commitment for a small family has been punishing but you've all, without exception, been heroic. And there have been some good laughs. Cheers everyone.' Tim raised his glass.

There were murmurs as we toasted each other and Jane asked us all to help ourselves. This was an evening off, time to relax. I knew that the proper summing up would take place at the next Saturday supper, once everything had been dismantled and Trelerric had slipped into its quiet reverie.

TWENTY NINE

The next day the prolonged period of hot dry weather broke with a colossal storm and Coco dived under her blanket bulgy eyed with fright. I stood at the French windows in Flick's day room and watched the rain sluicing down the glass. The Japanese-style garden came into its own in the wet, the stones and slates taking on a dimension far beyond their size. Rain splashed off the bronze Acer, polishing it to the colour of red gold.

He loves me, I was thinking, hardly conscious of the thunder rumbling outside. Sam Latchley, Samuel John Latchley loves me. Sam had told me that the Latchley men usually had the second name of John, in memory of Johannes de Lachele. I cradled these snippets of information. We'd talked on that bench for hours, that foolish talk you have when you first tell someone you love them. Sam said it happened the moment he saw me standing amongst the snowdrops. For me, I wasn't sure, it had grown slowly and steadily with each passing day. 'Like your sunflower seeds when you were a little boy, it's just gone on growing. I've looked at it in secret almost every day. That funny thing inside that says I'm falling in love with Sam Latchley.'

We'd kissed some more but mostly held each other in that special sort of shock you get when love first confesses itself.

'Is that why you told the bees about me so early on?'

'Yes. Because I knew you were special. I've never felt like this about anyone before.'

'Wow.'

Another clap of thunder sounded overhead and the rain redoubled its efforts, hissing in fury at the windows. I turned and knelt down by Coco's basket crooning to her, patting the blanket covered bundle. Flick came in and found me there.

'Lucy, they want me to start filming next week. It's only a couple of days, it's a very small part. But they're sending a car, and of course I shall come back here at night. They offered a nice

B&B but I said I preferred my home comforts.' She lowered herself onto her chaise. 'I was feeling fine until the weather changed. This rain is making my hip ache.'

As the thunder moved away I extracted Coco and cuddled her. Flick watched me.

'Did you hear anything I just said Lucy?'

'I did. Every word. Why?'

'Because you've got a soppy look on your face and I don't think it's because of Coco. Anyway, I shall repeat all my news at Saturday supper.' Her mobile phone pinged and she read a text but didn't answer it. Now who's got a soppy look on her face I thought.

The first Saturday in September had a tiny chill in the air and I put my black cashmere cardigan on over a teal coloured t-shirt with my black jeans for Saturday supper. Flick gave me an exasperated look.

'Well it's slow progress, but you could look so much better than that. Have you got a red belt you could add? Here, twist this round your neck.' She handed me a wispy orange crushed silk scarf. 'Don't argue, just try it. I've just discarded it myself.'

Once again the Flick magic worked. At least I was wearing mascara. Flick was looking fabulous of course in a dark blue and peachy orange long sleeved layered tunic with dark blue wide legged trousers. 'Cruise wear really, but I thought it could do with an outing. I have an announcement to make tonight.'

Sam picked us up. 'Bloody hell Flick, you look like a Strelitzia in full bloom. Amazing. You'd fit in well in the Eden Project in one of the domes.'

'What's he talking about?' I gave a stage whisper.

'No idea. He's an odd boy, I've always thought.' Flick said, jauntily taking Sam's arm.

'It's the bird of paradise flower, that fabulous blue and orange thing that looks like a bird's beak.' Sam explained to uncomprehending shrugs. 'Check your iPhone, you'll find it.'

'I would if I could spell it.' Flick muttered.

Discussion over dinner for the first part of the evening centred around the Trelerric Vintage event. With capacity for one hundred visitors per day, which we'd split into two groups of fifty since that was all the tea room could comfortably cope with, we'd managed approximately three thousand visitors. Not all the days had been fully booked but publicity had provided a fair number of holiday visitors who had called in on spec.

Jane had taken calls from yet more people who wanted to run articles or use the Tudor building as a showcase for exhibitions. 'A craft fair organiser would like to use us as a venue for a pre-Christmas fair, high-end crafts not tatty stuff, his words not mine. Someone else asked if we'd be available for corporate events but they want to include team building exercises, which could involve outdoor activities.' she reported.

'That's a no.' Tim said immediately and Sam agreed.

'I'm not having my gardens trampled on in the dark, and anyway, we live here.'

'And a lady called Fiona Rose Frazer called, she said she'd spoken to you Lucy. She's an artist and would like to have a look around. I googled her, she exhibits in a London gallery. She's also been in the local papers, her partner is someone called Daniel Pencraddoc.' Jane continued.

Everyone looked blank apart from Jonathan. 'Blimey. He's the local dot com millionaire isn't he?'

'Anyway, not bad for a tiny family run enterprise.' Jane said. 'Ticket sales put thirty thousand in the bag, less deductions for catering, Megan's expenses and so on. The estate is in profit.'

'Maybe we can have another greenhouse then.' Sam said. 'Plant sales were good, people were buying propagated cuttings and small plants because they didn't take up much room and were easy take home at the end of the holiday. It's taught me what I should concentrate on.'

Flick spoke up next. 'My takings on the merchandising were obviously a lot less but Matt's expenses were more than covered since the mark up on cards is quite a lot, and I'm pleased with the cash injection my own portfolio has received.' Flick commented. 'The interesting thing is that the event has raised my personal profile. As you know I'm filming next week and I've been invited to open some local fetes and shows.'

'And don't forget Trelerric House and the gardens are going to be in a full colour spread in "Living in the County" magazine next summer, and you're the focus in that.' I added.

'I've more to say,' said Flick. 'I'm also working on my semi-autobiographical book, which concentrates mostly on new and original photographs of the clothes. That's due to be published by next Easter. Meanwhile I've been approached by the Fashion and Textile Museum who might be interested in showcasing some of my things, the Royal School of Needlework and the London Embroidery School are interested in examining and possibly showing some items,' she was ticking items off on her long fingers. 'Then there's the V&A who are interested in separating the collection into designer labels and studio labels for a potential exhibition, there's someone else, oh I forget who they represent, who wants to get their hands on the shoes and bags and accessories. The list goes on. It's going to keep me busy for months, years even.'

We were all pleased by the news and sat quietly letting the information sink in. Tim had already said we probably wouldn't do the event on that scale again and anyway it was all Flick's to do with what she wished. Flick regarded us all with sparkling eyes and then spoke again. 'I've one final thing to tell you all, and I hope you'll be happy for me. Sir Hugh Flinton has asked me to marry him.'

There were gasps from me, Jane and Alice; Jonathan said 'Wow,' and Tim smiled broadly. Sam was looking at me, his expression changing from pleasure to concern. It was a bombshell and I was speechless.

'That's fantastic Flick, when did he propose?' Jane asked.

'Last weekend. I was up at Flinton Hall to meet my new photographer Miles Blyth. Lucy is acquainted with him.'

'We've got a lot to thank Lucy for haven't we.' Jane said. 'Trelerric Vintage and now this.'

Flick smiled at her and at me. 'Lucy, do you want to add anything to this? I mean about how your connections fit in?'

Apart from Sam the expressions around the table were either blank or curious. Oh well, I thought, in at the deep end, and stumblingly explained my family history and how I'd just discovered that I was related to Sir Hugh. Once again the family were silent as they absorbed the information.

'So you'd become Flick's niece by marriage once removed or something?' Alice was trying to work it out. 'No, a cousin. Anyway, wow, how extraordinary.'

'I haven't got my head round it yet.' I felt myself blushing. 'It doesn't change a thing about my mum and dad. They come first in my life, but Jenny, my mother, is a really nice person.' I thought the description rather lame but I just couldn't find the words.

Sam was still looking thoughtful and he turned to Flick. 'So when's the happy day, and where, and on top of all that, where will you live?'

Flick made us all laugh, saying that at their time of life she and Sir Hugh weren't going to have an engagement, but that they had decided to marry as soon as possible, where exactly, she wasn't sure. 'I expect I shall spend a lot of time at Flinton Hall, but it's not my home and of course if Hugh should predecease me I couldn't possibly live there. For one thing it's too large for me and anyway, his son Paul will inherit.'

Apparently Paul worked in the Foreign Office and was currently working abroad.

'So you'll be up and down the M5 and away a lot.' Sam persisted.

Flick wasn't stupid, Sam meant a lot to her and she could see his concern. 'I can guess what's troubling you darling and I promise you I shall sort everything out. No need to worry,' she smiled. 'And another thing, I nearly forgot. Sir Hugh loves the

Japanese-style dry garden in the courtyard, he'd like to engage Simon to do a design for a corner at Flinton Hall.'

'I can't bear it.' That night Sam was lying on his back in bed with one arm around me and the other behind his head. 'Will it mean that you'll be away for weeks at a time?'

I'd been wondering the same thing. 'We've not discussed it yet.' Something else was worrying me. 'I don't know if she'll need me anyway. I mean, I might not fit into her life since Sir Hugh has his own staff and arrangements at Flinton Hall. And once she's married she'll have all the company she needs, so I'll be redundant.'

'Crap, I hadn't thought of it that way.' Sam groaned. 'I'd been trying to see it from your point of view, thinking about how nice it would be for you to be staying nearer your mum and dad, and convenient for meeting up with Jenny too. It would give you a chance to get to know her better.'

'Well, I don't know what's happening. I expect Flick and I will talk about it on Monday.' But like Sam I had my concerns.

We went to The Wheal for Sunday lunch and were pretty hungry, since we hadn't had any breakfast. It was a busy, popular place so it was a good job that Sam had booked ahead. We had to share a table with another couple who were on holiday, staying in the holiday cottage the landlord owned in the village they told us. It meant that we couldn't have a private conversation. After the meal we drove up onto the moor at Minions and walked to The Cheesewring rock formation. The recent rain had cleared the air and we could see right across the extensive farmland to Kit Hill and to Dartmoor. Somewhere in those folding fields Trelerric lay hidden. Despite the lovely setting our mood was sombre and after a short walk Sam drove us back to Trelerric. We collected Mitch and walked round through the woods and down to the terraced gardens. Flick and Sir Hugh were sitting together on one of the seats and Mitch bounded over to greet them. Flick turned and waved, beckoning us over.

'Bum.' Sam said under this breath. 'I wanted you to myself today.'

'Darlings both.' Flick greeted. 'Would you mind joining us for a few minutes. I've had a few ideas I've been discussing with Hugh.'

'Let me fetch another couple of glasses Felicity. Let's do this properly.'

I raised my eyebrows at the use of Flick's full name and she waited until Sir Hugh was out of sight before she spoke. 'He likes to use my name when he feels there's a sense of occasion. I think it's rather sweet.'

Sam and I perched on the low wall opposite the bench while Mitch flopped down between us and Coco prowled around him. We made small talk about lunch until Sir Hugh reappeared and poured us all a fresh glass of white wine with a practised flourish of the wrist. 'A rather decent Sauvignon Blanc this. I think you'll enjoy it.'

'Lucy,' Flick began. 'I can guess you're a little unsettled by my news. And Sam too. The thing is, I want to keep you on, but not as my companion. For a start you've become a friend, and someone I trust. And you're almost family now. I'm going to need a friend I can trust with all the ramifications of the exhibition. Would you consider becoming my personal assistant?'

I was surprised and then doubtful. 'But I don't type, well I can use a keyboard of course, but, what would I do as your PA?'

'Well, there are all these people to liaise with and I'll need someone here at Trelerric since that's where everything is. People are going to want to visit and examine the clothes, borrow things and so on. It will all need cataloguing and recording, there'll be phone calls and arrangements to make and so on so it's going to be a lot of work. It has to be a professional job, it's not a casual task. Visitors will need looking after too, some of them anyway. Would you like to do it?'

'So I'd stay here at Trelerric?'

'Yes. Does that suit you?'

I told her it suited me very well. 'And what about Maggie?' I couldn't help asking.

'Well Hugh and I will be here a couple of times a month so I shall still need my suite to be kept up and meals to be provided. Her hours might be a little reduced but if you need assistance perhaps she might help. Maggie loves the clothes and both Hugh and I are keen that she should be kept on and taken care of.'

I sat there in the afternoon sunshine letting the news sink in and feeling a profound sense of relief, but wondering what that last comment meant. Sam covered my hand with his and squeezed it. 'That's great Flick, and Sir Hugh.' Sam said. 'Isn't it Lucy.'

I nodded. 'Yes, absolutely. It's fantastic. I'd love to give it a try.'

'There's another favour to ask Lucy.' Sir Hugh was looking me. 'I understand you're a hugely talented cake maker. Would you make a small celebration cake for our wedding. Nothing extravagant, it's going to be an intimate occasion.'

They had decided to marry at Trelerric and then go to Sir Hugh's flat in London. 'Neither of us wants a honeymoon.' Flick explained. 'Travel is so tiring these days.'

'Anyway we've seen most of the sights although we might pop over to Venice.' Sir Hugh smiled at Flick. 'One never tires of Venice.'

I enjoyed the statement and their obvious happiness. 'And when's the wedding going to be, and what sort of cake would you like, we need to discuss your theme.'

'Flick named a date in October. 'About a month from now if we can organise the vicar and get the announcement in The Times.'

'Oh.' I sat up straight. 'That's my birthday!'

THIRTY

'Lady Felicity Flinton,' I said the next morning to Flick, 'has a certain ring to it. That will help your book sell I'm sure.'

Flick looked delighted. 'That's more or less what Hugh said.'

On the subject of the wedding cake Flick, for once in her life, wasn't sure what she wanted. 'I don't know Lucy, I'm not a young bride and it's a second marriage for us both. What do you suggest?'

'You love flowers Flick, what are your favourites? And what about your very long friendship with Hugh, are there some special moments which I could interpret?'

'We met when I was in rep in London. He came backstage with some pals, they were all wearing evening dress and white silk scarves with fringes. People dressed up for theatre in those days. He gave me a single red rose.' I watched as her eyes misted. 'I was attracted to him at once. We had a long and passionate love affair, but then I had to take work elsewhere, and the films intervened and took me abroad. But we never lost touch, and even though he married Caro and I married Robin, and was very happy, we were always friends.'

Flick sat lost in reverie while I made notes, a silk scarf, a red rose, I could see the cake taking shape in my mind and we sat quietly as I started making a preliminary sketch. Slowly she began speaking again.

'Robin and I had a house party here a year after our marriage. Twenty years ago now. Caro didn't come, their son Paul was recovering from some childhood accident involving broken bones and she didn't want to leave him. Paul was their only child and she was protective. Hugh was a very handsome man, he still is. Maggie had just started working here doing some catering and she consoled him that evening. She's a very pretty woman. Clare was born nine months later. Are you shocked?'

'Is it certain that Sir Hugh is her father?' I wasn't shocked, I'd been entertaining certain suspicions and now the jigsaw of their lives was completing the picture.

'She has his dark hair, not unlike yours. And there's a particular look that distinguishes the Wingfield's, again I'm thinking of the portrait of Beatrice that you've still not seen.'

'So she's the pretty girl that Jumbo was referring to. Does her father know? And more importantly, does she know?'

'No to both questions. But it's why we look after Maggie, although she's a sweetie anyway. Hugh always wanted to make sure that Maggie had money. And of course it means that Clare is also your cousin. She's a Flinton but she has Wingfield blood. Hugh thought you should know in view of the things that have happened lately. And he trusts you.' Flick said sympathetically.

'Okay. Right. Well, I don't know what to say, but I'll keep it a secret. Will Maggie know that I know?'

'Perhaps not yet, but once someone lets slip that you and Hugh are cousins she'll make the connection.' Flick said. 'Possibly in the near future I should tell her.'

The way she said it made me feel that I was going to be around for a long time. But it also felt like being handed the baton in a race. It was news for me to carry, perhaps it was information for me to use at some time in the future.

I'd thought that Trelerric Vintage had kept me busy but I found myself flat out learning about clothes, the intricacies of cut and design and methods of embroidery using beads and gold thread. Flick was right, I needed to understand the alchemy of couture, how things were made and why. The people who had contacted Flick initially were now all flocking to make appointments to visit and to discuss options to hire clothes. I learned about acid free tissue and proper storage and I was introduced to the complicated world of contracts. I thanked my lucky stars that Flick already had some experience and that Jane was also able to provide some advice. As Jane said, running the estate, the farm and open days wasn't just about taking entry fees or paying animal feed bills.

The morning of their wedding was the day of my own birthday. Sam had woken me with tea in bed and a small prettily wrapped present. Inside was a key, very old looking and ornate.

'Oh, it's a pretty thing, what's it the key to?' I asked, aware that I was tousled and rumpled and probably not looking my best.

Sam didn't appear to be bothered by my appearance. 'You'll find out later.'

He'd given me a handmade birthday card as well, with a photograph of shooting stars on it. Inside he'd written in sepia calligraphy ink "Happy Birthday, with all my love to Lucy, under the shooting stars at Trelerric", signed and dated with his name and kisses. 'And tomorrow I'm taking you somewhere decent for dinner, and not to the pub. Now get up and start getting ready for Flick's wedding. I suppose it's going to take you women all morning.'

Mum and dad were staying in the guest room next to my flat and Megan and Mike were joining us at the wedding reception. They'd put presents on my coffee table, along with some from Tim and Jane, Alice and Jonathan and one from Maggie. I'd have to open them later.

We were running the event in a similar manner to that of Megan's wedding and Jane had decided that it was definitely something Trelerric could offer.

'After two practises I think that acting as a wedding venue for small weddings is something we can manage, don't you Lucy. I can't remember whose idea it was, but I think it's possible. And people can always bring their own caterers in and their own florist. In fact I'd encourage them to do that. Less work for us and I don't think I can bear the idea of doing all the necessary arrangements and organisation. The very idea is giving me grey hairs.'

Alice and I were both maids of honour and Grace was a little bridesmaid. Flick had us dressed in simple long sleeved cream dresses with deep red sashes and matching red detail at the neckline and inserted into the sleeves. It gave them a faintly medieval look. We wore red shoes and carried red roses. Grace was particularly taken with her red shoes.

'We all look rather good don't we.' Alice commented as we dressed in my rooms after Sunny had performed her usual miracles with our hair. 'I thought we might be covered in spangles and rhinestones but this is tasteful.'

I thought that Grace would have liked rhinestones but she did have a spangly beribboned red hoop to carry instead of flowers. This time I was less emotional about being at a wedding and was able to appreciate the little chapel decked out in red and white and organised by Red, of course. Mum was horrified. 'It's all blood on bandages Lucy,' she hissed. 'Don't they know that?' Mum was referring to an old nurses belief. When people had brought flowers to the bedside of their loved ones in hospital the nurses in her day had always made sure that red and white was never seen together in the same vase. I wasn't so bothered. I thought it looked great.

Sir Hugh was waiting with his son Paul as best man when Flick arrived with Tim and walked down the little aisle to his side, wearing a pale turquoise dress and jacket with red embroidery on the lapels. She carried no flowers.

'I'm not going to be throwing a bouquet because I shall probably put my hip out and I certainly don't need something dried or in silk to keep as a memento. I'm too old for all that nonsense.' She'd said firmly.

As Alice and I took our seats in the chapel my eyes connected with Sam's. He mouthed "happy birthday" to me and smiled, and my heart jumped as it always did when I saw him. He was wearing Robin's red waistcoat again, I noticed.

Afterwards at the reception mum and Megan stood with me. 'Well, I never expected to be here again so soon, and at another wedding.' Mum said, looking at me knowingly. 'It will be yours next I expect Lucy.'

'Mum please.' I said. 'Keep your voice down. I know nothing of the sort. Anyway,' I added, 'I'm always the bridesmaid and never the bride.'

Mum wasn't to be deflected though. 'We'll see, I think there's someone here with views about that state of things.' She looked over to where dad was deep in conversation with Sam. 'I'm guessing there'll be another entry in that Latchley Book of theirs.'

Megan followed her gaze. 'Oh dear,' she said softly to me. 'Mum's got a glass in her hand and she's just gone all Jane Austen on us.' We watched fondly as mum bustled over to join dad and Sam.

'Are you still having that recurring dream Luce?' Megan asked out of the blue.

'I don't know, but I'm sleeping well these days.' I said. Somehow I felt that the bad dreams were over.

'I wonder why that is?' Megan smirked at me. She clearly wasn't referring to the insight into my past I'd received from Jenny.

Again it was a relaxed and informal event although Flick's friends kept the tempo up. I had fun explaining to Megan why her friends had their nicknames. 'Stop it Lucy, I shan't be able to look that man in the face without wondering about what he's got stashed in his trousers. It's gross. You know I see things in pictures!'

Paul Flinton joined us and was even more urbane and polished than his father. Tall and well groomed he was completely laid back about his father remarrying. 'Delightful setting, charming house. Good to see the old man settled at last, been a bit lost since mater passed on. Old friends are the best aren't they.' He raised his glass to his lips but barely wet them and I noticed he didn't swallow. Mum was enthralled by him.

'Are you a spy Lord Flinton?' She asked. 'Isn't everybody who works for the Foreign Office a spy?'

Paul was both taken aback by mum's vague grasp of British upper class hierarchy and hugely amused by her question. I left him to explain himself to her and joined Sam, slipping my hand into his. He looked down at me, his eyes dancing with amusement.

'Fantastic value for money aren't they, Flick's friends I mean. They're all barking mad.'

'Define normal and you'll make a fortune.' I told him.

There were a couple of speeches and the cake to be cut. I'd made Flick a three tier cake. One layer was chocolate and coffee liqueur cake with a second tier of Madeira sponge and a small top tier consisting of a carrot cake because she'd be able to eat a bit of that. A white chocolate ganache covered them and I'd swathed that with slightly sparkly sugar work in the form of a silk opera scarf with red roses enclosed in the folds as they fell and a cluster of red roses on the top. It looked gorgeous and both Fizz and Red were excited by it.

'My girls Eleanor and Lydia would like this. I'm sure El is thinking about getting married.' Fizz said, taking a photograph on her phone and pressing buttons to send it. I looked at her with new interest, somehow I'd thought of her as the eternal party girl, I hadn't expected her to have family of her own.

Sir Hugh thanked me for the marvellous cake and raised his glass to me. 'And happy birthday Lucy, you're a wonderful girl and a very sweet cousin.'

He'd bought both Alice and me a fancy gold chain hung with a pearl drop, which we were wearing. When Megan had seen it she'd coveted it. 'My name means pearl, if you don't want that I'll give it a home.'

'In your dreams Mrs Bartlett.' I'd replied. 'By chance it goes with those earrings you bought me for your own wedding. All these weddings are providing me with some decent bling for once.'

Finally Sam joined me and stayed at my side as we circulated. We ate and chatted to people and danced a little and then he steered me out of the room, holding a plate with uneaten cake on it. 'Come on, we have business to attend to. Will those shoes cope on grass? And you better find a coat, it's cold outside.'

Oddly clad in a long dress with my hair up and wearing my old black quilted jacket and black ankle boots I walked hand in hand with Sam. I knew we were going to the bees. This time it was Sam who carried out the ritual of putting the little offering on the hives, and then he took both my hands in his and kissed me lightly on the lips before looking seriously into my eyes.

'Lucy under the stars.' He said, smiling slightly.

I was confused. Didn't something about diamonds follow that? I was about to speak but he stopped me with a finger on my lips. 'Lucy, the bees already know what this is about.'

I breathed out slowly. 'Shhh', he said, taking my hand again. 'The bees are resting now. Lucy, I love you, I love everything about you. Will you marry me and stay here forever?'

I think the bees hummed.

'You want to marry me?'

'Definitely. So what's your answer?' Sam's voice was serious.

'I thought this was about the little key you gave me this morning.' I said in confusion.

'It is. It's the key to a home at Trelerric, if you'll stay. The key to the tumbledown cottage, I found it one day when I was exploring there. I want to make it into a home for us. The old market garden is perfect for another apple orchard, but I think I'll plant some cherries as well.' Sam was looking down at me as he spoke. 'So what's your answer then lovely Lucy?'

I just stood there gazing up at him. Everything felt right. I was at home already, with a man I loved and trusted. 'Yes. Oh yes please.'

'And Lucy,' Sam pulled me close and kissed me. 'Do you mind skipping the engagement and just getting married. I'd like a Christmas wedding. I'd like to start next year with my wife at my side.'

Printed in Great Britain
by Amazon